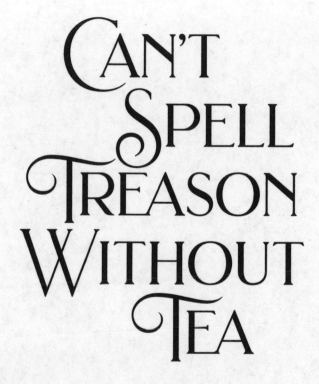

CAN'T SPELL TREASON WITHOUT TEA

rebecca thorne

CAN'T SPELL TREASON WITHOUT TEA

A COZY FANTASY STEEPED WITH LOVE

BRAMBLE

TOR PUBLISHING GROUP / NEW YORK

CAN'T SPELL TREASON WITHOUT TEA

Copyright © 2022 by Rebecca Thorne
"Meet and Greet" © 2024 by Rebecca Thorne

Map by Rebecca Thorne
Chapter ornaments by Amphi
Tip-in illustration by Eilene Cherie

A Bramble Book
Published by Tom Doherty Associates / Tor Publishing Group
120 Broadway
New York, NY 10271

www.brambleromance.com

Bramble™ is a trademark of Macmillan Publishing Group, LLC.

The Library of Congress Cataloging-in-Publication Data is available upon request.

ISBN 978-1-250-33329-2 (trade paperback)
ISBN 978-1-250-33330-8 (ebook)

Our books may be purchased in bulk for promotional, educational, or business use. Please contact your local bookseller or the Macmillan Corporate and Premium Sales Department at 1-800-221-7945, extension 5442, or by email at MacmillanSpecialMarkets@macmillan.com.

First Bramble Trade Paperback Edition: 2024

Printed in the United States of America

0 9 8 7 6 5 4 3 2 1

For anyone who really needs a cup of tea
and a nice book.

Take a break. You've earned it.

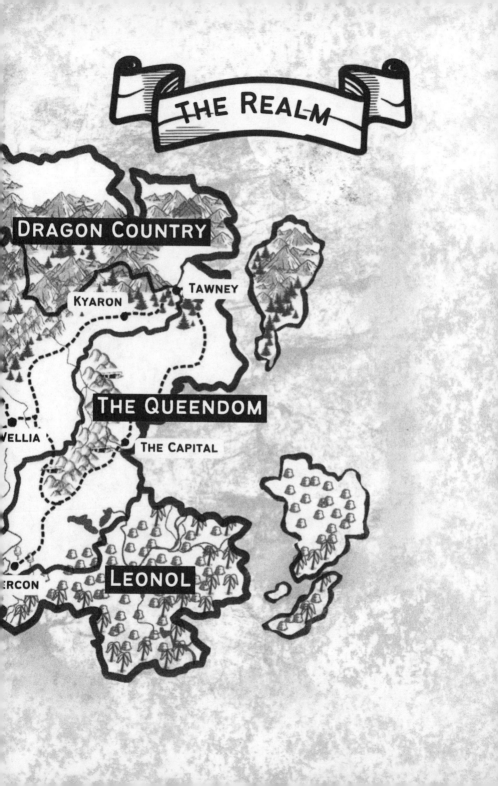

1

Reyna

Reyna stalked the edges of the gilded crowd, watching the assassin creep ever closer to Queen Tilaine.

The party was lively, the royal orchestra working hard to fill the cavernous ballroom with their sovereign's favorite scores. Even with the open windows, the brisk evening air smelled of sweat and perfume. Court folk clad in colorful silk attire danced with nobility from every corner of the Queendom. Servers with golden trays and matching smiles flitted between them, offering shrimp, chocolates, champagne—all imported from Shepara for the Arcandor, their absent guest of honor.

It was a bold place to attempt an assassination.

Reyna hadn't faced one this foolish in . . . oh, seven months? The Mid-Winter Celebration. An assassin tried to behead Queen Tilaine while she made her yearly address. Reyna would never forget his gurgling gasps, or the queen's impassive stare as his spattered blood stained her silk shoes. Reyna *certainly* wouldn't forget how Her Excellency nudged the body off the high balcony, then continued her address as if a corpse hadn't crunched to the ground ten meters below.

Kianthe called Queen Tilaine a sociopath.

Reyna was finding that easier and easier to believe.

"I specifically ordered faster dancing." Queen Tilaine's voice was melodious—but with a venomous bite. Everyone knew why she was irate: Kianthe, the Arcandor, the Mage of Ages, their foreign guest of honor—who also happened to be Reyna's very secret girlfriend—hadn't shown. Although the queen's cheery expression never faltered, it was obvious that the Arcandor's absence was picking at the queen's mind like a child with a scab.

"Entertain me, my loves," Queen Tilaine chimed. "Pick up your feet!"

At their sovereign's command, the music shifted into something more frenzied, and the court folk led their partners in a faster twirl. Their faces gleamed with sweat, but no one dared to slow their footwork.

Honestly, it was probably a good thing Kianthe had avoided this party. She may have done it out of spite, but whenever the Arcandor was near Queen Tilaine, it was an immense struggle for Kianthe to hold her tongue. All she'd need was to see Her Excellency's reaction to this assassin, and she'd have *choice* words.

Reyna, contrarily, had no words about this. Just a consistent, pulsing weariness for her profession, growing more profound each day.

The would-be assassin wove through the ballroom, expertly managing to avoid being trampled by the dancers. Although the man's outfit was a poor mimic of their professional servers, he moved with dangerous grace. There was no doubt he was a threat; even pretending to serve the public, his eyes never left the queen.

It drew the palace guards like moths to a flame.

Already, Reyna's partner, Venne, was matching her steps on the opposite side of the ballroom. Crimson cloaks and gold armor accents—indicators of the queen's private guards—meant they drew attention from the more discerning citizens, but no one dared approach. Behind Venne, two other soldiers were already securing the exits. Four senior guards, the ones proven worthy enough to stand near the queen, subtly tightened their circle around her.

Yet another carefully orchestrated dance.

Reyna's short sword slid from its scabbard with a whisper.

Turn around. Walk away, she thought. *You don't have to die tonight.*

But of course, it was far too late for that. He'd been identified as a threat—and threats were dealt with swiftly and mercilessly.

Not for the first time, Kianthe's offer rose from the back of Reyna's mind. *"Run away with me,"* the mage had said, her eyes alight. *"You like tea. I like books. Let's open a shop somewhere remote and forget the world exists."*

Reyna had rolled her eyes back then, her lips tilting in a forbidden smile. It used to sound crazy. She came from a long line of palace guards, even if most were dead now. Her duty had been inscribed with blood the moment she was born.

And yet, a part of her fantasized about lounging in a quiet, no-name town, sipping a cup of tea by the fire while Kianthe flipped aimlessly through a heavy tome. It was a distant dream, but one that left a warm glow deep in her soul.

The song ended, and almost immediately the music shifted into a brighter melody, if that were possible. But the pause allowed a breath of silence, one where the guards' coordinated commands reached the assassin's ears.

He knew they'd seen him.

His eyes grew desperate, the set of his mouth firmed, and he began shoving his way to the queen. People yelped as the man knocked them to the ground, cried out as he yanked two wicked-looking knives from sheaths hidden beneath his loose shirt.

Queen Tilaine watched the entire display with marked disinterest, chewing a delicate bite of shrimp. Her eyes flicked to Reyna, the closest of her guards, and she made a *Well? Get on with it* motion.

Gods be damned. Reyna hated this part.

Drawing a short breath and steeling her resolve, Reyna lunged. As easily as a knife through butter, her sword slid into the man's back. The blade nicked a couple ribs, meeting resistance, but she shoved it deeper, her face a distant mask as the bloody tip protruded from his chest, just below his heart.

She'd been raised for murder, for "protection," but Reyna could never get used to this. Pressed against the back of a dying man, his blood seeping through her uniform and slicking her sword's hilt, the coppery scent hanging thick in the air . . . it made her insides twist.

The assassin had made his choice when he arrived at this ball, but as Kianthe was so blunt to remind her, there were *other* methods of apprehension. And yet, this particular one had Queen Tilaine tilting her head, smiling amidst the screams.

"Well. Now it's a party," Her Excellency said over the faltering orchestra.

Blood dribbled from the man's mouth, and his body spasmed as Reyna withdrew the sword. He staggered, finally facing her, and gasped, "She d-deserves to die."

Reyna, who shouldn't have an opinion on that, didn't falter.

"Finish him," Queen Tilaine ordered.

Reyna raised her sword again, and inside her chest, that weariness quadrupled. She was so, so tired of this: of their sovereign, of palace protocol. All she wanted was a nice, hot cup of tea.

It was treason to think that.

She thought it anyway.

And then Venne shouted in alarm, and a dagger pressed against Reyna's neck. It sliced the skin, a drop of blood slipping along her throat before diving between her collarbones. Reyna stiffened, freezing instantly, her breaths shallow. Although her heart pounded, her mind slipped into survival mode, analyzing the person who'd grabbed her.

Most likely a man, based off the size of his hand on Reyna's arm, his tall stature for the knife's positioning . . . and his ripe scent. He moved too close, leaning against Reyna's back, fully expecting her to comply.

"Let us go," he called, fear lingering in his voice. "Or I'll kill her!"

His partner was dead anyway—palace blades were coated in poison, just in case the physical act didn't finish the job. Already, the first assassin was teetering, clutching at the blood gushing through his chest.

But all eyes fell to Queen Tilaine.

Her Excellency regarded the situation. Warm ocean-blue eyes slid over Reyna as easily as if she were a street dog. Her white, powdered cheeks crinkled in amusement. "Dear, if you think one guard will ensure your survival tonight, you are sorely mistaken. I won't show mercy for someone intruding on my party like this."

"Mercy" was Tilaine's favorite word, considering she'd been blessed by the God of Mercy on her coronation day. The tilt of the sovereign's painted lips proved she thought this was very clever to mention.

The knife at Reyna's neck pressed more firmly. Pain, acute and shocking, lanced through her. A thicker stream of blood dripped from the blade. How lovely for Tilaine, to feel clever at the expense of Reyna's safety.

Kianthe was going to be furious.

Hells, *Reyna* was furious. It prickled along her spine. She knew she was expendable, had known since she was five years old and her mother first handed her a blade and a mission. But Queen Eren, Gods rest her soul, had at least feigned sympathy at her mother's funeral.

"A good life lost," she'd said. *"We mourn her sacrifice."*

Reyna, barely a teenager, had watched impassively. Her emotions were cold and dark that day, and they shifted to something cold and dark now.

In direct response to her pain, the inscribed moonstone Kianthe had gifted her pulsed twice over her heart. It was intended to alert the mage to injury, but they used it to communicate too—the moonstone would warm or pulse against her skin, and they'd formed a code through it. Reyna had no idea where Kianthe was currently, but two taps meant the Arcandor would be on her way shortly.

She'd probably be in a nervous fit, too. Because even if Queen Tilaine didn't value Reyna's life, *Kianthe* did. She hated Reyna's job, reiterated over and over that she'd be devastated if something happened to Reyna.

Well, something had happened tonight—and Reyna was not going to let this be the final chapter in her life.

Barely a breath had passed since Queen Tilaine's proclamation, but Reyna didn't wait for more. Fast as lightning, she buried her elbow into the man's gut. Her heel followed, the stiff sole grinding down his shin.

He grunted, and the knife at her neck vanished as the man staggered back. It was a brief reprieve; seconds later, the assassin lunged, aiming for Reyna's chest. Reyna twisted to avoid the knife, swallowing a gasp as it sliced deep into her upper arm instead.

Enough of this. Reyna moved like a woman possessed, sliced the man's throat, then buried the blade into his heart.

He died instantly, his hazel eyes shifting into a dull sheen.

Blood poured from the wound in Reyna's arm, dripped sickly down her neck. Logic told her neither wound was life-threatening. It didn't matter; her body was numb, and true pain would follow shortly.

Somehow, the queen's betrayal hurt more.

Reyna shoved the corpse off her sword and faced the first assassin, only to see the man's head had been graciously separated from his body. It rolled to the base of the dais, eyes and mouth open in never-ending horror. Venne casually wiped his sword off on the intruder's black clothes.

"Are you all right?" His dark eyes flicked to her arm.

She cleaned her sword on her already-bloodied cloak and

sheathed it, then gripped the wound to slow the bleeding. Crimson oozed through her fingers. She felt faint with anger. But everyone was watching, so she casually replied, "It's nothing I haven't experienced before."

The spell pulsed again: Kianthe was smacking her from a country away. Reyna fought a wince. In an attempt to ignore her girlfriend, she bowed to the sovereign. "Your Excellency, what are your orders?"

The whole ballroom held its breath.

Queen Tilaine surveyed them, the frozen musicians, the panting dancers, the court folk who'd stepped away from the first assassin's severed head. After a long moment, she smiled. "Well, this is a party—regardless of whether the Arcandor deigns to attend. String up the bodies, then double entertainment efforts. Everybody enjoy themselves!"

It sounded like a threat.

Already, a tall man with a thin mustache was nodding to several partygoers who'd lurked on the edges of the crowd. The queen's spymaster, commanding his spies. They scattered like leaves on the wind, undoubtedly prepared to spread rumors of the royal ball's opulence to every neighboring town and country.

It was all above Reyna's paygrade. She planted her feet to keep from swaying.

Venne was beside her then, ripping the fabric of his cloak to tie around her wound. She didn't want to let him that close, but her circumstances didn't offer much choice. His smile grated on her, even as he murmured, "You are as fierce as an ice leopard, and just as beautiful."

"Flattery won't change my preferences," she replied pointedly.

He shrugged. "Can't fault a man for trying."

Were that true.

"Luckily, I can find fault in a multitude of other qualities. For example, your bandaging skills need work." She hissed as he tied the cloth too tightly, but the initial stab of pain faded into an uncomfortable thrum. Dimly, she dabbed at her neck with her crimson cloak. The blood blended right in.

Before them, another pair of palace guards were gathering the corpses. One held open a heavy bag, and the second dropped the severed head inside. He tied the bag to his belt, then hauled the body over his shoulder. The unburdened guard scooped up the other assassin's bleeding corpse, following suit.

Waiters stood nearby, armed with buckets and mops. Soon, there would be no tangible record of this assassination attempt.

Except, of course, in the shackles by the bank of windows, where their corpses would be strung for the partygoers to appreciate as the evening wore on. Already, the court folk were offering a slight berth as a guard pried open the manacles.

Reyna could be lounging on a velvet couch beside a roaring fire, running her hands through Kianthe's dark hair as they chatted about mundane things. No bodies. No prison-like palace routine. Just them, existing together.

And this time, something solidified in Reyna's soul.

"The queen gave permission to escort you to the medical ward," Venne said. She hadn't even noticed him addressing their monarch, but apparently she'd been distracted making drastic life decisions.

Treasonous life decisions.

Queen Tilaine's cheerful response ran through her head like a suffocating song: *"You are sorely mistaken."*

Leaving didn't feel like such a stretch anymore.

"I can escort myself." Reyna was dizzy, her body starting to go cold, but she could still walk. The bandage against her arm was beginning to soak through, and there was no doubt she'd need stitches and rest soon, but she wasn't on death's door.

And yet, her mind whirled. Kianthe shouldn't take long to arrive, distance depending. The moonstone was a quiet comfort over her heart, firm and warm as a kiss from the mage's own lips.

Gods, she was really going to do this, wasn't she?

Venne set a guiding arm over her shoulders and whispered, "You're my excuse, Rey. Save me from the pomp and circumstance."

Her entire life had been pomp and circumstance. Just once, Reyna was ready for something real.

"Reyna, I expect you back in service first thing tomorrow," Queen Tilaine called.

Reyna bowed deeply, automatically, and turned her back on Her Excellency, the ballroom, the palace . . . and the Queendom.

And it happened so quietly, no one else noticed.

She visited the doctor, sat stoically while he stitched the gash on her bicep closed, while he applied pressure to her neck wound until it stopped bleeding. Venne escorted her to her quarters in the palace's east wing, and she closed the door in his face. She slept until the ballroom cleared out, until the early-morning hours when the moon hung low and the palace guards had reduced to a skeleton staff.

Then she packed her meager belongings in two saddlebags, heaving them over her good shoulder. With her sword's sheath tied to her leather belt, she glanced one final time at her old home: at the bed where Kianthe had first whispered promises in her ear, at the desk where she'd penned dozens of secret letters to the Arcandor, at the stone window where the mage would sometimes appear with a bouquet of exotic flowers.

Reyna drew a deep breath and walked out the door.

She'd memorized the palace guard rotations years ago, so her cohorts were easy to evade. When the stablemaster's apprentice raised an eyebrow at her unusual arrival, she merely intoned: "The queen ordered me to run an errand. Saddle my horse, please."

He did so.

And Reyna did something brave, just for herself. Without resistance, she thundered out the north gates of the Queendom's capital city.

And this time, she wasn't coming back.

2

Kianthe

In a perfect world, Kianthe would have ignored Reyna the palace guard. She'd have met with the spiteful queen, scoffed at her paltry requests for magical assistance, and never let her eyes wander to the striking blonde clad in crimson and gold nearby.

She'd have bid that awful queen farewell and returned to the Magicary—the hub of magic within the Realm, placed firmly in the northern mountains of Shepara, where mages congregated and the legendary Stone of Seeing claimed its residence. Then she'd have spent her life basking in the disdain of withered old prunes who couldn't fathom that the Stone chose *her* to succeed the last Arcandor.

None of that happened.

Well, the last part still happened on occasion, mostly because Kianthe took gleeful pleasure in reminding those ancient mages of her continued existence.

But instead, Kianthe engaged in witty banter in that horrid queen's court—was shocked to discover the gorgeous palace guard had a sharp tongue and a sharper mind—and she fell.

And for the last two years, she hadn't stopped falling.

Which was why it vexed her when Reyna—gorgeous, capable Reyna—was stuck working as a lapdog for Queen Tilaine. And worse, Reyna had a protective streak, which came with utter disregard for her own Stone-damned safety.

She was an excellent guard. She was a terrible girlfriend.

Kianthe cursed Reyna's name, family, home, and values as she crossed Shepara's borders, guiding her griffon, Visk, deep into the Queendom. Beneath her, the magical beast flexed powerful wings over the bitter night air. Kianthe leaned nearly off his back, squinting through the darkness at moonlit stretches of volcanic rock dotted with sparse grass, trying to quell the frantic beating of her heart, the sick breathlessness that hadn't left since her moonstone—a perfect match to Reyna's—pulsed last night.

A full day had passed since then, far too long for comfort. Kianthe had been in Wellia, Shepara's capital, but even by air, travel from that distance took time. She'd left the council mid-meeting and didn't apologize. Let them plant their own crops for once, instead of begging her to seed their fields.

Her spelled moonstones had confirmed two things: Reyna had been injured. And more peculiarly, she'd left the Queendom's Grand Palace. The magic pulled Kianthe toward her, which was decidedly away from their capital city. About a day's ride north, judging by the angle.

"Maybe she finally got wise and stabbed Tilaine herself," Kianthe muttered, her words lost to the roaring wind. Fear sliced down her spine, and for a moment, the mage considered what it would mean if that were true.

If Reyna had killed the queen, she would be fleeing the entire might of the Queendom. Even Kianthe's magic couldn't save her then.

"Fuck. I take it back," Kianthe shouted, as if the Stone itself had been listening. "Her sensible nature has to be good for something, right?"

The wind didn't answer, and Kianthe huffed in frustration, urging Visk to fly lower over the lands.

For all Queen Tilaine's posturing, her country was rather barren. To the west, Shepara had claimed the best farming soil, the richest oceans, and the Stone of Seeing—protected within the immense walls of the Magicary. Farther south, a luscious jungle offered the Leonolans refuge from the blazing sun and sticky heat. And to the north, dragon country. Perhaps all these perceived threats were why Tilaine tried so desperately to position herself as a worldly power.

Kianthe stopped caring when she saw the bodies strung in the woman's streets—and imagined Reyna being next.

She flew on, growing more panicked as the Eastern Ocean glimmered in the meager moonlight. The Capital loomed to the south, its stone architecture a nod to the many quarries that marred the land. She nudged her griffon north, following the pull of magic, scanning for any sign of Reyna.

And then, near midnight, she found her.

It was honestly impressive Kianthe noticed her at all; Reyna had traveled far off the main road, making camp in a forest of pinyon pines, which grew low enough to hide her from anyone on the ground. She hadn't made a fire, either. The only indication that someone camped there at all was Kianthe's pulsing moonstone—and Lilac, Reyna's warhorse, tied to a nearby tree.

"Landing, Rain," she called over Visk's flank as the griffon slid into a lazy circle overhead. "Don't try to stab me this time."

A quiet laugh pierced the air, and Kianthe relaxed a bit.

The mage pushed off her mount's back, pulling magic from the air to cushion her fall. The Stone of Seeing designated her as a sort of . . . conduit, channeling its immense magic into smaller spells that benefited the world at large. Luckily, Kianthe had a lot of freedom to define "benefit," and right now, it benefited her to inspect Reyna as soon as possible.

The stars were bright overhead and the moon was half-full, so she had enough light to see Reyna picking her way from underneath a pine's low-hanging branches.

"Surprised to see me?" Kianthe spread her arms wide.

Reyna snorted. "Not one bit." But her breath hitched as she moved.

Concern tightened Kianthe's chest, and she crossed the distance between them in seconds. It was too dark to see details, and instantly, Kianthe's mind fabricated an intrusive thought of Reyna drenched in blood, seconds from collapsing. It was a bad habit; Kianthe had spent an entire day squashing terrible scenarios, and now they all flared back to life, hot enough to burn.

So Kianthe let them burn, channeling the emotion into a flame perched within her open palm. Its embers reached for the pine needles, but she hissed, "Not right now," and the flame sank into a tight ball, chastened.

It illuminated Reyna instantly, and she squinted against the light. "Key, I'm fine. Don't worry."

But her right arm hung at her side, and blood stained her clothes. She'd changed out of her palace uniform at some point, but her outfit now had clearly seen battle. And her neck—did someone try to slash her neck? Kianthe sucked in a breath, shooing the docile fireball into the tree to get a closer look.

"Don't worry, my ass. What in the five hells happened?"

Reyna sighed. "Well, first it was an assassin at Her Excellency's ball."

The ball. A twinge of guilt made Kianthe flinch. This wasn't the first time Tilaine had used opulence and flattery as an attempt to woo Kianthe into her service. Normally, Kianthe ignored her, and felt no remorse about it.

Tonight, she wished she'd chosen differently.

Reyna had already moved on, casually gesturing at the wound on her shoulder. While it must have received medical attention at some point, she'd stripped the bandage, and now it bled sluggishly.

"Stitches were pulled, but I was about to redo them. My neck probably looks bad, but it's just a cut."

"Just a—" Kianthe cut herself off. It was beside the point: "Wait. Go back. What do you mean, *first*?"

Now her girlfriend winced, like she didn't really want to expand on this very important topic. "Ah, this—" She reluctantly lifted her torn shirt, revealing scratched skin underneath, like she'd tumbled into underbrush during a fight. "—is because a troop of bandits thought I made a decent target."

"Bandits," Kianthe repeated, deadpan.

Above them, Visk circled the clearing. Despite Lilac's training for battle, she was still a horse—and in the wild, griffons preyed on horses. Now, Lilac was eyeing the sky, nostrils flared.

Kianthe would address it in a minute.

Reyna grimaced. "I thought I'd be finished with killing, but— well. It couldn't be helped." She swayed a bit, then replanted her feet. "Care to sit down, love? I need to restitch my arm."

Kianthe drew a few calming breaths, attempting to quell the panic blooming in her chest. She numbly nodded, flicking a finger to raise a bench-like rock from the ground. "Visk, land," she called, and when the griffon touched down—as far from Lilac as possible, since he had excellent manners—she rummaged through the leather bags he carried. Once she retrieved her supplies, she patted his flank. "Feel free to roam, bud. You're making Lilac uneasy."

The griffon chittered, a very cute sound from an incredibly fierce creature, and flew off. He'd have no problem keeping busy until they were ready to travel again.

Lilac relaxed, but only slightly.

Kianthe turned—and almost ran into Reyna. Her girlfriend's lips tilted downward.

"Key, I'm fine." Reyna's voice softened. "And I'm sorry I've worried you."

"I'm the one who took so long to get here." Kianthe moved to lead her back under the tree.

Reyna caught her arm, and when Kianthe glanced back, the woman kissed her. Her lips were warm and reassuring, her good hand tangling in Kianthe's hair just as she liked. Kianthe melted against her, wanting to hold her close, but she was ever-careful about Reyna's wounds. Delicately, she looped an arm around her girlfriend's waist, feeling their hearts beat together as magic literally sparked around them.

Relief. Slowly, the knot in Kianthe's chest unwound.

She'd be okay. And that meant this was now a rare night together—despite two years of dating, their jobs had kept them apart for most of it. A few stolen days here and there were all they managed, alongside their limited communication with the moonstones.

Happiness bloomed in Kianthe's chest. She grumbled when Reyna broke the kiss.

"Thought you had the sparks under control," Reyna said, laughing a little.

"I thought you had your life under control, but here we are." She waved the magic off, guiding Reyna to the bench she'd created under the tree.

Overhead, her spelled flame split to offer more light, glimmering like tiny candles amidst the pine needles. They warmed the air, too, and Reyna smiled. "Well, that's beautiful."

"You're beautiful."

As always, Reyna rolled her eyes, but a blush tinged her cheeks. It was delightful, and Kianthe grinned. Reyna shoved her shoulder, flushing now. "Don't look so smug. That was a mediocre compliment at best."

"Please. All of my compliments are mediocre at best." Kianthe opened her leather bags, rummaging through the supplies she'd brought. She set a few things on the stone beside Reyna, hunting for a needle and medical thread.

Meanwhile, Reyna picked up a deep blue potion inside a glass vial. "Anti-venom?"

"My spell didn't say how you were injured. For all I knew, you ate something meant for that Stone-damned queen and spent the night writhing on her fancy marble floor."

"Thank the Gods you're pretty," Reyna remarked.

"Ouch. Be glad you wore that moonstone, or I wouldn't know to be here at all." Kianthe heated a needle with a thimble-sized flame off her fingertip. "For the record, I hate sewing. Especially this kind of sewing."

"Don't we all."

Kianthe began stitching the wound closed, which was a struggle with her hands still trembling a bit. She hated this. She hated that the very definition of Reyna's job was waiting for danger to strike. The breathless horror that encompassed wondering if she'd survive the next day, every day, forever.

Reyna had accepted it long ago. She turned her face upward, her hazel eyes tracing the firelight overhead as she steadied her breathing. Kianthe had to force herself not to stare at the sharp lines of her jaw and nose, or the way her ice-blond hair fell in tendrils from a loose bun.

After she messily stitched and redressed the first wound, she turned her attention to the scrapes on Reyna's stomach. Basic armor—hell, even leather—would have helped avoid this. But palace guards didn't *wear* armor, except for ceremonial purposes. Even then, the plating was carved into decorative dragon skulls and coated in gold, useless for a proper attack. Reyna ranted about it often, and once Kianthe started paying attention, the queen's choices were comically bad.

Unsurprising, considering the source.

Reyna had shed her crimson cloak at some point, leaving her in a formfitting tank and trousers, but the gold rings curving around the shell of her ears were remnants of a formal evening.

Kianthe carefully dabbed the blood spotting a few deeper scrapes on Reyna's stomach. Her skin was warm under Kianthe's touch. "So . . . after all this, maybe tonight you'll give up on that miserable woman and run away with me?"

It was meant to be a joke. But when Reyna didn't respond, Kianthe glanced up, and their gazes locked. Reyna's eyes were light enough to be startling, dark enough to be mysterious—and now they were raw with emotion.

Something deep and impacting shifted between them.

"You're acting strange," Kianthe said. "It's concerning me."

Reyna drew a breath. "Ask me again. Just like you've asked me before."

She didn't have to reference what she meant. Kianthe knew. She knew, because every minute they stole felt like a luxury. Fleeting memories of beauty and happiness, bookended with the heavy knowledge that Reyna had committed to a lifelong career.

"You can't leave your life either," Reyna had teased, the first time Kianthe proposed it. *"You're the Mage of Ages. You have responsibility."*

Kianthe had rolled her eyes. *"Who's going to stop me? The Stone of Seeing? It hasn't intervened with an Arcandor's choices in a century. And it's not like I couldn't fly to the site of a natural disaster; that's what I'm doing now anyway. We'd just have a different home base."*

Reyna had snorted and waved a hand, dismissing the idea.

Kianthe didn't push. After all, Reyna had earned a position of power beside a vindictive queen, and unlike Kianthe, very real consequences would find her if she abandoned that post.

Those consequences didn't seem to matter now. Reyna held her gaze, steady.

"Ask me again, Key."

Kianthe's mouth was dry. She swallowed hard, and the whispered words felt like a promise. "Run away with me. You like tea. I like books. Care to open a shop and forget the world exists?"

The words hung like a melody between them. Reyna closed her

eyes, a soft smile curving her lips. Everything condensed to this moment: spelled firelight glimmering overhead, her blood seeping into the bandage, her face pale and drawn, and her expression so, so happy.

Kianthe was mesmerized.

"Okay. I'll run away with you. Let's find a shop and make a home and forget about everything else."

The spell shattered. Kianthe squealed, throwing her arms around Reyna's shoulders, utterly forgetting to be mindful of her wounds. They laughed together, their uncertain futures solidifying into something tangible and real and lovely.

A bookstore that served tea, perched in the most remote corner of the world.

Kianthe could see it already.

3

Reyna

After the shock had worn off, after Kianthe tended to Reyna's wounds, after the mage's featherlight touch on her stomach prompted something a bit more passionate, they lay together under the firelight. It had dimmed with Kianthe's simple command, casting them in a cozy glow, and exhaustion tugged at Reyna's mind.

But alongside it, excitement and happiness. They were going to do it. Open a shop somewhere, fill it with books and tea and a fireplace and cozy armchairs, and Reyna could finally, *finally* learn who she was without the queen looming over her.

She liked to cook—she knew that. She enjoyed testing new blends of tisane, and the warmth of her muscles after a good practice spar. She'd never been a reader, not until meeting Kianthe, but the mage's love of the written word had infected her. Beyond that . . . well, Queensguard weren't given much time off. It was an all-or-nothing job.

What kind of person could she become?

It was intimidating to decide.

Kianthe propped herself up on her arm, her fingers roaming along Reyna's stomach. "You look like you swallowed a lemon."

"I'm just . . . thinking." She paused. As much as she loved Kianthe, she didn't want the mage helpfully suggesting new ambitions. It was important that Reyna didn't replace the queen with the Arcandor. So, she diverted: "About logistics."

"The best part of any adventurous idea." Sarcasm dripped from Kianthe's statement.

Reyna snorted, turning on her good shoulder to face her properly. The ground had smoothed to be perfectly flat beneath her bedroll, no pebbles or stones or divots disrupting their sleep. That kind of thing happened around the Arcandor; the elements always wanted her to be comfortable.

"I found an insignia on the bandits who attacked me. The queen's spies identified a few of their hideouts over the last several months. One is north of here." Ever since Kianthe had first proposed this idea, Reyna kept a running tally of empty buildings reported to the queen. It used to be a "just in case" kind of thing, a laughable aside to keep Reyna's attention span from drifting during court meetings.

After last night, she was very grateful she had an excellent memory.

Kianthe quirked an eyebrow. "You want to steal a bandit hideout as our new home?"

"Not *steal*." Reyna winced, because she intended to earn her new life. Pay coin for property, even if she used a fake name. But owning in the Queendom—hells, owning anywhere—was expensive, and her savings over years of service felt very small when she checked the numbers.

She wasn't willing to let it delay them, not once the decision had been made. So, she explored other options. "Her Excellency takes pride in offering safe passage within the Queendom. It's one of the reasons her nobility tolerates her . . . other quirks."

"'Quirks' is kind for that witch."

Reyna paused. "Is it offensive to call someone a witch, as a magic user yourself?"

The mage snorted. "It's because I'm a magic user that I can get away with it, love." She pushed upright, swallowing a yawn. "If you're talking logistics, I'm going to need a cup of tea. What'd you bring?"

"Just a few bags. Black, white, oolong. There's rose and mint in the purple satchel." She nodded at Lilac's saddlebags, which she'd relocated under the tree before Kianthe arrived. Kianthe brightened at the mention of her favorite herbal blend, and wasted no time retrieving it and the copper kettle—Reyna's most prized possession, other than the spelled moonstone.

"You want a cup?"

Reyna pushed upright too, although her whole body screamed protest at the movement. She was exhausted—she'd spent most of the day riding hard to get distance, and the bandit attack hadn't helped matters.

Luckily, Kianthe was a quick learner when it came to tea. Already the mage was coaxing fresh groundwater to purify itself, easing it into the teakettle with a wave of her hand. She set the kettle on a tiny metal frame Reyna kept for camping. Then she snapped her fingers and a small fireball ignited on her palm, warming the water.

Reyna may have been tired, but she could never refuse a nice cup of tea, especially on a cold night. She tugged the woolen blanket tighter over her shoulders, winced as it applied pressure to her wound. "I suppose I'll take one."

"Of course you will." Kianthe winked, then gestured for her to keep talking. "So, the queen hates bandits."

"Mmm. So much that she offers payment for killing them. The ones I felled today would be worth at least a palidron."

"Which is . . . how much in normal coin?"

Reyna very much disliked how disconnected the Queendom was from the rest of the continent. She considered the current exchange rate, based on their last royal visit to Wellia. "It's . . . ah—"
But the total fell from her mind as fast as she calculated it—the

scent of brewing tea and the blanket's warmth were distracting her. "It's a sum. But not enough to buy a building."

"Hence the stealing." Kianthe offered a wicked grin.

Reyna hesitated. "If you have money, we can combine our savings and try another route." A pause. "Do you have anything?" Her face warmed; this felt like none of her business. She should know this after two years, but with just a few stolen nights every season, there always seemed to be more important conversation topics.

Luckily, her partner didn't seem to care. "Please. I'm the Arcandor." The words were spoken with a puffed chest and arrogant tone. Then she broke down laughing. "Which, of course, means all my funds are routed through the Magicary. So . . . no. Did you think I chose you for your looks?"

Reyna forced a smile. "I'm quite certain the Arcandor, Mage of Ages, could find a wealthier woman to bankroll her endeavors."

This was an age-old worry, nicking her brain like an ice pick on a sculpture. Carving out an image where Kianthe grew bored, flitted away on her high-flying griffon, and left Reyna alone.

Suddenly, it felt like Reyna couldn't breathe. Gods, what was she doing? Leaving a steady job, making enemies of *Queen Tilaine,* just to run off with her clandestine partner? They'd taken trips, but living together was a distant dream. Everyone knew the Arcandor was as fleeting as the wind itself.

Kianthe loved her, but what if that love wasn't enough? What if close proximity revealed new problems, and their entire relationship fell apart?

Reyna drew a shaking breath, keeping as quiet as she could.

With the water boiling, Kianthe lowered the intensity of the flame in her palm, then added the rose and mint leaves to the water. All the while, she squinted at Reyna. Her voice was kind, yet firm: "Don't do that."

Shit. Reyna ducked her head, making a show of checking the bandage on her arm. "I don't—"

"Yes, you do." Kianthe let the flame die, crossing the distance between them in seconds. She touched Reyna's cheek to redirect her gaze. "Rain. It was a joke. You know I wouldn't choose someone for their coin. I love you because you're amazing. You find worth in *me*, not my title or magic." Kianthe's voice cracked, and now she was the one averting her eyes. "No one else sees past that. Ever."

Reyna's heart broke. Every time she heard about Kianthe's travels as the Arcandor, it sounded isolating.

"I'd do it again and again," Reyna swore. She pulled Kianthe closer, kissing her hard. A promise. When they broke, hazel eyes met deep brown. "I'm not worried about you. I'm worried about your life . . . and whether or not you can truly leave it. If we try and discover you can't, I'm not sure where that leaves me."

After all, an Arcandor had never established a residence outside the Magicary walls. It just wasn't done.

Right?

The mage considered her for a moment, and Reyna appreciated that she didn't attempt to lie. "The mages in the Magicary won't be happy if I don't make regular appearances. And the Stone itself might get involved if I'm away too long." She drew a breath. "But I'm committed to you. I want to explore every facet of this new life together . . . even if I have to travel sometimes. Is that okay?"

It was as good a promise as Reyna could expect. And she wouldn't be sitting around, twiddling her thumbs while she waited for Kianthe to return. This was an opportunity for both of them, really.

Reyna inhaled slowly to calm her nerves, and this time, her smile was real. "Okay. You're over-steeping that blend."

"Well, *excuse me* for attempting to be fully present for this very important conversation." Kianthe stuck out her tongue, but dutifully filtered the tisane into two ceramic mugs. She tossed the used leaves to the ground, rinsed the kettle with another pull of groundwater, and added two scoops of sugar to her tea and a fleck of honey to Reyna's.

Then she tromped over, gave Reyna the mug and an almost

assertive kiss, and resolutely plopped down beside her. "Move over. I'm cold."

Together, they sat shoulder to shoulder underneath the wool blanket, pressed up against the rock she'd raised earlier. With a huff, Kianthe waved a hand at the pinyon pine tree, and its branches slid aside to reveal a window of stars. She extinguished the firelight with another unspoken spell, casting them in comfortable darkness.

For a long moment, neither of them spoke. Outside, Lilac munched on grass near the campsite. A pack of wolves howled in the distance, and crickets filled the air with music. An owl hooted nearby.

Reyna's body relaxed. She clutched her mug against her chest, leaning heavily on Kianthe's shoulder. "We're going to need more distance from the Capital. Her Excellency's spies will be searching for me."

"Can't just tell her to fuck off, huh?"

"Key!"

Kianthe chuckled, sipping her tea. "Just an idea." But they both knew Queen Tilaine would take to Reyna's absence about as well as the Magicary would take to Kianthe's. The difference was, Reyna held no power—all Queen Tilaine would see was a traitor to the crown.

Kianthe pulled her arm over Reyna's shoulders, being mindful of her wound. Her fingers traced the bandage, so light the touch tickled. "So, where are we going, then? The Magicary won't expect me for a while, and I'm sure you have a plan for this mystical building."

"Of course I do." Reyna pressed the mug to her lips, murmuring over it: "Have you ever been to Tawney?"

Kianthe quirked an eyebrow. "The town that straddles Shepara and the Queendom? Just south of dragon country? That Tawney?"

"It's remote, difficult to reach, and its trade routes rarely cross with the Capital. Plus, with the Sheparan and Queendom influences, we'll blend right in." Reyna sipped her tisane, savoring the sharp notes of mint overtop the mellower rose petals. "The bandits I killed today were part of the ring that recruits out of there. But with the questionable boundaries and ownership of the town, it's been in Queen Tilaine's best interest to ignore that hideout. We could secure it before the bandits realize what we've done."

Kianthe frowned. "Or, and hear me out . . . we just go to Shepara. Let Tilaine throw her hissy fit; we'll be sipping wine on the Nacean River out west."

Reyna grimaced. Kianthe was warm against her side, but she suddenly felt very cold. "Queen Tilaine operates an extensive network of spies, Key."

"And we'll be out of their range—" Kianthe stopped short, staring at her. "Oh. Shit. Seriously? All the way in Shepara?"

"Everywhere. She has outposts in Leonol, and even sent scouts to dragon country once." Reyna shook her head. "Fleeing to Shepara won't save me. But Tawney is remote enough that her spies might not explore it for a year, maybe two. It's small enough that we'll notice any newcomers quickly. And—well, the building is enticing, I'll admit. Shepara's construction costs significantly more."

Kianthe puffed out air. It ruffled Reyna's hair, just a bit. The mage slumped against her, taking a deep swig of her tea. "Oh, fine. I hate the cold, but I'm sure you can warm me up."

"Either me, or the dragon raids."

"Dragon raids?"

"Mmm. Happens a few times a year." Reyna quirked a smile. "Thank the Gods I'm dating an elemental mage. You know. For the fire control."

Kianthe looked skyward. "You're lucky I love you."

And so, they went to Tawney.

4

Kianthe

They stared at the ramshackle building.

"Well, it's not . . . uninhabitable," Reyna said.

Kianthe snickered.

Truly, though, the building itself wasn't bad. As the mage had feared, *Tawney* bordered on uninhabitable—pressed between a vicious mountain range and the cold, open plains of a vast tundra. Sparse forests of pine trees offered mild scenery, but a closer look proved that only the stiffest plants bothered to take root. Lindenback, the road they stood on, was on the edge of town and faced an open stretch of land.

The sunset views were incredible, but Kianthe was already too cold to appreciate them.

Aside from the scenery, the best word to describe this place was "seedy." Reyna was spot-on about it being a bandit headquarters—or at least a recruiting spot they sometimes visited. Broken glass and empty ale barrels filled the street, although the barn in question seemed unoccupied.

The neighbors had slammed their doors shut when Reyna and Kianthe approached, and a pair of men were staring greedily at Visk. Kianthe noticed them, and wrote them off just as fast.

Reyna was more alert. Her hand rested on her sword as she stared them down, reminding them that they weren't being sneaky—and she wouldn't back away from a fight. Her professional attitude was always sexy, but Kianthe had voiced that before and it never won any favors.

Under her breath, Reyna murmured, "I suspect your mount is attracting attention. And not the flattering kind."

Kianthe barked a laugh, waggling her fingers at the men. Contrary to her partner's, *her* voice was loud: "By the Stone, what a mistake that would be. Isn't that right, sweetie?" She cooed at her griffon, scratching the feathers on Visk's head. He preened under her attention, flexing talons larger than a dragon's tooth.

The men flinched and ducked into a nearby alley.

Reyna relaxed, but only a smidge. Kianthe wondered if she was having second thoughts about this place.

But Reyna had brought up excellent points—mostly on the topic of cost. Shepara's buildings would be nearly unreachable from an affordability standpoint, and anywhere properly within the Queendom was too close to Tilaine for Kianthe's comfort. Leonol might be a good option, but it was as humid and miserable in their jungle as it was cold and miserable here on the plains.

Plus, the mage had never been great with delayed gratification. There was a niggling fear in Kianthe's mind that if Reyna took too much time considering this, she might change her mind.

Kianthe didn't use the word "devastated" often, but if Reyna rescinded their new life—all the hopes and dreams Kianthe couldn't wait to explore—she certainly wouldn't be *happy* about it.

So, while Reyna's brow furrowed and her lips tilted downward, Kianthe slipped into cheery optimism.

The mage slid off Visk's back and strolled to the old barn's front windows. The lock was metal, but that was technically a type of earth—and technicalities didn't slow the Arcandor. She twirled her fingers, using magic to pull up the pins, and it unlatched with a heavy clunk.

"Anybody home?" she trilled into the space.

Emptiness echoed. Reyna slid off Lilac and followed the mage inside, unsheathing her poison-brushed sword with a soft *schwick*.

Visk stepped near Lilac, protecting the horse with his presence. A Queendom warhorse was a prize, after all. Visk's presence made Lilac stomp her hooves—but she had enough training to quell her basic impulse to flee.

Preposterous that Reyna thought griffons were "vicious." By all standards, Visk was an itty-bitty buddy and a good boy.

The two of them stood in the space, silent for a long moment.

"It's big," Reyna remarked neutrally.

It was that. At some point, it might have been used as a barn. Now cobwebs hung from the rafters, its cavernous ceiling dark and looming. There was a makeshift kitchen in the corner, a pair of rooms in the back, and . . . that was it. The floor was dirt and sawdust. Rat droppings and feces of something bigger—raccoon, maybe?—scented the air. A few wooden tables had been shoved in the corner, and they were slick with a dark, tacky liquid.

Kianthe was enamored. "This is *perfect*."

"This is a health hazard, love."

"No, your last career was a health hazard. This is raw potential." Kianthe winked at her, strolling into the center of the space. "Look. Clear out the dust and debris. Pine floors from the forest nearby. Bookshelves to the ceiling on this wall. A few more windows . . . some ever-flame lights strung from the rafters . . ." She twirled, starry-eyed. "And plants! I can keep the tropical ones alive, you know."

"Did you say 'ever-flame' near the brittle, wooden rafters?" Reyna reluctantly sheathed her sword, although a slight smile played on her lips.

Kianthe rolled her eyes. "You worry too much. A simple spell will keep them burning without *burning*."

"I think there was a miscommunication when we discussed fire control." Reyna's voice held a hint of worry—and it wasn't about the ever-flame. She looked doubtfully around the space, touching the healing wound at her neck.

She'd given a lot to be here; it was possible she'd built Tawney up in her mind and the reality was a letdown.

Kianthe was awash with ideas, seeing magic and fantastical notions everywhere. Reyna remained firmly on the ground, always. It was why Kianthe loved her . . . but it was also something she needed to be aware of. Her partner didn't like big change or exuberant gestures. She liked facts. Figures. Certainties.

Which meant she'd been nervous *before* they reached Tawney.

"Tell me how you're feeling," Kianthe said, her tone leaving no room for argument. This was their go-to discussion tactic, something they'd developed after their first real fight.

Reyna rubbed her arm, sighing. "We don't know if it's structurally sound. This building had an open call for bandits and thieves—and beyond that, renovating it will take immense effort and coin."

This had been Reyna's idea, but Kianthe was starting to think she'd pushed her girlfriend into a box with cheery optimism and grandiose ideas for renovation. Kianthe didn't care where they wound up, as long as they were together.

She could wait for the right place.

. . . Really.

"Okay." Kianthe forced a smile. "If you aren't comfortable here, we'll keep looking. This is the first area we've investigated; there's no reason to settle."

She just had to pray that Reyna wouldn't change her mind as this dragged on.

Her girlfriend blinked, taken aback. "Oh." Then, instead of arguing, Reyna turned a more critical eye to the space. As a Queensguard, she'd spent her life in a career where paying attention saved lives, and it showed in the careful way she moved through the old barn. She examined the floors, felt the walls, tested the sturdiness of the windows. She squinted at the roof, murmuring under her breath.

With the knowledge that they could leave Tawney behind, the whole place seemed to have more merit.

Kianthe moved to the doorway, keeping an eye on their mounts. Visk stood stoically, his eagle eyes glaring at the men down the street. Lilac had edged away from him, as far as her tether allowed, but otherwise seemed fine.

Granted, Kianthe didn't have much experience with horses, but the lack of panicked whinnying seemed like a good sign.

After several long minutes, Reyna emerged from one of the bedrooms. "There's a patio out back. Some trees and tiles, and we could make a nice sitting area for the summertime."

Tawney was cold most of the year, but Kianthe hoped the coming summer months would warm at least a little. And if not, a bit of fire magic would go a long way. If Reyna wanted to sip tea in a garden, Stone damn it all, she'd have the chance.

"That'd be excellent." Kianthe didn't offer more, allowing Reyna to draw her own conclusion.

Reyna paused at the western wall and tilted her head. "I think this lumber will need reinforcing. A few planks are coming loose. Propping the weight of a wall of books would test it in this state . . . not to mention the wind off the plains."

Kianthe felt giddy. She tried to keep an even tone, act like this was no big deal. "Sure, sure." And really, it wasn't—they'd already decided to make this happen. Whether it was here or in another building, Kianthe shouldn't care.

But this place was big and bright and faced a nice view, and standing inside it, watching the woman she loved, Kianthe could imagine them making it home.

Reyna sighed, finally. "There was a reason I suggested investigating this building first. The bandits don't concern me. We have the skillset to face them if more arrive. Tawney itself is where I'm hesitating, but . . . I can't imagine this building will cost much."

She seemed embarrassed about that, ducking her head as her cheeks tinged red.

Kianthe cleared her throat, even as the back of her neck burned. "If you want to explore someplace more expensive, I can pick up a few jobs. I have plenty of ability—that's got to be worth something." They'd never been in a position to share funds before. It made Kianthe immensely aware that she had none.

For a moment, they both stared at each other.

Then Reyna laughed. It was a rare thing, and filled the space with bright happiness. "I don't think I've ever been this nervous, Key. Afraid of what you're going to say, afraid of offending, afraid of losing our chance to do this."

"Offend who? Me? Have you *met* me?"

With the tension shattered, they both grinned. Kianthe's chest was warm. "I don't have money, Rain, but I'll do what I need to make this happen. Is that okay?"

"I don't care about money. I've saved all my life for a dream I never expected to reach reality. I'm only sorry if my funds aren't enough," Reyna replied.

"Don't apologize." Kianthe tossed an arm over her shoulder, then backpedaled when Reyna hissed in pain. "Shit, sorry!"

"Maybe we apologize sometimes," Reyna joked, her fingers feathering over her wound they'd rebandaged that morning. She turned her attention back to the street. "I think we can accomplish anything we set our minds to. But I am concerned about this street in particular. We won't attract the right clientele here, and location is the first step to a successful shop."

"Who said we're opening it for the public?" Kianthe scowled. "That means work."

Reyna crossed her arms, raising one eyebrow. "And profit."

The mage huffed, feigning exasperation. "Ugh. Fine. Let's check out the rest of Tawney, see what we think." She gestured outside, and Reyna stepped lithely from the building. Kianthe closed the door behind her, then welded the lock shut with a burst of flame.

At least she could protect it while they made their decision.

Reyna chuckled. "Was that necessary?"

But Kianthe didn't reply, because the men who'd been contemplating Visk earlier had resurfaced. They were perched on two wooden crates, murmuring to each other. Their eyes kept flicking to the griffon—and now, concerningly, Reyna. The rest of the street was oddly deserted, like the women had scared everyone else away.

Those two should have taken the hint.

Kianthe growled: "One moment."

And she stomped over to the men.

They startled at her approach. Kianthe stopped near enough to smell the alcohol on one, see the yellowing teeth of the other. They looked well fed, but one had a thick beard and sallow skin, and the other possessed a tall, wiry frame and beady eyes.

"Hello, folks."

They leered at her. Tall One said in a rough voice, "What do you want?" Sheparan accent, heavy on the consonants, but he spoke Common like the rest of them.

"We're new in town. Bit curious about that building." She jerked a thumb back at it.

Reyna appeared at her shoulder like a specter, one hand resting on her sword. The queen's royal insignia, stamped on the pommel, drew their attention.

The men were looking less confident now. Tall One hesitated. "It's just an old barn. No one lives there anymore."

"Anymore? Who occupied it originally?"

They exchanged glances. Tall One chuckled. "You're new in town, but here, people *pay* for that information."

"Any information, really. We're the best at it." Beardy smiled. His voice was higher-pitched, with a whistle at the end from a missing tooth. Even so, their dangerous demeanors had vanished, replaced with something more curious.

Reyna raised an eyebrow. "Town informants?"

"Unofficially." Tall One picked at his nails. "We watch everyone and everything. New folk come to town, 'specially with a griffon? Folk will want to know. You'd do best to get on our good sides."

Kianthe nearly rolled her eyes. They weren't a threat, then. Still, awfully audacious to ask for money from strangers who'd just moseyed into town. It felt like a scam.

Beside her, though, Reyna looked contemplative. She strolled back to Lilac, fishing in her saddlebags for a few coins. The men looked surprised when she willingly handed them over. "I'll pay for that."

They took the money, and Tall One squinted at the insignia on her sword. "You work for the queen?"

Reyna crossed her arms. "Used to. Now I pay handsomely for information about the queen's people. Guards, citizens, spies. Any newcomers to Tawney—I'd like to know."

Ah. Kianthe hated that this was necessary, but at least Reyna was taking steps to protect herself.

Beardy nodded, slipping the pents into a bag at his hip. He patted it, and the pouch jingled. "We can do that, long as the coins keep coming."

Reyna smirked. "They will."

"With that money, we deserve a bit more information. Seems only fair." Kianthe gestured again at the barn. "Tell us about the building."

The men exchanged another glance, and Tall One shrugged. "Used to belong to that Queendom lord, Julan." At her questioning frown, he expanded: "Passed a few years ago. Dragon attack killed him and his wife."

"So, who presides over Tawney now?" Reyna asked, brow furrowing. It was clear she both recognized the name, and had no idea Lord Julan had been killed.

Kianthe almost laughed. Tawney's borders were irregular at best, and both countries assumed ownership. It was interesting that the Queendom had placed a lord here, as if they had claim over the land.

Not unexpected, considering their snake of a ruler, but still.

"Well, we've been betting on that kid Feo." Beardy leaned back on the wooden crate, grinning wide. "They're Sheparan-born. Real fancy-like. Hoping to make themself a name. But Julan had a son, and he isn't happy someone's disputing his claim. Whole town's been waiting for the dust to settle." Now he nodded at the barn. "There were casualties. Figuratively speaking."

Reyna was smiling. Not just a quiet, amused smile, but an eager one: she'd just discovered a problem and was dying to resolve it. Kianthe snorted, bumped her shoulder, and asked, "Well, we're sticking around for a bit. Last thing: You two know a spot to bunk tonight?"

"Inn's just up the road," Tall One commented, jerking a thumb. "If you like ale, Hansen serves the best."

"We appreciate it." Reyna paused, then tilted her head. "Do you have names?"

Tall One held out a hand, and Kianthe felt bad about mentally calling him *Tall One* this whole time. "Sigmund. This here's Nurt."

"It's a nickname," Nurt said solemnly.

"Call me Kianthe," the mage said, because only a select few knew the given name of the Arcandor, Mage of Ages. "And this is—" She paused, glanced at Reyna awkwardly. If Tilaine's spies followed their trail, using Reyna's real name would make her too easy to track.

Reyna held out a hand. "Cya. Also a nickname."

They bid the men farewell, then mounted their steeds to ride deeper into town. As they left Lindenback Road, Reyna remarked, "Always good to know the town informants. Didn't expect they'd find us so fast; those two must be good."

"Sure, sure." Kianthe quirked an eyebrow. "So . . . Cya?"

"As in, see ya later," Reyna replied, putting on a thick—almost absurd—Sheparan accent.

Kianthe cackled. "By the Stone, I'm already rubbing off on you. That does *not* bode well for this town."

Reyna was still laughing when they reached the inn.

5

Reyna

Tawney's sole inn was a decent establishment. It had a bar on the main level, stables that could accommodate Lilac—griffons didn't like to be caged, and thus Visk vanished into the night on Kianthe's dismissal—and several cozy rooms available upstairs. At the welcome counter, Kianthe said, "One room, please. Preferably with one bed."

The innkeeper turned to collect a key.

As they climbed the staircase, Reyna murmured, "Only one bed? Are you planning something untoward, Key?"

They'd spent the last two nights camping in the wilderness, so any hints of unfamiliarity were gone. Kianthe offered a wicked grin. "Every night since that rendezvous last season, I've been planning something untoward. We've barely scratched the surface."

Reyna smirked and led the way to their room. It was small and simple, with just a bed, a chamber pot in the corner, and a desk positioned beside a window. They stored their saddlebags inside the chest at the foot of the bed, washed themselves down with a bucket of water. While Reyna changed into a new shirt, Kianthe set a well-loved book on the bedside table.

Reyna assessed it. "Let me guess. Forbidden love?"

"Hey. I like what I like." Kianthe patted the tome. "For obvious reasons."

Reyna snorted, but made a note to steal that book at some point.

With a bit of time before bed, they headed downstairs for a drink.

Evening had arrived, and the air was frigid every time someone opened the inn's door. Reyna could handle this weather, but Kianthe looked miserable hunched in her fur-lined coat. It made sense; the Magicary rarely experienced seasons, considering their large population of elemental mages. Reyna took pity and led the mage to a small table beside the roaring fireplace.

They settled in, ordered a drink—wine for Reyna, hot water for Kianthe, since alcohol and magic never mixed—and a plate of smoked elk. Based on the scent of the table beside them, it was served drizzled with a rosemary sauce. Reyna's mouth watered, and she took a sip of her wine to distract. As the innkeeper left, Reyna pulled a sheet of parchment from her bag, her mind buzzing.

"So, the barn. Before we purchase it, let's make a plan for the renovation. We'll need a few contractors, unless your plant magic comes with treated lumber."

"It does not," Kianthe replied, clutching her mug in both hands.

"Mmm. So, a carpenter, at least. Possibly a glassworker for the windows." She tapped her chin, then sketched a rough outline of the floorplan. "We keep the rooms intact. One for us, the other maybe a storage space. Add a washroom . . . here. And counter space on this back wall, against the storage room, and an oven for baking."

She paused, glancing at her girlfriend—double-checking that this was, in fact, what Kianthe expected. But the mage was more "big picture, sweeping ideas," and it was clear she hadn't considered where they'd steep the tea, or store pastries they might offer. Kianthe gestured for Reyna to continue, eyes wide.

A thrill rushed through Reyna too. Putting it on paper made it feel real, and seeing Kianthe's encouragement solidified everything.

"We put down wood floors. Tawney may have piped water, which would save us the time of hauling it from the well—" At this, Reyna stopped, realizing what she just said.

Kianthe sat beside her, an insufferable smile on her face. "What's it like, living without magic?"

"It comes with a lot less arrogance, for one," Reyna replied smoothly, taking another deep sip of her wine. It was a dry white from the Queendom's vineyards, which spread across the southern half of the country. The wine itself was only okay, but it did prove that Tawney received imports.

That might make getting tea leaves easier, anyway.

"There's a ley line running through town," Kianthe said after a moment. "Unsurprising; the Stone tends to guide me along its paths."

Kianthe's divine Stone of Seeing was—as far as Reyna could tell—a literal rock in the Magicary. The idea that a rock could move Kianthe on any certain path left Reyna very confused. She raised an eyebrow. "What does that have to do with the pipes, dear?"

"It means magic can be tapped here, instead of requiring me to use my personal reserves. There's always water in the ground." Kianthe knocked the floor with her boot.

"Which still depends on whether you're available. I'd like to explore piping in a more reliable source."

Kianthe looked offended. "I won't be traveling *that* often."

Reyna's expression softened, and her fingers drifted over the back of her girlfriend's hand. Kianthe's skin was the color of drying clay, a slight contrast to Reyna's own skin, which was light in tone and calloused from years of combat drills. "Key, you have other obligations. I'm aware that they'll steal you from Tawney at some point."

"You are my obligation," Kianthe said. "Those ancient mages and needy world leaders can go to hells."

"Those ancient mages ensure the world's magic remains in balance. And those leaders usually have mouths to feed." Reyna kept her voice as patient as possible, but inside her chest warmed. There was something special about being someone's top priority. "We can start a life here, but I don't want us to lose a wider perspective."

Kianthe sighed. "Sometimes it feels easier to run from my responsibilities, and never stop running."

"What an unfulfilling life that would be," Reyna said. "All the best things come alongside responsibility."

Kianthe made a face.

They settled on exploring the piped water option, then drafted out a few levels at Reyna's behest. Funds withstanding—and they should withstand, provided the building itself remained free—Reyna believed they could accomplish every renovation they hoped, along with a few side aspirations. Even so, she catalogued their must-haves, nice-to-haves, and if-there's-coin-left.

In the end, they had full bellies and several sheets of parchment penned with their hopes and dreams. The inn was bustling now—it was wholly possible this was the only place to grab a drink in Tawney—and the buzz of conversation became a distant backdrop. Reyna wasn't one for crowds, considering her old career, but the wine had warmed her from the inside out and perching beside Kianthe made her feel invincible.

It wasn't the best mindset for making a major decision, but Reyna made it nonetheless.

"I think we should do it."

Kianthe's expression brightened. "You like Tawney?"

Reyna gestured at the inn. "This is all I've ever wanted. A social atmosphere, new friends, and you holding me close."

"Aww, you always get so romantic after a drink." Kianthe smirked, clearly amused. Reyna wrinkled her nose, so Kianthe moved on quickly. "We haven't met much of the town yet."

"I can already tell I'll like the people, and that barn—" Reyna breathed out, tapping the parchment before them. "Look at this. This is a *plan*. You know I love those."

They were in a crowded room, but it didn't stop Kianthe from hugging Reyna's shoulders. "I was hoping you'd say that."

Reyna's body felt light with happiness. "You're okay with it? I know you hate the cold."

"I also hate the idea of spending months tromping around the world, hoping to find somewhere better." Kianthe averted her gaze, taking a sip of her water. "Can't give you a chance to change your mind, after all."

It cut through the fog of alcohol, and Reyna frowned. "Are you worried about that?"

A pause.

"A bit," Kianthe admitted.

Reyna groaned. Her mind buzzed, dulling the world's sharp edges, narrowing to Kianthe as the primary focus. "Key, my old life is over." She lowered her voice, bending closer so they were the only ones privy to the conversation. "Queen Tilaine is not a forgiving soul, and I've essentially committed treason to the crown."

Kianthe blanched. "Don't remind me."

Reyna's stomach twisted, because anyone with intelligence feared Queen Tilaine and her temper. To distract from that unpleasant thought, Reyna polished off her wine. "My point is that I love you, and that won't change. Even if we don't stay in Tawney, we're staying together now. Assuming that's what you want?"

"That's the only thing I want. Tawney suits me just fine." The mage breathed a satisfied sigh.

"Good. Me too. Should I have another?"

Now Kianthe laughed. "You should always have another. Drunk Reyna is one of my favorites."

"I'm not drunk," Reyna scoffed. Back at the palace, she wasn't allowed to drink on the job—and her life was the job. It maybe, possibly, lowered her tolerance to the wine. Kianthe's smirk widened, and she shoved the woman's shoulder. "I'm *not*."

"Go get another glass, love. I'll hold our table."

"From all the people vying for it?"

"We clearly claimed the best spot." Kianthe gestured to the nearby fire.

Reyna retrieved her glass and pushed upright, chuckling when she stumbled a bit. She wove through the crowds to the innkeeper, who'd contracted her husband for help at some point: a heavyset man stood by the ale kegs, pouring drinks for anyone who approached with a few pents.

Another man stood in front of her. He had a thick red beard and dark eyes, but he smiled jovially when she stood behind him. "Line's a bit long, but Hansen moves fast."

"An excellent trait for a bartender." Reyna squinted at the man. "You have a Queendom accent. Sounds like you're from the inner palace." She shouldn't be so forward, but the wine had loosened her tongue.

That, and suspicion drifted on the edges of her mind. The queen's spies were everywhere—but if this one planned to haul her back into service, he had another think coming. Kianthe was watching from across the inn, her chin resting in her palm, and Reyna could kill a man sixteen ways without her sword.

She might have to concentrate a bit more, wine considering, but still.

The man rubbed the back of his neck. "Grew up there. Met my wife, and we moved here." He paused, then said tactfully, "Bless the queen, and may her lands have good fortune . . . but we wanted some distance."

Reyna wove her arm through his. "Well, aren't we kindred spirits then? Where's your wife? She should meet my girlfriend."

Relaxing at her bold gesture, the man laughed. The sound shook his whole body, booming through the space. He didn't extract himself from her hold, but he did raise his empty pint at a woman perched at a table by the front door. "Matild, we made a friend! Bring the wine!"

"That's your wife?" Reyna exclaimed. She elbowed him, pushed to her tiptoes to whisper, "She's marvelous. That *hair*." It was inky with amber undertones, expertly braided into thick plaits that Matild had pulled into a loose bun on the top of her head. Reyna felt a pang of jealousy: Kianthe used to have long, vivacious hair, but she'd sliced it to shoulder-length after she burned the edges by accident. Reyna's own hair fell to her mid-back, ice blond, but the strands were too thin for her personal taste.

"Wait until you meet her. Looks have nothing on her personality," the big man said. Across the bar, Matild heaved a sigh and gathered her drink and the jug of wine. "Name's Tarly. You folk new in town, or just passing through?"

Reyna thought about the inked parchment under Kianthe's arm, the empty barn brimming with potential.

"We're staying, actually." It felt bold to admit. "Just moved here. We're hoping to renovate an old barn on the far side of town. Call me Cya. And that's Kianthe." They'd reached the counter now, and Tarly wasted no time having his pint refilled. Reyna raised her glass for wine, a pent in hand, but Matild reached them and waved the bartender off.

"Don't be silly," she told Reyna. Her voice was lower, almost rough, and she offered her husband an amused smile. Standing side by side, they looked like the sun mingling with a starry night. "I always share wine with my friends. Even more so when they have a seat by the fireplace." Now she hoisted the jug over her shoulder. It sloshed with deep red wine, which was something Reyna hadn't tried yet.

Reyna led them back to Kianthe, proudly introducing them.

Kianthe looked delighted. "You made friends already?"

"I'm social," Reyna said. At the mage's amused expression, she crossed her arms. "I can *be* social." Ironic thing was that between the two of them, Reyna was typically the extrovert. Kianthe's title kept potential friends at arm's length.

A lot of people attempted to befriend the Queensguard to reach Her Excellency. But now, that didn't matter. Reyna could befriend whoever she wanted. Kianthe clearly agreed, because she scooched their chairs to one side to make room.

Tarly hauled two more chairs to their table. Matild poured the wine, which had a startlingly earthen flavor. Reyna sat beside Kianthe, nursing her newly filled glass, and was pleased when the mage's leg pressed against hers under the table.

"So, an old barn," Tarly mused. "You talking about that bandit hideout?"

Reyna offered their plans, pushing the parchment forward for inspection. Matild scanned it curiously while Reyna said, "The bandits have . . . moved on. And if they haven't, we're equipped to deal with them. But this town looks like it could use a book-shop."

"This town could use a lot of things," Tarly drawled.

His wife elbowed him. "Hey. This is my home too, you lug." She tapped the list Reyna had made. "Do you two have experience with this? Building a new store?"

Kianthe shrugged. "We're in love. How hard can it be?"

Matild burst into laughter.

Tarly rolled his eyes, but a smile played on his lips. "Well, we've been here a while. Know most of the good folk, and some of the bad. If you two are getting started tomorrow, I can have a carpenter there by midday. You'll want to get that place refinished before the summer rain sets in—we enjoy a healthy wet season here."

Reyna leaned forward eagerly. "You know a carpenter? How about a glassworker? Or somewhere to rent a cart to haul out the trash? Does Tawney have piped water?"

It descended into shop talk, most of which Reyna retained. He did indeed know every kind of contractor they'd need; Tarly himself was the town blacksmith. After a time, he borrowed a sheet of parchment and began making notes, coordinating with an increasingly drunk Reyna on all the little things they'd need. The most exciting part was that Tawney did have piped water, which flowed from a glacier lake north of the town.

Kianthe, meanwhile, diverged to speak with Matild. Reyna kept their conversation on her peripherals, even as Tarly was mulling ideas. At one point Kianthe asked, "So, what do you do? You work in the smithy too?"

Matild laughed boisterously. "Gods, no. I'm a midwife. Closest thing this town has to a doctor, so keep it in mind."

"That's a lot of responsibility." Kianthe's tone was sympathetic.

The woman shrugged a shoulder. "I like responsibility. I was trained in the Grand Palace, but furthered my education for half a year in Wellia. I'm well positioned to handle the emergencies here. Dragon attacks and all."

Kianthe had deviated already. "Well, that's a stroke of luck, because Cya has a wound on her shoulder that isn't healing right."

That pulled Reyna's attention away from the renovation strategy. She winced, her cheeks coloring. "Key, please. It's fine. I'm hardly keeling over." Her shoulder throbbed, but she was well versed in watching her wounds heal.

Kianthe frowned.

Matild took another swig of her drink. "Well, swing by my clinic soon, and I'll double-check it. I'm just across the town square."

"I will," Reyna said, and that seemed to appease Kianthe. The conversation moved on.

Finally, the wine hit hard enough that Reyna could no longer deny her inebriated state. Matild capped the bottle when Reyna's eyelids started to droop. At some point, she'd leaned against Kianthe's shoulder, and now she wasn't sure she could stand up straight again.

"Time to call it a night," Kianthe said, helping Reyna to her feet. As Tarly and Matild gathered themselves, Kianthe murmured in

Reyna's ear, "Anything untoward will have to wait until tomorrow, apparently."

"I'm here all week," Reyna replied.

Kianthe snorted, looping an arm around her waist to steady her.

Their new friends recaptured their attention. "You two are really nice." Reyna clasped hands with Tarly, then pulled away from Kianthe to hug Matild. The midwife seemed surprised, but a pleased smile tilted her lips as Reyna retreated. "Like, *really* nice."

"The benefit of a small community. We help each other." Tarly winked. "Assuming you sleep off the wine, I'll be at your place midday with the carpenter."

"And I'll see you soon for that shoulder," Matild commented.

Kianthe shook hands with them both. "I'll make sure Cya visits you soon." She grinned, still delighted by the nickname.

It was unfair that their new friends didn't know her real name. Reyna almost whispered it like some kind of conspiracy, but the last vestiges of common sense stopped her. Pouting, she stayed silent as they bid each other goodnight and trudged back upstairs.

Tomorrow, the real work would begin.

6

Kianthe

The next morning, Kianthe paused over Reyna's sleeping form, chuckling softly. She hadn't seen Reyna let loose like that in . . . Stone-damned, nearly a year. Not since they'd taken a trip to Leonol and were offered coconut juice spiked with rum. After that occasion, Reyna had been out of commission most of the following day. Kianthe expected this would be no different.

She wouldn't have traded it for anything, though. Partially for the amusement of watching her girlfriend relax, but mostly because of their new friends. Despite Kianthe's teasing, Reyna was fantastic at socializing; her steady presence and confident nature put most people at ease.

After a decade of isolation as the Arcandor, it was a welcome change. Spending her childhood surrounded by crotchety mages with grandiose ideas of Kianthe's purpose didn't exactly lend to a decent social life.

She knelt beside Reyna, her fingers drifting through the woman's long hair. It was soft, smooth as silk. Reyna didn't stir at the touch, but she did start snoring. Considering her normally quiet nature, the sound was hilarious.

Kianthe pressed a kiss to her cheek, then left a huge glass of water on the bedside table. As an afterthought, remembering Leonol, she plucked a few hindenlery leaves from her bag. They were bitter, but eased a headache when chewed slowly.

"Rest up, Rain," she murmured to the sleeping woman, and slipped from the room.

A few pents earned Reyna breakfast in bed, and Hansen's wife begrudgingly agreed to wait several hours before attempting it. Kianthe slipped into her fur-lined cloak, then trudged into the bitter morning.

Today, the sun was bright overhead. The snow-soaked plains beyond the town glistened, and dew had settled on the rooftops and cobblestones. The air was so sharp its bite almost made Kianthe start coughing. She contemplated summoning Visk—a sharp whistle would do it—but decided the walk might be nice. No reason to miss out on their new home.

Under her cloak, she summoned a ball of ever-flame, spelling it to keep her clothes from burning. She tucked the ball against her chest, hunching into the wind. With this weather, maybe they *should* have kept traveling; Shepara's grassy plains were bright and warm this time of year.

But when Kianthe arrived at the barn, their new home, her apprehension vanished. It was even prettier in the morning light, standing watch over the tundra and forest beyond. The two buildings on either side were squat houses with closed windows, and the street was deserted yet again.

She unlocked the deadbolt with a twist of magic, then stepped into the space. In every wall, the old lumber pulsed with yearning. Besieged by time, weather, and insects, it was tired, and ached to be remade. Kianthe pressed a hand to it, sending out a mild thrum of magic.

"You'll be right as rain soon. Right by Rain, too." She chuckled and got to work.

First, she summoned wind. It whipped through the space,

pulling trash from every corner. Bottles, glass shards, parchment, dried leather scraps, even a bent knife—Kianthe spiraled it into a tight tornado, then whisked it out the door. She strolled after it, casually directing it to a dumping area at the end of the street.

As she approached the barn again, the next-door neighbor's door flew open. A little boy sprinted out, eyes wide. "Are you a mage? A real-life mage?"

"I'm one of them, yeah." Kianthe grinned, but her eyes caught the boy's mother. The woman was tall and thin, with pale cheeks and hollow eyes. A wicked scar ran along her eyebrow, giving an intimidating appearance. Kianthe felt the need to reassure her. "Ah, it's not dangerous. My magic is easy to control."

"Did the Magicary send you to clear out the bandits?" the mother asked warily.

Kianthe frowned. It seemed rude to ask if a bandit gave the woman that scar, so she diverted. "It's on our docket. Are they a danger to you and your son?"

The mother nudged her son back inside, closing him safely in the house. When she straightened, weariness had settled in her tone. "They aren't pleasant neighbors, but mostly keep to themselves— especially considering the sheriff is a few streets away. But mages handle magical creatures, don't they? Like dragons?"

Kianthe was beginning to suspect the Stone of Seeing sent her to Tawney for a reason. "Yeah, we do. Well, the Arcandor does . . . but I can contact her if necessary."

"You may want to. They attack a few times a year, and we're due for another one." The woman set her jaw.

"Noted. My name's Kianthe." She held out her hand.

"Sasua," the mother replied, but she didn't shake. "Good luck with your renovations. And the bandits. And the dragons." And she stepped back into her house, slamming the door shut.

Huh.

Kianthe strolled back into the barn, her mind whirling as she surveyed the uneven, feces-coated floor. She'd address the dragons . . . eventually. For now, she wanted to focus on Reyna and their dream together, like she promised. With a turnover motion, Kianthe pushed the worn dirt deeper underground, pulling fresh earth that filled the space with the scent of wet soil. Sweat dripped down her temples as she packed it tight, leveled it flat. Against the front windows, she created an indoor planting area, tilling that dirt with magic.

"I'm going to plant some excellent things here. Nothing better than plants welcoming people inside," she told the soil. "Do good for me."

The earth seemed flattered. It was hard to tell, but she got the sense of it.

The place was cleaner already, and she searched for more to accomplish. No matter what, Reyna would be impressed when she arrived. Pulling water from the ground, Kianthe sprayed the walls with a concentrated mist, coaxed the air to dry the lumber fast, then peeled off layers of mold from the deep crevices of the barn. The stained wooden tables were washed down too, removing the dark, tacky substance with stubbornness and grit. As an afterthought, she addressed the spot Reyna had noted as their washroom, and carved out a deep trench for the water piping.

By now, she was feeling a bit lightheaded, like how Reyna described being tipsy. Still able to function, but the drain of magic pulsed in her reservoirs. Apparently, Tawney's ley line wasn't quite as powerful as she'd hoped. The Stone would send more magic, but until it did, Kianthe would feel a bit off.

With a bit of time before Tarly arrived, Kianthe stepped into the back patio area. It was a decent-sized space wedged between Sasua's house and another building, with a grassy clearing behind it. Nothing immense, but private enough that they could enjoy a cup of tea in the mornings without bother.

Kianthe repeated her cleaning process here: trash tornado, upturned soil, packed flat. This time, though, she pushed magic into the dirt surrounding the area, and didn't wait to fill it with plants. She plucked several seeds from a bag at her hip, choosing them for aesthetic purposes. Two palms, and some shorter fronds framing the entrance to their new place. A swell of luscious ground cover to mask the hard dirt, accented by several brightly colored flowers. Red was Reyna's favorite; the hibiscus protested the cold weather, but Kianthe scowled at it, and it reluctantly bloomed wide.

Satisfied, Kianthe finished the space with two gorgeous pines in the back corners, their bark smelling of sugar. The mage paused to inhale the trunks, then used their sturdiness to steady herself.

She may have overdone it. Just a bit.

But it already looked a thousand times better. She was readying the spell to rim the pines in protected ever-flame, dazzle them with lights to illuminate their new oasis, when the back door pushed open.

Kianthe wiped her forehead, smiling at Reyna. "Welcome to the land of the living."

"Don't—speak so loudly," Reyna muttered, one palm on her forehead. She looked vaguely nauseated, but more confused. "Were you here all morning? Gods, I did *not* mean to drink that much."

"Well, I had a fabulous time last night. If it's any consolation."

"It isn't." Reyna frowned, examining her for the first time. "You look horrible."

Kianthe pressed a hand to her chest. "Rude."

"*Key*. Why didn't you spread it out a bit?"

She leaned against the tree, hoping it looked casual rather than necessary. The loss of magic was an emptiness in her chest. She had the ability to tap into the magic of other mages, but there clearly weren't any in Tawney—and she'd ask permission before that spell anyway. The ley line would have to be enough, even if it was far weaker than Kianthe had expected.

She waved off Reyna's concern. "I was excited. Look, it's fine. Probably good the Arcandor is reminded that she's not all-powerful."

"I'd prefer you didn't remind me of that." Reyna stepped forward, offering her arm, and helped Kianthe back inside the barn. There wasn't anywhere to sit, so she left the mage to retrieve one of the wooden crates Sigmund and Nurt had been using yesterday.

Kianthe was very grateful to sit down. Taking the water Reyna offered, she gestured at the barn. "Magic drain aside, what do you think?"

Reyna inhaled deeply. "I think it smells a lot better."

"I replaced the ground." Kianthe was not above bragging.

Reyna pinched the bridge of her nose.

The mage leaned back on the crate, nodding at the walls. "Took care of the mold problem, sprayed the lumber, dried it again. We can put flooring down once we install your precious piping." She pointed at the trench, then jerked a thumb at the back door. "And you already saw the back patio."

"It's gorgeous. I know you're excited, but there's no rush for this. Right now, this building is technically owned by the monarchy; we need the local lord's permission to move further."

The mage opened her mouth to reply, but a knock on the open door distracted her. Tarly and Matild. She'd expected him, but his wife was a surprise.

Tarly offered a basket covered by a white cloth. "You two care for some company?"

"How are you feeling, Cya?" Matild cut right to the chase. She strolled into the barn, offering a blue-tinted bottle capped with a cork. "Care for my hangover remedy? It's disgusting, but it works."

Reyna must have been hurting, because she took the bottle.

Matild's sharp gaze landed on Kianthe. "And you! I thought Reyna was the one with the shoulder injury. Why are *you* so pale?"

"Magic drain," Kianthe replied, waving off her concern. It was already getting better as she rested; the Stone of Seeing was nudging her more magic. It spread through her veins, as warm and cozy as cocoa on a cold day. "Tawney is a bit farther from the blessed Stone than I expected. Ley-wise."

That made no sense to anyone who wasn't a mage, or dating one, so the pair merely nodded.

Tarly whistled as he examined the space. "You've, ah . . . already done a lot, it looks like. Carpenter should be here soon. Figured you may want lunch first." He set the basket on Kianthe's lap, pulling the linen aside to reveal fresh bread and sliced cheeses.

"I'll pass," Reyna muttered, uncorking the bottle. She took a sniff and grimaced. "This smells—"

"Like the Gods' shit." Matild chuckled, patting her arm.

Kianthe laughed, and they settled down for a meal at the round table. Reyna nursed the vile liquid in the bottle, gagging more than once, but eventually she started talking more and wincing less. Kianthe, too, regained strength with food and good company— and the Stone's grace.

The carpenter arrived just as they finished. He was a gruff-looking man with bulging muscles and no mirth. He grunted when Tarly introduced them, then squinted at the ceiling and walls. "You two own this place?"

Kianthe shifted. Reyna pulled her shoulders back. "We'll be speaking with Lord Wylan soon, but per Queen Eren's Decree of Development, lords are encouraged by Her Excellency to repurpose abandoned buildings for the prosperity of the Queendom. I don't anticipate problems in obtaining permission."

It sounded so official, coming from her.

The carpenter frowned. "Decree or no, you'll have to clear ownership with Diarn Feo." He was obviously from Shepara to brush a Queendom law off so fast.

"Diarn?" Kianthe drawled. Last she'd heard, there wasn't a di-arn in Tawney. For someone to claim that title without approval of Shepara's council was a grievous offense . . . and luckily, Kianthe was not above a little blackmail to get what she needed. A smile tilted her lips. "Trust me. We'll be fine there, too."

Tarly clapped the carpenter's shoulder. "They'll get it. Neither Feo nor Wylan have given much attention to this part of town, and these two entrepreneurs are planning to turn it around. What d'you say? Bend the rules a bit for an old friend?"

The carpenter heaved a massive sigh. "Get the permission." Kianthe nodded eagerly. Satisfied, he let his eyes roam the barn before settling on Reyna. "Walk me through what you want, and I'll tell you what you need."

They set out, touring the space, discussing logistics and occasionally referencing Reyna's architectural sketch.

Meanwhile, Kianthe helped herself to more bread. It was light and fluffy and a bit warm, like they'd pulled it from the oven before coming here. Across from her, Matild leaned back in her chair, casting a curious glance at Kianthe.

"So. You're a mage?"

Kianthe shrugged. "Something like that."

"I've met a few in Wellia. They're a quiet bunch. You're . . . not like that." Matild tossed her long braids over her shoulder as she helped herself to a slice of hard cheese.

"I'm not," Kianthe agreed. "The Magicary wasn't my preference. I like the world. I like her." She nodded at Reyna. "So, I delight in breaking tradition."

Matild frowned. "Hard to imagine a world-traveled mage will be happy living in Tawney the rest of her life."

It wasn't accusatory, but Kianthe bristled anyway. "I'm happy wherever Cya is." Now she shoved the sentiment back to Matild. "What surprises *me* is that a palace-trained midwife is settling for this backwater town. Especially one motivated enough to get additional training in Wellia."

Matild just smiled wider, almost sly now. "My coursework was in medicine, the body, and the mind. Lately, I've been fascinated by human interaction. For example, it's theorized that most of our communication happens through body positioning." A pause. "We also tend to deflect from things that make us uncomfortable."

Kianthe squinted at her.

Matild laughed boisterously, patting the mage's hand. "I think your devotion to Cya is admirable. But a good relationship thrives on distance, sometimes." Now she leaned in close. "That's why I went to Wellia. Drinking in those rooftop pubs. Dancing with strangers. It's exhilarating."

Kianthe was startled into a laugh, and their conversation moved to lighter things.

After assessing everything, the carpenter charged two palidrons for the materials and labor, with a warning it might climb if they discovered problems. But he had loosened considerably as he heard Reyna's plans for the barn.

"This'll be a good addition to Tawney. If you can pull it off—" He paused, shrugging. "Color me intrigued. My kid likes books more than lumber; she'd love something like this."

Tarly grinned. "Hells, *I'd* love something like this."

Reyna and Kianthe exchanged pleased glances.

The carpenter headed for the door. "Talk to Diarn Feo, and show me their seal of approval tomorrow. I'll come with the tools and supplies we need, and we'll get to work. I'd say . . . two weeks of labor, provided you both help me."

"We can help," Reyna replied with a solid nod.

"I'm on my way to Feo now," Kianthe added. "See you back at the inn, dear."

Without waiting, she followed the carpenter out the door.

7

Reyna

After a bit more time bidding Tarly and Matild goodbye and inspecting the barn with anticipation fluttering in her stomach, Reyna finally locked up. The sun hung low on the horizon, and she shielded her eyes as light gleamed off the distant snow. Once the sun shifted farther north for the summer, this would be a gorgeous spot.

But first things first.

Kianthe had gone to see the Sheparan representative—which left the Queendom lord as her unspoken responsibility. And considering how much time Reyna had spent around Queen Tilaine and her favored nobility, she had plenty to assess about this Wylan fellow.

Tawney was built on the plains, but jagged rocks formed a rim-like barrier to dragon country behind it. She headed up, climbing stone steps to the most ostentatious home in town. Lord Julan had always preferred visual displays of wealth to any actual governing style, and she expected his old home to be no different.

No one greeted her at the entrance. Reyna knocked, heavy-handed, on the thick wooden door. It reverberated through the expansive courtyard, and she counted the seconds as they passed.

Thirty-seven. Which must mean the lord was short-staffed. It was an embarrassment to leave a guest on the stoop longer than fifteen.

The door finally opened to a homely servant. He dipped his head and stammered, "Ah, p-pardon me, miss, but the good lord is not meeting anyone today."

Reyna hadn't quite decided how she would play this yet—would she be Cya, the anonymous Queendom citizen, hoping for a lord's boon? Or was Reyna, the member of the queen's royal guard, a smarter option?

One would leave her with little bargaining power but anonymity. The other would ensure this lord caused no problems as they established their new residence . . . but put her at significantly more risk.

Reyna wasn't prepared to leave anything to uncertainty. She played it safe until given a reason not to. "Apologies. I know my visit is unexpected, and that it's getting late. But I'm new to town, and merely wanted to pay my respects to Lord Wylan."

He seemed surprised. "Pay respects?"

"I'm a steadfast servant to the queen herself," she said humbly. Vaguely. "Lord Julan was a benefit to our society. I expect his son to be the same, and would like to offer my loyalty in person."

"Oh. I see." He didn't *seem* like he saw—which told Reyna an awful lot. "Well, I'm sure the lord could make an exception. This way." And he allowed her entrance into the massive house.

As she followed him deeper inside, her eyes cut to the surroundings: polished wood floors—scuffed with neglect. Tapestries on the walls—yellowing with age. The statues, some of which were gifted from the queen herself, held a layer of dust. No sign of any other servants, no sign of any true care.

"Ah, I assumed the lord had a full staff." Her tone was innocent, but she noted the way his back tensed.

"He does. They're . . . out. Celebrating."

"Celebrating what?"

"The f-full moon, of course. An age-old festival, here."

The full moon was hours away, and she was nearly positive there hadn't been any celebrations setting up in the town square. She nodded mutely and continued examining the home. It was built in towering granite, same as everything else in the Queendom, which almost certainly benefited them during the dragon attacks. She wondered how long it had taken to rebuild the rest of Tawney after it burned.

Or if Wylan or his father had cared to try.

Finally, they arrived at the heart of the building: an outdoor courtyard rimmed in fire torches. With the setting sun, it was getting frigid, but Lord Wylan perched near a huge bonfire, sipping from a leather flask.

"My lord," the servant said loudly. "A visitor."

"Who is it?"

His voice was deep, annoyed.

"A-A visitor," the servant repeated. She almost felt bad for him.

"My name is Cya," she said, and strolled into the courtyard without waiting for permission. "I am a humble citizen of the Queendom, here to pay my respects." She stepped into the lord's line of sight and knelt, pointedly submissive.

And Gods, he was young. Reyna nearly laughed—the boy was barely older than she. To have claimed the title of lord, even as the dependent of Julan . . . it must have been a brave move. Lords, barons, dukes, and everything in between—if they owned land, they were subject to the queen's full scrutiny. Any found lacking were beheaded, replaced with a more suitable option.

Very brave, indeed. Or, quite possibly, desperate.

Reyna withheld judgment until she could differentiate that.

Lord Wylan ran a hand over his close-cropped, ombre hair, frowning down at her. He looked just like Julan—or what she remembered of him. Same square jaw, same attractive smile, although Wylan's skin was closer to smoky quartz. "Cya? I've never heard of you. Are you here on the queen's orders?" Now suspicion laced his voice.

Interesting.

Reyna ducked her head, still kneeling. "No, my lord. I've just moved here." Then, to force him away from the topic of herself, she said, "I heard of Lord Julan's passing. I offer my sincerest apologies."

For a moment, true pain flashed across his features. It had to be lonely, living in this big, empty house; even more so if he were reminded of his father at every turn. Sympathy raced through her veins, although she kept her expression earnest.

"Thank you," he said simply.

Reyna tilted her head. "Are dragons a pressing concern here?" She infused her voice with just enough panic to gain sympathy herself. After all, Cya—this persona who developed the longer she pretended—would most likely be *very* concerned about dragons.

"No," Wylan snapped. "No, they aren't."

Silence.

He sighed, massaging his forehead. "Now I'm sorry. The dragons are a touchy subject for me. They tend to interfere with progress. Your presence is noted, and if you need anything as you settle in, let Ralund know." He gestured at the servant at his side. "Welcome to Tawney."

A dismissal. Reyna assessed what she knew. Letting Wylan learn her true identity now would be foolish . . . especially since she might need to play that card later. She saw no reason to ruffle feathers if he stayed amicable.

But that depended on one thing, and one thing only. The carpenter only cared if they gained Diarn Feo's approval, but there would be citizens loyal to the Queendom who would ask about Wylan's seal on the deed. Reyna wasn't leaving without it.

"There's one more thing, Lord Wylan," she asked tentatively. Reyna was anything but tentative, but—well, Cya was shaping up to be a bit more malleable. Actually, it was fun diving into character.

And then he heaved a sigh and ruined it: "There always is."

A flash of irritation coursed through her. Lords were placed in cities to further the queen's rule, but also to bolster the local economy and guide the lands. Handling townsfolk's issues came with the territory.

Literally.

"My partner and I are hoping to open a shop."

"Good. Tawney needs more shops." He took another drink from his flask. "What are you planning? Cloth and attire? A general store?"

"A bookshop that serves tea, my lord."

He stopped short, eyes widening. "A . . . a bookstore?" For a moment, it looked like all his dreams were coming true. Reyna's irritation with him vanished, replaced now with mild amusement. He leaned forward, voice eager. "Where are you obtaining the books?"

That was an excellent question, but with Kianthe's connections, Reyna had no doubt they could gather them. "My partner has trade routes established. All we need is a space to call our own."

Lord Wylan contemplated that. "Well, there's a listing of open buildings at the registry in the town square. We've had more people leaving than coming of late, so your options should be decent."

"We've already found a building. And we'd like to own, not rent." Reyna lifted her head from her kneeling position, meeting his gaze. "The old barn on Lindenback."

Now his expression darkened. "Afraid that's a poor choice. You aren't from Tawney, but that area's historically been ransacked by bandits. We've had difficulties clearing them out."

She wondered, briefly, who "we" referenced. The sheriff? Or perhaps his rival, Feo?

"I've taken care of the bandits, my lord. All I'm asking for is permission to repossess the barn itself. Renovate it into something that benefits the town, instead of smudging it in blood."

Anyone with sense would accept the offer.

Wylan squinted. "You took care of the bandits? *You?*"

Perhaps Cya was a poor choice after all. Reyna pushed to her feet now, crossing her arms. Her right shoulder throbbed in lingering pain from her wound, a vivid reminder of the stitches she'd pulled. Shit. She'd meant to visit Matild's clinic before this meeting, and completely forgot.

"My partner and I are quite competent."

Wylan tilted his head. "Where did you say you were from?"

Reyna considered, then replied, "I didn't. I hail from Mercon, to the south. My father was a weaponsmith, and I spent my life testing his wares." Simply shocking, how fast Cya took form as a character. Perhaps Reyna should have explored the entertainment arts instead. That thought sent a thrill through her—maybe acting would become a new interest. It seemed as fun a hobby as anything else.

"Hmm." He studied her now, but any of the queen's markings were left at the inn. All she had to prove her old identity was her badge, an iron sigil etched with the queen's personal insignia— identical to the one stamped onto the pommel of her sword—but it was hidden in the folds of her shirt. Confident in her anonymity, she remained calm under his scrutiny.

Finally, he sighed. "If you've cleared the bandits, that's one less stone on my back. I'll have Ralund deliver a signed deed first thing tomorrow morning." Now his expression brightened. "I look forward to the bookshop you envision. I haven't had a good cup of tea in years."

Maybe he wasn't so bad.

Reyna smiled. "I appreciate the approval, my lord. Please inform me if you need anything."

With a deep bow, she saw herself out.

8

Kianthe

It was pretty telling that Feo, the fake diarn, was staying in a compound at the edge of town.

That was the best word Kianthe could use: a compound. A collection of tiny huts, aggressively fenced, with armed guards at the entrance. Beyond, chickens and geese roamed through empty gardens, sheltered from the wind by sparse pine trees. It didn't look like anyone lived there. In fact, it looked like the guards were watching a stash of coin, rather than a diarn.

Said guards pointed spears tipped with triangle blades at her as she approached. "Stop—"

Kianthe waved a hand to swath them in living vines. The plants burst from the hard soil like a child sprinting into a party, curling around the guards' legs, torsos, necks, faces before they could react. Their spears clattered to the cobblestones, and the vines muffled shouts of horror and fear.

"Can you direct me to Feo?" Kianthe asked the nearest guard, offering what she considered to be a polite smile.

He twisted in the vines, face red. "Witch!"

Kianthe inhaled sharply. "Excuse *you*. I'm a mage, you buffoon. And serving a diarn, you should know that mages of the Magicary always have free entrance into their, ah, estates." *Compound,* she thought stubbornly.

The guard clamped his mouth shut.

"Um—"

She glanced at the other guard, who was taking her living prison in stride. The woman pointed a finger, all she could wiggle free, in the direction of one of the huts. "They're in there. Second cabin on the left."

"Thank you," Kianthe replied. With a flick, the vines untangled from the guard's body and sank into the ground, allowing her to retrieve her spear. Kianthe frowned at the weapon. "Are they expecting an attack?"

The guard ducked her head. "They're . . . willing to fight for Tawney's future. The Queendom lord hasn't exactly been amicable."

"Excellent," Kianthe muttered. She swept inside, leaving the female guard to hack away at the vines entangling her partner.

The compound was empty aside from livestock and a few very sad-looking heads of cabbage. Inside one of the huts, a few guards played molem around a table. They paused in shuffling cards as she strode past, but obviously weren't concerned enough to investigate further.

The second hut from the left was locked, but Kianthe coaxed the metal pins upward, just like she did at the barn. The lock sprung open at her command, and she knocked once—courtesy—before shoving the door aside.

Only to come face-to-face with one of the Magicary's ex-apprentices.

She stopped short, jaw dropping. "Fylo?"

The person perched at a long wooden desk startled so fast, they spilled a jar of ink all over the parchment before them. They were wearing ashen-brown robes that matched their cropped hair. Their skin, a cool chestnut color, offered a nice contrast to their striking blue eyes, which were alight with horror. "Not the *com-mandment—*" They snatched the nearest page, desperately trying to wipe the ink off.

Typical.

Kianthe crossed her arms. "What in the hells are you doing here?"

"Do you know how long this took me to pen?" Fylo snapped, waving the ruined document. "Six weeks. Six weeks of research-ing border disputes, marking boundaries, interviewing locals, and documenting claims. This commandment was going to bring that bastard to his knees!" They groaned, sinking back into their chair. "And now it's ruined. *Damn* it all."

With little appraisal of Kianthe, they plucked out a quill, swept the inked pages aside, and tugged a clean sheet of parchment free.

Kianthe rolled her eyes, striding farther into the hut. It wasn't big, but every inch was covered in books—some of which Fylo had clearly stolen from the Magicary. She paused at a very old, very rare copy of *Dragons and Other Beasts,* and snorted.

"You are in so much trouble, Fylo."

"My name is Feo now," they replied, already distracted. "What do you want, Kianthe? Did the Magicary send you?" They stiff-ened, pausing in their work to glare. "Tell Jezof that he made his bed, and he can lie in it. I'm not going back."

She'd heard through whispered rumors that Fylo—ah, Feo— had failed their final apprentice exam. This was exceedingly rare, as most apprentice exams were a formality that concluded years of research into the magical arts.

Then again, most apprentice exams didn't produce a fifty-three-page rant about the Stone's very scripture and the "flaws" in its timeline. Feo had been promptly exiled, with extreme prejudice.

Kianthe crossed her arms. "Jezof didn't send me."

"The Arcandor, Mage of Ages, working independently?" Feo scoffed. "What a shock." Their words dripped sarcasm.

Rude. Feeling mildly vindictive, Kianthe dropped into the

chair opposite their desk, then waved a hand to pull the spilled ink—made of plant extract, after all—off the parchment. The ink grumbled at the hassle, but finally lifted free, leaving the already-dry words still penned beneath.

Feo gasped in delight. "The commandment—"

Kianthe lowered her hand, and the cloud of ink brushed the parchment again. "Good. I was worried I'd never get your attention."

"You always have to be the center of everything," Feo muttered, but they watched the newly cleaned parchment with rapt attention. At least they weren't writing anymore. She took the win.

"Only when I want answers. Why are you here, Feo? And pretending to be a diarn, no less?" The mage chuckled at their brazen ploy, leaning over her knees. "Assuming the identity of a noble . . . that's a dangerous offense to the council. You could be imprisoned for this."

To their credit, Feo wasn't fazed. "No one was sent to claim Tawney for Shepara."

"That's because it's Queendom territory." Kianthe didn't really believe that, but she also didn't care to dispute boundaries with a failed apprentice.

"A bold claim from a false queen," Feo retorted, and the irony seemed lost on them. They continued, oblivious to Kianthe's laughter: "Originally, Sheparan citizens settled Tawney. The Queendom only took control after the Great Awakening three hundred years ago, when magic forced the dragons to rise from their slumber. Tawney was in the Queendom's sights, and with the chaos, the queen wasted no time."

Kianthe raised an eyebrow. "So, you believe—because of an age-old history book—you're entitled to the riches and power of a diarn." She had their attention now, so she twirled the spilled ink into a thick black sphere and coaxed it back into the bottle.

Feo snatched the clean commandment pages, tapping them into a stiff pile.

"I took the liberty of getting this place under control. The people outside? They believe Tawney is Shepara's rightful claim. They're willing to fight for it, but I'm attempting the enlightened route before we begin an all-out civil war."

Whatever Kianthe was expecting, it wasn't that.

"Civil war?" she snarled, pushing to her feet. "You really think I'll let you massacre Queendom citizens in the streets?"

"Perish the thought!" Feo looked genuinely offended now. "I'm not killing anyone. But it's increasingly obvious that a physical display of power is all Lord Wylan will respond to." They set their jaw. "Insufferable, strong-arming bastard."

Kianthe slammed a hand on the desk. "If you move toward Wylan's estate with armed civilians, you'll throw a snowball that will cascade into an avalanche. Innocents *will* be killed. And when the snow settles, I promise you that lack of intent won't stop the hellstorm *I'll* bring on your entire compound. Do you understand?" She leaned forward, her magic crackling the air, eyes dark as night.

For the first time, Feo looked appropriately alarmed.

"I—I won't bring armed guards to his door," they said.

"You'll dispel these people. Send them home. You're finished playing diarn."

Now Feo bristled. "I'll send them home. I'll get rid of the weapons. But you are as much a fool as Jezof if you think I'm backing away from this fight. Wylan is an impostor, like his father before him. And worse, his ineptitude will bring dragon fire down on us all." They pressed their shoulders back, clutching the commandment like a shield. "There won't be a town to save if I can't gain control here. Do *you* understand that?"

Kianthe frowned. "You think he's causing the dragon attacks?"

"I think he's powerless to stop them, which is the same problem."

"Hmm." For a long moment, neither one spoke. Kianthe let them fester, meeting their glower easily, before commenting, "I admit, Feo, I'm liking this new fire. Where'd you find the passion?"

Now their cheeks colored, and they feigned disinterest. "Tawney grew on me. No one cares about it, but it has a very rich history, and the people here—" They cleared their throat. "Well. They're fine." An accusatory glare. "What are you doing here, then? Just came to threaten me?"

"Nah, I threaten lots of people. You wouldn't be high enough on my list to warrant a private visit." Feo relaxed at that, which was mildly amusing. "I'm here to get your stamp of approval, *diarn*. My girlfriend and I are repurposing that old barn on Lindenback, but the carpenter won't start work until you give me the building."

Feo had always been bold. A sly smile slid across their features. "The Arcandor, Mage of Ages, needs a building? The Magicary will never approve you living somewhere else."

"The Magicary can fight me." Kianthe rolled her eyes. "It won't go well."

"So, what I'm hearing is that I can expect the Magicary's most persistent mages on my doorstep within months."

"Years, if you keep your mouth shut. No one else knows who I am. They just think I'm a traveling mage."

Feo heaved a sigh, pinching their brow. After a pause, they pulled the blank page they'd been penning, scribbled out the stuff at the top, and wrote: *Give her whatever she wants.* Their cursive script was impeccable, and they signed the paper with a flourish. Then they folded it in thirds, dripped red wax from a nearby candle onto the seam, and stamped it with a very official-looking sigil.

Kianthe squinted at it. "By the Stone, you even got your new name and fake title put on a stamp."

They tossed the paper at her. "It's all about the details, Kianthe." Now they gestured at the door. "If we're done here?"

"Almost. I'm stealing this book, too." Kianthe plucked the rare copy of *Dragons and Other Beasts* off the shelf, tucking it resolutely under her arm. Feo looked like they wanted to argue, but one smile from the mage silenced them.

They waved a hand, shooing her out. "Fine. Please leave."

"Glad we've reached an understanding," Kianthe said lightly. "Good luck on your uprising. Next time I swing by, those people had better be gone."

Feo heaved a sigh, and Kianthe strolled out the door.

9

Reyna

The next morning, Kianthe and Reyna reconvened with their respective stamps of approval. Which was good, because as Reyna predicted, the glassworker Tarly recommended was a Queendom citizen, and wouldn't touch their windows until she knew that Lord Wylan had approved.

After that, work began in earnest. The carpenter made good on his promise to keep them busy, and they spent days hauling lumber, propping the rafters, essentially rebuilding the barn from the inside out. Any rotted wood was replaced, and any decent wood was refinished. The bedroom walls were secured, and they built a decently sized washroom with two doors—one from the bedroom, one from the main area.

They did some work on the rafters, then went outside and addressed the roof. The carpenter brought an apprentice skilled in slate shingles, and they spent two long days ensuring everything was waterproof for the coming rains.

Everything was going well, so it irritated Reyna that her shoulder wound hadn't healed yet. She'd half hoped that a visit to the clinic wouldn't be necessary, not with so much work to be done.

But they'd been in Tawney almost a week, and the wound went from oozing pus to puckering red. Manual labor wasn't helping; her stitches had been pulled so many times she'd given up.

When Kianthe found her one night dabbing the wound with a bloodstained towel, she was not pleased. The inn's room was already too warm, but it heated several degrees as the mage bristled in irritation. "I thought you were going to visit Matild!"

"I was," Reyna replied, resisting the urge to leap to petty defenses. It was an impulse she quelled with Kianthe around; her partner only wanted the best. So, she went with the truth: "With the renovations, I just forgot."

"You forgot. That's clearly infected." Kianthe's tone was sharp, although her touch was gentle as she peeled back the wet compress. Her fingers feathered the edge of the wound, and even that light touch made Reyna flinch in pain.

"I'll visit the clinic tomorrow." Reyna caught Kianthe's hand, and their eyes met. Warmth spread through her veins. Before Kianthe, no one worried about her. In the Queensguard, injuries were a fact of life; this wasn't the first infection Reyna had weathered.

Kianthe fidgeted, like she was debating pushing the subject. But it was late. "Tomorrow" was only a few hours away at this point. With a puff of exasperation, Kianthe helped Reyna rebind the wound. "Fine. First thing tomorrow, okay?"

Reyna agreed.

The next morning, while Kianthe strolled to the barn for another day's work, Reyna tracked down Matild's clinic. It was a small, cozy building with three beds lining one wall and an assortment of medicinal herbs and tools along another. Tarly's smithy was next door, which felt quaint.

"Why didn't you come to me sooner?" Matild lightly cuffed the back of Reyna's head. "You're playing with fire, Cya."

"I meant to. But this is nothing I haven't experienced before," Reyna replied steadily.

Matild squinted. "What did you say you did, again?"

She couldn't use the "daughter of a weaponsmith" excuse she'd pulled for Lord Wylan; that actually *meant* something to Matild. And Gods forbid Tarly showed up and tried to talk shop.

Instead, Reyna went another way. "Just a servant in the kitchen. Lots of sharp knives."

"And this was one of those?" Matild didn't look amused.

"No. We were attacked by bandits on the trip here." A pause, a lie: "Kianthe's magic saved us."

It was convincing. Matild heaved a sigh and moved to the back table, mixing a collection of herbs in a stone bowl. She tamped it down until it formed a thick green paste, then smeared it on the wound. After she'd bound it and cleaned her fingers, she pressed a hand to Reyna's forehead.

"Fever," she said disapprovingly.

Reyna had felt off for a couple days, but she'd attributed it to the manual labor. "Well. It's hot when we're lifting lumber and slate."

"Enough of that for you. You start resting until this gets better." She handed a clear bottle to Reyna, then covered the bowl with a piece of linen and twine. "Drink this morning and night, apply the salve, and see me in two days."

Reyna heaved a sigh and accepted them. At least knowing she had medication would appease Kianthe somewhat. "Is this like your hangover cure?"

"That worked, didn't it?"

"I suppose. Tasted terrible, though."

Matild jabbed a finger her way. "Medicine is like that. Morning and night. Salve. And no more lifting lumber. I'm sending Tarly to check on you tomorrow."

Reyna smirked. "Good. Then he can lift the heavy lumber."

Matild was startled into a laugh. "Fair enough."

Reyna went on her way. She took her medicine and went to bed early, and eventually, the wound faded to the back of her mind—just like always. Years of work at the Grand Palace made it easy to fall back into old habits, and there was plenty of work to be done.

When the apprentice asked for a hand with the roof work, Reyna volunteered instantly.

Kianthe, hunched over a particularly stubborn section of lumber, wiped her forehead. "Rain, hang on. You're still recovering. Let me—"

"Without a mage's help, this will be a four-day job," the carpenter interrupted.

They were building cabinets for the kitchen area, with cubbies for teas, racks for various bottles of spices and herbs. The cabinets formed a U shape, which would eventually offer a nice countertop to display the baked goods, tea-steeping station, and other things necessary to run a teahouse.

Right now, it was just a husk of wood, and every inch of it demanded Kianthe's attention. Reyna pressed a kiss to Kianthe's forehead. "I'll be fine. I've been taking my medication, and there's work to be done."

"There's always work to be done." Kianthe squinted at her. "Matild said to rest."

"Kianthe. Please."

A stalemate.

After a long moment, Kianthe hung her head. "Fine. But be quick."

It wasn't quick work. The temperature was beginning to warm during the day, but that also meant the spring rains were approaching fast. The apprentice's "quick check" wound up being an entire process—the slate tiles were huge and heavy, and one person couldn't lift them alone. Each one had to be meticulously placed to ensure they didn't slide right off the roof.

"They're useful against dragon attacks," the apprentice grunted at one point. "We switched from thatch before I was born, and it's helped offer fire resistance to the newer side of town."

"I'm surprised the wooden walls can support this," Reyna replied. "We use stone in the Queendom."

"Most buildings here have stone pillars to carry the weight. But the forest is a lot closer; cheaper to use lumber. Trees are strong." The apprentice smirked. "Especially with an elemental mage downstairs."

Their downturn of luck happened when the dark clouds gathering overhead finally burst. Rain poured over them, drenching Reyna in moments. The roofing apprentice responded instantly, dropping to his hands and knees. "Get down," he shouted to her. "Grab the wood instead; it's less slippery."

Reyna hunkered down, feeling faint. Long moments passed as they waited for the storm to ease.

The barn door slammed open, and on the ground Kianthe shouted, "Cya! I can hold the rain—"

The ley line was weak enough, and she'd already used her magic on the cabinets downstairs. The last thing they needed was Kianthe suffering from a magic drain in addition to Reyna feeling lightheaded.

"Don't bother," Reyna called. "We're fine. Just let the storm move through."

Kianthe huffed. "Come down for lunch when it's safe; I'll dry your clothes."

"Okay," Reyna agreed.

Now that she'd taken a moment to rest, exhaustion layered in her bones. The rain beat them senseless, chilling her, soaking her bandage, clearing the salve she'd painstakingly applied that morning. And then, just as fast, it thundered on. The slate tiles gleamed with water, and Reyna shuddered in the sudden cold.

"She can really dry our clothes?"

"Magic," Reyna replied, and they inched their way across the wet roof, then down the ladder. The storm had moved on quickly, and they sat in the barn as sunshine filtered through the windows, bright and cheery. Kianthe pulled the water from them with a wave of her hand. "All done up there?" With a pointed look, she set lunch on the table near the windows: slices of bread and cold ham slathered in melted cheese. She'd probably heated the cheese up herself.

The apprentice and carpenter sat down to eat, diving in with appetite. Tawney's primary roofer was working on another job, and his apprentice seemed interested in every trade he could find. They chatted about carpentry while Kianthe dropped into the seat next to Reyna.

"Mostly done. Shouldn't be much longer." Reyna smiled. She was feeling a bit dizzy, but it was nothing she hadn't powered through before. She took small bites of her meal while Kianthe joined the contractors' conversation, half listening.

The meal revived her, and while Kianthe was distracted with the placement of the cabinets, she followed the roofing apprentice back up the ladder. Just a few more hours, and she could relax at the inn. Just a few more days, and they'd be done with the major renovations.

Accomplishment settled into her bones.

Except the dizziness didn't subside as she'd hoped. It made sense, in a drunken, disconnected sort of way. The salve had washed off. Half a day had passed since she'd taken Matild's medicine. She touched her forehead, but her hands were so cold they were numb. Her skin felt fine. Cool enough, considering the temperature.

A wave of nausea passed over her, followed by a period of absolute unsteadiness. Ah. Then she wasn't fine—and she'd made a massive mistake climbing this roof a second time. Reyna gripped wooden beams, dimly aware the apprentice was maintaining jovial conversation.

"—that's the way. What do you think?"

The apprentice was talking politics. Or maybe current events. What was the difference? Reyna glanced at him, but her vision took a second to catch up . . . and then the world kept spinning. She clenched her eyes shut, her focus shifting from *Shit, Kianthe is going to be furious* to the very useful *Don't let go of the roof.*

Rough hands grabbed her shoulders. "Hey, are you all right?"

But he'd touched her wound.

Hot pain lanced up her arm, spiking deep into her chest. Reyna gasped, wrenching away from him on instinct—and then she was falling, slipping from his panicked grasp and sliding down their newly installed slate roof. She heard him scream, an actual, devastated scream, but everything was muddled and her world had narrowed to darkness and pain.

Another shout, this one in alarm.

The feeling of weightlessness as she tumbled off the rooftop.

Wind.

It whipped her hair, blinded her fading vision, cooled her cheeks, and froze her limbs. She was stationary, hovering fifty stones off the ground, and her mind was drifting like a turtle in the bitter ocean. She caught a glimpse of the barn, the devastated apprentice, the ground, Kianthe—

And then none of it mattered.

When she came to, she was flat on her back. Kianthe was bent over her, gripping her cheeks. It took precious seconds to realize the mage was speaking, *shouting,* and precious more to place what happened.

Ah. Reyna had slipped.

Gods, she felt like shit.

Kianthe had a hand on Reyna's forehead, her panicked words fading in and out. Reyna was losing her everlasting battle with consciousness, but she was present long enough to croak, "I m-might have overestimated—my ability."

"*Might* have?" The mage laughed, a desperate sound. "What the fuck was your first clue, Rain? When you *fell off a roof*?"

Reyna had to concentrate to truly understand her, and that

made her head throb viciously. A shudder wracked her body. She shouldn't have collapsed like this, shouldn't have—not with the medicine—

Shit. Even her thoughts were garbled.

She was dimly aware of Kianthe whistling sharply, dimly aware of feathered wings appearing overhead. Visk.

Reyna opened her mouth to reassure, but all that emerged was a groan. Her vision was tunneling, ears roaring, and as Kianthe hauled her onto the magical mount, Reyna's world went black.

10

Kianthe

The wind whipped past Visk as he flew to the town's center, toward Tarly's smithy and the clinic beside it. On his back, Kianthe hunched protectively over Reyna's slack form. The wind was biting, and it seemed hard to draw a deep breath. Her chest was tight, her mind spiraling.

Matild would help. Matild had to help.

Against Kianthe's chest, Reyna was burning up. Her body radiated heat—something Reyna *should have noticed* when she was perched on that Stone-damned rooftop for literal hours. Why didn't she come inside sooner? Why did Kianthe let her *back* up on that rooftop?

Well. She'd trusted Reyna to take stock of herself. She'd figured after the last time, when Reyna was injured in a swordfight and stood behind Queen Tilaine's throne during a day-long meeting, then collapsed from blood loss, that Reyna would have learned.

Reyna said she was fine, and Kianthe believed her.

Clearly, that was a mistake.

Kianthe wanted to cry. Or scream. Or sweep a tornado across the plains and rip every single tree in that forest apart. Instead, she leapt off Visk the moment he landed—barely noting as the earth rose to meet her feet—and hauled Reyna toward the clinic.

"Matild," she shouted. "*Matild!* Tarly! I need help!"

The blacksmith burst from his shop almost in time with his wife. His eyes widened when he saw Reyna, and he moved to relieve Kianthe of her—but unconsciously, the mage flared with internal fire. Magic rippled the air and he immediately stepped back, hands raised.

Visk screeched in response to his mistress's emotion. A small crowd was gathering; they were making a scene. And yet, Kianthe didn't have the wherewithal to wave the griffon back into the skies.

Matild wasn't so intimidated. She hauled Kianthe—and Reyna—inside by the arm, cursing: "Gods damn it, I told her to rest."

Tarly gently closed the door behind them, his bushy brows knitted in concern as Kianthe set Reyna on a nearby bed. He stood stoically, an extra set of hands just awaiting direction.

Kianthe, meanwhile, fought to control the surge of anger. She couldn't be furious at Reyna—not now, anyway—but panic had her looking for an outlet. She rounded on the midwife, who seemed like the next easiest target.

"You said you'd help her. She came to see you, right? Why is she still sick?" Kianthe's voice was hot with fury.

Matild raised one eyebrow, even as she bustled about her clinic collecting supplies. "Do you really want to argue about this now?"

It was an abrasive comment that slammed Kianthe's curt words into perspective. "N-No. I don't."

"Good," Matild said, and continued working.

Kianthe dropped to her knees so she was eye level with Reyna, lying on the cot. Her fingers were trembling as she nudged sweat-slicked hair off Reyna's forehead. She was burning up. She hadn't been this hot at lunch, had she? Surely Kianthe would have noticed.

Reyna's eyelids fluttered, and she moaned.

Fear swept through Kianthe, compounding into the panic she tried so hard to control. The mage could feel herself growing cold, feel her thoughts spiraling. She was shaking all over, not just her hands. The mage had saved her girlfriend from a dangerous fall, but fevers killed more often.

And unlike tipping off a barn's roof, an infection wasn't something Kianthe could stop.

When a mage's thoughts spiraled, when they lost control, dangerous things could happen. Things that impacted the elements around them—the earth below the clinic, the water in Matild's salves and tonics, the air inside their lungs.

Already, fire was rippling along her fingertips, embers in her veins waiting to ignite with the Stone's magic.

She could burn down this whole clinic if she didn't get a hold of herself—but watching Reyna collapse had tipped her over a cliff's edge, and she couldn't seem to slow the vicious fall.

The mage staggered backward, looking again to Reyna. "I'm-I'm sorry. Stars and Stone, I'm sorry. I can't stay here."

"Are you sick too?" Matild asked, concern tilting her tone.

Kianthe felt sick . . . but not from infection. "N-No," she croaked, stumbling to the exit. Tarly stepped aside for her, but she paused there, shaking so badly that she could barely grip the door handle. "Will she be okay?"

Matild squinted at her. It felt like Kianthe was the one on the cot, being examined by a medical professional. Luckily, Matild seemed to realize now wasn't the time.

Unluckily, she also wasn't one to mince words. "Fevers need to be monitored closely. If she gets too hot, her organs could shut down." At Kianthe's sharp inhale, Matild stepped to Reyna, felt her cheek. "But—it doesn't seem that bad yet. I'm personally hoping she just overdid it."

"Overdoing it" was working hard enough to pull a muscle. "Overdoing it" was renovating an entire barn and needing lunch to recover from the magic drain. "Overdoing it" was not toppling off a roof with a raging fever and an infected wound.

The walls were closing in. No one could feel it, but beneath her feet, the earth rippled, desperate to tear itself apart.

Kianthe had to get out of here.

"I'll—I'll be back. I just need a moment," she gasped, casting one last glance at Reyna's unconscious form. Her girlfriend was breathing fast, face red with fever, sweat dripping down her temples.

Shit.

Kianthe sprinted into the sunshine, hoping to step around the corner, compose herself in the crisp afternoon air. But the townsfolk had gathered, peering curiously through the clinic's windows, brows knitted as they murmured sympathies for Reyna.

She and Reyna didn't even *know* these people.

Overwhelmed, Kianthe clenched her eyes shut and whistled sharply for Visk. The griffon hadn't gone far, and within seconds she'd hauled herself onto his sturdy back, gripping his feathers as he leapt into the air.

It was colder higher up, and the wind positively chilled her. It did nothing for the tremors that wracked her body, but it helped clear her mind. Rushing air overtook the muted conversation as she gained distance from town. At least up here, she could breathe.

It helped, but only a little.

She urged Visk over the rim-like ledge, beyond Tawney and straight into dragon country. It was reckless to travel in that direction, but dragons were immensely magical creatures. Being around strong magic—even if it wasn't compatible with normal mages, and was barely stomached by the Arcandor—might help ease her physical symptoms.

Although only a miracle would slow her careening mind.

What would happen if Reyna . . . didn't make it? Vividly, Kianthe recalled the aching loneliness that pervaded her life in the Before Times. Long days in foreign lands, surrounded by strangers who only cared about what she could do for them. Dark nights visiting various rooftops, conducting conversations with Visk because she had no one else. Intense fights with enemies and natural disasters, knowing that if she fell, she might be mourned—but only as long as it took the Stone of Seeing to choose her replacement.

Without Reyna, Kianthe was faced with a world of people who bowed to the Arcandor first and never realized there was anguish behind her eyes.

Surely, the Stone, the Gods, the Stars . . . they couldn't be so cruel as to rip her away.

Kianthe choked on a sob, hunching over Visk's musky feathers. He was a warm, solid presence beneath her, twittering reassuringly. At her subtle motion, he landed—mostly because they couldn't keep flying north without heavy opposition.

They were deep in dragon country now; the tundra stretched wide around them, sharp mountains rising to the west. The storm that exacerbated all this had drifted here over the last several hours—and instead of pelting rain, it now snowed viciously. Kianthe breathed in the foreign magic, tinted deep blue in her mind's eye. But even being here wasn't enough; her heart still thudded painfully. Relentless and disconnected thoughts pelted her with every possible, terrible scenario.

In the distance, a deep-throated roar rocked the land.

Ah, the dragons.

Kianthe sank to the ground, drawing measured breaths, running her fingers over icy stone. Trying to feel something here, now. Physical things to remind her that the world wasn't a real nightmare. Except her magic was responding to her distress; the snow whipped around her like a blizzard, and her fingertips melted the ice. The earth grumbled distaste.

Kianthe never used to have these kind of mental attacks—not until she was gifted the Arcandor's magic . . . and responsibility. An overwhelming stress had settled on her shoulders then, and only worsened with age. Only Reyna's calm influence and logical approach to life had lessened the snarl of emotion. For a few blessed seasons, Kianthe could relax.

And then Reyna had fainted in the throne room last year, bleeding from a hidden wound while Kianthe and Queen Tilaine debated politics and policy, offering yet another problem Kianthe couldn't control. As the other Queensguard carried Reyna to the Grand Palace's infirmary, Kianthe had faked an excuse and fled.

Days passed before she resurfaced with her composure intact.

Kianthe had obtained the spelled moonstones so that kind of surprise would never happen again.

Now, she was cold with the certainty that if she'd stepped out of that barn a breath later, hadn't reacted fast enough to catch her girlfriend with that gust of wind—Reyna would be gone.

Forever.

Visk butted Kianthe, nearly knocking her flat on her face. A bold interruption, one that proved the mage was terrible at meditation. She glared at the beast, but he chirped and buried his head in her chest, his presence a steady warmth. The dragon magic settled around them like a fog.

"I'm scared," Kianthe admitted to the griffon.

Visk whistled softly, nibbling her clothes with his beak.

Reyna is okay. She'll be okay. Everything is fine.

Petting Visk, thinking that, slowly began to help. The knot in her chest eased. Her roiling stomach settled. Her breaths came easier. The elements themselves calmed down, the snow slowing into something almost pleasant.

"*You always have a choice,*" Reyna had told her over and over. "*Even if it seems impossible to notice in the moment.*"

Now, Kianthe tried to identify her choice. She could sit here in devastation—or she could return to Tawney, to Reyna, and be there when her girlfriend awoke.

In the distance, silver dragons beat wings as dark as a mountain's shadow, their guttural roars warning against the intrusion.

They weren't going to entertain Kianthe much longer. Snow piled around them; Visk's outstretched wings did little to protect them from the drifts.

Time to go home.

Wearily, she climbed onto Visk's back. He took to the skies without order, angling away from dragon country, back toward Tawney. A steady presence, something she leaned into as they flew.

And Kianthe's tears dried in the bitter wind.

11

Reyna

The first thing Reyna noticed was a pounding headache. The second thing was that her whole body ached, like someone had taken a hammer to her joints. Her cheeks burned, the fever hot on her skin. Her stomach roiled. People murmured around her, a man and a woman, but neither were Kianthe, so Reyna didn't care.

"—be dangerous. I hope she's okay."

"I mean, better there—"

Reyna let herself drift, sinking into the numbness. She hoped Kianthe would come back. Her mind niggled that it was concerning Kianthe wasn't here—but that, too, faded with time.

She awoke again later, this time to darkness. The room was quiet and still, and Reyna blinked slowly, staring at the ceiling. Her mind was a bit clearer, her face warm but not burning. She felt like she'd run every flight of stairs in the Grand Palace.

A steady pressure rested on her stomach. Reyna lifted her hand to feel it, and an unbidden smile touched her lips as her fingers entangled with short, wild hair. There was Kianthe. The hours of misery tumbled from her mind as she gently rubbed her girlfriend's scalp.

She was starting to drift again when Kianthe stirred under the touch.

"Rain?" the mage breathed, pushing off Reyna's belly. Her voice was rough with sleep, but under the silver moonlight filtering through the windows, Kianthe's face was painted in relief. She shifted, setting a book on the nearby table: a tome Reyna hadn't noticed before. The mage must have fallen asleep reading, as always.

"That's me," Reyna mumbled, disconnected.

Kianthe chuckled, brushing Reyna's cheek. The world narrowed to the featherlight touch of Kianthe's thumb on her skin. Her physical aches faded. Reyna drifted, anchored by the single point of contact.

But she didn't want to sleep again, so instead she whispered, "Are you all right?"

Kianthe's touch vanished, a tangible loss. Reyna opened her eyes—when had they closed?—to see the mage's expression darken with anger. Or maybe fear. Magic sparked the air around them, fireflies in an open field.

Reyna had meant that to be comforting, but clearly it wasn't. She pulled herself upright, swallowing a moan as the world spun viciously. Her good arm reached for Kianthe. "Key?"

"I'm—" The mage choked on her words. "Stone damn it all, of course *I'm* okay. You're the one—" She cut herself off, irritation creeping into her tone. With a huff, she pushed away from the bed, stomping to the door and back. Then she did it twice more for good measure. "Do you know how easy it would have been to avoid this? You just . . . climb down the ladder. You don't stay on the roof during a rainstorm. You don't *go back up*."

Well, this was better than the haunted look she'd had before. Reyna slumped against the goose-feather pillow. "You're right."

"Of course I'm right. I'm always—" The audacity of it sent Kianthe on another tirade.

Reyna's arm hurt. Fairly confident that her girlfriend was

preoccupied, that she'd feel better after she vented, Reyna glanced at the thick bandage on her bicep. Flaking bits of dry salve pulled at the skin, which told her the wound was positively slathered in healing ointment.

It was probably the only reason her fever had receded. She was lucky they'd met Matild early.

Might have been luckier if the medicine had worked yesterday, but . . .

Memories flashed back into existence, and Reyna winced. Everything was murky, like ink-stained water, but she recalled enough to ask, "Did I . . . fall off a roof?"

"Yes. Yes, Reyna, you did." Kianthe collapsed into the chair at Reyna's bedside with a heavy sigh, rubbing her temples as magic rippled the air around them. It was obviously taking conscious effort to stay calm.

"Huh." Reyna should probably be concerned about that. Or the roof thing. Or . . . well, anything. But all she could think was that it looked cold outside, and her bed was warm, and she wished Kianthe would curl up beside her again.

The mage offered an exasperated stare. Her voice was uncharacteristically hard. "That's all you have to say?"

Reyna stared back blearily. Her mind was having trouble processing this discussion, deep fatigue tugging at the corners of her soul.

Kianthe looked simultaneously ready to shake her senseless . . . or kiss her senseless. Reyna would have preferred the latter, if she had a choice. Before she could voice that, Kianthe groaned. "Now isn't the time. I just—" A pause. "Never mind. Get some sleep, love."

She moved to fluff the pillow at Reyna's back, but Reyna caught her hand. Her mind was distant, fading, but this was important. Even with her fever-addled brain, she could recognize that Kianthe was worried, and it made her heart ache more painfully than her muscles.

"Tell me how you're feeling," Reyna murmured.

Kianthe crumbled, squeezing her hand roughly. "I will. Just—you need to rest. We'll have time." She closed her eyes for a moment, then forced a smile. "We have time. Concentrate on getting better, okay?"

Reyna nodded, sinking farther into the pillow. She really didn't feel well . . . and the small, childish part of her mind wanted physical comfort. "Lay with me?"

The bed was small, but Kianthe didn't need further encouragement. She climbed under the thick woolen blanket, pulling Reyna into an almost aggressive hold against her chest. She was mindful of Reyna's bandaged wound.

In the ensuing quiet, Reyna released a sigh, letting her eyes slip closed.

"I think I love you."

"Wow. What a relief," Kianthe replied sarcastically. She tucked Reyna's head under her chin, her breaths solid and even against Reyna's body. It was hot under the blanket, but Reyna was still shivering a bit, so it didn't bother her. The silence ticked by, long moments of comfort, before Kianthe whispered, "I love you too, Rain."

Reyna smiled and let herself drift off again.

❅

"Three times a day," Matild told Kianthe, handing her a bottle of clear liquid.

Buttoning her shirt, perched on the edge of the mattress, Reyna frowned. "Three times? You told me two."

The midwife shot her a glare. "That was before you fell off a roof and nearly killed yourself. Now, because of your stubbornness, it's three times a day—and Kianthe is going to make sure you don't get out of bed before I say so."

The mage looked smug. "Doctor's orders."

"Damned right."

Reyna supposed she deserved that. Truthfully, exhaustion still prickled along the edges of her mind. Her body had glimpsed a rare chance for sleep and was seizing every opportunity with gleeful pleasure. Even sitting upright was a bit of a struggle.

Granted, it had only been two days. Her fever broke yesterday, but Matild wanted to keep a close eye for a little while longer. No one argued.

"Anyhow." Matild turned back to Kianthe, offering a bowl covered in wet linen. "Keep that wound covered in salve at *all* times. If she tells you she's feeling better, she's lying. Infections like this take several days, maybe a week, to shake entirely."

"Noted," Kianthe replied, shooting Reyna a pointed look.

Reyna sighed. She deserved this.

As they headed for the door, Kianthe paused and whispered quietly, "Thank you for your help, Matild."

"Deep breaths," the midwife said, clasping her shoulders. "You'll get a handle on it."

It was never defined, but Kianthe nodded glumly.

Matild bid them goodbye, and Kianthe's arm snaked around Reyna's waist, taking most of her weight as they exited the clinic. It was a cold, rainy day in Tawney—the earlier sunshine had faded, and Reyna winced as icy drops pelted them. She pulled the hood of her cloak over her head, swallowing a gasp as the motion twinged her wound.

"That's going to take some getting used to," she muttered, not pleased. "And now we're losing time with the renovation."

Kianthe was unmoved. "The carpenter is there today, working inside. The roof was almost done before all this. You're the one who said we can take our time." The mage's grip tightened. "Some things are more important."

Reyna recalled their hazy conversation the first night and felt embarrassed at how disconnected she'd been. Yesterday, they lacked the privacy to talk about things. Now, anchored to her girlfriend's side, she could see the tight lines on the mage's face, her clenched jaw, her tense muscles.

She wasn't pleased, even if she was trying her best to hide it.

They were quiet all the way through town, although several people stopped to tell Reyna to feel better. She thanked them, her tone riddled with confusion, until Kianthe said, "We, ah . . . drew a crowd. Well, Visk did. My shouting probably didn't help."

"Key—"

"It's fine."

It was most assuredly not fine. Reyna frowned.

As they neared the inn, she caught a glimpse of Lilac—chomping happily on a carrot while Hansen brushed her down—before Kianthe ushered Reyna inside. The large interior room was nearly empty, occupied by a couple eating near the fireplace and the innkeeper perched behind the counter.

The woman appraised them, brows knitting together. "You feeling better, hon?"

Reyna was taken aback by this hospitality. She'd sustained many injuries at Queen Tilaine's palace, and no one—except maybe Venne—stopped to ask how she was feeling. "Ah, yes. Much better."

"Even better with some food and rest," Kianthe added, and towed Reyna upstairs.

A bouquet of luscious flowers tied with twine had been left on the storage chest. Both women stopped short, eyeing it suspiciously. It looked innocent enough, but . . . Reyna moved to pick it up.

Kianthe tugged her away. "Uh-uh. If it's poison from that pernicious queen, *I'll* handle it, thank you." She deposited Reyna in bed, waited until the woman had settled under the covers, then plucked the flowers off the chest.

A simple card fluttered to the scuffed floor. Kianthe retrieved it, then made a face as she handed it to Reyna. "Ugh. You have a suitor."

That was a stretch. The heavyset parchment square simply read *Feel better soon*, and was signed *Lord Wylan of Tawney*. More likely, the lord was trying to gather as much support as he could in his fight against Feo.

Reyna nearly chuckled. "Your diarn has him worried, I think."

"That diarn shouldn't worry anyone," Kianthe replied. "Especially after my visit." She moved dispassionately through the room, hanging their cloaks, retrieving a cloth to dry her hair. Everything was done in uncharacteristic silence.

Finally, Reyna couldn't stand it. She pushed upright, tucking a pillow at her back so she could relax and talk. "Tell me how you're feeling." There was no room for argument.

And this time, Kianthe spun to face her, like she'd been waiting for that.

"I feel like you're an absolute, unbridled idiot. I feel like all of this was avoidable, and you're just too stubborn to admit it. I thought you could take care of yourself, but now that we're living together, I'm wondering how often you let injuries get to that point. I'm still angry and I hate that, because all I want is to be happy you're recovering."

Her voice rose in pitch and tone until she was nearly spitting.

Reyna waited. It had taken a while to perfect, but this was their failsafe now. Once one of them asked that question, they stayed quiet until the other was absolutely finished. Sometimes, a person just needed to verbally work through their feelings.

Sometimes, the first thing out of their mouth wasn't *really* the problem.

Gods, Reyna hoped Kianthe's first sentence wasn't the true issue here. Her chest prickled with despair thinking about it.

Kianthe paced, scrubbing her face with a hand. "And the worst part, Reyna, is that I couldn't handle it. The Arcandor is supposed to remain calm and levelheaded. My magic can get dangerous otherwise, but I spent hours up in the snow just trying to *breathe* without gasping. I really thought we were making progress before, but—something about seeing you like that sent me careening back into that space." She stared numbly at the towel in her hand, then tossed it onto the rack beside their cloaks to dry.

Her final sentence was quiet, defeated. "No wonder the Magicary hates me."

The mage slumped into a chair by the window, the dark clouds outside casting her face in shadow. Her entire body was limp as string, like she might ooze onto the floor in shame.

Reyna swallowed past a suddenly dry mouth, but still, she waited.

Kianthe waved a dejected hand. "I'm done. And I'm so, so sorry."

"You're sorry?" Reyna wanted to slap her silly. "Key, I fucked up. If I knew it'd get that bad, that fast, I'd have stayed here and slept it off. I really thought Matild's medicine would fix it."

Kianthe scrubbed her face, but didn't speak.

Reyna's gaze dropped to the blanket over the bed. It was crocheted, each stitch meticulously crafted, the yarn soft and dyed a deep blue. It was pilling a bit from age and use, but it was warm and comforting. She picked at a piece of fluff on it, her voice quietly contemplative. "This isn't how I want to live our lives: me getting injured, you worrying about it. I'm just . . . not used to having someone worry. And it was easy enough to recover from injuries between your visits."

"Did that happen often?" Kianthe whispered. Her eyes were tracing Reyna's bare arms, and the scars that marred her skin. They told the story Kianthe had been able to ignore or forget until now.

Reyna winced, tracing a particularly jagged scar left from an attack during Her Excellency's last visit to Leonol. "My job was dangerous. It isn't now." She raised her gaze, determination settling on her features. "You *are* improving, Key. The fact that you were here while I recovered told me you got the anxiety under control."

"It didn't feel like it." Kianthe's voice was defeated.

"I don't think it's a straight path, dear." Reyna pushed out of the bed, staggering to Kianthe's lap. Her good arm draped over

Kianthe's shoulder, and she rested her head in the crook of Kianthe's neck. "I'm the one who's sorry. And if those Magicary mages hate you, they're old bats who can wither in the five hells."

It startled Kianthe into a laugh. "Pretty sure that's blasphemy."

"I don't care." Reyna's voice was muffled, but fierce.

The mage pulled her into a careful hug, minding her healing wound. It felt like coming home, and Reyna basked in her affection.

"You're the most incredible person I've ever met." Reyna pressed a kiss to her lips.

Kianthe opened her mouth—to make a joke, to laugh it off, anything to keep it from being real—and Reyna cut her off, pulling back just far enough to meet her gaze. "No. I'm serious. You're dedicated and attentive and caring, and I'm lucky to know you. Not because you're the Arcandor—but because you love me, and that's everything."

"I think it's the other way around." A flush crept over Kianthe's cheeks. She didn't release Reyna from their hug.

Reyna smirked. "Incorrect. Which proves the almighty Mage of Ages doesn't, in fact, know everything."

"Okay." Kianthe shoved her away now, jokingly, and Reyna grinned. "I've said what I need. How are you feeling?"

"Like I want to sleep for a year." Reyna paused, considering, and staggered back to the bed. "Maybe more."

Kianthe drew the curtains. "Sounds like an excellent plan." As Reyna got comfortable, Kianthe considered her for a moment, then slid into bed beside her. "I was going to read, but—this looks cozier." Her body fit against Reyna's perfectly, and the mage carefully rested her head on Reyna's good shoulder.

Reyna didn't protest; they were due for a lazy day, after all. She snuggled close.

Kianthe inhaled deeply, then grimaced. "You need a rinse."

"I was *unconscious*."

And life went on.

Perched on a ladder nearby, Kianthe raised an eyebrow. "What are you doing out of bed?"

It had only been a few days, which didn't seem long enough by Kianthe's standards. She was hardly surprised, though; Reyna was built for motion, for duty, not for lounging around on a forced vacation.

"Matild approved it. The infection is nearly gone." Reyna raised her right arm as proof, and Kianthe had to admit her dexterity seemed to have returned. Even as recently as yesterday, she hadn't been able to complete a sword drill—an unsanctioned activity that Reyna begged to attempt "just to see." She'd spent the rest of the afternoon in bed, silently seething at her failure.

Now, the mage waved a hand. "If you drop off another rooftop, dear, we'll have words."

"We've already had words. I learned my lesson." Reyna squinted at the bucket secured to Kianthe's ladder, the white walls behind her. The color didn't cover the dark wood perfectly, but it made the walls look more tasteful. "What . . . are you doing?"

Ah yes. Kianthe forgot the Queendom didn't like paint, or fun of any kind.

She dipped her brush—one she'd crafted herself from tufts of Visk's shed fur—back into the bucket. "Painting. Water-based, pigmented with elderflower. Easy to wash off if you don't like it." A pause. "Do you like it?"

"If I say no, is that a week of work gone?" Reyna approached the ladder's base. She stepped without staggering now, back to her fluid motions. It was poetry and pleased Kianthe immensely.

The mage glanced at the walls she'd already painted . . . which was most of them. In fact, she'd been hoping to finish up before Reyna arrived, another surprise. "Two days, maybe."

"Is this a Sheparan custom?"

"It's an 'everywhere but the Queendom' custom," Kianthe replied, although she had no clue if that were true. In Shepara, murals were common. The Leonolans built their towns into the

12

Kianthe

After that, Kianthe poured herself into repairs at the barn. The roofing apprentice finished his work with her help, and the carpenter framed the west wall with towering bookshelves, just like Kianthe wanted. Because Kianthe hated being cold, she had the carpenter design a fireplace dividing the wall of books. It was big and deep, framed in stone with a thick wooden mantel, and would make the cold winters in Tawney almost bearable.

A metalworker came by to install piping. He called himself a "plumber," which seemed very suspicious, but even she couldn't deny the convenience of a pump that pulled water directly to their washroom. As an afterthought and a surprise to Reyna, Kianthe had him lay extra pipes in the storage room, so they could get the water for tea easier too.

When he left, Kianthe and the carpenter laid flooring together— a smooth pine that brightened the space immensely. After that was finished, Kianthe dove into painting the walls—which busied her until Reyna arrived.

The carpenter noticed her first, clearing his throat. "Visitor."

"Hardly a visitor," Reyna said.

towering trees of the rainforest, and most of their walls doubled as windows for heat circulation. Admittedly, painting the barn one flat color was uninspiring.

But in Kianthe's vision, the walls were background scenery—her plants would be the focus. And green sparkled against white paint.

"So? Yes or no?" Kianthe wasn't worried about the answer.

Reyna smiled and delivered exactly as expected: "I like everything about you. Even your wild choice in décor." She strolled away from the ladder, leaving Kianthe to finish up. In the meantime, she admired the roof, windows, flooring, before stopping at the bookshelves. Her eyes fell to the fireplace. "Ah, thank the Gods. I was meaning to suggest a hearth."

Kianthe had been hoping for a bit more swooning, maybe some *Oh, Kianthe, you're so smart, dearest* comments. The carpenter, who knew this, ducked to hide a smile. Kianthe sighed, waving a hand that sent paint splatters across their new pine floors. "That's because you're so smart, dearest."

Reyna missed her sarcasm. She'd already turned her attention to the wall of bookshelves, tilting her head to survey their height. "Are we going to add a ladder, so the customers can pull books they want?"

The carpenter and Kianthe exchanged glances. The man replied, "We hadn't planned on it, but I can make one, sure."

"We did add a spot for an oven." The brush spread the paint evenly and quickly, but it was still tiny compared to the very large wall. If Kianthe didn't finish quickly, the paint would dry out and she'd be left mixing another batch. Again. "And I had your . . . *plumber* . . . bring water into the storage room, too. For tea."

Reyna squealed, which was an adorably rare sound, and disappeared into the storage room. When she emerged a few minutes later, her cheeks were pink with excitement.

"It works! I'm so impressed Tawney has this. Did you taste the water? It's delicious."

"I prefer my own water," Kianthe said. "You know. The stuff from the ground, not weird metal pipes."

Reyna waved a hand to dismiss her, then inspected the new kitchen area.

Atop Kianthe's cabinets, they'd sanded a long tabletop, perfect to separate customers from the staff. The wood had been stained deep brown, like several other accents along the barn's interior. On the back countertops, the carpenter had devised a clever shelving system for a future assortment of teas and herbal blends, and even built a folding menu they could prop outside.

Reyna looked amazed. "How did you finish all this in a few days?"

"Well." The carpenter rubbed the back of his neck, hunching over his current project. "Townsfolk felt bad for you. A few of them came by while you two were resting and pitched in a hand."

Reyna hesitated, her brow knitting together. "Do—do we need to pay anyone?"

The carpenter shot her an exasperated look. "They weren't here for coin, kid. Tawney folk just try to help when we can."

This was a foreign concept to Reyna, clearly.

Even Kianthe had to admit it made her feel uneasy. In her experience, being indebted to people meant they'd be asking for a magical favor later. But she'd been keeping an eye on Reyna while they were helping, and no one had arrived since to ask for payment, so she'd dropped it.

Now, the mage waved the damp paintbrush in Reyna's direction. "We'll make it up, love. The bigger concern is where we're getting our books and tea. Can't open the shop without them."

"Mmm." Reyna frowned. "I'm sure we can locate a good selection. Might need to take a quick trip to Wellia to do it right, though."

Wellia was a two-day flight, at least, and an even longer ride. Leaving Tawney for nearly as long as they'd been residents felt like relinquishing an already tenuous dream. Kianthe didn't want to do it.

Luckily, Feo had an excellent collection of literature at their compound, and Kianthe was positive they could obtain more with ease. They might even lend her a few of their rarer tomes— although she'd have to return the books later.

Huh. Return the books.

The thought took root in her mind. "What if we open the space to the public and let them take the books home?"

"That *is* how a bookshop works," Reyna said evenly.

Kianthe shook her head, getting excited now. The motion rocked the ladder, and she gripped it tighter to keep from falling. "No. No, this happens in the Magicary libraries sometimes. People here must have tomes they aren't reading anymore. We could ask for donations. And as a thank-you, we can let people read here . . . or, if they want, take a book home for free. They could bring it back when they're done."

"That sounds like a very kind venture." Reyna paused, as if she were trying to phrase this just right. "But my funds aren't unlimited. And lending out books means we can't *sell* them."

Hmm. Kianthe pouted a bit, deflating.

The carpenter spoke up. "What if you do both?" When he realized he had their curiosity, he shrugged, gesturing at the shelves. "You have plenty of space. Set aside a shelf as a lending center. Fill the rest with books to sell. Then people can decide if they want to return a book or keep it."

Kianthe grinned wide, glancing at Reyna.

The ex-guard sighed, massaging her brow. "I suppose we can test it, see the public reception. We'll still need to go to Wellia—"

And then, a shock of magic sliced through Kianthe's chest.

It was so startling—and *painful*, Stone damn it all—that she nearly tipped off the ladder. Only a white-knuckle grip saved her. The paint bucket swayed dangerously, and in an instant, Reyna was at the base of the ladder, holding it steady.

Her gaze was sharp. "What happened?"

"A summons," Kianthe gasped, feeling the magic pulsing along its sad little ley line. The Stone might as well be screaming at her. "Something's wrong. A natural disaster, or—or a battle I can stop." She slid off the ladder, planting her feet on the pine floors. Everything felt distant, out of sorts.

Reyna cupped her cheek, studied her. "Then you have to go."

Kianthe considered it for exactly one breath.

Then she shoved it aside, tamped the magic down, and extracted herself from Reyna. "I'm not a slave to the Stone's whims. It can warn me of impending doom—and I can choose to ignore it."

Behind them, the carpenter raised an eyebrow. "Is this a mage thing?"

"Something like that," Reyna said. "Key. You are not the kind of person to ignore 'impending doom.'" Her light brown eyes searched Kianthe's. "People could get hurt."

It was too much. Too soon.

"*You* got hurt," Kianthe couldn't help snapping. It felt like she was back in the open tundra of dragon country, hunched in Visk's shadow, mind swirling with worst-case scenarios.

Reyna cocked a hip. "I'm fine now, and I promise, it won't happen again. Just because I've sheathed my sword doesn't mean I can't retrieve it if needed." Her lips tilted upward. "I love you, but I signed up for a partner, not a protector."

The power imbalance between them was a raw thing—one that Kianthe had solidly decided to ignore, because her girlfriend was fantastic and incredible and someone didn't need all-powerful magic to have worth. But she knew Reyna didn't see it that way. *Reyna* felt that Kianthe was on par with royalty.

And Reyna used to serve royalty.

So, when she said that, it stung . . . but it was probably fair.

Kianthe exhaled. "After last week, I think you need a sitter."

"I'll speak with Matild." Reyna plucked the paintbrush out of her hand. "In the meantime, you aren't going to defy your deity's direct order."

As if on cue, the Stone pulsed again, shoving urgency across the ley line. Kianthe swallowed another gasp as her chest wrenched. Reyna was right, as always. And honestly, Kianthe had no idea what would happen to her—physically, mentally, or magically—if she disobeyed a summons like this.

Like the dragons or Feo, this was yet another reminder that their quaint, mundane life was a pretty façade. Even in Tawney, she couldn't escape it. Kianthe would always have a duty to the world's magic.

Bitterness and exhaustion settled over her shoulders. All she wanted to do today was paint a wall, maybe sit with Reyna tonight at the inn and chat with the locals.

Reyna saw it. She sighed, squeezing Kianthe's hand. "Besides. I'm just learning who I am without, ah, my old life's influence. It'll do me good to get some perspective alone. Figure out where I belong in Tawney when you're away."

Well, Kianthe couldn't fault Reyna for that. Everyone needed a life independent of their partner.

And truly, Reyna was a gem for tolerating Kianthe's clinginess: a nasty side effect of years of independent travel with few friendships in between. If leaving gave Reyna some much-needed space, Kianthe would seize every opportunity to offer it.

Before she could agree, Visk landed on the dirt road outside with a *whump*, whistling for her through the open doorway. He felt the magic too, and was eager to answer the call. It had to be boring for him, prowling the edges of a town like this, awaiting a summons that rarely came these days.

"I hear you, bud. We're going." Kianthe turned back to her girlfriend. "Don't plant anything without me."

"Anything I plant will die in hours, so never fear." Reyna pulled her into a strong hug, then offered a quick kiss, lips warm and firm.

Happiness fluttered in Kianthe's chest. She wanted to keep kissing Reyna, wanted to stay here forever—but maybe it would make her return all the sweeter.

When they separated, her eyes were alight with an old excitement. Reyna would never admit it, but she loved gossip; hearing about the Arcandor's triumphs always thrilled her. It made Kianthe feel wonderful, warm from the inside out.

"Please don't die in a tsunami. And stop by Wellia on the way back. We really will need some exotic books and teas to gather attention."

An errand. Kianthe should have known.

She laughed, kissed her again, and sprinted for Visk. Mage and mount took to the skies, but she craned over his massive wings to wave at her girlfriend, their new place, and the entire town of Tawney.

It was exhilarating. Kianthe loved having someone who genuinely anticipated her return, but this felt bigger. Not just returning to Reyna . . . but to the home they were building together.

She only hoped Reyna would finish painting before that bucket dried out.

13

Reyna

The days without Kianthe passed in a blur of activity. There were so many little things to accomplish for the shop, and Reyna was determined to get every detail right.

She also started wearing her moonstone again—mostly to put Kianthe's mind at ease, but partially because the mage would send pulses of magic across the continent, like taps against her heart. They'd formed a code through it, and it was nice to know that even when she was physically alone, someone cared about her.

Matild checked on Reyna at the barn one spring afternoon, whistling at the progress. "This looks like a suitable place to stay now! Are you moving in soon?"

"Not until Kianthe gets back. I can't move in without her."

"But you already bought a bed, I heard," Matild replied with a sly grin.

Reyna quirked an eyebrow. "Does everyone in this town gossip about *everything*, or is this a special occurrence for us?"

Matild shrugged, setting a basket of bread on the counter for later. "You two are the most interesting folk to pass through since that 'dragon tamer' last year. He thought he could stop the attacks. All he got for his trouble were some burns and forced recovery time in Wellia."

"Yikes. It still doesn't answer the question: Why is my bed purchase public knowledge?"

Now Matild peeked through the open door into their new bedroom. The mattress was lavish, something Reyna was willing to drop a palidron or two on. The carpenter had built a stunning frame for it, and she'd furnished the extra space with a storage chest and bedside tables. The window offered an idyllic glimpse of their back patio.

The midwife smirked, shrugging a shoulder. "Feather mattresses are pretty rare outside the Grand Palace." Reyna flushed, but Matild had already moved on. Her eyes roamed the shop itself. "And this is all coming along, too. Did you need any help?"

"Not really. We've stocked the storage room with bags of flour, sugar, and a few other things. A Leonolan tradesman at the market had sweetened cacao, so I might try a recipe with that soon." Reyna stepped behind the counter, gesturing at the cubbies of tea. "I finally stocked up on teas, too. Just need the books now, but that's Kianthe's job."

Matild dropped heavily into one of their little booths, built against the wall opposite the bookshelves. The midwife bounced on the cushions Reyna had made—the ex-guard was more adept at sewing wounds than fabric, but the process was similar enough—and smiled wide.

"Color me impressed. What kind of teas do you have?"

Reyna wrinkled her nose. "Tisane—ah, herbal blends—seem more common here. I have some with lemongrass and pine needles that are local, but I have a lovely black tea from the Capital if you're interested."

Matild tugged out a pent and slid it dramatically across the table.

Reyna was startled into a laugh. "I wouldn't be here without you, Matild. Keep your coin." And she slipped behind the counter to pour water into the heavy copper kettle. She lit the flame with a spark of flint and blew on it gently, then rummaged through her private stash of teas.

Matild pocketed the pent, drumming her fingers on the booth's table. "Hmm. Black tea from the Capital. Is it the queen's favorite?"

"Second-favorite, actually. Her first favorite is Leonol's Stripe Blend—which is made with tiger dung."

"You're joking."

"I swear I'm not." Reyna chuckled at Matild's horrified look. "I wouldn't trust her taste. But this tea has hints of cacao and flavors well with sugar and cream."

She set the leaves in a cup, then poured hot water over them. She really needed a sand glass to track the steeping time, but for now, she relied on her own feel for the teas, the scent as they steeped, and the color of the water.

Matild, meanwhile, raised her eyebrows. "Okay, now I'm confused. How do you know the queen's favorite teas, Cya? I worked alongside her at the palace, and even I didn't know that."

Reyna paused briefly.

"I'm a royal enthusiast," she lied.

Matild didn't buy it. She hesitated, then leaned back in her seat. "I was running from something too, you know. A decade ago. The queen's third cousin delivered a baby boy, but—we couldn't save her."

Reyna vaguely recalled that. She'd been a teenager at the time, training under her uncle's tutelage. Her mother had died in an earlier assassination attack, but the family business meant she was immortalized forever.

"That's the best you can hope for," her uncle had said, lifting her practice sword and tapping her feet into position. *"An honorable death, after a life of loyal servitude."*

She hadn't questioned it until Kianthe did.

Now Reyna winced. "I'm sorry to hear it."

"My mentor was killed on the spot . . . but the blame fell to me, then. I reported to Queen Eren." Matild's gaze went distant, grim. "She was not pleased. She ordered me to sit penance in the palace courtyard for one week. No food. No water. I knew a death sentence when I saw one."

"You fled," Reyna said carefully.

Matild pinched the bridge of her nose. "I got word to Tarly, and he attacked my guard. We ran. And can you blame us?"

The tea was done steeping. Reyna poured it into a mug, flavored it with a spoonful of sugar. Her steps were measured as she handed it to Matild, who looked at her like she was an executioner.

Reyna's heart twinged.

"My real name is Reyna," she replied quietly. "I was a Queensguard; I dedicated everything to serving the throne. Kianthe—she convinced me there's more to life than an honorable death."

It was like she'd crystallized a hidden truth. Matild relaxed immediately, taking a careful sip of her tea. "This is excellent." A pointed gaze. "And Kianthe is right. You can help more people outside the palace walls . . . Reyna."

Hearing her true name on Matild's lips made Reyna smile slightly. "I know. And I intend to."

Their discussions dissolved into other things, and the day slid past.

❉

The barn was finished.

Reyna hesitated to accept it while Kianthe was absent, but— well, it was obvious. She and Matild had decorated the walls, laid rugs on the floor, and Reyna received shipments of plush armchairs from the furniture maker in town.

The shop's western side was Kianthe's haven: bookshelves, heavy rugs, comfy seats. A reading oasis. The east was Reyna's domain, with three booths, four small tables, and a larger round table that came with the barn. The perfect spot for sipping tea and conducting conversation.

She imagined the townsfolk would find their preferred space once they opened. But the barn doors stayed solidly closed until Kianthe returned.

A few more days passed while Reyna busied herself. She helped in Matild's clinic for a time, organizing herbs and sorting bandages. Tarly put her to work in the smithy, gleefully teaching her to hammer red-hot blades into a proper shape. She visited the more obscure tradesmen in town, such as a local exterminator who prided himself on poisoning rats, and a woman who specialized in "trading cards," which she insisted would be rare and valuable "someday."

Finally, Reyna was bored enough to pull Lilac from her pampered life at the inn's stable. The horse whinnied distaste as Reyna saddled her, mounted, and headed southwest. A quaint Sheparan town was close, maybe half a day's ride, and Reyna needed more teas.

The town's name was Kyaron, and it was at least five times Tawney's size. Buildings displayed traditional Sheparan architecture: stone pillars framing structures of mostly wood and glass. This never made sense to Reyna, unless stone was more of a status symbol and difficult to get here. With the Queendom and its quarries right next door, it seemed laughable.

But the people were solidly Sheparan, and several raised eyebrows at her accent. One tradesman scoffed when she inquired about specialty tea blends. "I hear your precious queen loves a good tea. Although, knowing her, it might be brewed with blood." He rolled his eyes and continued walking.

Reyna scowled, hand drifting to her sword, but there was nothing to protest.

She perched in the town square around the twilight hour, feeling morose. The moonstone was hard between her fingers, and she rubbed its smooth surface. The spell carved into one side pulsed at her longing, and she wondered if Kianthe could feel it.

But if the Arcandor noticed, she couldn't send a magical pulse back.

For some reason, that made Reyna even more lonely.

She spent the night at a local inn and met no one. The ale had been watered down, the seats were uncomfortable, and anyone she spoke with heard her accent and shrugged her off. In a striking moment of clarity, Reyna *missed* Tawney. It was obvious no one cared for Queendom citizens outside of the Queendom itself.

She left her ale half-finished and went to bed early.

The next day, Reyna tackled her tea hunt with renewed vigor, and finally uncovered a rare goods shop. It was brimming with Leonolan rope weapons, trinkets carved from dragon horns, and odd clothing from the islands west of Shepara. She scoured the shop and laughed when she landed on their tea selection.

"Who's your tradesman?" she asked the owner, plucking several bags of leaves for the shop.

The woman squinted at her. "Why do you care? You trying to compete?"

Reyna truly missed Tawney. She narrowed her eyes. "Are you worried your business will flee at the first competitor?"

It was the wrong thing to say. The woman huffed, pulling a swirl of parchment from behind the counter and opening it with a flourish. Ignoring her. Reyna collected more teas and a few herbal blends, slowly, contemplatively.

This could be important.

She swallowed her pride, approaching the counter. "I'm not a competitor. My partner and I are opening a bookstore."

"Where does tea fit into that?"

Reyna gestured at the unique goods around them. "Where does tea fit into this?"

The woman frowned.

"I'm just—" Reyna sighed, choosing the humble route. "I've

never done this before. I live in Tawney, and they don't have many options for trade. I find myself at a true loss in stocking supply."

The woman loosened. "Queendom?"

Reyna nodded reluctantly. It wouldn't make the woman more amicable, but it wasn't like she could hide her accent. It reminded her to practice a Sheparan accent in her spare time; that would certainly be a useful skill now that she'd separated from the queen's employ.

The woman plucked the teas from Reyna's hand, bundling the bags into a piece of parchment. "My sister lives in Tawney. Can't imagine why, with those dragons." The owner rolled her eyes. "But I won't fault a Queendom citizen making something of themselves. My tradesman visits Leonol four times a year, and spends the remainder touring Shepara. I can have him retrieve extra teas for your shop, if you place your order here."

"That'd be incredible," Reyna said.

A gleam overtook the shopkeeper's eye. "Five percent sounds fair."

Of course. Now Reyna frowned. "Just for placing the order? I believe three percent will be perfectly appropriate—and I'll ensure I'm here within a day of his delivery deadline, so it doesn't steal your shelf space."

The shopkeeper rested her hands on the paper bundle of teas.

Reyna held her gaze, waiting.

"Fine," the woman replied. She pushed the large bundle at Reyna, accepted four sils for it, and spent a few moments riffling through a set of parchment under the counter. When she emerged, it was with a long list of available teas.

Reyna chose her favorites, plus a few Kianthe would like.

"Come back in twenty-five days," the woman said. "He visits every full moon, give or take."

Reyna thanked her and left, feeling almost giddy. She would explore her own tradesmen as they got settled, but for now, this was a fair exchange. And as she packed the teas into Lilac's saddlebags and mounted her horse, it felt like her future stretched before her.

❋

Of course, she'd barely arrived back in Tawney before Nurt intercepted her. He waved as she approached the barn to drop off the teas. "Miss! Over here."

Perplexed, Reyna nudged Lilac into the alleyway, something the steed was none too pleased about. The horse huffed, shifting her weight, as Reyna slid out of the saddle.

Nurt was alone, but his eyes were wide: with panic or anticipation, Reyna couldn't tell. And frankly, she didn't care. Unease settled in her limbs; this wasn't a social call.

"What's going on?"

He scrubbed his balding head. "Visitors came while you were gone. Three men. Snooped around your barn, visited the inn. Sigmund went up, sneaky-like, but they wouldn't tell their business." Nurt hesitated. "To be honest, they weren't dressed like anyone I've seen. Red cloaks and expensive swords. Possible you've attracted the wrong kind of attention."

Red cloaks. Expensive swords.

The wrong kind of attention, indeed. Reyna set her jaw. Gods damn it all, she thought they'd have more time before Queen Tilaine's people narrowed their search. Although she expected spies, not the Queensguard themselves knocking on her door.

It was possible they were doing a casual sweep of neighboring towns . . . but the fact that they located the barn was concerning. The only positive was that there wasn't anything to tie Reyna specifically to the renovations. If Her Excellency's folk peeked through the windows, they'd see a nice shop—nothing more.

She couldn't think about what would happen if she was home next time.

This was worth more than a few pents. Reyna fished out a sil, handing it to Nurt. "For the warning. Did they leave town yet?"

His eyes widened at the silver piece, but he pocketed it without question.

"Aye, this morning." His words were stern. "Cya, you'd do well to keep an eye out. These folk didn't seem to have good intentions."

Reyna sighed. "I have no plans to intercept them. I appreciate the news, Nurt. If you hear anything else, please let me know." She hadn't expected Nurt and Sigmund to be so good at their jobs, but she wasn't about to let their keen eyes and prying curiosity go to waste.

"Of course, miss." A pause, a quiet smile. "Sigmund and I stopped by the barn to help while you were . . . ah, laid up. We stained the countertop. Did you notice?"

That was touching. Warmth filled her, and she squeezed his arm. "I did. It looks amazing, Nurt. Thank you. Come in for a cup of tea once we open."

"I just might. Shop like that? Good place to overhear conversations." With a sly smile and a wave, he slipped into the shadows again, whistling as he navigated the town's alleys.

Reyna's own smile faded. Rather than stopping at the barn, which suddenly felt dangerous and tenuous, she trudged back to the inn, the teas forgotten in Lilac's saddlebag.

14

Kianthe

"Unicorns," Kianthe exclaimed, throwing open the barn's doors two days later, "are *assholes*."

Outside, Visk screeched agreement, shook out his feathers, and took to the evening sky. It was telling that he didn't even wait for her dismissal. Not that Kianthe could blame him for being absolutely, wholeheartedly finished with their magical duty. Being nearly gutted by a unicorn's knifelike horn would do that to a griffon.

And to a mage, actually.

Behind a newly polished counter, Reyna paused in kneading a ball of dough. She was wearing a sleeveless shirt that showed off her muscular arms, even if they were covered in flour right now. She even had a smudge of flour on her cheek, and she looked so domestic that Kianthe couldn't help stomping over and sweeping her into a dramatic kiss. For added flourish, Kianthe bent Reyna backward, dipping her toward the floor, mostly to hear her startled laughter.

Good to be home.

No unicorns to be found here, either. Excellent.

Reyna's cheeks were flushed when they straightened, but her sharp eyes roamed Kianthe's form. It was cute, how she casually checked for injuries. "Things went poorly, then?" She wiped her forehead with her shoulder, which had apparently healed beautifully while Kianthe was gone. A thick scar puckered along her arm, but it was a far cry from the angry red mess it'd been before.

The mage grunted, exhaustion slipping into her bones. "Horses are bad enough. Truly, Rain, I can't imagine why you'd choose one as a mount. They're either dull as a rock or sharp as a royal's tongue, and there is no in between."

"Regrettably, I was not offered the option of a griffon at the queen's palace." It didn't sound regrettable to her. It sounded sarcastic. Reyna wiped her hands on her apron, which was dyed deep blue. On the breast, someone had stitched the words *I cook, you clean* in white thread.

Where she found that, Kianthe had no idea.

Every muscle in Kianthe's body ached. She sulked away from the kitchen, eyeing the comfy armchairs that had appeared on the western side of the shop while she was gone. They were perfect, plush and wonderful and velvet, but right now they looked *extra* comfy. Two faced each other near the front windows, a small table between them, and she sank into one and propped up her feet.

Shit. She might never move.

"You've been busy," Kianthe mumbled, letting her eyes slip shut. She smelled like horse and sour magic, and it was making her vaguely nauseated.

A few moments passed and Reyna appeared at her side, offering a small pastry. It was puffed sweet bread, and she'd drizzled melted Leonolan cacao over the top. "After all the progress made while I was recuperating, it wasn't difficult. All we're missing are the books now."

She set the pastry down, pushed Kianthe's clumpy bangs off her face. Kianthe was smeared in dirt, but Reyna didn't seem to care. Her expression softened. "You look tired, love. I'm surprised you didn't go back to the inn."

"I wanted to see you first," Kianthe admitted. "Can I have some tea?" Her tone was pleading, almost childlike in its petulance, and Reyna's lips quirked upward.

"Mint and rose?"

"Stars and Stone, it's like you're reading my mind."

Reyna laughed again and strolled back to the kitchen. The sound of pouring water, gentle clinking of copper over a flickering flame made a peaceful soundtrack, only interrupted by Reyna's soft singing. She'd even lit the fireplace, filling the room with a pleasantly smoky scent. Considering Tawney's cold climate, they could probably keep it lit year-round.

Kianthe's eyes slipped shut as she immersed herself in this dream. Responsibilities met, her partner healthy again . . . the stress of her life unwound slowly. Now *this* was meditation.

After they met, it had taken an entire year before Kianthe heard Reyna sing. When Kianthe confronted her, she spluttered some drivel about it being unprofessional, better left to musicians at the palace.

Contrarily, Kianthe sang loudly whenever she was soaring over the country on Visk's back—but she chose that height out of courtesy, because *Kianthe* wailed like a banshee. Reyna had a lovely voice . . . and even lovelier, this proved Reyna was happy here, to sing like that.

The thought warmed Kianthe's very soul. The mage felt herself drifting, settling into utter relaxation in the space they'd made their own.

Which meant she was wholly unprepared when the barn door was thrown open.

"What in the five hells happened here?"

Kianthe jerked upright, nearly knocking her pastry to the floor. The man at the door looked positively livid, his mustache twitching as he glared at the two women, the bookshelves, the new floors, the paint.

Reyna swept out from behind the counter, a few flour-dusted fingers brushing her messy bun. Her smile was as sharp as a dragon's fangs. "We're closed, sir. Happy to help you when we officially open for business."

"Open for—You two are about to be dead." He drew a vicious, bloodstained sword.

Reyna appraised it, wholly unimpressed. Considering her sword was always pristine, oiled to a shine, this must speak volumes to her.

"You really don't want to do that," Kianthe snapped, agitated at the interruption. But it was all posturing—her magic had been drained fighting an excessively stubborn unicorn herd, and the Stone hadn't deigned to refill her reservoir yet. Returning to Tawney, the Town of Little Ley Line, didn't help matters.

Reyna seemed to realize it, because she swept in front of Kianthe, seamlessly taking center focus. "I can see your confusion." She held up her hands, palms facing outward. "Lower the sword. Let's have a discussion."

He hesitated, although anger still coiled in his muscles. One wrong move, and there would be blood all over their new floors.

Considering she was unarmed, Reyna had no problem facing down his sword. In fact, she leaned closer, like they were discussing a secret. "This is a *front,* dear. Locals were getting frustrated, and Lord Wylan reached out to the queen herself to coordinate an intervention."

At the mention of Tilaine, the man flinched.

It was all the confirmation Kianthe needed: they were dealing with a bandit. They knew other members of the bandit ring might trickle in eventually, but it was impressive Reyna had identified one so quickly.

Granted, his sword probably helped solve the mystery.

Stone damn it all, Kianthe was tired.

"It isn't wise to test the queen. One of her Queensguard massacred a troop of our men five weeks ago." Reyna tsked, like this was a tragic loss.

"I heard of that," the man muttered, lowering his sword even farther. "Gods rest their souls."

Reyna had this handled. Kianthe dropped back into her armchair, fingers drifting to the pastry. It was flaky and delicious. Reyna used to sneak away and learn from the royal chefs as a child, and the lessons held. Kianthe didn't bother hiding her moan of delight.

Exasperation flashed on Reyna's features, there and gone faster than a bolt of lightning. It almost made Kianthe want to moan again, far more obnoxiously, just to see her reaction.

She didn't, but it was a near thing.

Reyna's expression was perfectly neutral, almost sympathetic, when the man glanced back at her. She beckoned him farther into the shop.

"Put that sword away; if anyone sees it through the window, we're finished."

He grumbled, but reluctantly obliged. At her pointed gesture, he dropped into a two-seater table near the back of the barn.

"There we go. You like tea? I'll get you a cup." She moved behind the counter, speaking as she worked: "We were hired to keep the storefront running. But to mask our true operation, this must be convincing. I need you to spread the word. No more waving swords the moment you step inside. We can't host malicious plans and co-conspirators here anymore. Now we serve tea, and offer books."

"Books are a work in progress," Kianthe called tiredly. She'd made short work of the pastry; with her belly full, she eyed the mugs of tea steeping behind the counter.

Reyna waved a hand. "Yours is coming, love."

"So . . . where *do* we meet, then?" the bandit asked, accepting the ceramic mug as Reyna handed it off. He sniffed it, made a face, and took a careful sip. When she placed a tiny container of crystalline sugar and an itty-bitty spoon in front of him, he didn't hesitate to load several scoops into the mug.

"We're shifting to a contracting method. I'll hand off assignments, and you complete them. Whatever you earn is yours to keep . . . except for a small finder's fee. Two pents to receive an assignment."

The bandit balked. "I'm not *payin'* you for that."

"Not me." Reyna winced, like the very word was blasphemous. "I'm merely a soldier on the front lines of this war." She carried the second cup to Kianthe, offering a private wink. Kianthe was having a very hard time keeping a straight face, especially when Reyna added ominously, "Troops that adapt, survive. Troops that don't . . . well." She pressed a hand to her heart.

The bandit set his jaw, sipping in silence. "Tea's good," he finally grunted.

"I am excellent at my job." Reyna stepped behind the counter, wiping the excess flour. "Are you excellent at yours?"

He heaved a sigh. "Two pents?" And then, Stars and Stone as their witness, he slid coins across the table.

Kianthe snorted into her tea. Unbelievable.

Reyna swept them up, tucking them in her apron's pocket. "One moment." And she slipped into the back storage room. Long, uncomfortable seconds passed, where the bandit and Kianthe sipped their tea in cold silence. When Reyna resurfaced, it was with a folded envelope.

"The spoils are yours. Spread the word, if you please. I don't need bandits blowing our cover once we truly open for business."

He muttered something, pocketed the envelope, and left.

Reyna locked the door behind him, waited until he'd vanished down the street before chuckling. "Well. That was something." She stepped back to the dough she'd left on the counter, clapped her hands with flour, and began kneading it again.

A few moments passed before Kianthe drawled, "What would you have done if he'd used that sword?"

Her girlfriend shrugged. "Considering I have multiple knives on my person, I wasn't worried. And he might do some good if he actually follows that 'assignment'—Mercon has had trouble with wild boars this year. He'll fetch an excellent bounty for one." Reyna tilted her head, and Kianthe tried to ignore how a single strand of hair fell over her ash-brown eyes. "Granted, that's assuming he doesn't claim he's a bandit to anyone with ears. For my own reference, what is Shepara's response to bandit troops?"

"Multiple knives?" Kianthe squinted, studying every piece of her attire. "*Where?*"

"Darling, please stay focused."

Kianthe puffed in exasperation. She was rarely focused around Reyna. "Sheparan law responds in kind. If a bandit attacks, they'll be imprisoned. If they kill indiscriminately, they'll be killed."

Reyna hummed. "Good to know. Keep your ears out for any other Realm-wide problems. It might be nice to send these bandits to help various towns." She pressed her lips together. "Anything to avoid a fight here . . . Scrubbing blood off pine floors will take ages. Trust me."

"Sure, sure."

Reyna kneaded the dough, patted it into a ball shape, then set the lump on a metal sheet. She took the sheet and disappeared into the storage room, where they'd installed the oven. Then she returned a few moments later, sans the dough, and began cleaning flour off the countertop.

"Our bedroom is done, by the way. We can move in anytime," Reyna said, changing the subject.

In response, Kianthe squinted harder. "Seriously. Where are the knives?"

Reyna just laughed.

15

Reyna

A few days later, the bookshop opened for business, and it was an anticlimactic affair.

This was because, while Kianthe had indeed stopped in Wellia to order a multitude of books, she hadn't been able to carry them back. Which meant a merchant sent the tomes on a wagon that wasn't due into Tawney for another week. Which *meant* they either had to stall for time or do a soft opening.

While they decided, Reyna allowed Kianthe to add the plants—which proved to be a huge mistake. Within hours, the barn was bursting with them: towering figs and shorter palms in the dirt near the front door, wisteria winding along the empty bookshelves, short green shrubs on every table, ivy in the rafters, and a dozen more Reyna couldn't even hope to name.

"Ah, dear? Is this a bit much?" Reyna asked.

The mage swept her arms in a circle, eyes alight. "No, it's perfect!" She seemed wholly unconcerned.

Reyna, meanwhile, was very concerned—mostly about how *she'd* keep them alive when Kianthe next traveled. But if this was part of Kianthe's dream, Reyna wouldn't interfere, so she forced a smile and left her to it.

The final touch was Kianthe's precious ever-flame, balls of magic that spread through the rafters like stars. Reyna began filling a bucket, waiting for their new home to catch fire—but the Arcandor proved to be skilled at her magic. The ever-flame remained in the rafters, glowing like warm candles. Nothing burned, which was a relief.

Finally, they checked out of Tawney's inn and relocated to the barn, their new home. Lilac was having the time of her life at the inn's stables, so Reyna reluctantly paid a few sils from her ever-dwindling pile to keep her mount housed a while longer.

After putting up with Visk for years, Lilac deserved a vacation.

The first morning they woke up together, entangled in the bed Reyna had purchased, birds chirping on their patio and a warm cup of tea awaiting them, happiness filled Reyna's soul. As they began their day, she admitted, "I think we're ready to open."

"The books aren't here yet." Kianthe tousled her shoulder-length dark hair—which somehow made the wavy locks more unruly—and nodded in satisfaction at the mirror.

Reyna pulled hers into a bun. A few blond tendrils fell free, framing her face. She pushed them behind her ear with a practiced motion and tugged on a loose-fitting shirt. "Well, we can serve tea. A soft opening."

She waited.

"Heh. Sof-tea opening."

Reyna heaved a long-suffering sigh.

Kianthe, meanwhile, was just starting: "Sorry. That felt like a strain. Get it? Straining tea leaves?"

Reyna might die. She refrained from rolling her eyes, instead pressing a kiss to Kianthe's lips on her way out of the bedroom. "Brilliant, my darling. You're as witty as you are skilled with a sword."

"Ah, shit." A pause. "That was pretty . . . brewed . . . of you."

Reyna closed the door in her face.

And so, they opened the bookshop. And when Kianthe swung the doors wide and they put the A-frame sign outside to announce their new business, Reyna realized—far too late—that they hadn't discussed what to call it, not once.

As they lounged inside waiting for customers, Reyna drummed her fingers on the counter, contemplative. "I think we'll need a name to properly advertise."

"I think we'll need books to properly advertise," Kianthe replied, cooing lovingly at a stiff-looking plant on one of their tables. At Reyna's exasperated stare, she shrugged. "All right. Look. The shop's name is New Leaf Tomes and Tea."

Reyna blinked. "New Leaf? That was fast."

"No, it's hilarious. New leaf? Tea leaves? Turning over a new leaf? A leaf of a book?" Kianthe smirked. "Please, Rain. I've had this name picked out for two years. I was just waiting for you to join my chaos."

Reyna delicately chose a pastry from her piles. Earlier that morning, she'd baked both cacao and blueberry scones, and completed their supply with powdered croissants. The latter were buttery and flaky, sweetened with a dusting of ground sugar. Not bad, if she said so herself.

"You're hardly chaos compared to Queen Tilaine."

Kianthe snorted. "Well, I would hope I'm not that kind of chaos."

The conversation diverged, but the name stuck. To pass the time, Reyna retrieved the sign from inside and borrowed Kianthe's paintbrush, writing in perfect cursive: *Welcome to New Leaf Tomes and Tea.*

They both admired the board for a moment. Reyna glanced around the shop they'd built, decorated, *perfected,* and a warm sense of accomplishment washed over her. It was bright and friendly and wonderful. Even if the place was empty for now, it brimmed with potential.

And most importantly, it was theirs. Reyna had framed both

deeds—one from Lord Wylan, one from Diarn Feo—with dark wood, and hung them behind the kitchen counter. Absolute proof of ownership.

It made her feel absurdly pleased, nearly giddy.

"I'll place this at the town square." She penned smaller, cursive directions at the base of the board. "Maybe invite Matild and Tarly over for a cup of tea. They wanted to know when we opened."

"I'll be here, tending my plants like the crazed elemental mage I am."

"You're not crazed." Her eyes roamed the foliage of the shop. "A bit obsessed, possibly."

"Obsessed with you."

"Ever the romantic." Reyna hooked the sign over her shoulder, blowing Kianthe a kiss. As she stepped into the street, she noticed a few windows had opened to welcome the crisp spring breeze. A child played on the stoop of the home next door, waving as Reyna approached.

The child's mother tilted her head, arms crossed. Kianthe had mentioned she met the neighbors—this woman must be Sasua.

"So, we'll finally get to see what you've been up to?" Suspicion laced the woman's voice. "I saw that bandit visiting yesterday. The dragons are bad enough; I thought you were here to clean up this street."

An ugly scar sliced across Sasua's eyebrow, and Reyna recognized the fear in her gaze. The Gods only knew what trials this woman had faced in her lifetime. Reyna stopped, facing her fully. "I'm Reyna."

It took the woman aback. "Ah, Sasua."

"We'll make sure your home is safe, Sasua." Reyna offered a kind smile. "That man misunderstood what we were doing, so we sent him on his way. This is our home now, too. If anyone gives you trouble, just let me know, all right?"

Sasua hesitated, glancing at the barn again. Her dubious expression softened. "It looks good. The plants are a nice touch."

"We think so." Reyna hoisted the sign higher up her shoulder. "Come in anytime for a cup of tea, okay?"

Sasua watched her son press his nose to the glass windows of the barn, squinting inside. Fluffing the leaves of the fig tree by the door, Kianthe waggled a few fingers. A twirl of the mage's hand had a strand of ivy craning from the rafters, stringing into a heart shape over the glass windowpane.

Sasua's son laughed gleefully, tracing it with his finger. "Mama, look!"

"I see," Sasua chimed, rubbing the back of her neck. Her tone was abashed now. "I didn't mean to assume, Reyna. It's just been . . . rough. It'll be good to have you two here. We'll visit for some tea when you open."

"We look forward to it." Feeling warm, Reyna bid her goodbye and headed for the center of Tawney.

Tarly burst from his smithy as Reyna set up the board in the town square. He whistled at the name. "Your shop is open to receive customers?" Anticipation had his bulky frame bouncing.

Reyna laughed. "Finally, yes."

Taking the cue, Tarly cupped his mouth and bellowed: "Hey, everyone! That bookshop is open. Down on Lindenback—take an early lunch and go support our newcomers!"

"Ah, Tarly, we don't have books yet."

He blinked. "Oh." At a much higher volume, he amended, "No books yet, but good tea. A casual meeting spot for the curious and open-minded!"

Well, he was good at pivoting.

A few people chuckled, but several more moseyed to the sign and squinted at the name. Reyna's insides flipped. She didn't really care if their shop was successful anytime soon, but there was something nerve-wracking about presenting their dream on a wooden board and hoping it was received favorably.

Fact was, her funds were already half-gone, and they couldn't survive in Tawney forever without a positive revenue stream.

So, she assumed a friendly smile and accepted congratulations from strangers who were slowly becoming neighbors. Tarly loomed nearby, arms crossed, appearing pleased with the modest reception.

Matild had emerged to her husband's shouting, and she wiped poultice off her hands with a messy rag. "Tarly, I think it'd be more helpful if you send them to the shop, not to her advert board."

Reyna's cheeks colored. "Possibly."

"Well, go on then." Tarly made a shooing motion at the crowd, interrupting their curious chatter. "Go get a cup of hot tea. It's too cold to stand out here."

And to Reyna's delight, a few broke off, heading down the street toward Lindenback.

She mouthed *thank you* to Tarly, waved at Matild, and followed them back to the store. Inside, Kianthe was brewing tea like a master—she'd spent enough time around Reyna to pour an excellent cup. Two mugs were already steeping, and as the crowd milled inside, the mage's eyes widened.

"You . . . are very good at this," Kianthe said.

Reyna slid behind the counter, retrieving the copper kettle to refill in their storage room. Already, compliments and casual observations were spilling from their customers' lips as they toured the refurbished barn. She tried not to eavesdrop.

It was a losing battle.

"Tarly did most of it. Can't blame them for wanting a nice, warm cup." Reyna raised her voice slightly. "Thank you all for coming! Please, stay and enjoy the space. No purchase necessary, although we're pleased to offer teas and herbal blends from as far south as Leonol, and as far west as the Roiling Islands of Shepara."

Excited murmurs overtook the place. A few lined up to place an order, and the day slipped away in a blur of pleasant conversation and lovely company.

The sun was beginning to set when Lord Wylan stepped into the barn.

The crowd had thinned considerably, and the few stragglers hastily finished their tea. Reyna watched, exasperated, as they all but fled the young lord's presence. Whatever loyalty he thought he had in Tawney, it was clear the public was more intimidated than awe-inspired.

Then again, she expected nothing less from a Queendom lord.

He surveyed the shop, noted the deed she'd hung on the wall—and the paper below it scribbled with the diarn's informal note of ownership. His expression twisted into irritation. "That fraud's signature hardly holds weight—"

"Watch your tongue," Kianthe said curtly as she gathered leftover mugs from the empty tables. "That fraud is a friend."

Reyna pinched her brow. "Kianthe, this is *Lord* Wylan." Emphasis on his title. The mage had the decency to look disconcerted. "My lord, welcome to our shop. Can I get you a cup of tea?"

"Green, if you please," he replied stiffly.

She gestured at a nearby table, and he sat, looking for all the world like ants had crawled up his leg. So, it was perfect, *truly* serendipitous timing, that Diarn Feo strolled into the shop moments later.

"Oh. This should be interesting," Kianthe murmured, passing Reyna with the mugs.

"Hells. I knew you followed me," Lord Wylan snapped, pushing to his feet.

Diarn Feo—skinny, with short hair and a stern expression—heaved a sigh. "Perish the thought. But when my competitor takes note of a new establishment, it's only fitting that I show my support as well."

Reyna dipped her head. "Diarn Feo. I've heard so much about you."

"Ah, the girlfriend." Feo appraised her, and she met their gaze head-on. Whatever they saw, they must have liked, because they nodded once. "Stands your ground. I approve."

"You don't need their approval, love," Kianthe called from the storage room.

The diarn waved her off, chose an herbal blend of ginseng, dandelion root, and raspberry, and dropped into the chair across from Lord Wylan. Reyna busied herself with preparing the teas, even as the two leaders glared at each other.

Lord Wylan spoke first. "I read your commandment." His voice was cold as a winter wind.

"A convincing case, I hope?" Diarn Feo paused. "That was rhetorical. It's the most ironclad proposition for township control ever written. And I'd know—I've read most of them."

"My father, and his mother before, lived and died here. You haven't even stayed a full year." Lord Wylan looked ready to reach across the table and strangle them. "The people of Tawney deserve a lord who won't flee at the first devastating dragon attack."

Diarn Feo scoffed. "I've endured dragon attacks. Perhaps, instead of wearing those raids like a medal of honor, you should turn your attention to *why* they're happening in the first place."

"Ah, yes. The mythical stolen egg." Lord Wylan's tone dripped sarcasm.

Kianthe appeared over Reyna's shoulder. She watched the leaders with excitement, looking for all the world like the Mid-Winter Celebration had come early. Her voice was a bare whisper, meant for Reyna's ears alone: "This seems like a very ten-tea-tive conversation."

Reyna nearly snorted. "Been saving that one?"

"Maybe."

She poured hot water into two mugs, then portioned the leaves into linen bags, which she tied with twine and rested in each cup. This tense atmosphere was a vibrant contrast to the casual tone of their other customers. It wasn't the environment Reyna wanted to foster—but it *was* entertaining. It reminded her of her old life, standing on the outskirts, watching the conversations of powerful people go wrong.

She did love a bit of gossip. Maybe Reyna fit into Tawney better than she thought.

Because there was little else to do while the leaves steeped, Reyna retrieved a rag to wipe down the counters. Meanwhile, Kianthe draped over the polished wood, not even pretending like she wasn't eavesdropping.

Neither leader noticed them. Or maybe they did, and they simply didn't care.

Lord Wylan tapped his finger aggressively on the wooden tabletop. "Dragons hatch in broods of dozens. If one egg went missing, they likely wouldn't even notice."

Kianthe and Diarn Feo snorted at the same time.

"Dragons mate once a century, and their gestation period is a decade long. Their eggs take half of our lifetimes to hatch." Diarn Feo rolled their eyes. "Your grandmother's biggest problem was convincing Shepara they had no true claim over this town. The dragon attacks didn't begin until your *father* allowed an egg to be stolen."

"That's a lie," Lord Wylan hissed. "I have journal entries from my grandmother proving they've happened ever since the dragons awakened."

"And I have journals from dozens of Shepara citizens proving otherwise."

Reyna plucked out the linen bags, then presented the mugs to each leader. They didn't acknowledge her, too busy fighting each other. Lord Wylan gripped his mug like he could throttle the ceramic instead of his enemy. Diarn Feo traced the glaze of theirs as if it were a lover, eyes glinting with malice.

"There's sugar," Reyna said, partly to stoke the fires, partly to fulfill her role as hostess. She set the jar on the table, alongside the tiny metal spoon.

"You know an awful lot about dragons for a diarn." Lord Wylan ignored the sugar.

Diarn Feo, in contrast, scooped a healthy serving into their tea. "All diarns are required to know about threats to their townships."

Lord Wylan took a deep swig. His tea was more bitter than Feo's, but he seemed to savor the bold flavor. "Ah. And what would happen if I visited the Sheparan council and inquired about you? Would they back your claim?"

"What if I tell your precious queen that you're losing control to a Sheparan national? I would think very carefully about bringing our governments into this dispute."

"Our governments are the entire reason *for* this dispute."

"I have a question." Kianthe raised her hand like a student in a schoolroom.

Both startled, and Reyna nearly laughed. It was like the leaders existed in their own little world, which was . . . very interesting, actually. She busied herself in washing out the copper kettle, drying it for the night, but kept one ear toward the conversation.

Meanwhile, the mage grinned. "If the dragons are attacking for a lost egg, why aren't they here more often?"

Lord Wylan smirked, leaning back in his chair. "Yes, Diarn Feo. The dragons only attack a few times a year. Surely you can explain why?"

The diarn shot Kianthe an exasperated glare. "My theory is that the egg's magic flares occasionally. It's hidden somewhere in Tawney, and when it pulses, it summons the dragons."

Lord Wylan didn't immediately respond, but he did roll his eyes.

Kianthe, meanwhile, raised her hand again. "What causes the flare-ups?"

Reyna suspected the mage was just messing with Diarn Feo now.

They fumbled for a response. "I—I haven't figured that out yet." When Lord Wylan's smirk shifted into true arrogance, Diarn Feo bared their teeth. "That's a distant issue. If you truly want to do right by this town, Lord Wylan, you'll explore your family history. And you'll realize I was right."

Lord Wylan drained his tea in a single gulp, which must have burned. But he looked like he'd rather suffer a sore throat than sit here one more second. He tossed a few pents on the counter, shot Diarn Feo an acidic look, and left.

The diarn attempted a bit more grace. "Well. I think I won that round."

. . . Relatively speaking.

Kianthe laughed out loud. "How d'you figure?"

"I'm still here, aren't I?" Diarn Feo replied. "Nice shop. Good to meet you, girlfriend."

They were out the door before Reyna could offer her fake name.

Silence filled their wake, and Reyna carefully locked the front door. Her eyes met Kianthe's, and they both burst into laughter. Reyna slid into Feo's vacated seat, rubbing her eyes. "That was a charged conversation. Romantically speaking."

"The angriest flirting I've ever seen."

A successful opening day, all things considered.

16

Kianthe

The books arrived several days later on a pair of carts pulled by two downtrodden donkeys.

Kianthe squealed, shamelessly abandoning a customer to greet the merchants. It was raining outside, more spitting than actual drops, and the water clung to her hair as if it were greeting an old friend. She waved the liquid off, shooing it into the mud.

Her voice was giddy: "Are they books?"

"Dunno," the first merchant replied. "Are you Kianthe?"

"Yes!"

He grunted and climbed off the cart, motioning for his partner to do the same. Together, they began unloading crates: there were at least sixteen of them, and they looked as heavy as a Magicary mage's glare. Since Kianthe was standing nearby, the merchant handed one to her.

She wheezed at the weight, scrabbling to keep her hold.

The man rolled his eyes. "Ain't that heavy."

"I'll handle it," Reyna said, suddenly at her shoulder. She swept the crate away with ease, because unlike Kianthe, Reyna had spent years ensuring she was in peak physical condition. "Remind me to give you a briefing on proper business protocol, dearest. It's better for the shop if you don't leave a customer mid-order."

"Rain, I will never remind you to give me a lecture on business protocol."

A rare gleam overtook Reyna's eyes, and she lowered her voice as she brushed past Kianthe. "Pity. I'm certain I can keep that lecture interesting."

Kianthe grinned. "Is that so?"

"Only if you go back inside and finish what you started."

"Well, now I'd rather finish this." Kianthe whistled, stepping an appraising circle around her girlfriend. There was something spectacular about Reyna's sly smile, the way she flipped her long hair over her shoulder with a graceful twist. Her muscles were tight under the weight of the books, but it didn't seem to faze her.

"*This* is already over, love. We have customers." Reyna strolled inside.

Kianthe trailed behind, admiring her girlfriend. Stone *bless* whatever magic put Kianthe in this woman's path two years ago.

Between Reyna and the merchants, they had the carts unloaded quickly. Then Reyna invited them for a cup of tea, introducing them to a few customers as they settled into one of the booths.

It was both unsurprising and disconcerting that Reyna had learned their regulars' names, when Kianthe was only beginning to recognize faces. Even as a child, Kianthe had struggled to remember the names of every crotchety mage she reported to—and after she left the Magicary, they'd slipped from her mind as fast as water down a mountainside.

Reyna probably had a list hidden somewhere of Tawney townsfolk. She'd probably divided them into household or family name. *Probably,* Reyna had already begun identifying their hobbies, their friends, their love interests, their favorite vacation spots, all discerned through friendly socializing and meticulous recording.

Actually, Reyna and Feo would get along well if they ever spent time together. Kianthe made a mental note to keep them apart as long as possible.

The merchants enjoyed their tea, commented on how nice the shop was, and asked about the books inside the crates. A conversation about the bookshop's origins developed, during which Reyna forgot Kianthe to showcase the finer points of New Leaf.

And thus, Kianthe ignored them, descending on the wooden crates with a metal bar and vicious glee. She wrenched the lids off, tore into the sawdust to find heavyset tomes inside.

They were perfect.

"Cya, look! *One Baker's Dozen: Recipes for the Culinarily Adept.*" She waved the book at Reyna, who quirked an eyebrow over the copper kettle.

"Is that a hint?"

"Nooo." Kianthe tugged out another book. *A Gentleperson's Guide to Sex and Sensuality.* She didn't bother quelling her suggestive smile as she tucked *that* one away for later.

Always good to have reference guides.

It took the better part of the day to open every crate and sift through them. This was mostly because Kianthe kept pausing in her exploration to read. There was a thrill to losing herself within the pages of a new story, and it'd been a while since she'd had this wide a selection. The tome on her bedside table had been reread four times, and while she didn't mind the familiarity, there was a novelty to something new.

"Heh. Novel-tea." She almost shouted the pun across the space, but Reyna was in the storage room again. Kianthe distracted herself quickly.

The merchants left with full bellies and bright smiles, and after their remaining customers vacated for the night, Reyna locked the front door and joined Kianthe on the tightly woven rug near the fireplace. Their knees touched as she retrieved a mystery novel and flipped through heavy yellow pages.

"This isn't handwritten." Her ash-brown eyes widened.

Kianthe almost laughed. "An astute observation."

Reyna ran her fingers over the blocky letters. "I heard Shepara developed some way to mass-produce their words. But I've never seen one before."

Oh, Stars and Stone, she was serious. Kianthe lowered her own book, unable to hide her bone-dry tone. "Ah, yes. I forgot the Queendom snubs progress, innovation, and entertainment of any sort. Frankly, I'm shocked Tilaine didn't adopt the technology to spread her precious thoughts to the masses."

"Dear, would you care to explain how it happens, or would you rather gloat about Shepara's modernization?"

Well, Kianthe deserved that. She cleared her throat, appropriately scolded. "It's called a printing press. A wordsmith sets the letters, and the press copies multiple pages in one sitting. All done with tiny blocks of wood and a metal machine."

Reyna examined the typeset. "How old is the technology?"

"New enough to be exciting to a Queendom citizen, apparently. Old enough that printed books in Shepara are cheaper than handwritten ones."

At the mention of money, Reyna winced. Her eyes roamed the open crates, the books beginning to fill their shelves. It would take several more deliveries to truly occupy the massive bookshelves, but Kianthe planned to hide the empty spaces with plants and oddities in the meantime.

"Even considering that, these tomes couldn't have been cheap. What did this cost?"

Kianthe had been dreading that question. She rubbed the back of her neck. "It didn't cost us anything. The Magicary, on the other hand, will be getting a very large invoice—and they probably won't be pleased about it." At Reyna's exasperated stare, the mage shrugged. "What? I handled those awful unicorns. It's only fair I receive some form of payment."

"That's not—" Reyna pinched her brow. "Key, we're supposed to be doing this independent of our old lives."

"You sent me to Wellia to buy books."

"I know, but this feels like a shortcut. If we want to earn New Leaf Tomes and Tea"—now Reyna gestured at the shop at large—"we have to do the work, and pay for it slowly." Her cheeks tinged pink. "That's how I imagined our life together, anyway."

Shame flooded Kianthe's veins, and hot on its heels was irritation. "Ironic, considering we basically stole this building on your recommendation." Her words were deadpan, and maybe a bit sharp. She pushed to her feet, slid her current book onto a nearby shelf between ten others.

Reyna pressed her lips into a firm line. "We're dealing with Tawney's bandit problem, so I considered this building payment for services rendered. But I agree it was through less-than-traditional means, and I've already begun putting coin aside to buy it properly."

"Why would we buy it? We already own it!"

Silence hung between them, tense as a sword to the neck.

The longer it lasted, the stupider Kianthe felt.

"I'm sorry," she muttered, although she didn't feel sorry. "I'm just—you got your teas. The books were my contribution, and I already messed up." Apparently.

Doubt flashed on Reyna's face. She looked again at the books, then muttered a curse under her breath and pushed to her feet. It only took a second to cross the distance between them.

The mage stiffened as Reyna gripped her forearms, gentle and comforting. "No, I'm sorry. I never meant to imply that you messed up. After you left Tawney, I realized I forgot to give you coin to buy these books. Of course you had to get creative."

That's right, Kianthe thought stubbornly, but already her tension was easing. Proximity to Reyna had that effect.

Reyna pulled back now, gaze flicking to the floor. "I didn't mean to get hostile. It's just . . . When my mother was alive, she used to lecture that everything was earned. My cooking lessons were paid with dish duty. My combat training came through my mother's indebtment to the crown. I achieved my spot beside Queen Tilaine by eliminating an assassin no one else thought to track."

"That's admirable." It was all Kianthe could say without losing her neutral expression—because inside, she was exhausted by this concept. A person could work and work and work, and still never "earn" their dues.

Sometimes success meant determination . . . and sometimes, it was just luck.

Kianthe was the perfect example. She'd done nothing to earn her place as the Stone of Seeing's chosen one. She'd just existed, studied alongside twenty other children—and when the old Arcandor died, power infused her with no real explanation. There were still mages in the Magicary who loathed her for it.

Some days, Kianthe loathed herself for it too.

Reyna massaged her brow. "That's how we're raised in the Queendom. If we work hard, good things come. It's possible that I'm still trying to figure out how to earn you, Key."

Now Kianthe stared, because she must have misheard.

Must have.

"Reyna, you don't have to 'earn' me. You *have* me."

"Yes, and it's baffling." Reyna spoke like it was a common truth. Her eyes roamed the bookstore, the small touches Kianthe had added over the weeks. The plants. The paint. The ever-flame. A smile tilted her lips as she retrieved another book, stroked its leather cover. "I'm not sure I deserve this . . . but if I pay for it, that gives me something tangible. Proof, if anyone in the Queendom comes asking. If I come asking myself."

It made sense. It was messed up and wholly incorrect, but it made sense.

Kianthe still wanted to shake her girlfriend until logic settled behind those gorgeous eyes. "You deserve this. Stars and Stone, you deserve everything."

Reyna hugged the book to her chest, looking small and sad

in their spacious home. "I love you for saying that. I'm not trying to secure sympathy—just explain myself, I suppose. If I pay
for the barn, the tea, the books . . . maybe that will be enough to
feel worthy of dating the Arcandor, the Mage of Ages, the most
incredible woman alive. Who loves me, even though sometimes
I'm not exactly sure why."

Kianthe might die.

"*Fuck,* Rain."

Without another word, Kianthe pulled Reyna into a bone-
crushing hug. The book fell to the floor. Reyna wheezed a bit, but
Kianthe couldn't bear to loosen her hold—as if she could convey
her absolute adoration with physical touch.

"I want you to feel loved without earning it. Because that's how
you make me feel every Stone-damned day." Kianthe muttered
this into Reyna's neck, her lips brushing the sensitive spot just
below Reyna's ear. She delighted in how her girlfriend shivered,
and Kianthe pulled back to kiss her. Her words were a passionate
promise: "You are worth every moment of my time. Do you understand that?"

Reyna traced her back, laughing a little. "I understand it."

"Do you believe it?"

Now her silence was telling.

Kianthe thought for a moment, still gripping Reyna as if she
were as precious as the Stone of Seeing itself. Her girlfriend's
insecurity went deeper than Kianthe ever imagined. She'd discovered a glimpse that night under the fire-lit pinyon pine, and
should have known it hadn't just . . . gone away.

Kianthe's tone was fierce. "Okay. If you don't believe it, I'll
worship you until you do. Prove it through action."

"Starting with that new book of yours? *Sex and Sensuality*? I
saw you sneak it into our room."

"This isn't a joke."

Reyna chuckled. "Everything you say is a joke."

Deflecting when faced with something uncomfortable, just

like Matild had said weeks ago. Kianthe's pulse thrummed like she was partaking in a life-or-death fight—like one wrong move would send this incredible woman away.

She proceeded carefully.

"Reyna. This is important: you never have to earn me. I'm not 'payment for services rendered.'" A pause for breath, almost pained. "*Please* don't reduce me to that."

That, finally, made Reyna flinch. Her eyes lost their amusement, her lips down-turning slightly. "Ah, Key, I'm sorry. It wasn't my intention to make you . . ." She paused, forced a smile. "I know you love me."

"I do love you. More than anything."

Reyna lowered her gaze. "Then I need you to understand that this is my problem. Not yours. You're so wonderful, you make me feel like I've . . . cheated . . . somehow. But I want to be your equal. And maybe, with this shop, I can be."

"How aren't you my equal?" Kianthe asked, her voice strangled. "This is so insane, Reyna, because every time I look at us, I wonder how *I* snagged *you*. This stunning, capable, confident woman who's loyal enough to guard that ass of a queen with her life. Somehow, now, you're loyal to me instead, and that's—that's everything. That's more than I've ever had."

Reyna's face flushed. "You're the Arcandor—"

That *title* again. Anger thrummed in Kianthe's veins, sudden and infuriating, but it quelled into devastation almost immediately. Around them, the plants began to wilt. Kianthe laughed drily. "Ah, yes. The title I was handed merely for existing. Talk about earning my accomplishments."

"I didn't mean—"

"I know what you meant."

For a long moment, Reyna stared at her. Then, with a frustrated huff, she stepped to the nearby watering can, dipped her fingers in it, and flicked the water on Kianthe's face.

It shattered the tension instantly.

Wiping the drips, Kianthe spluttered: "W-What the hell was that?"

"You're misreading. All I meant was that your title puts you in the realm of queens and councils. It's *intimidating*, Kianthe, but it isn't why I love you. So, get that out of your head."

The mage squinted at her.

Then she coaxed the remaining water out of the watering can with a wave of her hand.

Maintained eye contact as she tugged it across the floor, pooling around Reyna's ankles.

Reyna tensed, already dancing backward. "What are you— Don't you dare, Key—"

"If you're going to scold me with a splash of water, you have to know I'm going to retaliate." And Kianthe pulled the water upward in a geyser-like blast. It soaked Reyna instantly.

Reyna yelped, holding her arms away from her sopping clothes. A murderous glint overtook her eyes.

"You are going to pay for that, darling."

When they were both soaking wet, dripping over the pine floors, they held each other's gazes—and burst into laughter. The mugs Reyna used for her half of the fight sat on a table, forgotten, as they collapsed against each other, laughing until their bellies hurt and tears streamed from their eyes.

"I think we're both pretty ridiculous," Reyna said finally.

"I think you're ridiculous. I'm perfect."

"Modest, too. Yet another trait I love about you."

Kianthe kissed her.

17

Reyna

It was calming, being finished with the bookstore. New Leaf Tomes and Tea was about as successful as Reyna could have hoped, now that the construction was complete and books lined their shelves. Nearly everyone in Tawney had stopped by at some point, and many had become true regulars. At least four or five people occupied the bookstore at any given point, sipping tea and thumbing through handwritten or typed pages.

Kianthe and Reyna worked side by side, and occasionally Kianthe would make comments about their prior conversation:

"Just so you know, Rain, that kiss earlier really earned my affection today."

"If you wanted to earn my love this afternoon, you'd clean the mugs piling up in the storage room."

"Your hard work is really proving to me that you deserve a nice dinner tonight."

It became so insistent, so sarcastic, that Reyna was ready to smack her. But it *did* reinforce how silly she'd been, and Reyna found herself paying close attention to her own emotions. Were her errands done for her own benefit, the bookstore's benefit . . . or were they done to prove her love to Kianthe?

She finally settled on a mix of both—but it was encouraging that her girlfriend didn't seem to care either way if the dishes were done or the washroom was cleaned. She brought fancy dinners home regardless, and kissed Reyna senseless when she hesitated.

It was cute, and made Reyna's chest warm with love.

Word began to spread within the bandit troops, too. A few stopped by—mostly identifiable by their grungy attire and disgusting weaponry—for a cup of tea. They'd slide two extra pents across the table, give Reyna a knowing look, and she'd smile and hand them a mug and a sealed envelope.

It was impossible to know if they completed the assignments, but word did come from Mercon that the boars were no longer a problem. And the bandits kept coming, kept paying, so Reyna happily maintained the ruse.

One day, Kianthe tracked her down in the storage room while she mixed tisane blends. The mage's face was pinched. "Ah, Rain? We have a problem."

Reyna frowned. "The *royal* kind of problem?"

As the weeks passed peacefully, it was difficult to tell what felt more ominous: Queen Tilaine's silence, or the lapse of dragon attacks on Tawney. Kianthe joked that maybe the dragons sensed her magic and were leaving the town alone—but she never seemed convinced by her own words.

Reyna resisted worrying. Either the problems would arrive on their doorstep, or they wouldn't, but fretting wasn't productive in the meantime.

Now, the mage waved a hand to dismiss the thought. "No. Sigmund came earlier for a cup of tea and said Tawney has been quiet. This is a bandit problem. Ah, *potential* bandit problem."

Reyna had been reaching for her prewritten envelopes. The sheriff's cousin, down in Shepara's southernmost town of Jallin, was having issues with illicit items smuggled into their ports. Bandits could investigate that problem much easier than law enforcement.

But at Kianthe's corrected statement, Reyna paused.

"What do you mean, 'potential'?"

"I think you'll want to handle this one." Kianthe left the storage room, beckoning her along.

When Reyna saw the "bandit" in question, she almost broke down laughing.

It was a skinny boy, thin and wiry, with skin the shade of waterlogged driftwood and eyes a stormy blue. He was wearing a broadsword in a homemade back scabbard; he wouldn't even be able to *draw* that sword, a scabbard like that with a blade so large, but he seemed satisfied to show it off. He tapped four pents sitting on the counter—which might be half his life's savings, considering he was a teenager—and said, "I'm ready for my assignment, ma'am."

Ma'am, Kianthe mouthed to Reyna, nearly in fits herself.

Reyna smoothed her expression, ignoring the coin. "I think you've made a mistake, dear. We're not handing out assignments." *To children,* she amended in her mind.

He stiffened. "I've paid. You have to give me a job."

"Oh, do I?" Reyna's smile bordered on amused. "This is a bookstore. We serve tea. I'd be happy to steep your preference, but we only charge two pents a mug." She slid two back toward him, a pointed gesture.

The boy glared, shifting the straps over his shoulders. He possessed none of the muscle she'd boasted at that age. It reaffirmed that he almost certainly didn't know how to use that blade.

"I'm a *bandit,*" he whispered harshly, casting a surreptitious glance at the other customers. None of them paid much mind to the counter, and Reyna was grateful for it.

She leaned over the polished wood, resting on her elbows. For a long moment, they considered each other, and Reyna finally chuckled. "Dear, do you think we accept just anyone?"

Kianthe snorted, carefully excusing herself. Almost like she realized this ruse was about to get complicated, and she didn't trust herself to keep a straight face. Her lithe footsteps *tap-tap-tapped* on the pine floors as she returned to the storage room, hopefully to finish blending the teas Reyna had started. As the door squeaked shut, Kianthe shushed it—a cute quirk Reyna hadn't seen before they started living together.

The boy frowned. "I was told I could receive an assignment here; he didn't mention other requirements. Just the two pents." He tapped the coin again, but now he seemed less sure.

"And who is 'he'?"

The boy clammed up. He could keep a secret, which was a decent trait to have.

Reyna quirked one eyebrow. "*He* is correct, but he probably also has experience."

"He doesn't! He's not a bandit. But I need to join a troop; that's why I'm here."

Hmm. Reyna filed that information away. "I see. I'm afraid you're out of luck; I'm not some bandit matchmaker. And I won't waste an assignment on someone who's likely to get himself killed. It doesn't reflect well on our superiors."

"I won't get myself killed," he exclaimed, indignant now. "I can use this sword."

Reyna smiled wider, almost viciously. She hadn't lifted her sword in weeks, and she missed it. So, there was an ulterior motive when she drawled, "Can you now? How about we spar, and you prove it?"

He puffed out his chest. "Fine."

Reyna beckoned toward the back patio, then left him outside. The temperatures were warming for the summertime, which meant she could finally utilize the cozy space. It was big enough for a quick sparring session, and private enough to avoid curious eyes.

Kianthe peeked out from the storage room, shaking with laughter. "What the hells? Are you really going to fight him?"

"Sometimes, it's a good lesson to be knocked on your ass. And it's either me . . . or someone far less forgiving." Reyna slipped into their bedroom to retrieve her sword. She considered the queen's insignia stamped to the hilt, cursing. "I need a new weapon, I think. Is Tarly skilled in sword smithing?"

"You'll have to ask Matild. In the meantime, here." Kianthe pulled bare earth from the side alley, meshing it into a sticky, spelled clay. She rolled it into a small disc and pressed it over the insignia. Another muttered spell, and it hardened, firm as stone.

The weight messed with the balance a bit, but Reyna could work with it.

"Enjoy fighting the child, dear." Kianthe shook her head. "Please don't skewer him."

Reyna rolled her eyes and stepped onto the patio. The boy had moved the center table to free space, and somehow unsheathed his sword. She was sorry she missed it, because that must have been hilarious—back sheaths were only practical when the sword was significantly shorter.

He straightened self-importantly when she approached. "Ready if you are." Only a teenage boy could have such arrogance.

Reyna was going to enjoy this.

"First to touch," she said. Unlike Shepara's sparring ordinances, which required wooden swords unless certified for better, the Queendom abided by a ruthless *If you can't survive a spar, you are not fit to serve* mentality. Kianthe would count Reyna's scars late at night and curse Her Excellency's name, palace, and country.

Reyna, on the other hand, felt they were a visual accomplishment of duty served. When she removed her restrictive outer shirt and rolled her shoulders, the boy's eyes fell to the scars on her arms, and he blanched.

Despite her posturing, she had no intention of pinning a sword to this teenager's neck, so real blades with milder rules seemed fitting.

He gripped his with both hands, wielding it like a mallet.

She slid into a defensive position, sword in one hand, balancing her weight with the other.

"Whenever you're ready," she said smoothly.

He yelled and lunged forward, raising the sword over his head. It was definitely too heavy for him. In the moment where the blade hovered over her skull, Reyna darted closer, and her sword sliced against his shirt. She didn't nick the skin, but his clothes ripped cleanly.

He yelped in surprise, stumbling away from her, but Reyna had already resumed her original positioning.

The spar was over in seconds.

She waited to see how he'd react.

His sword dropped heavily to the tiles, and his fingers feathered over the torn fabric. "Gods damn it all," he muttered, clenching his eyes shut.

It pulled at her sympathies. Satisfied that he wasn't going to lunge for a cheap shot, Reyna sheathed her blade. "As I said, I won't distribute an assignment for someone unproven." She almost wanted to come clean, admit it was all a scam—but until she determined who "he" was, she couldn't be sure this boy wouldn't go running back to his informant and admit everything.

So, she played the lie. "However, I do believe you have potential. How much coin do you need?" Someone like this, determined as he was—he must owe someone something. No one with money turned to that kind of life.

"Four palidrons," he whispered.

She winced. "A hefty sum for someone your age."

"It was my father's debt. I don't have a choice." Now he gestured vaguely. "Bandit work seemed reliable. And fast. And . . . well, it'd be nice to not work alone."

Shit. If she let him go, he'd be killed. Reyna breathed a sigh. "What's your name?"

"Gossley."

Oh, the puns Kianthe would make about that. A little gosling. He even had spotty facial hair, a beard as fuzzy as down feathers. Reyna already felt exasperated, anticipating her partner's glee.

"Call me Cya." She paused, then made the decision: "And it so happens that we have an opening in our shop. Bussing tables, cleaning mugs, steeping tea. And more subtly, redirecting folk like yourself to their assignments." Reyna put a hand on her sword's hilt, running her finger over the clay that hid the queen's sigil. "We'll pay one sil a week."

Gossley's eyes widened. It was admittedly high for the work— but Reyna was not going to throw this boy to the wolves.

And Kianthe always said how much she hated dishes.

"The debt has to be paid by summertime, or he'll come after me." He lowered his gaze. "It'd be easier if you just give me an assignment. Let me finish this once and for all."

"I'm quite confident the debt collectors won't make it past our front door." Reyna smirked, a glimmer of her old life shining through. "The blacksmith in town has a hayloft where you can bunk; he might even teach you an honest trade if you pay attention. And in our slow times, I'm happy to teach you swordsmanship."

Gossley brightened. "Really?"

"Only if you're reliable working here. What's your decision?"

He hesitated. "It'll take me a long time to pay off four palidrons."

It would indeed, but Reyna was already planning to identify the boy's connection and eliminate him. She wouldn't tolerate anyone encouraging children into such a terrible profession. "I'm certain you'll find more benefit in honest labor, rather than risking everything for one lucrative job."

"That's what my mother said before she died." He heaved a frustrated sigh. "Fine. But when I'm able to beat you in a spar, you have to give me an assignment."

Well, that was like waiting for snow to run hot. Reyna smiled. "Deal."

She pulled Kianthe aside and set Gossley loose on the shop, telling him to wipe the tables while she informed her partner. The mage cheerily followed her into the bedroom, then appeared crestfallen when Reyna kept her clothes on.

Her expression soured further when Reyna explained the situation.

"So, you picked up a stray?" Kianthe peeked out of their bedroom to watch Gossley putter around the shop. He'd traded his sword for an apron, his violent intent for polite smiles.

Based on her tone, she thought this was suspicious as hells.

Reyna meticulously wiped an oil-soaked rag across her sword. It scented the air with cloves, so familiar she breathed in deep before replying, "He's in over his head. We can help."

"Are we helping *everyone* who comes into our home?"

Reyna snorted. "Dear, you once rescued a litter of kittens, then realized you didn't have the wherewithal to raise them and handed them off to me. I don't think you're able to dispute this."

Kianthe had saved a few animals over the years, but rarely wanted to follow through on the midnight feedings, the nurturing, the overall care of a living soul. She'd done it once for Visk, and according to her, once was enough.

The mage crossed her arms, pouting. "When I imagined running a bookstore with you, this wasn't what I had in mind."

"Well, I didn't expect I'd be picking your clothes off the washroom floor every morning. And here I thought the Arcandor would be more tidy." Reyna smirked as Kianthe's cheeks colored. "He'll stay in Tarly's shop. I'm sure Matild will approve it." A pause. "And he'll do the dishes. All of them."

It took Kianthe exactly half a second to process that.

"Sold."

And so Gossley stayed, ever-assuming that Reyna and Kianthe were brokers for a huge ring of bandits, and that he was apprenticing to become one himself. They never bothered to correct him.

18

Kianthe

Feo, the almighty diarn, was getting bold.

Kianthe squinted at the summons, delivered by the second-best baker's wife. (Not the baker's *second-best* wife, as that would cause far too much confusion.) The woman had accepted a mug of tea as payment for the delivery, and was perched at the outdoor table, admiring the flowers Kianthe had planted to liven up the barn's exterior. Their next-door neighbor, Sasua, had stepped outside to chat with her, and the two women were laughing.

Kianthe wasn't laughing. *Kianthe* was annoyed.

"Do you believe this?" she demanded, waving the sheet of parchment at Reyna.

Gossley was at the market buying flour, and Reyna stood behind the counter, tallying their coin for the week, comparing it to the costs they'd incurred in obtaining ingredients for her pastries and tea. Their book-lending program was a success, and they had a steady business selling the tomes that lined their massive shelves, but her tea was their biggest draw.

Thank the Stone itself that Reyna liked all that accounting nonsense. Kianthe had no patience for it.

Now, her girlfriend lifted hazel eyes from her work. Her tone was mild. "Believe what, darling?"

Kianthe lowered her voice. "This! Feo wants me to 'report at the site of a disturbance,' blah blah blah, 'must arrive posthaste.'" The mage scoffed, tossing the page to the polished wood. "Posthaste, my ass. Like I'm a lackey awaiting their orders."

Reyna tugged the letter toward her, reading it swiftly. "This sounds important."

"Everything's important when the Arcandor is involved." Her voice was nearly inaudible now, so their patrons didn't overhear. Or accuse her of treason, for ignoring a diarn's direct summons.

Imagine the outrage: a fake diarn, not getting the respect they deserved.

Reyna's lips had drawn upward, watching her.

Kianthe paused. "What?"

"You're ranting. In your mind. Your face twists a bit." Reyna mimicked it, lifting her lips in pretend disgust, brow furrowing, before letting the expression shift into amusement. "You know what I think?"

Kianthe was still sore that she had a *ranting face*, apparently. She sniffed. "I'm not sure I want to know, after that."

"Oh, don't. It's cute." Reyna kissed her, just a brief peck of fondness, which lightened Kianthe's mood considerably. "You're powerful, respected . . . and I think you're accustomed to it now. Being treated like a normal citizen, ordered around by someone with less status . . . it annoys you."

"It does not—" Kianthe spluttered.

Reyna smiled, her eyes flickering to their customers. No one was paying them any mind. She drummed her fingers on the counter. "In Tawney, you're just a mage who opened a bookshop. Do you want to continue that, or would you rather the town know your true identity?"

Kianthe shuddered. "Word would get back to the Magicary. They were already furious when I left after the unicorn debacle.

I'd never have a moment's peace." A pause. "Not to mention, the anonymity is nice."

"Exactly. So, since you delight in proving me wrong—"

"I don't—" Kianthe started to say, but cut herself off when Reyna's shaking shoulders proved she'd played right into that.

Reyna finished, amused: "—you'll report for your diarn's summons. And I'll have dinner waiting when you return."

The mage muttered under her breath, snatched the paper, and stomped out of their shop.

Feo wanted her to meet on the opposite side of town, of course. Kianthe thought about walking—but Visk had settled into a nomadic life in the forest southwest of Tawney, and it'd do good to remind the creature of his training. She stepped away from the shop so she wouldn't startle the customers, and once she'd cleared a safe distance, she pinched her thumb and pinkie fingers together in her mouth. Her whistle was sharp and short, piercing the cool air.

It took Visk longer than expected to arrive. He fluffed his feathers, nuzzled her chest, but looked mildly annoyed at the interruption—as annoyed as a griffon could look, anyway.

Kianthe patted his beak. "Sorry, kiddo. Some of us work for a living."

Considering that Visk required no help in finding meals or surviving in the wild, his side-eye made her laugh.

She mounted, urging him into the air. They circled Tawney a few times, Kianthe appreciating the feeling of freedom and breathless anticipation as they soared over the winds.

Stars and Stone, she'd missed this.

Finally, she found the location Feo had indicated. It was a charred building in a sea of charred buildings: the dragon-crisped portion of town. No one lived there anymore—apparently it served as a sort of false town, somewhere to direct the dragons in order to mitigate damage to the actual households.

The diarn was standing in the center of a dusty road, squinting into the sunshine. With summer nearly upon them, the days were getting long and bright, and the temperatures had finally warmed from scathingly cold to merely chilly. Feo had dressed down from a heavy cloak to a wrap that covered their shoulders, pinned with a stately clasp.

They looked like a real leader, which was impressive. Kianthe hadn't realized they were such a con artist when they'd been puttering around the Magicary.

She delighted in how they startled when Visk thumped to the ground. Kianthe didn't dismount; she merely leaned over Visk's bulk as the griffon folded his wings. "Well? I've been summoned. And we *will* be having words about that, believe you me."

"It was necessary," Feo retorted.

"Debatable."

With a huff, Feo set off down the street, beckoning for Kianthe to follow. Visk chittered in displeasure, and Kianthe finally slid off his back with a gruff, "Fine, *fine*. Dismissed." After all, griffons weren't made for walking; from the moment they hatched, they existed in the skies. With a pleased chirp, the beast took off again, angling toward the forest.

Kianthe watched him go, silently wondering what kept his attention in those trees. Maybe he'd found a wild griffon mate; they were in the right physical locale for one. *Aww, that'd be so cute. Tiny baby griffons flying around—*

Feo snapped their fingers. "*Arcandor*. Focus. I brought you here to feel for magic."

There was magic in every living thing, and several unliving ones—and as an ex-Magicary apprentice, Feo should know that. Kianthe arched her eyebrows. "You're going to have to be more specific."

They pinched their nose, stopping their swift pace abruptly. "Isn't it odd that the dragon attacks are always concentrated here? They keep building farther south and west, and the newer additions are in far better shape. Why wouldn't the dragons raze the entire village? They're capable enough."

Kianthe had considered all that, but she was too busy enjoying her new life to focus on it. Not that she'd admit that to Feo. "I assume it's because the buildings are newer. Less time to be targeted during the raids."

"I suspect otherwise." Feo flicked two fingers, motioning for Kianthe to follow them into a dilapidated . . . church? Eating hall? It was unclear what it used to be, but Kianthe could now say it had become a death trap.

She paused at the threshold, putting a hand on the wood. It ached, decades charred, its feeble magic pulsing in remnant pain. And there was something else thrumming beneath it—something in the soil itself. Kianthe's eyes drifted to the floor, which was barely more than gruesome metal nails and black ash now.

"Arcandor," Feo called impatiently. "Come along."

Their tone irked her. It was honestly astounding how well they took to a diarn's conceited mindset.

She didn't move. "See, the thing is, my girlfriend will be very angry if I die in a building collapse." Feo stopped, utter disbelief on their features, which only spurred Kianthe on: "She has a tendency toward dramatics. If I were killed by a falling roof, she'd dissolve into hysterics. Lurking in the shadows, polishing her knives in the dark, seeking revenge in all the wrong places. It'd be a nightmare for you."

If Reyna were here, she'd be rolling her eyes . . . but a magic-hating cult had once used fire arrows and cannons to shoot Visk out of the sky, stranding an injured Kianthe in enemy territory. Once she realized what happened, Reyna rallied the queen's military to storm the gates. The entire experience took less than two days.

It was flattering.

It was also terrifying.

Kianthe grinned, getting into this now. "You'd better tell me what we're doing here, so I can gauge if this—" She gestured at the crumbling doorway, which creaked in the gentle wind. "—is worth the risk."

"This is already a nightmare," Feo muttered.

Kianthe offered a winning smile. "There. Now you see. I'll just be on my way—"

"Don't you feel the magic?" Feo said sharply. When she turned back to them, they stomped a foot on the ground. "Below. Seeping into the clay like a poison. It's not a ley line, Kianthe; there's something bigger below this building."

Well, she did love a good mystery. Threats forgotten—because realistically, if the building collapsed, she could just order the wood to stay upright for a few seconds and get them both out—Kianthe ducked into the building.

It had indeed been a church. Beyond the foyer stretched a long room lined with remnants of painted glass and pews. At the front, a mural of stars indicated this was a monument to the cosmos overhead—the traditional deity of Sheparan locals. It was commonplace for the Stars and the Stone of Seeing to be lumped together, but only mages worshiped the Stone's power. Normal citizens preferred something more easily identifiable.

Feo ignored the mural, arching their head toward the decaying ceiling. It had collapsed in five areas, letting the bright morning sunshine paint the floor with mottled spots. Whatever they were looking for, they seemed satisfied; probably checking that the rafters wouldn't fall at the next strong breeze.

"So, there's magic here. You think it has to do with a stolen dragon's egg?" Kianthe didn't have all day, after all.

They crossed their arms. "I think it's here because of the dragon egg, yes. And I think the dragons can sense it, and that's why they keep invading. And why it's possible for the townsfolk to redirect them here during an attack."

Kianthe's brow pinched. "How are you able to sense it?"

Tawney's ley line was weak, but even it pulsed like a bonfire compared to the candle's flame of this hidden magic. She found it in the soil because the earth *told* her it was there—but only the Arcandor had the ability to communicate with elements like that.

"I used a transfixation spell. Narrowed it down to this building, but that's all I could produce." A frustrated huff. "The road ended here for my solo journey. Even researching the history of this church offered nothing of note."

"Transfixation?" Kianthe wrinkled her nose. Any spells not based in nature were based off alchemy: twisting magic into unnatural means with animal sacrifices and dark texts. It was practiced within the Magicary walls, but rarely touted in the world at large; most people would be horrified if they knew the finer details of it.

"Alchemic magic is far easier to control, and it's a decent option for those of us not skilled in the elements." Feo brushed it off, wholly unconcerned. When Kianthe didn't respond, they huffed. "If it comes down to alchemical magic, or merely researching theory . . . is it so surprising I'd choose the former?"

"It's a bloody kind of magic."

"A chicken here and there to solve the mysteries of Tawney? Come on, Kianthe." The fake diarn gestured at the ground. "What do you think? Is the egg still here, or—or is there something else happening?"

At the end of that sentence, their voice tilted into uncertainty, lost its arrogant swagger. It made Kianthe feel like she could help, and like they'd truly appreciate it—even if Feo would never admit that out loud.

Heaving a sigh, she knelt to the ground. The old wooden floors dissolved under her fingertips, exposing ashen dirt. And below that . . . the odd magic thrummed.

Her magic, the elemental kind, was bright and yellow. If she closed her eyes, she could visualize it racing around her body, twirling like a hummingbird dancing near a flower, touching everything around them. But now, it wasn't yellow that engulfed her.

It was blue, deep and dissimilar. Less sunshine, more ice.

An echo. Hmm. Dragons did control their own, unique magic. The Stone of Seeing occasionally prodded dragon country, and it was theorized that the Stone's curiosity had awakened them three hundred years ago. Dragon magic was partly elemental, partly alchemical, and entirely mysterious. They weren't like griffons, unicorns, or any other mythical beast: they *shouldn't* be able to fly, not with their bulky muscles and solid bones. They shouldn't be able to summon flame in the back of their throats. They shouldn't live longer than any other creature in the Realm.

And yet.

Feo was suddenly very close. "You figured something out, didn't you?"

"I figured out that I like personal space."

They rolled their eyes, the motion so exaggerated it tilted their head. "Arcandor, please. Focus." They knelt beside her, tapped the earth. "Something's down there. If it isn't the egg, it's a residual imprint left from it."

"You're not wrong," she admitted.

Feo seemed one second short of pumping the air with accomplishment. Instead, they cleared their throat, turning their gaze to the rest of the church. "Is there a crypt belowground? A secret area of worship, maybe?"

Kianthe rolled her eyes. "How should I know? I'm up here, with you."

"Can't you pull the earth open? Get us down there?"

"Sure I can. Doesn't mean I *will*." The pulse was so far below that it'd take immense magic to carve a path to it—and that wasn't magic Tawney's ley line held. The magic drain of attempting something like that would be more dangerous than rewarding.

Kianthe filed this information away, but today wasn't the day to address it. She pushed to her feet, dusting her pants off.

Feo scowled. "Do you enjoy being this combative?"

"Do you enjoy ordering people around?" Kianthe's tone was

sharp. "I respond a lot better when I'm approached as a friend, not a tool in your arsenal. And my magic isn't going to make you someone important in this town." She stepped into their space, her dark eyes glinting now. "If you truly want to help Tawney, why don't you interact with the people here instead of obsessing over some ancient magic?"

"This town will never be safe until the dragons abandon it." Feo scowled.

Kianthe barked a laugh. "Why are the dragons your primary focus? There are a lot of things a town needs to run smoothly. You should be more concerned about the fact that a midwife is our only medical professional. Or that the road into town is so degraded it's deterring valuable tradesfolk."

Feo stiffened, but their eyes cut to the side, unable to hold her gaze.

Kianthe wasn't finished.

"You know what else I learned talking to the locals? Food is always a question here. Tawneans survive on a seafood-based diet thanks to the glacier lakes, but with dragon country so close, fishing is a dangerous job. If you focused on constructing a few greenhouses, you might be able to grow emergency supplies."

Now Feo hesitated. "Lord Wylan should have—"

"You're truly going to let a Queendom lord outperform you? Wylan is planning a trip south, to incentivize merchants to make the trip here." After all, Wylan had stopped Reyna earlier to ask about "Cya's hometown," and the trade routes they could establish with the south Queendom, and Leonol farther beyond. They'd discussed options for half the afternoon.

Feo had the decency to look abashed. They rubbed the back of their neck, casting a doubtful glance at the ground. "I suppose . . . it's possible I've been swept away by a good mystery."

Kianthe sighed, clapping their shoulder. "It's an admirable mystery to solve. But in the meantime, there are people who believe you're a council representative, here to improve their lives.

You want to be a diarn? Start acting like it. The dragons are my problem now, anyway."

Much as Kianthe hated to admit it, when the alternative was a hot cup of tea and a good book. But any magical creature over-stepping human boundaries required mediation—and it was the Arcandor's job to intervene.

The next time dragons attacked, she would have to fight.

Ugh. Her stomach twisted in anxiety. Kianthe *really* didn't want to think about this. One day, she might return to this church and locate the magic below. Today, though, Reyna was preparing a yeast roll filled with cinnamon sugar and crushed walnuts, and Kianthe planned to taste-test.

"You have a real chance here, Feo. I hope you make something of it."

And with a resolute wave, the Arcandor strolled out of the rickety church, leaving the self-appointed diarn and weakly puls-ing dragon magic behind.

19

Reyna

Kianthe took a while to return, which would have been alarming if Reyna weren't so busy preparing her new treat. It was a Queendom favorite—sweet enough to be enticing, but the walnuts tempered the sugar. She'd spent the better part of her twelfth year perfecting the royal chef's recipe, and now it filled the bookstore with a homey scent.

She set a few aside for Kianthe before selling the rest—which turned out to be a smart move, since the pastries were immensely popular even with Sheparans. Soon she had multiple reorders of tea to accompany the treat, and spent her time flitting around the shop, refilling hot water as people perused novels along the shelves or basked in the fireplace's glow.

Kianthe reappeared later that afternoon, rubbing her brow. "Remind me never to get into government," she told Reyna. The mage collected her favorite mug—glazed deep purple with flecks of white, like the stars overhead—and abandoned Reyna and their customers to sulk with her tea on the back patio.

Reyna stifled a laugh, finished up their final patrons' orders. Then she turned to Gossley. "Can you handle the shop alone?"

The boy scoffed, pulling his shoulders back. He'd spent his morning opening the smithy with Tarly, and his confidence was growing into something smugly superior. His tone was extravagant. "As easily as I can demonstrate the drill you taught me last week."

That didn't inspire confidence, but Reyna doubted he'd burn the place down while she chatted with Kianthe. She untied her apron, retrieved the sweet rolls she'd set aside, and followed her girlfriend into the sunshine. It was mid-afternoon now, and their north-facing patio was cut with shade from the pines and the barn's angled roof.

Kianthe had dropped to her wrought-iron chair, propped her feet on their metal table, and was sipping her tisane.

"I take it Diarn Feo didn't inspire confidence." Reyna squeezed Kianthe's shoulder, presented the rolls, and sat on the chair beside her. "Wait, let me guess. They asked for a favor."

The mage plucked one of the treats off the plate, squinting at it. "I thought these had walnuts?"

"I'm testing it with strawberry jam filling instead. You'll like it."

Reyna admired how easily her partner took a blind bite of the food, on just her word alone. It made her chest warm, especially when Kianthe moaned in delight. "This is divine."

"High praise. The diarn?"

Kianthe grumbled around her food. "They wouldn't call me for anything but a magical favor. Hey, how would a diarn claim ownership of a town, anyway? Is there some legal end to their dispute with Wylan, or will this go on until they form a truce?"

Reyna shrugged, settling into her chair. It was hot in the barn, with the fire roaring and the oven heating the walls of their storage room and the copper kettle steaming with water, but outside the air was crisp. She almost wished she'd brought a mug of tea too.

"Well, Her Excellency will never admit Shepara has ownership, and I doubt the council would hand Queen Tilaine the town without a fight. So, my guess? Either one of them dies and isn't replaced, or yes, they form a truce."

"Hmm. We should probably nudge them in the direction of a truce, then."

A redspar chirped overhead, flitting between the branches of the trees. Reyna chuckled. "I thought you weren't interested in government." A pause, a smirk. "Which is ironic, since your position means you're basically a ruling entity yourself."

Reyna didn't mean to add the self-deprecating air, but it came up anyway. She ducked her head, hoping Kianthe didn't notice. They'd put that "earn or receive" conversation to rest, but kicking the belief was proving harder than Reyna anticipated.

Kianthe squinted at her, voice cautious. "I don't command anyone, or make choices that affect an entire town."

Reyna offered a wry look.

The mage groaned. "Well, I don't do it *intentionally.*"

"That might be worse, darling." Before Kianthe could latch on to that, Reyna changed the subject: "What did Diarn Feo request?" Whatever it was, Kianthe looked weary after their meeting. Curiosity prickled Reyna's arms, and she shifted to face her partner better.

The Arcandor sighed, taking another large bite of the sweet roll. Her words were muffled. "They're hunting for the rumored dragon egg. They found an old church on the burnt side of town, and they're right—something is belowground. Probably an old crypt or underground tunnel system." She swallowed, took a swig of tea. "Might be a dragon's egg. Might be something else."

"You're not curious?" Excitement spiked up Reyna's spine. If there was one thing she loved more than baking and tea, it was a solid mystery. There was something exhilarating about investigating dark alleys, meeting shady folk, and ultimately uncovering the truth.

In her old job, she'd been excellent at identifying royal assassins before they had a chance to do something stupid. Very few plots escaped her notice when she'd served Queen Tilaine.

Kianthe opened her mouth—but that's when the back door flew open.

Gossley said frantically, "Ah, um, s-sorry to bother, but the *lord* is here." He whispered the word, eyes wide with panic. "The queen's chosen. He's asking for you, Cya."

Kianthe grinned, her sardonic look almost unbearable. "Your turn."

Reyna shoved her shoulder. "I'll be back."

"Are there more rolls?"

"No; then you won't be hungry for dinner. Keep our customers' mugs filled, please." Reyna kissed her swiftly, then followed Gossley inside.

Lord Wylan was indeed standing in the center of their barn. Like last time, a few patrons were moving to stand, but he graciously waved them off. "Enjoy your drink."

A few of the Sheparan citizens rolled their eyes. The Queendom ones seemed relieved.

Considering he was the weapon of Queen Tilaine here, Reyna couldn't blame any of them. And yet, she almost felt bad for him—he clearly wanted to know these people, but didn't have a clue how to start.

"Did you need something, my lord?"

Lord Wylan dipped his head. "Deepest apologies, Cya. I was hoping to have a private chat."

"The bedroom is private. Or the storage room, if you'd prefer?"

If Kianthe had been here, she'd make a joke about this man stealing her girlfriend. It'd be raucous and borderline obscene, and she'd do it just to see who blushed first: Reyna, or the esteemed lord.

Reyna was partly grateful the mage hadn't trailed behind her, and partly disappointed about it.

"Ah, not private enough." Lord Wylan's gaze was stern, and he lowered his voice. "Report to my estate as soon as you can. Make sure you aren't followed."

His estate. *Followed.* Reyna's lighthearted mood vanished in a breath, replaced by dangerous thoughts. The only people who would tail Reyna were Queen Tilaine's spies. And she already knew they'd been poking around several weeks ago.

Lord Wylan glanced over his shoulder, tipped his tri-point hat, and walked out. Reyna didn't miss how he doubled back on his path, disappearing before she could blink.

Of course. He'd been evading the queen's spies for years, considering his father's reputation. It was probably why he'd come himself, instead of sending Ralund or someone else.

Gossley bounded over. "What was that? Are we blown?" The kid looked ready to bolt.

For a moment, she forgot her ruse with the bandits. It took precious seconds to realign herself. "Oh, we've been expecting this." She forced a bright smile. "There's a reason our superiors positioned me here; I have a way with the queen's people. Now, back to work, please. There are tables to clean."

Gossley frowned, but dutifully picked up a rag.

Reyna, meanwhile, retrieved her sword from the bedroom, then stepped back outside. Kianthe's small plate had been cleaned, either by finger or tongue, with only crumbs to imply she'd eaten at all. Her mug steamed under her nose, and she was scowling at one of the pine trees—which seemed to be wilting under her ire.

"Key."

The mage startled, and the pine's needles perked up again. Kianthe glanced her way. "Anything important?"

"A private meeting with Lord Wylan, as soon as possible. At his estate."

"Tell him you're taken." She paused, offered a sly grin. "Wait. Tell him you'll do it for sixteen palidrons."

Reyna raised an eyebrow.

Kianthe slapped her leg, wholly amused. "What? You're the one who said you should *earn* everything. Was it a lie?" The mage dissolved into laughter, shoulders shaking.

"Are you finished, dear?"

"For now."

Reyna sighed, massaging her forehead. She glanced around the patio, but they were solidly alone, wedged between two buildings and the empty lot. Nevertheless, she lowered her voice to a bare whisper. "I suspect the queen has asked for his help in locating me."

That got Kianthe straightening. Her dark eyes flashed. "Then I'm coming with you."

"Entirely unnecessary."

"*Unnecessary?*" Kianthe repeated, indignant. "You're going to face a Queendom lord alone, with your history?" She kept her voice low, quiet enough that Reyna had to strain to hear, but her sudden fury was flattering.

Reyna tied the sword's sheath to her belt. "Dearest, I love you, but I am capable of handling Lord Wylan."

"And if the queen's spies ambush you?"

"Then I'll summon you with the moonstone, straight away."

That seemed to placate the mage. She grumbled, sinking back into her chair. "First the dragons, now this. Can we go back to yesterday, when my biggest question was which tea to wake you up with, and trying to remember to pick my clothes up off the washroom floor?"

Reyna kissed her softly. "I love you, and I'll be back shortly."

"I'll raze the town if you aren't."

Reyna couldn't tell if she was serious or not. She laughed and left the bookstore.

The path to Lord Wylan's estate was a straightforward one, nestled against the rocky rim on the far side of town. It was getting darker by the second, but Reyna took her time, using techniques she'd perfected as Queen Tilaine's guard. After all, Her Excellency had secret passageways all over her palace, and patience was power in avoiding those who prowled within them.

When Reyna rapped on the estate's back door, she didn't bother hiding her sword or her determined expression. And when Lord Wylan's butler finally arrived, she barely waited for his acknowledgment before striding past him.

"The lord is expecting me," she said.

Ralund's watery eyes dropped to the sword, but he stammered, "Ah, yes. Of course. This way." He led her through winding hallways and empty parlors.

They reached a massive study, one that easily could have housed half the scholars in Queen Tilaine's palace. A huge chandelier stocked with melted candles blazed overhead, and the upper level was decorated with ancient artifacts: leather battle armor, chipped swords, clay pots, golden statues.

The lower level was brimming with books, and Reyna normally would have asked to borrow some for their lending center. She *normally* would have requested permission to unleash Kianthe here, because books were her inclination, but *this many books* would be her absolute, unbridled pleasure.

Reyna didn't do either of those things. She stepped to the center of the room, faced Lord Wylan as he perched at a huge desk, and asked, "Can you explain what's happened, my lord?"

Is anyone dying tonight?

He looked surprised at her expression, and his gaze dropped to her sword. A slight smile lifted his lips. "Come for battle?"

"I'm not one to be caught unprepared."

"Do you think I'll attack you?"

Reyna considered. "That depends on what's happened."

Lord Wylan pushed to his feet, walked around his desk. He leaned against it, the motion casual, but his eyes were sharp and calculating. "I was approached today. By a man from the queen's palace, bearing her official seal."

Approached. Which meant he hadn't merely noticed unsavory folk lingering on the outskirts of his town. Reyna filed that away. "I see." It was surprising that Sigmund and Nurt hadn't warned her about this, but perhaps they'd been busy elsewhere.

Lord Wylan continued: "He inquired about a rogue Queensguard named Reyna. Apparently, she's accused of high treason for abandoning a royal post. He read me Her Excellency's decree—it's scathing. Nothing good awaits this woman in the Capital."

Reyna kept her expression relaxed, mildly intrigued. But inside, her heart pounded, and nausea settled like sour milk in her gut. Gods, she thought she'd have more time . . . but every dream ended.

Her tone feigned confusion. "That sounds concerning. I'm unsure how I can help, however."

"Drop the act." Lord Wylan shook his head. "I may be a minor lord from an inconsequential town, but I'm not blind to the politics of the Queendom. You fled. And now, you've set a precedent that anyone under her employ can flee. That is a dangerous notion for Queen Tilaine."

Reyna considered him, keeping her mouth shut. It was possible he was baiting her into admitting something he hadn't confirmed— but based on his knowing expression, she doubted it. He'd clearly accepted the information, checked the math, and drawn his conclusions. Those conclusions were correct, and he knew it.

The question now was . . . how much had he told the queen's representative?

Her hand drifted to her sword. Her thumb absently rubbed the stiff clay that hid the queen's insignia from view—but that only reminded her of Kianthe, and their bookshop, and everything she could stand to lose here.

It was so much more than just her life, now.

With that in mind, it only took her a moment to make her choice. She dropped to her knees, bowing her head to the floor. "If you know the truth, my lord, then you've already determined my fate. While I pray for courtesy, it's necessary to warn you that anything less will not occur without a fight."

Lord Wylan started to laugh. It was a bold sound that echoed off the books, the tall ceiling, the heavy windows, although Reyna's muscles remained tense.

But the man just scrubbed his face with a hand. "By the Gods,

Reyna, I'm not an executioner. Maybe it's the Sheparan influence here, but I believe everyone deserves a second chance."

Hope soared in her chest, dark and unbidden. "Then you kept my secret?"

He sighed, turning his face to the ceiling.

"Once upon a time, my father visited the Capital on his hands and knees, pleading for help fighting the dragon attacks. Queen Eren saw it as a sign of weakness."

Reyna recalled hearing of this visit. She'd been a child at the time.

In an unbidden display of empathy, Lord Wylan offered a hand, helping her stand so they were on even footing. His gaze was hard, bitter, as he reminisced. "The queen let her daughter choose his punishment. Princess Tilaine ordered him to the dungeon for a month. He returned to Tawney defeated, skin and bones, his pride stripped . . . even if his land remained."

That was what Reyna remembered. Her mother watched the entire affair from behind Queen Eren's throne, tsking at the lord who failed to manage his assets. She'd murmured to Reyna, late that night: *"Never beg the queen for help, my darling. You exist to serve Her Excellency, not steal her time and solutions."*

When Reyna did think of Lord Julan, Wylan's father, she thought of feebleness, poor management, and a weak constitution. The lord who begged. If Queen Eren, Gods rest her soul, had made the decision instead of her young daughter, Wylan wouldn't even have an estate to protect.

The whole family would have been killed.

Reyna was rethinking everything, facing his son. Time with Kianthe had taught her that asking for help wasn't weakness, and now she was embarrassed the ideation ever entered her mind.

"I'm very sorry, Lord Wylan. Your father didn't deserve that."

"No, he didn't." Lord Wylan pinched his brow, redirecting back to the topic at hand. "I told the queen's man I haven't heard of anyone with that name in Tawney. It will reflect poorly when that report reaches the Capital; Her Excellency expects her lords to know their lands inside and out. I'll take the punishment, if I must." His lips quirked upward briefly. "I'm not above admitting it: nothing pleases me more than harboring a traitor of the queen's court."

Now it was Reyna's turn to laugh, bubbly as sparkling wine. "If we're speaking honestly, nothing pleased me more than *leaving* her court."

Lord Wylan snorted, and a bridge formed between them.

His next words were sobering. "Her man seemed reluctant to leave. His name is Venne. Does that mean anything to you?"

Reyna's lips set into a firm line. Venne, her partner in the guard. The man who'd been wholly convinced they'd be together someday. He'd viewed every smile, every touch, every spar as flirtation, and as they aged, ignored that she'd developed other preferences.

If Venne was hunting her, it would be because he'd asked permission. Requested to the queen personally that *he* be assigned this search.

A fake name wouldn't distract him for long.

Lord Wylan read her expression and frowned. "I wanted you to know. Be cautious, Reyna. You've become a staple of Tawney, and I would hate to lose you, your partner, or your bookshop."

It was a dismissal, but the kindest one she'd ever received. And he hadn't asked for anything in exchange. Reyna regretted assuming tonight would become hostile, when faced with this generosity.

She bowed respectfully and didn't hide the gratitude in her voice. "Thank you, my lord. If you ever need anything . . . well. I'm quite adept in many avenues."

He chuckled. "I'll remember that the next time dragons attack."

Reyna left, mulling over his warning. With Venne involved, she took three times as long returning to the bookshop, and now that night had fallen, every shadow seemed like an unwanted caress.

Kianthe would need to know about this.

20

Kianthe

The evening dragged without Reyna. Kianthe tabled the thought of dragons, and stopping dragon raids, and investigating a missing dragon egg—or whatever was below that church—but quickly realized that *deciding* to table it and *actually* tabling it were two different things. Couple it with the fact that Queen Tilaine may have found Reyna, and now her girlfriend was out there alone, at the mercy of that ridiculous lord, possibly already at swordpoint—

Kianthe growled and plucked a random tome from the shelves, dropping into one of the armchairs beside the fire. With the setting sun came the evening cold, and the barn creaked under the wind. She tugged a heavy knitted throw over her shoulders, glaring at the book in her hands.

Tabled. Dismissed. Moved on from. Reyna was fine and capable and the dragons might not even be a problem with her here; Kianthe didn't want to think about all this responsibility, damn it.

The customers had sensed her discontent earlier and quietly vacated. Gossley ducked out shortly after, barely offering a goodbye on his way to Tarly's smithy. In the echoing emptiness, Kianthe almost wished one of Tilaine's spies would arrive and challenge her.

It didn't happen, of course, and as the night wore on, her chest tightened dangerously and her hands started to shake. Where was Reyna? This was taking too long, wasn't it? She should—

Kianthe forced herself back into the chair. No, she shouldn't. Reyna would poke her with the moonstones if she needed help.

Unless Wylan had taken the moonstone.

No. Reyna wouldn't let that happen.

Fuck, she was regressing again. Knowing it didn't stop her thoughts from spiraling until she was on the edge of her seat, novel forgotten on her lap. Sitting here wasn't helping. Kianthe was about to go hunting when the barn doors slid open, and Reyna stepped inside.

Thank the Stone of Seeing itself. It didn't help much with Kianthe's tight chest and shaking hands, but relief was still preferable to intrusive thoughts.

They'd hung heavy curtains over the front windows for evening privacy, and her girlfriend wasted no time drawing them. "Apologies for the wait, love."

"How was Wylan?" Kianthe wasn't in the mood for jokes or teasing. Instead, she pushed off her chair, feeling unsorted.

Reyna sagged a bit, exhaustion rimming her eyes. "Fine. He received a visitor today: Venne."

That did not help Kianthe's disposition. Venne was a nice guy on the surface, pleasant and reliable, but he pined for Reyna in an almost possessive way. There were many times in the Grand Palace where Kianthe ached to intervene at his pointed touches, the way his eyes roamed Reyna as she entered a room. Kianthe couldn't manage it without revealing their relationship.

"Let it go, man," she muttered. "Stars and Stone, can't he survive without you orbiting his ego?"

Reyna pulled her into a tight hug. Her fingers were icy cold, and she raised them toward the fire when they separated. "You know the answer to that. According to Wylan, he's unsure if I'm still in Tawney, but it won't be long before he finds this shop."

Her inflection changed to apprehension, and for the first time, her voice wavered. "I'm . . . not sure where this leaves us, Kianthe. What do you want to do?"

If the queen's dogs were sniffing around their shop, it might be time to pull in a favor from the Arcandor herself: strike a truce in exchange for Reyna's freedom. Kianthe pondered how, exactly, to pull that off—especially without starting a war over the outrage of handing a vicious queen control of her magic—and then realized Reyna was staring at her.

Not just staring. Waiting. A terror hid behind her eyes, like Kianthe could crush her dreams with a word.

The mage was beginning to think she'd missed something.

"Um. I need you to speak like I'm five, because I'm not sure what you're asking here."

Reyna released a trembling breath. "Queen Tilaine is dangerous, Key."

"So am I, Rain."

"Exactly. You're the Arcandor—countries will crumble if you make an enemy out of her. When Venne finds me, I'll have to flee. The queen's spies will never take the target off my back." Reyna gestured around the shop, a little breathless now. "Or . . . I can leave before that happens. Alone. And you can enjoy what we've built."

Kianthe stared at her, a spike of panic twisting in her gut. She opened her mouth to refute—or maybe to kiss Reyna senseless—or *something*—but at that exact moment, something thudded outside the barn. Both women stiffened, but hard claws scratched the wood, and a birdlike shriek filled the air.

Visk. And the griffon wouldn't bother them for just anything.

They exchanged a glance, then sprinted for the shopfront. Kianthe used magic to pull the barn doors open, and immediately, a wall of flame welcomed them. Visk was pressed against the wood, wings folded tight, his eyes glinting with panic in the rippling waves of heat.

Tawney was on fire.

"Shit, stay back," Kianthe snapped, yanking the griffon through the wide doorway. She pushed outside, feeling the eager anticipation of the flames as they licked the barn. "Not today, not *ever*. Douse yourself or I'll do it for you!"

The flames responded to her magic, heaving smoke-spluttering sighs as they slunk toward the earth. She pulled a wave of dirt over the smoldering ashes, cutting the flames out entirely.

The sad little ley line pulsed as she tapped its energy, but they weren't done yet. Visk wiggled back outside, shaking off ashen feathers, and screeched another warning. Overhead, a deep-throated bellow responded, and dark shapes cut across the stars.

"Dragons," Reyna said, reaching for the sword strapped at her hip.

Kianthe nearly had a heart attack. She grabbed her girlfriend's arm. "Reyna, I love you more than Visk, the moon, the stars, and all the flowers in Shepara. But if you try and attack a dragon with that toothpick of a blade, I *will* tie you to a chair and leave you to contemplate your actions."

The mage kissed her then, deeply, passionately.

Reyna's exclamation of surprise shifted into a sigh of delight. She clung to Kianthe, and their bodies felt warm and solid against each other. Her nose buried in Kianthe's shoulder. "So, I guess we're in it together."

"Tonight and always, for as long as you'll have me, queens and dragons be damned." Kianthe smoothed the hair off Reyna's forehead, traced her cheek, and pulled away. "Now, I have to negotiate peace. Please don't be upset with me later; there's a very real chance I won't be conscious enough to protest it."

"What? Key—"

But Kianthe was already leaping onto Visk's back, taking to the skies in a flurry of feathers.

The town was burning, flames crisscrossing buildings and streets as the dragons—at least six of them, maybe closer to eight—took turns diving at different areas. They'd created a blazing perimeter around most of the town, trapping the citizens inside.

Her neighbors, her *friends*, were shouting, fleeing their homes, carrying babies and towing toddlers and pets as they searched for somewhere safe. So far, they had enough sense to avoid the diving creatures, but it was only a matter of time before someone got seriously hurt.

Thundering hooves: Reyna had retrieved Lilac from the stable, and now was shouting commands to the townsfolk. Tarly bellowed alongside her, evacuating people to New Leaf, the safest spot simply because a mage lived there.

Kianthe would ensure that held true.

Magic swelled inside her, bright and yellow and blinding as the sun itself. The ley line didn't have much, but if she was smart about this, she could stop the attack.

She didn't let herself think of the consequences if she couldn't.

"Dragons! Over here! You're dealing with me now, not them. We need to talk!"

It gained all the wrong kind of attention.

Unlike Lilac—whose training seemed to be faltering under the chaos, causing her to skitter as she faced the flames—Visk was meant for battle. All griffons were; that's why mages bonded with them as mounts. So, when a dragon noticed them, unleashed a torrent of flame in their direction, Visk didn't flinch.

Kianthe didn't either. Her magic met the dragon's head-on, redirecting the flame toward the clouds overhead. "All right. Not negotiating. Time to make them listen." Smoke billowed around her, but Kianthe cut through it with a muttered spell, preserving their air quality as they dove into the darkness.

The dragon was too big to hide in the smoke, scales gleaming silver in the moonlight—and it wasn't prepared for Visk slamming onto its back.

With the added proximity, Kianthe shouted again. "You have

to listen to me. This town is not at fault—this has to be a misunderstanding!"

The dragon snarled, twisting midair to claw at Visk. To protect her mount, Kianthe pulled the air from the creature's lungs in one magic-intensive move. The dragon wheezed, faltered, and crashed into the barren tundra.

It gained the horde's attention.

Sweat dripped off her face as Visk soared in a wide circle, screeching a warning at two more dragons that swerved toward them. One broke off to check its wounded horde-mate.

The other came at Visk, claws brandished, teeth flashing.

But Visk was part eagle, and they weren't slow in the skies. He chirped, and Kianthe barely had time to grab his feathers before he dove sharply, aiming at the rim outside of town. Wind sliced her face, but she didn't waste magic protecting herself. Heat billowed at her back, dragon fire coming hard toward them.

She wrenched a hand behind her, catching the flame, dissipating it.

At the same time, Visk spread his wings and banked hard.

The dragon chasing behind them veered up at the last second to avoid a nasty crash, but its wing clipped the rim. With a howl, it slammed into the edge of dragon country, the *thud* echoing across the summer-warmed tundra. Trees shook in the pine forest to the south, and Visk barely had time to escape the cloud of dust that washed toward them like a tidal wave.

"They need to *listen* to me," she called, coughing. "If this goes on, one of them will die."

And if one of the dragons was killed, all negotiation would cease. Dragons weren't like griffons, more animalistic than not. They were intelligent, conniving, and fiercely protective. A death would mean war—a war even the Arcandor would be powerless to stop.

Visk chittered, angling back toward the dragon that crashed

above the rim. It was wheezing for breath, its wing held at an awkward angle, but it was alive. A small blessing, tonight.

Visk had stamina for literal days, but Kianthe was fading fast. This ley line was too weak for this kind of magic, and without fellow mages to draw from, her reserves were dipping dangerously.

Time was running out.

Kianthe fought a wave of dizziness, pinching her arm as they angled back toward Tawney. Most of the townsfolk had fled to their barn, and Reyna was still riding Lilac, commanding the evacuation. Kianthe's heart leapt in her chest when another dragon turned toward them, opening its massive jaw for a flame strike.

"Shit!" She leapt off Visk in a very stupid move, whipping the wind to redirect her fall. This time, she was close enough to *feel* the air inside its lungs, swirling to her command. A firm spell had the fire pausing in the dragon's throat, even as she sprinted up its back to shout near its ears. "Stop attacking! Please; we need to talk!"

The dragon coughed, belching flame, like the magic equivalent of indigestion. Smoke poured out its nostrils, and Kianthe released her hold on its fire. But the dragon wasn't giving up that easily—and it clearly didn't care about her desire to negotiate. It snarled and sent a burst of flame against the ground, narrowly missing the barn.

"*No,*" Kianthe screamed, and wrenched the flame inside its throat back further.

This time, the dragon huffed, wheezed, and teetered toward dragon country. It sounded like it was choking on seawater, like she'd singed its innards with that final spell.

The sudden shift had her grabbing its scales while Visk repositioned himself underneath her. Sharp edges sliced her fingers and hot blood welled, but she couldn't think on it. The timing aligned, she shoved off the dragon's back, using another burst of wind to land on her mount instead.

That dragon limped back to dragon country.

"Kianthe—" Reyna called from the ground. Her voice held a razor's edge, rimmed in panic, but still quiet considering the distance between them. "You've done enough!"

It couldn't be enough; the town was still burning. In a trance, the mage turned her attention to the buildings. Fire eagerly consumed whatever hadn't been reinforced with stone or metal. Irritated, she smacked the flames on their ass, and the earth swallowed them whole.

Only smoke remained, drifting lazily into the nighttime sky.

The stars were very bright now.

Visk screeched a warning. Apparently, in stalling three dragons, Kianthe had earned the attention of the rest of them. The remaining four circled like vultures.

Reyna was still on the ground, desperately gripping Lilac's mane. Visk flew close enough that Kianthe could see the pale horror on her partner's face.

Regret was quickly quelled by the realization that *four dragons were circling her like vultures.* They'd go after the townsfolk—and Reyna—next if Kianthe didn't do something about it.

With little choice and her magic flickering, Kianthe bent over Visk's back and shouted, "We got their attention! Let's lead them as far from Tawney as we can, buddy." A pause, a scattered thought. "Find me magic. Something that isn't tapped out."

Visk tilted his wings and flew north, straight into dragon country.

It was a bad idea. A *very* bad idea. Only the Arcandor could absorb and utilize dragon magic, but that didn't mean they were compatible. The last Arcandor who tried wound up . . . not well. The sketched images of that Arcandor withering to skin and bones had been seared in Kianthe's brain as a teenager.

"Mixing magic is for the Stone of Seeing and any foolish enough to believe themselves on its level," her tutors had preached. Elemental mages worked with elements. Alchemical mages tested alchemy. And dragons thrived with their special blend.

But this was the only choice Kianthe had left. The nearest powerful ley line was a day's flight. Even with three dragons distracted, four were following at top speed. She'd never make it to a more natural, Stone-blessed source.

Dragon-topped mountains sprawling in the distance, with more creatures in question taking notice of their brethren chasing a rat through their domain. Several broke from their mountain perches, their roars shattering the air.

But at the same time, their magic flooded her.

It felt abrasive: her magic was bright yellow and moved with the elements, and dragons were far more than that. But it was easy to steal—even if the very act of absorbing some made her stomach lurch and her head pound.

No time to think on it. She craned her neck, urged Visk to skim along the rocky ground, and when the dragons got too close . . . she yanked the *very earth* upward to pin them. Her magic set the barriers for the spell, and the dragon magic surged through the lines, obeying her command.

One, two, three dragons were captured before they realized what she was doing. The fourth climbed with purpose, gaining too much altitude to raise the earth.

So Kianthe attacked with the sky.

A shouted spell and a grunt, and she pulled the air out from underneath its wings. Without lift, it fell. Not far enough to do serious damage, but enough to stun.

Seven dragons down. The sweat had dried on her face, and she was shaking uncontrollably with the magical effort. If there were a cohort of mages nearby, she could possibly avoid collapsing. If she were at the Magicary, where several ley lines converged in sweet, succulent magic, she could kiss Reyna goodnight in a few hours.

More dragons were coming.

Visk realized the perilous state of his mage and quickly angled back toward Tawney. But Kianthe grabbed his feathers and urged him to the ground instead. The griffon screeched protest, but she snapped, "More on the way, Visk! If we don't talk to them now, everything is finished."

Her voice was weak, ripped away by the icy wind. Dragon country was apparently cold year-round.

Visk chittered angrily, but landed beside the final dragon Kianthe had grounded, the biggest of the horde. That would also make it the oldest—dragons never stopped growing as they aged. With luck, it had some sway in their horde.

It was dazed, but seemed physically all right. Behind it, its brethren were trapped in stone, writhing against the unforgiving earth. It took even more control to hold them in place, now that their own magic was testing the bonds.

"Look at me," she called, sliding off Visk. A wave of exhaustion washed over her, and for a moment, the world spun. Visk stepped beside her, wings folded tight, and Kianthe steadied herself on his solid bulk.

The dragon hissed, opening its mouth for a flame strike. Heat rippled from the back of its throat. Its silver scales almost entirely blended with the ice—or maybe that was her vision fading in and out.

Kianthe blinked hard, reaching for the dragon magic again. It pulsed deep blue, so dark it was almost purple, and hit her like a poisoned meal. Like the unknown magic deep below Tawney . . . but not quite. That magic was too mild to make her stomach churn like this.

"Wait. Please. You know who I am."

It wasn't a question. Even with the language barrier, this dragon could understand her. There was a reason neither Shepara nor the Queendom had attempted to conquer dragon country. The creature's black eyes glittered, but its magic pulsed against hers, translating her language.

Curious. Kianthe linked their magic together, weaving deep blue and sunflower yellow like a tapestry, forming images. First of Tawney, the townsfolk, the things she held most dear. When the dragon raised its head, peering past her at the town, Kianthe emphasized, "That's *mine*. Under my protection. From now until forever, understand?"

The dragon snarled, digging its claws into the earth.

Kianthe was fading fast. She leaned heavier on Visk, but didn't remove her eyes from the threat at hand. The dragons in the distance were nearing.

"Don't—" Her words stuttered with a bone-rattling cough, but she tried again. "Don't argue. Look, I know what you're searching for. I'll find it for you." Now she shoved images into the dragon's mind.

The decaying church. The dirt beneath soot-stained flooring. The pulse of purple magic, thrumming like a child's persistent questions.

The dragon stilled. It tilted its head, contemplating her. Visk tensed, as if it might bite Kianthe in half at any moment—which, to be fair, was entirely possible. But the dragon just snorted, wispy smoke trailing from its nostrils.

Another image slid between their link. Three gleaming eggs, their leathery, lavender shells shining in the moonlight. A raiding party of humans, bold or foolish enough to climb the dragons' mountains, infiltrating their lairs. Most of the mortals were killed. A few escaped, eggs in tow.

Not one.

Three.

"Fuck," Kianthe muttered. "Feo was right."

The dragon pushed upright, wings spread wide as its brethren landed hard around her. Surrounded on every side, Kianthe raised her hands. Her dark eyes never left the dragon she'd connected with.

"I'll find them; you have my word. But you have to leave that town alone. Deal?"

A deal with a dragon. The stuffy mages at the Magicary would have a fit.

Kianthe was too weak to care. She held out a hand, barely able to focus on the creature swimming before her. A handshake—so very human. The dragon regarded it for a moment, then hissed something. The other dragons let their fire die in their throats, although there were growls and roars from every angle.

Visk appeared increasingly uncomfortable. It took a lot to shake her griffon, but this was enough.

The dragon she'd been speaking to tapped the earth with a claw, sketching an odd, circular language into the snow. When it finished, the magic formed a spell so powerful it shook Kianthe's teeth.

A bindment. She would locate the eggs, and in return, the dragons would allow it. Tawney would be safe for exactly as long as Kianthe upheld her side of the bargain.

But if that would protect Tawney—protect what they'd built here—Kianthe would do it. She couldn't fight the other dragons. This was the only way to ensure they didn't fly over her corpse and burn Tawney to the ground . . . for good this time.

So, she stepped inside the circle. Instantly, blue magic flared, prickling her skin like needles. Wind rushed around her. Then it died, quick as it came, and a magical chain locked in place between them. Blue linked with yellow, which would remain until the mission was complete.

"You're lucky I like you," Kianthe slurred, tugging the stone prisons she'd created away from the three captured dragons. One by one, they shook themselves loose, spread their wings, and soared away with their horde-mates, apparently satisfied with this ritual.

The big one she'd interacted with stayed, watching her impassively.

Kianthe was losing her battle with consciousness. "I tried not to kill anyone." Was she even speaking Common? Did the dragons have a name for their language? The world spun, and a strange wind roared inside her head. "But your friends may need help."

This one huffed, inclined its head in understanding. With a rush of wind, it leapt into the air, heading south. Three of its brethren followed, ready to help their horde-mates. Their wing-beats faded with distance.

The resulting silence was agony.

"Visk, get Rain," Kianthe breathed.

And with little decorum, the mage dropped like a stone.

21

Reyna

It was a fun secret that the Arcandor, Mage of Ages, was an absolute fool.

For someone who hated the stress of life-threatening danger, it was dramatic irony, watching Kianthe engage with the world. Staring in frustrated disbelief as she made enemies with the wrong people. Watching her test spells by leaping off the back of her high-flying griffon, just to "see if they worked."

And most recently, knowing the mage had drained herself of magic seven ways to the summer solstice, yet still staggered back into battle.

Reyna didn't get angry often, but she was *livid* now.

Lilac's hooves thundered against the rocky ground as they approached the rim of dragon country. In the distance, a dragon, one of three her beautifully stupid girlfriend had stopped, was spreading unsteady wings. Another circled above, checking its progress. Neither seemed to notice her, or care, so Reyna ducked her head and urged Lilac to gallop faster.

Her sword thumped against her leg as she braced herself in the saddle. "Toothpick" or not, if one of those beasts was hurting

Kianthe—*If?* her mind whispered viciously, and a stiff lump formed in her throat—Reyna was going to kill a dragon today. If there were two, or ten, or a hundred, Reyna would kill two, ten, a hundred.

Kianthe was coming home, safe and sound. She'd make Gods damn sure of it.

She gripped the reins until her knuckles turned white, shivering in the unnaturally icy wind as they crested the rim of dragon country. Lord Wylan's estate loomed below them, almost out of sight; he'd been in the thick of it, commanding fire brigades while Reyna evacuated their friends. Even Feo had pulled up their sleeves and written some kind of spell in the dirt. It wasn't powerful, but they claimed it would soothe burns.

But Kianthe—

Kianthe had single-handedly saved them.

Reyna knew the Arcandor's power was immense; there was a reason everyone wanted her favor. There was a reason the Magicary couldn't dispute her disappearance from their circular walls. Reyna had seen Kianthe working firsthand many times.

She'd never seen her accomplish something like this.

Foolish. *Reckless.*

In the distance, blending into the snowstorm, several huge figures loomed. For a moment, they looked like mountains . . . but then they moved, and her eye traced how big the dragons truly were. One by one, they climbed into the air. Almost like they'd accomplished what they needed.

Four soared back toward Tawney, and Reyna swallowed a shout, breathing the word *no* like a curse. Because if four dragons were heading back to town, that meant Kianthe was—was—

"Faster, Lilac," she begged, digging her heels into the warhorse's flank. "*Please,* faster."

The horse huffed, but lowered her head and seemed to pick up speed.

Then a screech sounded overhead and feathers swept past, so

abrupt that Lilac whinnied in panic, shoved her hooves into the ground. In the span of a gasp, Reyna went flying over the horse's head. She barely had time to yelp before sharp talons snatched her cloak, plucking her out of the sky.

Visk set her on the ground. He screeched again, and Lilac reared back, her calm shattered. With little decorum, she bolted. Reyna tried to lunge for the reins of her mount; her fingers brushed the leather straps, missed, and Lilac was gone, thundering back toward Tawney.

The griffon didn't care. He dove at Reyna with a razor-sharp beak, and she flinched—but he just grabbed her cloak and tugged her toward his back.

Visk didn't show up alone unless Kianthe was hurt. Reyna had very vivid memories of the last time this happened, and didn't care to repeat the experience. And if a griffon caused Lilac to forget her training, Reyna could only imagine what a dragon's presence would do. Swallowing her unease about Visk, she mounted, fitting her legs in front of his expansive wings.

"Take me to her," she said.

He lunged into the air, and she barely had time to brace herself against his thick neck. Kianthe did this without a bridle, without a saddle. It only reinforced how *careless* the mage was. Reyna clung to the griffon for dear life, but the ride was short.

All the dragons were gone now, but Visk still circled once— which gave Reyna enough time to see the upturned earth, a strange circle etched in the snow, and . . . a dark shape, so small it was dwarfed against the sizable stretch of ice.

Kianthe.

Fear leapt into Reyna's throat. Was she injured? Had a dragon gouged her? Burned her skin and left her for dead? Sunken in terror, she barely flinched as Visk dove fast, flashed his wings at the last second, and landed lithely beside the mage.

The mage, who didn't move.

Kianthe wasn't moving.

"No," Reyna breathed, leaping off the griffon's back. Her boots landed hard in the snow, and then she stumbled to her knees beside her partner. Kianthe was facedown, and Reyna unceremoniously scooped her into her lap. "Key. *Kianthe*. Look at me."

No bleeding wounds. But the magic drain—it was worse than Reyna had ever seen it. Kianthe's face was ashen, thin blue veins spidering away from her half-lidded, glassy eyes. Her lips tinged blue, and dried blood stained beneath her nose.

Reyna pressed a hand to her cheek, but the mage's skin was waxen, unnaturally cold even in this weather. Breaths, barely rasping whispers, formed icy clouds that vanished almost as soon as they appeared.

"My love, please." Reyna pressed a hard kiss to her forehead. "You were so brave. Keep fighting for me, all right?"

Not for the first time, Reyna wished she'd been born with the gift of magic. No one in the Queendom was, since they worshiped the Gods instead of the Stars or the Magicary's Stone of Seeing, but right now . . . Reyna would have denounced her deities if she thought it would save Kianthe. If she thought the Stone would gift her something, *anything* to heal its chosen one.

But whatever Kianthe felt pulsing in the earth, the air, the clouds, it was unknown to Reyna.

Visk leaned over her shoulder, his black eyes glinting. Reyna *swore* she saw concern in them—and finally, she believed Kianthe's grandiose tales of the creature's intelligence. Visk cared for his mistress, but this went past animal understanding.

It didn't feel like such a stretch to speak to him.

"We're going to save her, Visk." Unlike Kianthe, Reyna didn't resort to anger, didn't suffer from anxiety when her partner was hurt. No, Reyna's temperament solidified into something calm and dangerous, like the eye of a hurricane.

For that moment, nothing else mattered.

Kianthe would be fine. No matter what.

"She needs magic—" Reyna cut herself off when Visk suddenly

bristled, feathers fluffed like a sparrow in a rainstorm. He screeched again, spreading one wing over Reyna and Kianthe, hiding them from view as a huge, dark shape landed nearby.

Overhead, through Visk's feathers, Reyna saw one dragon carrying another with what appeared to be a broken wing. They soared toward the mountains, talons latched into the heavy bodies, somehow staying aloft with huge beats of their leathery wings. Four more followed—two unsteady in their wingbeats, two trailing like escorts.

The dragon that landed nearby was huge, bigger than any of them. It grumbled, which sounded like a boulder tumbling down a mountainside, and Visk reluctantly folded his wings.

Reyna could see the creature properly now, and Kianthe's earlier fear suddenly made sense. There was no way a single sword would take down a dragon. Its scales glinted like chainmail, its talons longer than her arm. Twisting horns protruded from a thick skull. It opened its mouth, revealing malicious teeth.

It hardly mattered. Reyna wouldn't let new harm befall Kianthe. She eased the mage back onto a cushion of snow, pushed to her feet, and unsheathed her sword.

Her hands didn't shake.

Her glare didn't waver.

"Make your choice," she told the beast, her voice steady and dangerous. "If you attack, you'll die tonight."

But the dragon rumbled what sounded suspiciously like a sigh, then lowered its head so they were eye level. Its black eyes glittered with a thousand stars, and it seemed to stare into her soul.

She remained loose, adjusting her stance slightly. One lunge, and she could blind it. It wouldn't fell the creature, but it would buy her enough time to find another weak spot.

Everything had a weak spot, after all.

Reyna's was Kianthe.

Kianthe, who suddenly moaned. She'd been unconscious before. Truly, honestly gone, far enough that Reyna doubted she'd wake for weeks . . . if she awoke at all. Reyna's heart wrenched at the sound, but she wasn't stupid enough to abandon the immediate threat.

Meanwhile, Visk chirped, his lion's tail swishing in catlike pleasure. He bent close to Kianthe, nudged her with his beak. And the mage groaned again, sounding far more conscious this time.

She was waking up.

Reyna hesitated, torn. Fight the dragon and protect Kianthe—or risk a glance at her partner?

The dragon huffed, making her decision for her. It gave Reyna one last, hard look, then spread its wings and leapt into the air. Loose snow washed over them. As it soared north, following its horde-mates, the icy clouds overhead vanished. Stars gleamed, and on the horizon, the faintest glimpse of sunlight painted the sky a stormy gray.

"T-Tell me you weren't—" Kianthe rasped the words, and then cut herself off to heave into the snow. Reyna dropped her sword, steadying the mage's shuddering shoulders until Kianthe was finished.

Her forehead was burning, her skin far too pale . . . but she was awake. Kianthe spit, made a face at the mess, and turned fever-glazed eyes on Reyna. "You weren't g-going to fight that dragon—right?"

"Of course not," Reyna said.

The Arcandor laughed, and it turned into a rasping wheeze. "Liar."

Reyna gathered Kianthe against her chest. "It was a tactical assessment. Nothing more."

"Tactical—" Kianthe broke off, coughing roughly. Her eyes fluttered shut as she moaned: "Shit. Dragon m-magic is the *worst*."

Dragon magic. Reyna traced the creature's path through the sky, then glanced wonderingly at Visk. The griffon chirped again, like he knew the whole time the dragon was going to give Kianthe enough magic to survive. Maybe he had.

It felt like she was trespassing in a world she was half-blind to. All the dragon did was stare at her, at Kianthe, but apparently it gave the mage enough power to step away from the five hells. Reyna was embarrassed she'd almost sliced its eye out.

"Will you be all right?" Reyna smoothed Kianthe's sweat-soaked bangs off her forehead. The mage's skin tone wasn't as pale anymore, but was still a far cry from its typical warm ochre.

The mage grunted, her eyes sliding closed: "M-Might vomit a few more times. Gave me t-too much. Stuff is *rancid*."

And she was out, her face smoothing into sleep.

Reyna pressed another kiss to her girlfriend's forehead, drew a few short breaths to calm her frenzied heart, and lifted Kianthe off the ground. The Arcandor had saved Tawney—now it was time for Tawney to return the favor.

Kianthe was slightly taller than her, but Reyna was stronger, and she carefully positioned Kianthe on the griffon's back. She paused to retrieve her sword, sheathing it with a soft prayer of gratitude. Then she climbed onto Visk's back as well.

Again, the griffon didn't wait for a command, but he flew slower this time, wings tilting with the wind instead of against it. Reyna gripped his feathery neck tight enough to pull a couple by accident, but the griffon barely flinched.

Kianthe's body was a pointed weight against Reyna's chest. She wanted to sink her face into the mage's wild hair and breathe deep, wanted to fall into bed together and hold her close. She wanted to reverse time, return to this morning, before Diarn Feo's summons, before Lord Wylan's appearance, before the dragons caused so many problems.

She wished they'd kept moving all those eons ago, found a different town, and never had this day to begin with.

Well, no, that wasn't true. Reyna adored Tawney, fell deeper in love every day. But she didn't want to think about life there without Kianthe.

She suddenly, vividly understood why Kianthe had been so

confused when Reyna proposed leaving alone. The idea was laughable, now—or would be, if Reyna had any humor left for laughing.

Visk circled Matild's clinic, but Reyna shouted at the griffon to stop. The place was overrun with traumatized citizens; most of the injuries thankfully appeared minor, but they were loud distractions. Kianthe wouldn't have any peace.

Reyna couldn't bear it. "Back to the barn, Visk. I'll summon Matild."

There wasn't much the midwife could do for magic drain, but maybe she could treat Kianthe's symptoms. The fever was worrying; Reyna didn't need it dissolving into more.

Visk obeyed, dropping instead outside their shop.

Lindenback was empty except for Sigmund and Nurt, who were speaking with Sasua. Her son was nowhere to be seen, but hopefully that meant he was safe inside. The adults waved, then stilled when they saw Kianthe's limp form. Nurt paled, and Sasua immediately stepped closer.

"Is she alive? Can I help?"

Reyna scooped Kianthe into her arms. "We need Matild. Now."

"Is she okay?" Sasua demanded.

"Not really." Reyna winced. "She should be fine. She just . . . needs rest."

Rest. Magic. Both would be necessary for recovery. Reyna was suddenly terrified that the Stone of Seeing might forsake Kianthe, leave her with unpalatable dragon magic and a raging fever. It pushed her to glance at Sigmund and Nurt, both of whom had their brows knitted in concern.

"Can you find someone willing to travel to Wellia? If we can get a mage or two here, Kianthe can draw on their magic. They can use my horse, if needed—I think she ran back to the inn's stables."

"Allow me to handle that," a voice said behind them, and Diarn Feo swept into the picture. Their eyes studied Kianthe, limp in Reyna's arms, and rare sympathy and regret flashed over their features. "Let me borrow her griffon and I'll bring who she needs. Just give us a few days."

Visk chittered, butting his head against Feo in a friendly fashion. Clearly, the griffon would do anything to help Kianthe recover.

Reyna breathed a sigh. "Thank you." She didn't mention that a true lord should rally around their community after a time of crisis; she frankly didn't care, with Kianthe in this state. Wylan could handle the politics, if Feo would retrieve magical help.

Sigmund crossed his arms. "Ah . . . your girl isn't just a mage, is she?"

Diarn Feo rolled their eyes, leaping onto Visk's back. They took off without another word, angling southwest toward Wellia.

Reyna felt a thousand years old. In her arms, Kianthe was too warm, shuddering occasionally. "We'll discuss it later. Please retrieve Matild, if you can."

Sasua divvied out babysitting duty to Sigmund and Nurt, then jogged toward the center of town and the clinic. Reyna left the men in the street, pushing the barn door open with her shoulder.

The hearth was merely burning embers now, but the everflame glimmered in the rafters, casting an almost somber hue over the space. "Almost there, Key," Reyna murmured, heading for their bedroom.

Hard to believe just a few hours ago, they'd been chatting by the fire. Gods, so much had happened.

Exhaustion tugged at Reyna's bones, but she couldn't sleep yet. She eased Kianthe into bed, set a wooden bucket nearby as an afterthought, then busied herself with collecting melting snow from the plains outside, wetting cloth for the fever, retrieving a jug of drinking water, and anything else that might help.

Matild arrived shortly after, and Sasua gave Reyna a small smile before leaving the bookshop, closing the barn doors firmly behind her. Matild, meanwhile, swept into the bedroom, eyes widening.

"Was wondering when you'd call; no chance she escaped that fight unscathed." The midwife felt Kianthe's forehead, pried open an eyelid, measured her breathing. "Gods. You'd think she'd been sick for weeks, with these symptoms."

Reyna might shake Kianthe senseless when she awoke, but for now, there was work to do. Her voice was measured. "Magic drain. You saw a bit of it when she renovated the shop, but this is . . . much worse. She attempted too much tonight."

"She saved us all, you mean." Matild met her gaze briefly, then busied herself with retrieving things from her bag. It was bursting with supplies, and at Reyna's curious look, Matild explained, "Didn't know what happened to her, so I brought what I could."

The next hour passed in a blur, with Matild stripping Kianthe of her snow-soaked clothes, packing her bed with watertight bags filled with ice. She used a strange bellows-like device to force air into the mage's lungs. It all helped take the deathly tinge off her skin, helped Kianthe breathe a bit easier. Twice, Kianthe awoke to vomit into the bucket, and twice she mumbled an apology before slipping back into unconsciousness.

Morning sunlight peeked through the windows when Matild finally clipped her bag shut. The midwife had dark smudges beneath her eyes, but she forced a smile for Reyna's benefit.

"It's my expert opinion that she's stable. Not *well*, by any means, but—I don't believe she'll get worse if we're monitoring that fever." She paused. "Get some sleep, Reyna. This whole town will be banging on your door soon. Lord Wylan is holding them off, but everyone wants to know what Kianthe did. Or rather, *how* she did it."

"You know how she did it." Reyna's fingers feathered over Kianthe's waxen skin. She wasn't as warm anymore, especially after hours surrounded by snow-packed bags, but her state still made Reyna's chest twinge.

"Let me rephrase. I think they're more curious about how the Arcandor, Mage of Ages, lived alongside them for so long . . . and why." Matild shook her head. "Everyone will want to thank her, if nothing else."

Reyna massaged her forehead, edging away the headache that had taken hold. "If they start to worship her, Matild, we'll leave, and to hells with this place." She didn't really mean it, but the idea of the townsfolk, their friends, their *patrons*, visiting the bookstore just to get a glance at Kianthe . . . it made Reyna feel terrible.

The midwife raised her hands. "I'm not worshiping her. I think she's an idiot, pushing herself this far."

"But a brave one, right?" Kianthe mumbled from the bed, the words slurred.

Reyna sighed.

Matild grinned, relief evident on her features. "The bravest. Bucket's right there, oh wise and heroic Arcandor. I'll check up on you tomorrow."

"Peachy." Kianthe was already fading again.

Matild saw herself out, a wry smile on her face.

After she was gone and the bookshop was quiet, Reyna leaned over Kianthe, pressing a kiss to her forehead. Her thumb traced the mage's cheek, which seemed to revive her, because Kianthe's bleary eyes opened, and she smiled at Reyna. "You think I'm b-brave."

Never, in all her life, would Reyna have believed it was possible to love someone *this much*. The intensity made tears well in her eyes, and she turned away fast, too fast, blinking hard to clear her vision.

"Aww, Rain." Kianthe grabbed her hand, pulling her back. If she'd had the strength to sit up, she'd certainly have done so—but all she could manage was a half-hearted attempt that ended in a groan.

Now was *not* the time for this. Reyna squeezed her hand, then fluffed her pillow. "It's fine, love. Just sleep. You've done something amazing tonight."

More than amazing, if that dragon offering his magic to

Kianthe was any indication. Unease settled in Reyna's gut, but Visk was the only other being who'd witnessed . . . whatever happened . . . and Reyna couldn't exactly ask him. She'd pry further when Kianthe wasn't on death's doorstep.

"P-Please don't cry," Kianthe said, and she must have been exhausted, because tears rimmed her eyes too. Kianthe rarely cried, not unless she was laughing too hard or in the deepest throes of anxiety—but right now, she looked at Reyna like either of them could shatter with one wrong word.

Gods, Reyna had to be stronger than this. Of the two of them, *she* wasn't the one who'd fought dragons and saved a town. She scrubbed her face, offered a genuine smile. "Key, if I'm crying, it's because I am so, so proud of you. Now please, do me the biggest favor and get some real sleep. Okay? How's your stomach feeling?"

The mage wrinkled her nose, blanching at the reminder. "S'fine."

Reyna wet a cloth with icy water and laid it over Kianthe's forehead. The fever was still present, but it wasn't raging anymore, so either the dragon magic or the ley line had started replenishing her reservoirs. It was happening far too slowly for Reyna's taste, but then again, she always hated seeing Kianthe after a true magic drain.

"You sleeping?" The words came out slurred together, and Kianthe's eyes fluttered shut.

"Yes, dearest. I'll rest too. And I'll make an herbal tea to settle your nausea once you're up for it."

Kianthe didn't reply. She was asleep again.

Reyna clenched her eyes shut. Diarn Feo and Visk were heading to Wellia, and magical help would be here soon. Kianthe was safe in bed, and the dragons hadn't returned. Everything would be fine.

But instead of relief, a cold sense of duty settled over her shoulders. Reyna dragged a plush armchair into their bedroom from the shop, locked the front door, and got comfortable beside Kianthe's bed. After all, she'd pulled many sleepless nights standing guard by Queen Tilaine's bedchamber.

Now, she was guarding someone far more precious, and she wouldn't fail in that task.

22

Kianthe

Kianthe awoke feeling like she'd been frozen in ice, and somehow simultaneously submerged into the lava pools of the Vardian mountain range. She shuddered violently, and it took several seconds to place where she was—and what was happening.

Ah, right. The dragons. Reyna crying. Missing eggs and more responsibility.

Kianthe's stomach roiled, and nausea slid through her veins like poison. Normal mages couldn't use dragon magic for a reason; it sat like bad meat in her gut. There wasn't enough energy to heave. There wasn't even enough energy to moan. She just existed in misery, drifting.

Her dreams were nonexistent, right until the moment they weren't. Elemental magic swarmed her, sickly sweet, drowning her in good intentions. Dark blue tinted the waters, and she gasped for breath, struggling to claw to the surface.

A hand reached for her. Reyna. Kianthe grasped it desperately, but when she was hauled out of the sea—no, an ocean of snow—it wasn't her girlfriend that greeted her. Instead, Queen Tilaine smiled and whispered, "She's mine."

"Like hells," Kianthe tried to snarl, but the words were ripped from her chest. She was falling, sinking again, and everything went dark.

More time passed. It was impossible to tell how much.

Nausea rose and fell in waves. Sometimes, her face felt too hot; sometimes it was cooler. On occasion, she would pry open her eyes—and Reyna was always there, perched in a chair reading a book, sipping tea, moving fluidly through sword drills that made her look like she was dancing. Once or twice, Matild was there too, but any memory of banter with the midwife vanished like stones into a pond after she left.

Days must be passing. Must be, and that frustrated Kianthe, because she'd awaken with a niggling insistence that something was wrong every single time. She tilted her head toward Reyna, grimaced when her girlfriend offered a glass of water, and mumbled, "How long?"

And sweet Reyna, calm and kind, smiled as patiently as a schoolteacher repeating a lesson for the umpteenth time. "Only three days, love. Diarn Feo should be in Wellia by now."

Kianthe forgot that as soon as it was said.

Later, Matild tried to feed Kianthe a mess of slop that tasted like both citrus and shit. Kianthe gagged, shoved it away, and spent the night heaving from the memory. After that, Matild returned with an immensely strong anti-nausea tonic, and a bottle of dark liquid intended to rehydrate. That combination worked, although it made Kianthe so tired she slept another day away.

When she opened her eyes one morning to a pair of stiff-looking men in Magicary robes, Kianthe cursed liberally. "Stone damn it all, go to hells. 'M not going back." Her words were accompanied by a half-hearted wave.

Reyna lurked on the outskirts, one hand on her sword. But she didn't intervene as the taller one—a fusty mage named Harold who had enough seniority that he insisted everyone call him

Master Harold, even though it wasn't an official Magicary title—remarked, "Ah, Arcandor. A delight as always."

"So, this is where you've been hiding," the other mage said. This person's robe was trimmed in silver, which meant the mage *had* earned a middling rank within the Magicary. Gender-neutral pronouns, based on the bronze pin attached to the mage's lapel, but that could mean any number of options.

Luckily, Reyna had been paying attention when Kianthe explained those identifier pins last year, because she interjected to say, "What pronouns would you prefer?"

"Ask the name, too," Kianthe mumbled. She couldn't quite place how she knew this mage.

The person heaved a sigh. "You may use 'they' or 'them.' And Arcandor, I'm slightly disappointed you don't remember me. We partook in the air manipulation class as children. I'm Allayan?"

"Excellent." Her eyes slipped closed. Stars and Stone, she was so *tired*. Her magic nudged against the bright yellow of these mages, like tapping a tree for syrup. "Fix me or go 'way, Allayan."

They sighed. "Good to know her attitude hasn't changed."

But Harold was frowning. "What did you *do*, Kianthe?" He moved forward—only to be swiftly intercepted by Reyna. Although she was much shorter, her stern look stopped him in his tracks.

Huh. If Kianthe were feeling better, she'd kiss her girlfriend. Maybe tomorrow.

Maybe by then, these mages would be gone, too.

"The Arcandor is very ill," Reyna said, as if that wasn't obvious. "You two flew here, so you understand the urgency. Before you start questioning her choices, perhaps you can offer your magic."

But Harold scoffed. "Rich words from someone who knows little about our ways."

Kianthe bristled, but Reyna's expression never wavered. "I was under the impression, Master Harold, that you were here to help.

If that is incorrect, you two may see yourself out—or it will be my pleasure to show you the way."

It was very clearly a threat.

She was so *sexy*. Kianthe opened her mouth to make a comment about it, but fog had settled over her brain, and nothing witty arrived. Disappointed, she pressed her lips together, sinking deeper into her feather pillow.

"I'm here to help," Allayan said helpfully.

Reyna smiled. "Then you may stay. Master Harold? What is your choice?"

The mage seemed a bit unnerved now, and his eyes dropped to the sword at her hip. There wasn't enough room to swing it between them, but Reyna probably wouldn't use a sword anyway. She *probably* had nine daggers hidden in her formfitting clothes.

Dazed by the fever, Kianthe laughed.

They ignored her. Harold pinched his brow. "As much as I'd love to entertain this protective act, the Arcandor's magic supply is tainted somehow. And that spells disaster for all of us, if you don't let me help."

"Spells," Kianthe muttered. "Heh."

They ignored her.

"Then you *will* help." Reyna sounded satisfied. She stepped aside, looming like the palace guard she used to be.

Harold huffed. "Yes, yes. Look, Allayan. You can see her reservoirs—mostly empty, except for what this ley line can provide. But there." He gestured at something near Kianthe's heart. "Poison."

Reyna stiffened almost imperceptibly. She'd probably just assumed this was a bad magic drain. Kianthe should have informed her about the dragons, and their deal. She had no idea when she'd have managed that, all things considered, but there was no time like the present.

"Dragon magic," Kianthe rasped, her dry throat rubbing painfully at the words.

"*Dragon* magic?" Harold's eyes widened.

Allayan flinched. "Arcandor, you know we aren't able to— Well, maybe *you* can, but—" They broke off with a huff. "How can we fix that?"

Harold didn't seem confident anymore. He shifted his weight, brow furrowed.

It was Reyna who stepped into the conversation again, seamlessly. "Can someone explain what's happening? I'm rather invested in her well-being."

"It's a mage problem," Harold snapped.

Kianthe struggled to push herself upright. "Magic's like—a mug of tea. Fill it up with one kind or another, but the capacity's limited." Speaking this much was truly exhausting, but if there was *one* conversation to pay attention to, it was this one. Like it or not, Kianthe needed these mages' help to recover anytime soon.

"Darling, I didn't mean you. Save your energy," Reyna said gently, smoothing Kianthe's hair off her face. The Arcandor huffed, but Reyna had already looked to Allayan. "So, your magic fills this mug. And when you use it, it drains."

"Unless there's a ley line present . . . or other mages for the Arcandor. She can tap into both; we're restricted to the ley lines and our own limits." Allayan ran a hand over their short brown ponytail. "But now, the Arcandor's mug is filled with *dragon* magic. It sits on ours like oil on water."

"So . . ." Reyna raised an eyebrow. "Use the dragon magic. It's making her sick anyway—if she uses it, depletes it, she can refill with yours. Right?"

The mages exchanged glances. Kianthe offered a pleased sigh. "The love of my life, everyone."

And so, with the expectation that dispelling dragon magic would be destructive, and *not* something to do near Tawney, they went outside to get some distance.

Visk was in the street, communing with two other griffons. While his fur and feathers were closer to that of a golden eagle, dark brown tufted with white, the new pair could have been copies of each other, with more traditional beige coloring. All three were chittering, as if deep in conversation.

When Reyna and Allayan hauled Kianthe into the brisk sunshine—her arms over their shoulders while Harold followed like a king in a procession—Kianthe blanched at the gifts outside their shop. Flowers were stacked on both outdoor tables, every chair, and piled against the barn in bright reds, pinks, oranges, and blues. Kianthe noticed a few bottles of liquor and wine buried beneath the madness.

"What—"

"Our neighbors are grateful," Reyna said. "Visk, if you please?"

That almost made Kianthe stumble. Reyna was always wary around Visk, distrust evident in the way she stood, or how she kept her distance. Hearing her address the griffon now made Kianthe wonder what the hells she'd missed.

Visk trotted over, his awkward claws digging slashes in the dirt as he preened Kianthe's messy hair. It probably smelled horrid, but no one commented. Happiness flashed in the mage's chest, overriding the exhaustion that had settled there like a suffocating blanket.

"Hello, beautiful," she cooed at him.

He fluffed under her words.

Kianthe clumsily—dazedly—slipped over his back, gripping his feathers. She was relieved when Reyna followed suit and settled behind her, wrapping strong arms around her waist to prop her upright. Reyna rested her chin on Kianthe's shoulder, whispering in her ear, "You doing all right?"

"Just dandy," Kianthe lied.

"If you feel ill, try to aim *over* Visk, please."

"How romantic."

The other mages climbed on their mounts, and the three griffons launched into the air, angling toward the pine forest south of Tawney. Reyna didn't seem willing to take them closer to dragon country—or maybe she was afraid Kianthe might accidentally absorb more magic. Either way, the Arcandor was too tired to argue.

When they landed and dismounted, Reyna was the only one who didn't immediately give Kianthe some distance. Instead, she steadied her, frowning at the barren space around them, the trees that rose like claws at their backs. "I hope this works."

"Me too." Kianthe was thoroughly done feeling this way. "Stand back, love. Harold, if anything happens to her, I'm using this magic on you next."

Harold had the decency to look alarmed. He stepped in front of Reyna, and at his feet, the earth rippled under a whispered command. A wall of stone, waiting to form a protective barrier.

Good.

Kianthe wobbled on her own, her energy quickly draining. Using the Stone's magic was as easy as breathing, but this magic required a lot more concentration. Her brow furrowed as she reached into her reservoir, grasping the intruding blue, yanking it to the surface. It coiled around her like a barrel of snakes, writhing, snarling.

Her feet lifted off the ground. Kianthe was barely aware of it, but there was the flying magic. And more: communication magic, a lilting language she suddenly understood even if she couldn't speak it. Time magic, like the years meant nothing, like immortality was a choice, not a birthright. She peeked into the future and saw the earth hardened over, jungles sprouting over deserts, creatures she didn't recognize roaming the plains.

And finally, fire. She controlled it as the Arcandor, but now she realized her command was like that of a child with a stylus. She'd stopped one dragon by burning its throat—but with this magic, it could have ceased her ministrations with a thought. She was lucky its mind had been elsewhere.

The magic boiled around her, roiling like a riptide, and then *exploded*.

It singed the plains, sending a plume of smoke billowing into the sky. Time seemed to halt for a long moment, a breath, two, sixteen, as Kianthe watched the stars realign and the world tilt to catch her. Her feet landed hard on the icy ground, then her knees, and finally her shoulder slammed into the earth.

Awareness inched back in slivers of light. The nausea was gone, which was a massive relief. She blinked at the sky, and when Reyna's face appeared overhead, brow pinched in concern, Kianthe smiled.

"Dragon magic. Not for the fainthearted."

And ironically, she fainted.

※

Kianthe didn't stir until later that night, once again tucked into bed within their cozy bookshop. Reyna startled when Kianthe yelped awake. The Arcandor's heart raced and her breath was short, but they calmed as she oriented herself.

"Shit, Rain, I might need something stronger than tea." Kianthe pressed a hand to her pounding forehead. But despite the headache, she did feel a thousand times better. Relief settled in her chest.

"You don't drink, love." Reyna's lips quirked in amusement. "How are you feeling? Matild said your vitals are better now than they've been all week." She set her book aside, a romance novel that would have made a mother blush.

Kianthe grinned after seeing the title stamped on the leather cover. "You must have missed me, to be reading that."

Reyna's cheeks colored. "That's not why I picked this up."

"Can't let a girl dream, can you?"

Reyna spluttered an apology, which was both adorable and hilarious.

Kianthe pushed upright, reveling in how easy the motion was now. She really did feel much better. Still physically weak, but there wasn't a weight on her chest anymore, or poison in her veins. In fact, her magical reservoirs were capped full, so this must be the lag from whatever dragon magic she hadn't expelled. "Aw. Harold did help."

Reyna relaxed. "We were worried it might not take, without you awake to confirm it. They went to the inn to sleep off their magic drains, but Master Harold wants it known that he saved the Arcandor in her darkest hour."

"Shit, he'll be impossible after this. Makes me glad I don't live in the Magicary anymore."

A pause. "Will they allow you to stay here? I don't think any of us realized how little magic Tawney has . . . You might be better off somewhere with a stronger ley line." Reyna frowned, running her fingers over the tooling of her armrest, clearly nervous.

The mage huffed. "First, they don't 'allow' anything. I'm the Arcandor. The only being I answer to is the Stone of Seeing. Second, *I* knew exactly how much magic was here, and it didn't change my mind when we arrived. It isn't changing it now."

Reyna didn't seem convinced, or maybe she was in a morose mood, because all she did was nod and remain silent. Very unlike her.

"Are you okay?" Kianthe asked. "Tell me how you're feeling."

And for the first time since they implemented that method of conversation, Reyna deflected instead of answering honestly. "I feel like you might need a cup of tea by the fire, if you're up to it."

Well, that would be a nice place to converse. Kianthe was tired of this bedroom. She scrubbed her face, then grimaced. "I need a wash first. Then, yes. Absolutely."

"Tea preference?"

"Surprise me."

A little while later, Kianthe had settled by the roaring fire. Reyna had insisted on tucking a blanket around the mage's legs, insisted on toasting bread and cheese in the oven for her to eat, insisted on Kianthe not walking farther than the armchair without support.

There's a word for this, Kianthe thought wryly. *Doting.* And considering Kianthe had spent so many years alone, admired but never cared for, it was both awkward and wonderful.

"Spiced tea all right, love?" Reyna called from the back counter. "Or would you prefer something milder before bed?"

Kianthe wrinkled her nose. "I'm not sleeping for a while." That was probably a lie—her magic was back, but exhaustion from the week settled over her bones. Still, she was cozy as hells and *missed* Reyna, as ridiculous as that sounded. She didn't want this night to end so soon.

The cheesy bread was divine, and Kianthe attacked it with vigor. Reyna had only given her one slice, and after polishing it off, she craned her neck over the plush chair. "Is there more bread?"

A smile ghosted on Reyna's lips. "There is. But Matild suggested we go slow. Wait a bit and see how that settles."

"You know I have an iron stomach, right? At least concerning anything but poisonous magic?"

Reyna's expression bordered on amused. "I know I'd rather not clean up another mess."

Kianthe's cheeks colored. This whole week was embarrassing, and she hated it. She picked a few crumbs off the plate, then set it on the table between their chairs. Her tone was petulant: "Haven't vomited since I was six, but sure. Judge me all you'd like."

"Key, I'd never judge you." Reyna carried two steaming mugs from the kitchen. Her expression was pinched, laugh lines gone under a pressing weight. She handed Kianthe her mug, then perched on her chair, looking like she'd rather be fighting an enemy than having this conversation.

Kianthe waited, holding the mug close to her chest for warmth. The fire crackled a few stones away. Outside, the evening was quiet, the curtains drawn. They existed in their own little world.

"You were so brave," Reyna said gently.

"Thank you." Kianthe, contrarily, was very suspicious.

Reyna went silent for a bit longer.

Finally, *finally,* she clenched her eyes shut and snapped, "Why are you also so stupid?"

There it was. It was so unlike Reyna's typical personality that Kianthe snorted into her tea, spilling it over the knitted blanket. She gasped at the heat, patted the blanket futilely, laughed. "Shit, Rain. Warn me next time."

"I'm sorry. But also, I'm not." Reyna didn't flinch, although she did retrieve a cloth. Her expression was a mix of exasperated and irate, and she loomed over Kianthe as the mage dabbed at her blanket. "You tackled seven dragons. *Seven.* Gods, Kianthe, entire armies have been wiped out by fewer."

Kianthe swelled a bit at the praise. "I know. Did you see me?"

Reyna drew a slow breath. She looked like she'd spent the week coaxing herself through this conversation, and in just a few words, her careful plans were falling to ruin.

So . . . not praise, then.

"Oh, I saw. I saw you realize you'd done too much, and entice four more to follow you into *dragon country,* of all places. Why didn't you fly south, toward a ley line near the Capital? Or west, to Wellia? Anywhere else would have been—"

Reyna cut herself off then, pressed her palms to her eyes, and paced toward the bookshelves. "Never mind. You're still recovering. I meant to wait for this conversation."

So, she had prepared for this. That made Kianthe want to engage more, because if it weighed on Reyna's mind this long, it needed to be addressed. Reyna didn't hold on to trivial matters.

"I considered it, believe me. But the dragons wouldn't have followed." Kianthe's brow knitted together. "My next source of magic is half a day's flight. They'd have turned around and burned Tawney while I was gone. They'd have destroyed the barn. Hurt you. I couldn't risk it."

Reyna looked very close to throttling her. She clenched her eyes shut again, drew a slow breath. "Tawney survived before we got here; no one asked for this kind of intervention. This place is just a shop, and I'm just a person. You're so much more important."

Irritation flickered in Kianthe's chest. Just a person? She opened her mouth to argue—then stopped.

This was dissolving from a productive conversation into a defensive debate. Kianthe was prone to that, but usually Reyna guided her to a better path.

Except *Reyna* had spent the entire week watching Kianthe writhing with fever, unconscious from magic that was poisoning her from the inside. There were no wounds to address, no herbs that could cure a magic drain. Even Matild's expertise was useless. It must have been terrifying, exhausting, and unnerving. If their positions were reversed, Kianthe would have been an anxious mess.

And yet Reyna stood before her, solid as the Stone of Seeing. She prepared food and tea and covered her with a blanket, and the only reason they were having this conversation now was because *Kianthe* pressed for it.

Her irritation dissolved.

"I'm sorry, Rain."

It disarmed her girlfriend immediately. Reyna's voice trembled. "No. Stop it. You have nothing to apologize for." She spoke like she'd whispered that over and over, like they were finally getting back on script.

There was something pleasing about having productive conversations, rather than burning bridges with fiery emotion. When they first started dating, Kianthe had never considered the little tactics Reyna often employed: separating from impulse, practicing empathy, repeating another's sentence to prove she'd been listening. But they were brilliant, just like Reyna was, and they made the entire relationship better.

Now Kianthe didn't bother hiding her remorse. "Maybe not in how I saved the town. But you must have been scared, and for that, I'm incredibly sorry." She set her spiced tea down on the table, leaned over the blanket. "Hells, Rain. You know I'd be terrified if our situations were reversed."

Tears welled in Reyna's eyes. It was the second time Kianthe remembered her crying this week. They dripped down her cheeks, shining in the firelight, before she swiped them away. "Oh, I was." She laughed, a bubbling sound filled with sorrow.

Kianthe tossed the blanket off her legs, pulling Reyna into a firm hug. It was reassuring, steady, and her heart ached to feel her girlfriend trembling. "Reyna, you don't need to protect me from how you feel."

"Well"—Reyna buried her face in Kianthe's clothes—"I feel like I want to strangle you for being so brave and reckless and stupid. But that's hardly productive, and I might make enemies out of the entire town."

Kianthe was startled into a laugh.

Reyna laughed too.

They held each other in silence for a long time, long enough that it was impossible to tell who was propping up whom by the time Kianthe pulled back. She kissed Reyna's hair, smoothed a few strands. Her soap was tinged with honey, and she smelled heavenly. "I'll be more careful next time. But I've stopped any future dragon attacks, so this particular fight won't be a problem again."

Reyna readjusted her grip, resting her chin on Kianthe's shoulder, eyes facing the bookshelves. "How did you manage that?"

"Feo was right. The dragons are missing three eggs, and they enlisted me to find them."

"Eggs—" Reyna stopped short, perking up at a new mystery. She pulled back, eyebrows raised. "Do you think they're under that burnt church?"

"Maybe. Don't worry about it; I'll investigate. Figure this out." Kianthe kissed Reyna on the lips, then rested their foreheads together. "The nice thing is that time is negligible for dragons. I don't have to rush out and solve this today."

"Excellent. Because for the foreseeable future, you're on house arrest." Reyna's voice was teasing, but somehow, Kianthe didn't think she was kidding.

"Excuse me?"

"You heard me, dear." Reyna guided Kianthe back into her chair, squeezing her hand before covering her again with the blanket. It had warmed from its spot by the fire, and Kianthe was secretly grateful to sit down. Reyna took her own seat, drawing a casual sip of her cooling tea. "House arrest. Imprisonment. Incarceration. Whatever you'd like to call it, you're not allowed to leave the bookstore. Not until I deem you better."

"Love, as sexy as it is to imagine you trapping me here, I highly doubt you'll be able to enforce that."

"Oh, feel free to test me." Reyna's lips tilted upward in a sly smile now. "I promised you I'd be careful after the roof incident, and then you turned around and put me to shame. This is a fitting punishment, and nothing you didn't impose on me."

Kianthe wanted to argue—but somehow, the words died on her lips. There wasn't anywhere pressing in Tawney to visit, nowhere more important than New Leaf Tomes and Tea. Nothing more important than ensuring Reyna wasn't worrying anymore.

So Kianthe sighed. "You are correct. As always."

"Excellent. Be glad I'm offering the option of tending to our customers. For a few days, Matild and I considered bed rest until fall." Now Reyna's eyes gleamed.

It was almost like . . . Reyna was turned on by this. By ordering the all-powerful Arcandor around, watching with pleasure as she acquiesced. It made Kianthe's heart pound, made her question if she was truly tired, or if they could accommodate a bit of physical activity tonight.

"Bed rest until fall. Hmm. Whatever would we do to pass that time . . ." Kianthe grinned, feeling more and more like her old self.

Reyna seized the opening, but not as she'd hoped. "Oh, sleep, certainly. Especially with the shop reopening tomorrow."

Back to work. Kianthe pouted.

Reyna pushed off her chair, pausing near Kianthe. She bent low, her lips brushing the mage's ear. "But I have a few other ideas, too. When you're up for it." And with a wink that told Kianthe she'd been *exactly* on point, Reyna strolled to the kitchen. "Another slice of cheesy bread, darling? I want you to enjoy your forced vacation."

"Trust me, I'm already enjoying this."

In the kitchen, Reyna chuckled. Her words were earnest, almost vulnerable. "I missed you. I'm glad you're feeling better."

Kianthe's heart fluttered, and she settled back in her chair to enjoy the warmth of the fire. "Me too, Rain." And the evening slipped away with good conversation, fabulous food, and exceptional company.

23

Reyna

The next day dawned bright, and Reyna prepped to open the shop for the first time in almost a week.

She placed the A-frame sign in the town square again, this time with *Grand Reopening—This Afternoon* penned below the directions. Several people had already passed by, peeking through the windows and offering support while Reyna wiped the outdoor tables. She relocated the vast array of gifts that cluttered the front of the barn inside, cutting their floor space while scenting the plant-filled oasis with new flowers—all of which were blooming days longer than they should have.

Kianthe slept through most of this prep work. The one time she appeared in the doorway, it was to remark, "Cleaning? This place is spotless."

Reyna wiped her brow, rearranging the free books in their lending shelf. "I cleaned while you were sick, but there's always more to do."

"Cleaned, as in *tidied,* or cleaned, as in *obsessively scrubbed*? Because I don't think I've ever seen that kettle gleaming before."

Kianthe nodded at the copper kettle perched on the burner, one eyebrow arched in exasperation.

"It kept me occupied." Reyna shrugged, and let the days where she'd paced anxiously, consumed sixteen books off their shelves, and yes, scrubbed every surface of the shop vanish from her mind.

No use dwelling on the past, after all.

Kianthe frowned, but trudged to bed soon after.

Reyna was baking when Gossley rapped on the barn's door. The boy carried a basket of medicinal tonics and a bottle of red wine. When she stepped aside to admit him, he hefted it. "Matild told me to bring these."

Reyna tucked the basket under her arm, leading him to the kitchen. He massaged his shoulder as he walked, which prompted her to ask: "Did you injure yourself?"

"Just sore." Gossley puffed long bangs out of his face. "Tarly's putting me to work. Blacksmithing is *hard*."

Reyna laughed. "There's a reason I left the family business, dear." Cya's fake backstory was alive and well, especially now that Matild and Tarly were privy to the truth. Tarly even offered to teach her the jargon so it'd be more convincing.

One day, she might take him up on it.

"How's Miss Kianthe?" Gossley turned out to be rather polite, once the goal of death and robbery had shifted. He retrieved a rag to wipe the tables. Reyna didn't bother telling him she'd already done that today, twice. She wanted their grand reopening to be perfect, even if Kianthe slept through it.

"She's recovering . . . slowly."

"She's the Arcandor," Gossley said, matter-of-fact.

Reyna stiffened. It wasn't a secret in Tawney anymore, but she hadn't considered how that would affect Cya's life, especially where Gossley was concerned. "Indeed." She waited, cautiously, patting dough for their daily scones.

Gossley chuckled. "Now I understand why you weren't worried about the debt collectors."

Reyna tried not to be offended by that.

The boy continued, bless his heart: "The Arcandor. I can't believe our boss got her on the payroll." He shook his head, then dove into the day's work.

Reyna had to duck into the storage room to hide her laughter.

✤

They opened to a huge crowd. Sasua was first in line, towing her boy behind her, smiling at Reyna. After the dragon attack, she seemed to fully accept the fact that Kianthe and Reyna cared for Tawney as much as she did. As a result, she'd loosened considerably around them.

She fished out two pents. "I've always wanted to try vanilla cacao tea. I have a bit of a sweet tooth."

Reyna laughed good-naturedly and collected the coin, then fired up her teakettle. "One day soon you'll have to test my chocolate croissants. They pair well with this tea."

Sasua's little boy grinned at the mention of chocolate, showing two missing teeth.

His mother, meanwhile, bounced on her heels. "I love to bake! Janice, Tawney's baker, is my best friend. We should raid her kitchen someday." Sasua paused, coloring. "Ah, not that *your* kitchen isn't wonderful—"

"It's hardly extravagant. True countertop space sounds divine." Reyna couldn't hide the pleasure in her voice. "Once Kianthe is back on her feet, I'll duck out for a baking day, all right?"

"Excellent," Sasua replied. With a promise of tea once it was done steeping, she and her son claimed the comfy armchairs beside the fireplace. Sasua promptly retrieved a children's book, inked with both words and painted images, and beckoned the boy to pay attention.

Reyna watched them, warmth in her chest. She'd never considered children, not seriously, but . . . perhaps someday. If Kianthe could ever sit still long enough to co-parent.

After that, Reyna lost herself in the morning rush. The line stretched, but people were patient, taking seats at the tables, booths, and armchairs, and perusing tomes while they waited. Gossley was Gods-sent, delivering the teas almost faster than Reyna could make them.

Lord Wylan appeared halfway through the day, removing his hat with a kind smile. Despite his amicable body language, several tables flinched away from him—same as they would to Queen Tilaine herself.

He really was fighting an uphill battle, especially with the Sheparan citizens so exasperated with Queendom policies. A flicker of disappointment was evident when a few people scooted away, clearing the space by the counter.

Still, he took the opening, sliding three pents across for a cup of tea and a blueberry scone. They'd just come out of the oven, scenting the air with sugar, and Reyna set one on a plate for him.

"How are things, Cya?" Her fake name fell off his tongue naturally.

Gratitude surged in her chest. "Bustling, and I'm quite relieved about it." It was nice, knowing he knew the truth, knowing he respected her for it. But behind him, people watched the lord like he was a rabid animal.

Either he didn't care about their opinions, or he tried not to. "And how's Kianthe? Still recovering?"

"She's feeling much better." Reyna paused, then asked, "Have you seen Diarn Feo lately? I have something to ask them, but they haven't visited since dropping off those two mages."

"Ask them . . . about Tawney?" Now Lord Wylan looked irritated. "I'm happy to help resolve any issues. You are a Queendom citizen, after all."

Those subtle hints were exactly why people didn't trust him, although she wouldn't say it aloud. She merely quirked an eyebrow. "My lord, I'm a *Tawney* citizen, and would appreciate the distinction. And furthermore, I'm allowed to address whomever I would like. It doesn't change my gratitude for your service."

He had the decency to look abashed. "Of course. My apologies. I haven't seen Feo."

He didn't use their title, she noted.

She pushed his mug and scone across the counter, then leaned forward, lowering her voice. "I have no intention of exploring Tawney without your knowledge, Lord Wylan. But I do believe Diarn Feo was right, and there is something to investigate."

Now he frowned. "There can't truly be an egg—"

"Kianthe says there are three. Although they may not be in Tawney anymore."

Lord Wylan stiffened, every muscle tensing. For a long moment, he was silent. Then he cursed under his breath. "Gods, Feo is going to be insufferable now. I suppose I *will* dig up my father's journal."

Reyna smiled serenely. "Excellent. I'll be in touch." Now she paused, glancing over his shoulder at the booths. "If you're hoping to earn ground over Diarn Feo, the first step is meeting your citizens. This shop is an excellent spot to socialize, and that particular booth has an opinionated mix of Sheparan and Queendom folk."

He cast a dubious glance their way. "I doubt they'd want my company."

"Depends on how you spend it." She flicked two fingers, indicating he should follow her, and led him to the booth. The occupants—the local tanner and his husband, and one of Tawney's string musicians—glanced at her in surprise.

Reyna smiled, gesturing at Lord Wylan. "It seems we've run out of seating today. Would you folk mind accommodating one more? It'd mean so much; after a week closed, we can't turn away patrons."

The subtle manipulation worked, and the musician hastily scooted over. "Take a seat, my lord." She was the Queendom citizen, and she stiffened like a child under a teacher's scrutiny. "We're always happy to socialize with a representative of Queen Tilaine."

It was false cheer. The Sheparan couple across the table grumbled, but couldn't say otherwise with Reyna standing so close.

Lord Wylan awkwardly sat down.

Reyna sighed, bending over the table. "It's worth mentioning that this shop isn't under Queen Tilaine's jurisdiction, any more than it belongs to the council in Wellia. We're neutral, and expect the same from our customers."

That made everyone relax, just a bit. Lord Wylan tilted his head. "Actually, while I have you three, I was wondering what your thoughts are on the rebuilding process after the attack. Is there something I can do to get people into their homes faster?"

That opened a torrent. All three exchanged eager glances, and opinions started flying. Reyna winked at Lord Wylan, then strolled back to the counter.

❧

The sun was setting, and their customers were clearing out when Reyna realized she hadn't seen Kianthe since they opened shop. She let Gossley take over the counter. Their assistant moved through the motions of cleaning the teakettle and steeping containers, and restocking teas for tomorrow.

Reyna ducked into her bedroom, only to find Kianthe both awake . . . and staring glumly out the back window. Their patio wasn't *that* interesting, but the mage didn't acknowledge when Reyna closed the door behind herself.

"Are you contemplating life, dragons, or me?" She added a teasing tone to her voice.

Kianthe heaved a sigh. "Oh, mostly regretting my choices."

"Gods forbid you're contemplating me, then."

"No," Kianthe yelped, realizing what she'd said. "Stars and Stone, no. But—I could hear people talking. They were expecting me to make an appearance, and I just . . . sat here. I've been awake for hours, too scared to face them."

Hmm. Reyna sat on the bed, shoulder to shoulder, and rested a comforting hand on the mage's thigh. "They want to thank you. That's all. Nothing you aren't familiar with."

"But this is different." Kianthe groaned, clawing through her messy hair. "They're going to ask me how I'm feeling. They're going to look at me with sympathy, with pity, because I was laid up for a week. They're going to wonder if the Arcandor is, in fact, all-powerful. And then they're going to realize I'm just . . . human."

Reyna opened her mouth, then reconsidered. Because the fact was people *did* expect the Arcandor to be all-powerful. The Mage of Ages was a beacon of hope, someone who protected the world when nothing else could. It was a lot of pressure to place on Kianthe's shoulders, especially while she was recovering.

"Key, what you did . . . ? If that isn't the definition of powerful, I'm not sure what can compete." Reyna leaned behind Kianthe, gently massaging her tense shoulders. "Do you feel like it wasn't enough?"

"Yes. Well, no. Maybe," Kianthe said.

"You want to know what I think?"

"No. Because you're going to spout logic, and I'd rather ruminate, thank you."

Reyna chuckled, pressing a kiss to the mage's temple. "You shouldn't carry the weight of inhuman expectations. You'll never meet them, because like it or not, you aren't the Stone of Seeing. You're just a person with a job, same as any of us."

Kianthe groaned. "That's what I've been telling you since we met."

"What can I say? Watching you vomit in a bucket reminded me."

The mage's cheeks colored, splotchy and red. "Are you ever going to let me forget that?"

"Mmm. It's proportionate to how idiotic you were, so . . . probably not." Reyna smirked, pushing to her feet. "Gossley's about to leave for the night, so I need to run a few drills with him outside. There are still some customers in the shop. I'm sure they'd love to see you."

She retrieved her sword, kissed Kianthe's forehead, and beckoned Gossley to the patio.

They were deep into the middle of their drills when Kianthe pushed off the bed and vanished from their window. For a brief moment, Reyna wondered if she was using the washroom, but long seconds passed and she didn't return.

Perhaps she had gone to greet their final customers. Reyna had utterly abandoned them, after all . . . but they'd closed the tea station for the evening, and she trusted her neighbors not to steal books without leaving the proper coin.

Distracted wondering about Kianthe, Reyna missed Gossley swinging his blade—a more appropriately sized piece, courtesy of an exasperated Tarly. The boy nicked her cheek with the sword, and everything seemed to stop. For a long moment, they simply stared at each other.

"I got you." Gossley sounded dazed. "*I got you.*"

Reyna wiped her skin, smearing a drop of blood over her fingers. Her heart dropped into her stomach. "So you did." The words were begrudging, filled with regret. She still couldn't give this boy a true "assignment," but . . . well, their deal was that when he bested her, he'd win her favor. And an envelope.

Shit. She shouldn't have gotten distracted.

"I let my guard down, and fair is fair." Her sword lowered to the ground, and she dipped her head in a slight bow. "You've won, Gossley."

The boy was still in shock. He stared at the tiniest drop of blood on her cheek, the tip of his sword, Reyna's lowered blade.

Then he took a physical step back, his jaw slack beneath that sad, fuzzy mustache.

"Well—" he stammered. "I don't really count that winning, see? You were watching Miss Kianthe through the window, and . . . given everything that happened this week, I think maybe you aren't at your best."

"I'm also not one to defend a loss," Reyna replied, sheathing her sword.

She didn't offer an envelope.

Gossley hesitated. "It doesn't count. In a fair fight, you're still leagues ahead, and—and I'm learning a lot, but not enough to beat you. Not yet. I think I need more time."

Relief smacked Reyna hard enough to make her laugh. She hid her shaking shoulders by retrieving a cup of water from the patio's table. "Even if you beat me, Gossley, you're welcome to remain in my employment. I still maintain that paying off debt the honest way is far more valuable in the long run."

Now he slouched, his sword brushing the stone tiles. "I got a letter while Miss Kianthe was recovering. Somehow, the debt collector found me at Mister Tarly's shop. He asked me to send everything I've earned so far, as promise of payment . . . but I don't think it'll be enough for his timeframe."

"Tracked you down, hmm?" Reyna contemplated him. She had some palidrons left, enough to pay off his debt if she chose. But rather than dropping coins at the problem, she was far more concerned with a debt collector locating this kid so quickly. "Your contact didn't have anything to do with that, did he? The one who sent you here in the first place?"

Gossley ran a finger over the leather grip of his sword. He had a proper sheath secured to his hip now, but he still looked very young. "Well, Branlen—the debt collector—has been in touch with my father for years. But he was the one who referred me to the bandit contact, yes."

There it was. Better to send a teenager on a death mission on the off chance they were paid faster, rather than wait for a decade or more for the kid to produce solid coin in an honest job. It wasn't the smartest collection mindset, but Reyna had seen it before.

She ran a finger over her own hilt, smiling slightly. "Well. If someone arrives in Tawney asking for you, send word for me, please. And if he visits the blacksmithing shop, ask Tarly for help."

She would have words with this debt collector, if he ever showed his face.

"And don't send him your coin. Something tells me it's wasted money."

"Yes, Miss Cya," Gossley said, brows knitted together. "If you think that's best."

Reyna patted his shoulder. "Everything I say is for the best. Now, get on home. I need to check on Kianthe."

When they stepped back inside the shop, swords sheathed and sweat drying on their faces—they returned to the Arcandor, Mage of Ages, actively discussing the unrealistic events of a new novel with one of Tawney's herbalists. The herbalist was laughing, and the other eavesdropping customers seemed more relieved than pitying.

Reyna smiled and sent Gossley on his way.

24

Kianthe

Kianthe was bored.

It was a dangerous thing, mistaking relaxation for boredom. But even for someone who loved her downtime, this was a bit ridiculous. The first week of conscious recovery, she slept more, spent a few hours every day socializing with their customers, and gradually rebuilt her tolerance to the world as the dregs of dragon magic trickled from her system.

It was difficult to accept gratitude from these people she viewed as neighbors. Sasua stopped by daily to purchase a mug of tea, read a book to her little boy, and ask Kianthe how she was feeling. Four days in, she squeezed Kianthe's arm and admitted, "The flames scorched our house. Right by my son's bedroom. If you hadn't been here . . ." She trailed off, drew a deep breath. "Thank you, Arcandor. I'm so glad you two moved in."

Across the barn, rearranging the empty spaces left by purchased books, Reyna winked.

"It's really nothing," Kianthe said.

"It's *everything*." Sasua left it there and escorted her son to the plush armchairs to read.

If they thought the shop was busy before, now it was bustling. People stopped by for tea, certainly, but the bookstore half couldn't be ignored. In fact, several customers arrived with book donations, stuffing the store's shelves to free space in their own homes. Most of the donated books were divvied into the lending center, but one evening after the shop had emptied, Reyna mused, "We should sell some of these. They're in excellent condition."

Kianthe slipped a bookmark into her most recent read—ironically, about a magic user who battled dragons—and replied, "What, like a 'resale' section?"

"Mmm. 'Used Books,' maybe."

Kianthe snorted. "All books are used."

Reyna ran her fingers along the spines of a few recent additions, shipped from Wellia in a standing order. They scented the air with leather oil and vellum, and Kianthe had already scoured them for her personal pleasure.

"The tomes from Wellia have never been read or owned." Reyna tilted her head. "We can charge more for them because of it."

"Yes, but it's not like a book that's been read is worth less. Labeling it 'used' makes it seem like no one rereads their novels." They'd found a healthy debate, and Kianthe was here for the distraction. She'd been planning to go to bed—she retired to the bedroom earlier than normal lately, and despite Reyna's earlier teasing, it wasn't for any *fun* reason—but this was intriguing.

"I don't reread novels," Reyna replied simply.

Scrap intriguing. Now Kianthe was horrified. "What? Ever? But—what if you find a favorite story? Don't you want to relive it?"

Reyna looked amused at her shock. "I find a new tome, one that makes me feel the same way. Rereading a book won't result in the same thrill, not when I already know how it ends."

Kianthe stared at her, jaw unhinged.

Reyna kissed the mage's hair, strolling into the kitchen to refill her mug. "You're gaping, dear."

"I'm rethinking my life choices, is what I'm doing."

"Ah. Do let me know what you determine." And this time, there wasn't a tremor of doubt in her words—just flat-out satisfaction.

Kianthe dropped the debate, craning over the chair to watch Reyna rummaging around the kitchen. She'd prepped the dough for tomorrow's scones, and was covering them in linen to store in the icebox while her tea steeped. Her hair fell over her shoulders, and a private smile tilted her lips—something she probably didn't even notice.

She was happy.

After a long moment, Reyna noticed Kianthe's eyes on her. She paused, teakettle in hand. "Love, when you stare like that, I wonder if a bug landed on me. Or if some wart appeared and sprouted fuzzy hairs on my face."

Kianthe didn't seize the distraction. Her voice was filled with wonder. "You're enjoying yourself here, aren't you?"

"Here, in the shop of our dreams? Living exactly as I've always wanted?" Reyna laughed. "Whatever are the odds of that?"

"No, I mean—that comment I just made, about rethinking my life choices. It was a joke, and always has been, but even last season, something like that would have made you doubt. You'd keep it quiet, pretend it didn't bother you, but it would. You'd wonder if there was truth to it."

That was why Kianthe kept poking, to be honest. Desensitization: the more she mentioned it, corrected Reyna's inaccurate response, the less it might affect Reyna next time. And maybe, eventually, her girlfriend would realize that while Kianthe was flaky, yes, and fleeting, sure, she was also committed to Reyna as a person and to the life they wanted together.

Reyna's cheeks colored. "I always tell you if something's bothering me."

"Eventually, sure. After days of self-doubt." Kianthe grinned. "But now, you aren't even questioning my humor. It's nice. No, it's *excellent*. It's like you finally believe me."

Reyna went silent, stirring honey into her tea. She inhaled

the scent, contemplative. "You're right . . . I suppose I was worried you'd leave after the Magicary discovered where you are. Or maybe something big would happen and the stress would tear us apart. Or—I don't know. Forever seems like a long time after short, passionate visits the last two years."

Kianthe shrugged. "Well, I do love that passion. But I like this more." When Reyna returned to her armchair, the mage captured her free hand. "Reyna. The last time I was injured, I awoke to six mages arguing over who'd be chosen as the next Arcandor. As if I'd already died. As if they might be gifted just by proximity."

"What?" Reyna stiffened, her face darkening like a winter storm. "Tell me you're joking."

Kianthe always tried to forget that day, forget the moment she realized she was worth more as the Arcandor than she'd ever been as Kianthe. The mages had seemed disappointed when the doctor said she'd make a full recovery.

Disappointed.

To this day, it filled her soul with anger—but beyond that, devastation. Like she was utterly worthless as a human being, utterly meaningless in the grand scheme of life. Maybe it was jealousy on the mages' part, or maybe she hadn't ingrained herself in their community, but it left her feeling very isolated.

"No one would have mourned me, before I met you." Kianthe's voice was quiet, her dark eyes holding Reyna's gaze. "They'd mourn the loss of an Arcandor, but they didn't give a Stone-blessed shit about me. No one would sit by my bedside for ages to make sure I was safe. Only you, Rain."

It was one of the most vulnerable things Kianthe had ever admitted. It made her heart pound, made her skin feel tight around her bones. She knew the confession was safe with Reyna, but she'd spent a lifetime hiding these feelings, and that was a tough habit to break.

Part of her wanted to laugh it off, flee the words.

She didn't.

Reyna didn't either. She set down her mug, dropped into Kianthe's lap, and hugged her tight.

"You've done everything for me, too, Key, and I love you for it. Fuck them all. We'll just have to take care of each other." The passion in her voice, the way she swore, was like an inferno consuming the world with dangerous promise.

Kianthe hugged her back and wondered if it was too soon to propose.

❋

Three days later, Reyna deemed Kianthe well enough to survive a few hours alone. When Kianthe asked where she was going, she merely smiled and replied, "Dear, I'm allowed to run errands without your knowledge. Some things are better left to mystery."

"Well, that only makes me want to know *more*."

Reyna patted her shoulder, utterly unconcerned. She set Gossley in charge of the shop, told Kianthe to "supervise, but not at the expense of rest," and left.

She didn't take her sword, so that was comforting. And yet, Kianthe's chest tightened at the idea of Venne and Tilaine's spies prowling Tawney, setting their sights on Reyna, stealing her away to the Capital to atone for her crimes—

Ugh.

She busied herself with recommending books to a few teenagers who visited with their parents' coin, offering a free book to the carpenter's daughter—who had, indeed, become a regular here—and critiquing the way Gossley brewed tea.

"No, you divide the leaves into these linen bags, then steep *that* in the water. Not the kettle itself, young gosling, or you'll poison it with opposing flavors."

Gossley set his jaw, scowling at her. For such a quiet kid, he truly had a spark of fight. "Miss Cya said you were supposed to rest."

Kianthe waved a hand. "Luckily, the Arcandor has no keeper."

"Pity," Gossley muttered, and turned his back on her. But he did adjust how he was steeping the tea, fumbling to tie twine knots around the bags of linen.

Kianthe supervised for several more hours before realizing she wasn't needed, and glumly retreating to a table against one of the barn's front windows. She fluffed the leaves of a cheery poinsettia, her yellow magic swathing the plant in nutrients and a directive. The flowers bloomed a deeper crimson than naturally possible, striving to please.

It was nice, using magic again.

Kianthe left the table and began making rounds, checking the health of every plant in the barn. Turned out, Reyna hadn't been lying when she said they might die under her care. It was obvious an attempt was made, but she'd overwatered the cactus and underwatered the ferns, and utterly ignored the metal mister bottles Kianthe had left for the tropical plants.

While she checked a spider plant beside a pair of older women, one pushed spectacles up her nose and tutted. "I love coming here. These plants you keep are lovely, Kianthe. This barn looks like a greenhouse."

Her friend nodded eagerly, her Queendom accent thick when she spoke. "Nothing like greenery to liven a space. If I didn't have such a black thumb, I'd ask to take a few home! But my husband would be so exasperated if I killed another." She chuckled good-naturedly, but regret was obvious on her features.

Kianthe paused. Even before the Stone had blessed her, she'd never had an issue keeping plants alive. Now she stroked the tall leaves of the spider plant contemplatively.

"So, you're saying you'd like a houseplant, if you knew how to care for it." This made her sad; everyone should be able to enjoy greenery in their space. "I could teach you."

"A lesson from the Arcandor?" The Queendom woman's eyes widened. "They said you were brave. They never said you were generous, too."

Kianthe shifted awkwardly. It had been fun to play the arrogant mage before, but was another thing entirely to face true admirers now. "It's really nothing. I just think you should be able to have a plant, if you want one."

Her friend snorted, a shocking sound from a sweet old woman. "Oh Stars, even a lesson wouldn't save me. There isn't enough magic in all the countries of the Realm. It's just too cold a climate, and our houses are either scalding or freezing. Poor dears would never stand a chance."

The Queendom citizen patted Kianthe's hand. "That, and our memories! If I'm not forgetting to water them, I'm forgetting that I already did."

The two women laughed their age away and switched topics. Kianthe wandered to the next plant, but now she squinted at the very fabric of its magic. All things, living and not, were woven with it—pinpricks of light that gleamed under a practiced eye. Her magic encouraged these plants to thrive, but once they'd accomplished that, the magic recessed, moving on to other things.

If she took the barest hint of magic, however, just a pinprick in the fabric of everything, she might be able to extend a plant's life. Coat the leaves with shining yellow, seed a flower's petals and soil with it. Houseplants that never died, even if one forgot to water, even if the climate wasn't quite right.

Greenery for anyone to enjoy, anytime.

After all, magic was timeless. A human lifetime spent tied to a few plants would be nothing at all. It'd just take the right combination of spells . . .

Kianthe was pondering that as the barn's door opened, and Harold and Allayan stepped inside. Both mages looked worse for the wear; she'd honestly thought they'd returned to Wellia or the Magicary by now, somewhere with a true convergence of ley lines. But apparently they'd given her enough magic to require extensive time in bed themselves.

Guilt prickled her chest, and she forced a smile. "Gentlepeople, welcome. Good to see you up and about."

A few customers craned their necks to see who the Arcandor was addressing, but without their mages' robes, the visitors were nothing special.

In case they'd stopped by on official business, Kianthe waved them toward the bedroom. "We can chat in here. Did you want tea? Reyna made scones before she left. Buttermilk and blueberry."

Allayan nodded vigorously, eyes wide. "I'm quite hungry."

"I'll wait until we return to civilization." Harold sniffed.

Kianthe snorted, fixed Allayan a healthy plate, and led them into the bedroom. She asked Gossley if he could handle the shop, but he'd already waved her off and was greeting a new customer, so she shut the door.

Allayan cheerfully took the biggest scone and perched at the desk, sinking their teeth into the firm treat. "This smells incredible." They paused, glancing over their shoulder. "Ah, I hope you're feeling better, Arcandor."

"I am," Kianthe replied, her lips quirking upward. "And before you ask, *Master* Harold, I'm not going back to the Magicary."

Harold spluttered, his face reddening.

Allayan ducked their head. "Told you." The taunt was barely audible.

"You are the Arcandor." Harold scowled. "Do you truly believe the Zenith Mages will accept you playing house in some country town? You have been gifted a true responsibility, and you'd squander it here?"

The Zenith Mages. Kianthe's nose wrinkled. There wasn't a hierarchy in the Magicary, not really. There were old mages (the Zenith) who felt they knew best, young mages (like Allayan) who often did know best, and middling mages (Harold) who loathed them all. Technically, the Arcandor commanded them, a mouthpiece for their deity. But the Stone of Seeing never spoke, except through magical nudges to the Arcandor—and thus the Magicary constructed itself around the whims of a mage who, historically, wasn't the most mature of the bunch.

There was an alchemical equivalent—ish—to the Arcandor, but they were historically . . . ah, how to put this delicately?

Reclusive jackasses.

Come to think of it, no one complained when the current Alchemicor left the Magicary to take solace in the Vardian Mountains of Shepara. Suddenly, Kianthe felt very spiteful about it.

"How have I squandered it, Harold? Please, enlighten me."

"You ignore the summons—"

"The summons of mages, yes. The summons of our venerated Stone? Absolutely not." Kianthe crossed her arms. "Are you telling me that your superiors know more about the Stone of Seeing's whim than me?"

At the desk, Allayan's shoulders were shaking with laughter.

Harold's lips pinched into a thin line. "I have no superiors. But there are murmurs at the Magicary about your dedication. And frankly, after Allayan and I gifted you our magic, I do feel we're owed an explanation. Are you here by our blessed Stone's command, or are you here because your significant other offered a life you couldn't refuse?"

Deep bags hung under his eyes, and he still looked sickly. At the desk, Allayan seemed a little better, but the magic drain had taken a toll on them both. They'd helped in a time of desperate need. Which meant, much as she was loath to admit it, Harold wasn't wrong.

Kianthe sighed, pinching her nose.

"The answer is yes, Harold. Both. All. I'm loyal to the Stone . . . but Reyna is everything to me. She's also a Queendom citizen. The Magicary would never accept her, even if I muscled her through the gates, and she'd be miserable if I tried. So, we've picked Tawney as a middle ground. You may report to the Zenith that I'm here, and I will respond for duties as required." Harold opened his mouth, but she silenced him with a hand. "But I'm staying. And no one can force me to leave."

"There's no magic here," Harold snapped. "How can you choose this place as a base of operations?"

Allayan cleared their throat.

Kianthe gestured for them to continue, because she'd rather be chatting with them than Harold.

Allayan had absolutely devoured both scones, and now they pointed at the plate. "This was wonderful. And there's almost certainly a reason this ley line is so weak. A whole forest grew southwest of here—there *must* have been magic at some point."

Kianthe raised an eyebrow, because they were right. She felt kind of silly she hadn't considered that before.

"Well, I'll explore it. But I need to puzzle through a mystery first. Actually, if you can check the Magicary archives for any mention of dragon eggs stolen—maybe thirty years ago?—that'd be very helpful to my Arcandor-ly duties." Now she set a pointed look at Harold.

But Harold dragged the conversation back to its starting point. "Your partner is a Queendom citizen. And based on her accent, it's obvious she's from the inner palace itself."

Now Kianthe went ramrod straight. "Tread carefully here, Harold. I'm not so indebted that I won't bury you in the earth for speaking ill of her."

"I'm not the one forgetting my place in the world. The Magicary resides in Shepara, but mages are *neutral* entities. We exist in every country peacefully, even if we aren't born within the Queendom. You should be the most impartial of us all. What will happen when Queen Tilaine realizes one of her citizens has earned your favor?"

At the desk, Allayan frowned.

Before, when Reyna and Kianthe fantasized about how they could reveal their relationship to the world, Reyna always pointed out that Tilaine would take any advantage she could. If lavish parties didn't gain the Arcandor's favor, one of her private guards might be the perfect plant.

But Reyna always expected she'd sweet-talk, use gifts and fancy titles, elevate Reyna to the status of court folk—woo one to persuade the other. That was before Reyna fled the Capital, before she became a traitor to the crown.

Now, if Queen Tilaine got her hands on Reyna, it'd be a completely different story. Violence. Blackmail. Kianthe already knew she'd be vulnerable. She'd never do anything to put Reyna at risk.

"You hadn't even considered that, had you?" For once, Harold didn't seem smug or arrogant. He just sounded disappointed. "Tilaine is brutal, Kianthe. Imagine what she could do with an Arcandor's power."

"She'll never get it," Kianthe snapped.

But fear clenched her chest regardless.

The older mage heaved an irate sigh, massaging his brow. A long moment passed. "I have to trust you know what you're doing, Kianthe. Either way, we won't be around to watch. Allayan, are you ready?" He barely waited for a nod before sweeping past Kianthe and out the bedroom door.

"I like your girlfriend, for what it's worth," Allayan said, handing Kianthe the plate.

"It's worth quite a lot. Thank you."

Allayan offered a smile and followed Harold outside. When Kianthe composed herself enough to step back into the bookstore, their griffons had already landed in the street. The two mages mounted and were gone.

Hopefully Reyna would be home soon.

To distract herself, Kianthe went back to her houseplants. She could get this spell right; she just knew it. An ever-life spell. Perhaps an adjustment on her ever-flame . . .

While she mused, the hours drifted away.

25

Reyna

Diarn Feo lived in a compound.

It was rather unimpressive, and quite large for one person. Multiple buildings clustered behind a single wooden fence, which had charred in certain places from the dragon attacks. A few people milled on the street, but none stepped through the open gate except Reyna. She passed by a wilting garden—if Kianthe were here, she'd be scowling at the mistreatment, especially with the warming weather and planting season in full swing—and a few empty barracks.

This place must have housed soldiers, once upon a time. Maybe it had existed since the dragons awoke, before the lines of dragon country were defined. The buildings looked old enough.

She approached the only closed door and rapped on it. The weather was brisk now, bright and cheery, and she basked in the sunshine as she waited for Diarn Feo's answer.

"Enter," they called.

She stepped into a cozy office, with Diarn Feo perched behind a huge desk, hunched over parchment. They glanced up, did a double take, and reluctantly set down their quill. "Did Kianthe take a turn?"

It might have sounded callous, but concern was evident in the set of their mouth. It made Reyna far more amicable toward them.

She shook her head. "She's still doing well. Resting, mostly."

"Ah."

Silence stretched between them.

Reyna crossed her arms. "I'm here for a related reason. It would appear when Kianthe was fighting the dragons, she made a deal. A bindment, she called it. To hunt for three missing dragon eggs in Tawney."

That got their attention. They shoved to their feet, eyes alight. "I knew it! I knew there was a reason for the attack. Who stole them? Was it Wylan's father?"

The timing was serendipitous.

A sharp knock rapped on the open door, and Lord Wylan breezed inside. He was dressed in a loose-fitting shirt and black pants, and plucked a three-pointed hat off his head. "No, but you'd love that, wouldn't you?"

Diarn Feo's eyes raked Wylan's form. It was barely a second, but they definitely gave the young lord a once-over. Reyna stepped aside, her lips quirking in amusement.

"I would, in fact. It'd give me every right to seize command for the betterment of Tawney, and not even your citizens could deny it." Diarn Feo puffed their chest.

Lord Wylan pinched his brow. "This was a bad idea."

Diarn Feo looked between them, eyebrows raised.

"I summoned Lord Wylan to accompany us. Kianthe mentioned a church in the burnt half of town. I wouldn't mind touring it, just to ensure we haven't missed something. The Arcandor shouldn't be bound to dragons; it puts the world at risk. We need to resolve this quickly, and that means our goals align."

"Mine will never align with his," Diarn Feo muttered.

Lord Wylan gestured, as if to say: *Do you see what I put up with?*

Gods, this was going to be a *day*. Reyna suddenly wished she were back home, serving tea alongside Kianthe. But first things first. She beckoned them out of the building, and together, the three of them headed for the east side of town.

Walking with the two leaders was a surreal experience. The townsfolk didn't seem to know how to handle a unified front. Whispers scorched their backs as they trekked through Tawney.

But the town was small, and it didn't take long to arrive at the old church. Ash tainted the air with an acrid scent. The dragons had once again hit this area hard, and several buildings that had previously stood were now splintered wood and charred stone. Diarn Feo huffed. "Incredible how this building is still standing. Almost magical." They cast a sideways glance at Lord Wylan, their tone nearly insufferable.

Lord Wylan scowled. "Yes, yes. You were right. Shall we resolve a decades-old dispute, or stand here bickering?"

Reyna snorted and delved into the ruins. She had to climb over a fallen beam, pick through religious pamphlets and trash that littered the floors, but eventually the entrance area opened into a wide space not unlike their barn. She squinted through huge holes in the ceiling, then noticed Diarn Feo had dropped to their knees at a specific point in the center of the room.

"Here's where Kianthe felt the magic. There must be something below. We could dig, but . . . it sounded like it was deep."

"Hmm." Reyna prowled the space, squinting at old tomes and abandoned statues. The Grand Palace was layered with secret passageways, and she'd become an expert at finding them. Queen Tilaine's great-grandmother had burned every map detailing their locations, so the palace guards were left creating their own internal records to counter threats. More than once, an assassin got close to Her Excellency simply because her guards hadn't known about an ancient passageway.

Now she put those skills to work, feeling for airflow where there shouldn't be any, casually testing statues for false bottoms, leaning her weight against walls and doorways to see if they gave under the pressure.

A bit dangerous in a building about to collapse, but Reyna didn't stop.

Lord Wylan was the only one who hadn't moved from the doorway. Instead, he tugged a thin leather-bound book from his bag, flipping to a bookmarked page. While Diarn Feo felt the floor and Reyna checked the room, he remarked: "There's a staircase somewhere. Stone, lined with old candles. My father inspected the room when it was built, before they put the church on top of it."

Reyna paused. "Is that Lord Julan's journal?"

"He admitted to stealing the eggs, didn't he?" Diarn Feo asked smugly.

Lord Wylan rolled his eyes. "Nothing of the sort. He didn't know about the dragon eggs, if they were stolen under his watch at all."

"They were."

Lord Wylan pointedly ignored the diarn, reread the journal, then strolled to a small room divided from the church with an ornate wooden lattice. Reyna knew from traveling with Her Excellency that it was common practice in Shepara—not with the mages, who worshiped the Stone of Seeing, but the majority of the other citizens—to confess perceived sins to their divine Stars in rooms like that. Traditionally, that area alone was fitted with a glass ceiling, for better communion with the sky.

Now, Lord Wylan ran his fingers along the seams of the room. It was too small for more than one person, so Diarn Feo and Reyna peered over his shoulders.

Reyna finally spoke. "Look for a loose stone in the floor, or somewhere the grout has worn away."

Lord Wylan shifted his attention to the floor—and with a bit of digging, one of the stones did indeed come loose. It revealed a metal handle, which he pulled. Everyone held their breath as something heavy thudded into place behind them. One of the wooden panels behind the altar had dropped, revealing a dark staircase descending into the earth.

Diarn Feo had lost their haughtiness amidst the thrill of discovery. They were the first to the passageway, peering deep into the darkness. "Did anyone bring a candle? Or an Arcandor who can create fire?"

"This might sound fallacious, but a mage isn't the only one able to create fire." Reyna shook her head, plucked a torch from her bag, and lit the wick with a match. "Let me." She stepped in front of the lords, brandishing the torch, one hand on the dagger hidden in the folds of her shirt.

Slowly, they descended, taking the stone steps carefully in case of decay. The air was damp, and quickly chilled. Cobwebs lined the corners, dark spiders skittering out of their path when the firelight hit. The air was scented with mold and rat droppings, and the passage tightened until they had to move single file.

The hushed silence was broken when Lord Wylan asked, "Why do you want this town at all, Feo? What does Tawney have that's so interesting to you?"

Reyna almost said, *It has you, my lord,* but she doubted Diarn Feo would appreciate that.

Diarn Feo huffed, their boots scuffing on a loose stone. "It's a cultural phenomenon. Two countries enmeshed, each allowed to peacefully worship their chosen deities, untouched by policies from the governments that claim ownership." Their voice was tinted with wonder and respect. "Tawney is proof that prejudice can be overcome. It's proof that your home country, your hometown, your home values . . . they don't have to define you."

Wow. Reyna wasn't expecting something so profound. She almost craned her neck to look at Feo's face, but wasn't willing to trip down the staircase to do it.

"Huh," Lord Wylan said. Long moments passed, and he begrudgingly added, "That's exactly how I feel."

"Then we can agree on something," Diarn Feo replied curtly.

A short while later, they arrived at a wooden door. Reyna signaled for them to stop, wait while she tested the handle. She handed the torch to Lord Wylan, then slid a wicked-looking knife from its sheath with a smooth *schwick*.

"*Where* were you hiding that?" Diarn Feo muttered.

Reyna shot them a silencing glance, then pushed open the door. The room beyond was empty—which she expected, mostly—and must not have been touched in decades. Heavy dust settled on both a desk and chair, as well as an old chest in the corner. Everything was dark and cold and eerily quiet. The floor was dirt, the ceiling and walls were stone, and as far as she could tell, it was a dead end.

She sheathed the knife and moved inside, only to be wrenched backward by Diarn Feo. Instinct had her spinning, nearly slamming them to the wall, but they raised their hands placatingly.

"Wait. There's magic here."

"Yes, dragon magic." Reyna forced herself to relax.

"No. Alchemical. Look here." Diarn Feo pointed at the dirt. A huge circle had been drawn around the wooden chest. It was rimmed with rust-red dirt, almost like someone had infused the circle with blood.

After a lifetime with Queen Tilaine, Reyna wasn't unfamiliar with blood . . . and yet, seeing it in an alchemical circle sent a chill up her spine. No wonder Kianthe scorned this magic as unnatural.

She crossed her arms, but didn't move from the doorway. "What were they trying to accomplish?"

For a long moment, Diarn Feo perused the edges of the circle. They didn't step over the marks, didn't try to reach the chest. "It's a displacement spell, but modified. Fairly ingenious. These indicators at the circle's edge directed the spell to drain the natural magic from something—the dragon eggs, most likely—and store that magic here."

"In the chest?" Lord Wylan asked, risking a step closer. He peered over Diarn Feo's shoulder.

The diarn waved him off. "No. The magic is kept within the spell's circle, but there's no height limit. Kianthe probably felt it directly above us, and the dragons targeted this area of town because of the magical signature." They scratched something into the circle, then held out a hand. "Girlfriend, your knife, if you will?"

Reyna rolled her eyes. "I won't."

"Her name is Cya," Lord Wylan said stiffly.

"Actually, her name is Reyna, but it's wholly unimportant to this topic," Diarn Feo retorted, which caused both Queendom citizens to stiffen. They realized it, raised one eyebrow. "Did you honestly believe I wouldn't keep tabs on the Arcandor's significant other? Or that I don't keep a running tally of who's truly visiting my town?"

"My town," Lord Wylan muttered.

"*Our* town," Reyna corrected.

Diarn Feo waved a hand. "Regardless, you're a risk now—staying so close to the Queendom means you could be attacked anytime. Have you thought about applying for immunity with the council?"

Reyna felt a hundred years old. "It won't stop her spies."

"You might be surprised. Immunity is a rare offering, gifted to only the most important dignitaries." Diarn Feo shrugged a shoulder. "Attacking someone the council has approved is akin to an act of war. I'd be shocked if Tilaine risked it."

A glimmer of hope, but Reyna wasn't optimistic enough to fall for it headfirst. She set her cautionary walls in place and diverted attention. "Perhaps. Either way, my blade is poisoned. Trust me when I say you won't want it."

They heaved a long-suffering sigh and slashed their finger

against a sharp stone instead. Blood welled, and Lord Wylan winced, but Diarn Feo was already squeezing their finger over their new additions to the alchemical circle. The blood splattered to the dirt, flared with sickly red magic, and faded just as fast.

Diarn Feo nodded, then stepped into the circle and safely opened the chest.

"Well?" Reyna asked.

"Empty." They sounded immensely disappointed, something she understood intimately.

Already, her mind was whirling. Kianthe still owed the dragons their eggs . . . if they weren't even in Tawney, how far would the mage have to travel to track them down? It wrenched Reyna's soul, knowing Kianthe would be trapped by this bindment for much longer than she'd expected.

"It's obvious the eggs were here. Three imprints, packed in straw." The diarn began rifling through the chest, as if the eggs might appear with a bit of blind hope. "They must not have a magical signature, not after this spell. Once they trapped the dragon magic, they were free to transport the eggs like normal cargo."

"Excellent." Lord Wylan massaged his forehead. "Then they could be anywhere."

Reyna examined the remainder of the room. There were a few papers left on the desk, each blocked with several numbers and destinations: shipping ledgers. That could prove useful if they timed the abandonment of this room with a shipment out of Tawney.

Otherwise, there wasn't anything here. Just the magical circle, which Diarn Feo was carefully stepping out of, and the now-empty desk.

Reyna waved the papers. "Perhaps with Lord Wylan's family journals and Diarn Feo's bookkeeping, we can decode these ledgers and discover where the shipment went."

Diarn Feo reached for the files, but she stepped out of reach. They huffed. "I can't help without studying those."

"This requires teamwork, Diarn Feo." Reyna set her jaw, and her glare was fierce enough to make the diarn pause. "Kianthe can't scour the Realm looking for ancient dragon eggs, and I won't let our only lead be damaged or destroyed because of your petty arguments. Now, I want a promise before I hand these off. Will you two cooperate?"

Lord Wylan snorted.

The pair of them seemed to forget who held the weapons here. Reyna's voice was stern, unwavering. "I repeat. Will you two co-operate?"

Diarn Feo and Lord Wylan exchanged glances.

Finally, Lord Wylan tugged out his father's journal and offered it to the diarn. "For the good of Tawney and the Arcandor, I'll do anything I can to help. My estate is open to you, Feo. I have an extensive library you may find useful."

Diarn Feo grumbled, snatching the book. "Fine. I'll report to your home first thing tomorrow for . . . collaboration."

Kianthe would have a field day with *that,* if she were here.

Reyna smiled and handed Lord Wylan the papers. "There we go. Now, my girlfriend will be wondering where I am. Please keep me informed when you determine the dragon eggs' next destination."

"Do you think this is going to happen at the snap of our fingers?" Diarn Feo rolled their eyes. "We're following a decades-old paper trail. None of this will be fast, Reyna. Did the dragons give Kianthe a deadline?"

"Nothing pressing for now." Reyna hesitated, wincing. "The bigger concern may be Queen Tilaine, with Venne poking around Tawney. Were you serious about that immunity, Diarn Feo?"

To their credit, the diarn's gaze was determined. "I don't say things if I'm not serious. We can't risk you getting hurt—or pulling anyone in town into an unintentional battle."

Reyna contemplated that. "Then that should be our next step. Let me know what to expect."

"A visit to Wellia, at minimum, to be presented before the council." Diarn Feo glanced at Lord Wylan. "Offering sponsorship for this is an official stake on my role as Tawney's diarn. If a council representative comes knocking, you may have to admit I hold at least some power in this town, or Reyna could be at risk."

"Sneaky," Lord Wylan drawled.

Diarn Feo smirked.

Gods, it felt like Reyna was back in the Grand Palace all over again. She breathed a sigh and said, "Let me speak with Kianthe. In the meantime, get working on that paper trail. Even if it's a lengthy search, we have to at least prove we're taking steps. Now, if you'll excuse me, I'd like a nice cup of tea."

She left them deep underground.

26

Kianthe

"You went looking for the eggs?" Kianthe said, exasperated.

It was early morning; usually the mage preferred to sleep a few hours past this point. But Reyna was up baking the day's goods—fresh cookies this time, the thick, sugary scent weighing the air like a warm blanket—and Kianthe didn't want to miss the chance of tasting them hot out of the oven. So, she leaned against the counter, watching Reyna scoop the next batch of dough from a metal bowl.

Her girlfriend waved a hand. "I followed the lead so you could rest. That's all."

"I'm feeling a lot better," Kianthe said, almost petulant. "I wanted to see the creepy underground room."

"It hasn't gone anywhere, love."

Kianthe pouted. "But now you're busy here, and the mystery's been solved."

Reyna chuckled. "Well, we'll just have to wait for the next clue, won't we?" Then she paused, slipping thick mitts on her hands. "You said it wasn't pressing, but I think we need to know. How long before the dragons get impatient?"

Kianthe read the underlying concern. "Aww. You're worried about me."

"Key, from the day we met, you've worried me." Reyna plucked the tray of unbaked cookies off the counter, disappearing into the storage room for a moment. Seconds later, she emerged with a freshly baked batch, setting the second tray on a few thick cotton squares so it didn't burn their wood counter.

Kianthe reached for one, and Reyna slapped her hand. "Let them cool."

"I'm the Arcandor."

"As far as I can tell, your magic doesn't extend to cookies." Reyna pinched her brow. "Gods, you have the patience of a five-year-old. Will the dragons inspect your progress? Is Tawney in imminent danger? Are *you*?"

Kianthe swallowed a yawn, hunching over her tea. Reyna chose a yerba maté to wake her up, and tossed a few cacao bits into the leaves. The result was a strong earthen flavor with a hint of sweetness. It'd pair perfectly with a cookie.

"Dragons live so long we can't even quantify their lifespans. Trust me when I say that I could feasibly procrastinate for decades before they come to collect on that bindment." At the bold statement, remnants of dragon magic pulsed, turning her stomach, making her wince. She glared at her chest, at the last tinge of blue dragon magic tinting her reservoir. "Don't start with that. I'm not going to."

Reyna seemed to realize that the second part of her statement wasn't directed at her, because she rolled her eyes and began sliding cookies onto a cooling tray. "Well, after the council grants me immunity, I'd feel better if we prioritized it."

"You really think immunity will stop Queen Tilaine?" Anxiety twisted in Kianthe's chest, and she drew a slow breath to stop the physical response.

Reyna noticed. Her tone was gentle. "It's a step. Better than sitting here, hoping Venne doesn't grow wise. Anywho, regarding the dragons. Lord Wylan and Diarn Feo are conferring, and if they find something, I'm prepared to—"

"Wylan and Feo are *conferring*, now?" Kianthe seized the conversation change, her grin turning wicked. "Whatever happened below that church?"

Reyna offered a knowing smirk. "Nothing like a good mystery to attract opposites." Then she finally set a cookie on a plate and pushed it toward Kianthe. The mage squealed in delight and began picking it apart—hot, *hot*—when someone banged on the door.

"An early customer?" Kianthe craned her neck to look, but whoever it was didn't step toward the windows.

"Or another bandit." Reyna casually picked up her sword. Considering she was wearing a kitchen apron, it was a true mishmash of attire, but somehow Reyna made even that look threatening. She strolled to the barn door and wrenched it open. "We're closed; you'll—Oh, Matild!"

The midwife crossed her arms. "Morning, all. You two better get down to the smithy. Tarly's holding a visitor for your kid."

"We don't have a kid," Kianthe said. "Do we?"

Reyna barely missed a beat. "Gossley, dear."

"Ah. Must have missed the moment we finalized the adoption." Kianthe pushed away from the counter, testing her magic. Nearly replenished—even the sad little ley line pulsed at her feet, as if anticipating a fight. "What the hells. I'll defend anyone who does the dishes, if we're being honest. Rain, permission to break house arrest?"

Reyna hummed, removing her apron. Deft fingers tied the scabbard to her belt, then rested on the sword's hilt. "Permission granted. But don't overdo it, or I'll let Matild choose your punishment."

"How do you feel about tilling my garden?" The midwife's lips curled into a devious smile.

"I feel like that's a euphemism."

Matild cackled. "Quite possibly."

Reyna snorted, ducked into the storage room to remove the most recent batch of cookies, and quelled the oven's fire. That handled, they locked up shop and strolled into town.

It was almost warm this morning; summer in Tawney was a pleasant surprise. The sun shone bright overhead, and there was fresh local produce flooding the farmers' market. They passed by a few merchants setting up shop, waving at some of their regulars.

"After this, remind me to visit Patol's stand. He has some fresh honey for the shop," Reyna mused, as if they weren't on their way to threaten or maim a "visitor."

Kianthe patted her back. "Anything you want, love."

Matild led them to her husband's shop, which had an ominous "CLOSED" sign hanging on the door. She went right in, holding the door open for them both. Then she latched it, the iron lock sliding into place with a final-sounding *thunk*.

Inside, Gossley was standing awkwardly beside a ladder to an elevated wooden platform, one he'd been using as a loft. Across from him, Tarly glowered at their visitor. To the stranger's credit, Tarly's massive muscles didn't seem to alter his easygoing stance. The man—a thin, bearded fellow with skin like ash—lounged on a hard wooden chair, acting like it was immensely comfortable and not at all required by his captor.

"What the forge is going on here?" Kianthe said.

For a moment, everyone just stared.

"You've been waiting to use that, haven't you?" Reyna pinched the bridge of her nose.

Kianthe shrugged. "Maybe."

"I thought it was funny." The visitor in the chair offered a sleazy smile, one that made Tarly scowl even deeper. He ignored the blacksmith, offering a hand. "Name's Branlen. I'm Gossley's mentor, so to speak."

"And here I thought we were his mentors," Kianthe drawled.

Reyna stepped forward, shaking the man's hand. She moved

like she was born with a sword at her hip—which, to be fair, she might have been. Branlen's eyes fell to the blade, but his casual expression didn't falter.

"It's a pleasure. I'm Cya. That's my partner, Kianthe. Gossley has been helping us at our shop, so I'm a bit confused at your statement." Reyna smiled, her voice silky smooth. "Are you related to Gossley?"

"I'm more of a family friend."

At the ladder, Gossley raised a hand. "Miss Cya, this is the debt collector."

Kianthe stepped forward so she was shoulder to shoulder with Reyna. A unified front. "Oh, right. You're the kind of 'family friend' who pressures a teenager to repay his father's bad gambling debts."

"An orphan, dear. You forgot that he's an orphan." Reyna's voice was deceptively lighthearted.

Disappointment flickered on Branlen's face. He sighed, leaning back in the chair like he *could* stand, even with Tarly looming, but chose not to bother. "Gossley's father understood the arrangement when he borrowed from me. And I'm not an unreasonable man. Gossley's had time to earn his keep."

"I have a few sils—" Gossley said at the ladder.

"Quiet, gosling. The adults are speaking."

The boy scowled, but clamped his mouth shut.

Meanwhile, Reyna chuckled, and the sound evolved into a bold laugh. It cut through the tense atmosphere, finally breaking Branlen's easygoing attitude. Unease slid into his features, gone in a flash.

"I love a good joke," he said pointedly.

Reyna squeezed his shoulder, never breaking that pretty smile. "Oh, that's because you are one."

Kianthe nearly snorted. It was like watching a carnivorous plant: bright colors, cheerful optimism, beneath which lurked something far more sinister.

Her girlfriend continued: "Gossley doesn't belong to you anymore. His father's debts will be paid, but they'll be paid to us, not you."

"Now see here—" Branlen started.

Her grip tightened on his shoulder, enough to make him wince and break off. "Didn't you hear my partner? The adults are speaking." She paused, offering Branlen the ability to interject. He didn't. She removed her hand, patting his cheek. "Good boy."

Heat washed down Kianthe's body. A lifetime of servitude had cracked at the seams, and Reyna was obviously enjoying the control that emerged. It was sexy as hells, and the mage struggled to keep a straight face.

Reyna ignored her, focused on this act. "Now, Branlen. Some time ago, you entangled Gossley in a bandit ring. Isn't that right? You referred him to Tawney, to our barn, for a less-than-legal assignment."

Branlen stiffened. "Everything I do is legal in the Queendom. The papers of his debt were signed by the lord of—"

"Oh my, there's been a miscommunication. You seem to think we care about that."

"We don't," Kianthe added, just because Reyna was having far too much fun without her.

Reyna sighed, trailing around his chair. "The moment Gossley followed your instruction and met us, he was lost to you. Because you see, dear, this bandit ring is a tight-knit group with even tighter control, and our supervisor has taken a liking to young Gossley."

"You're a smart man. You can see where she's going with this." Kianthe smirked.

At the door, Matild hid a smile. Tarly was wholly in character, never wavering in his stance. Gossley, who believed Reyna's words were true, hunched under Branlen's questioning stare.

Finally, the debt collector craned his neck to look at Reyna. "Look. I'm only here for the palidrons. A woman of your stature, operating within such a profitable ring? Surely you can weigh the risks."

She laughed again. All the while, her fingers brushed his shoulder, the back of his neck, her touch featherlight. She bent to his ear, but unlike when she whispered to Kianthe, her tone now was cruel.

"Oh, but why would we pay you, when you so carelessly wandered into our territory?"

He shuddered at her breath, her touch. "You can't hurt me. You wouldn't get away with it."

Now Reyna stepped back, reaching into the folds of her shirt. Somehow, she produced a knife, one small enough to be overlooked until it was pressed against her victim's neck. She twirled it with expert ease, never breaking that smile. "I get away with a great many things." A pause. When he didn't respond, she continued: "I assume your next step is to approach the local lord with your papers. Perhaps he summons the sheriff. Perhaps they knock down our door . . . and somehow, you get paid. Is that right?"

"Well, considering the sheriff's wife takes tea at our bookshop every other morning, I doubt that last part would happen." Kianthe rocked back on her heels. "Her point, Branlen, is that you mean nothing here. Gossley is ours. Make peace with it."

For a long moment, Branlen glanced between them. Tarly still lurked. By the door, Matild was chuckling—in disbelief, Kianthe knew, but to a bystander it could be conceit. Gossley, meanwhile, had never known the truth to begin with, so he couldn't blow their cover.

The debt collector pinched his brow. "I have superiors too, you know."

"I hear bandit work is profitable. Or you can remain on this path and test me further." Reyna drew the blade across his neck, just a whisper of a touch, before stepping away. "Make your choice."

"You haven't given me much of one, have you?" he muttered.

Reyna slipped the knife back into a hidden sheath. "Ah, then you do understand. Off you go. And we can all agree that this supposed 'debt' is null and void, if it was ever Gossley's problem at all."

Branlen stood, and Kianthe braced for him to lunge at Reyna or try something equally stupid. But he merely scowled, collected his jacket from a coatrack near Tarly's front door, and stepped past Matild into the sunshine.

The door closed, and silence echoed.

Without waiting, Kianthe stepped up to Reyna, pressing a deep kiss to her lips. She bent near Reyna's ear and whispered, "That was *hot*."

At the door, Matild snorted. Tarly cleared his throat, a pointed gesture.

"That was another day on the job." Reyna delicately separated herself, offered a wink that had Kianthe's heart pounding, then addressed Gossley. "Your debt is resolved, which means you're free to leave if you'd like. You've saved some sils. They'd pay for a trip to Wellia, at least."

But the boy set his jaw. "I can't leave Tawney. Who'd help you with your shop? And Mister Tarly's teaching me blacksmithing. Even Miss Matild said she'd share some herbalist practices." He gestured at the smithy, at all of them, his face coloring. "I like it here."

Well. No one could argue with that.

With Gossley in tow, they returned to New Leaf to open for the day.

27

Reyna

One morning, Reyna returned from the market to find Kianthe waiting with a surprise. Reyna slid through the open door with a bag of flour on one shoulder, a bag of sugar on the other, and rolled her eyes when Kianthe stopped in the middle of delivering tea to whistle appreciatively.

"Look at how strong my girlfriend is," she told Tarly, who'd swung by that morning for a new book.

The blacksmith snorted. "It's impressive. Not as impressive as *these*, but close." For emphasis, he flexed his arms, showing off muscles far bulkier than anything Reyna boasted.

Reyna paused, quirking an eyebrow. The flour was settled, but the sugar shifted in its bag, and she had to hoist it back up her shoulder. "Care to test that claim, Tarly?"

"Two pents on Reyna," Matild called from the romance section.

"Matild!" Tarly deflated immediately.

"I'll bet on you, Tarly," Kianthe chimed in, delivering a mug of tea to one of their patrons. Her eyes met Reyna's across the shop, and competition sparked between them. Reyna offered a fierce grin, one Kianthe matched. "But let's postpone it for now; she's already tired."

Reyna grunted as she nudged the front door closed with her foot. "I'm hardly tired."

To her surprise, both Tarly and Matild were nodding agreement. "Later, yeah. Not today." And they all resumed their activities.

Odd.

"Let me help, Miss Cya." Gossley was beside her in a second, offloading the sugar bag. Reyna followed him dubiously into the storage room, where they dropped off both bags. The moment she straightened, Reyna noticed a little basket perched on the center table.

Awaiting her.

Inside, someone had packed fresh-baked bread and sliced thick yellow cheese, then padded the extra space with grapes, apples, and strawberries. Reyna was certain apples, at least, didn't ripen until the fall, but here they were, deliciously red and enticing. There was even a tiny bag of cacao squares for dessert.

A picnic. Kianthe had prepared a picnic. It would explain why Tarly and Matild were here so early; Matild's bread was legendary in Tawney, and Kianthe wouldn't bother trying to bake it herself.

So, that was why they were acting strange.

"Miss Kianthe is giving me command of the shop today," Gossley said, noticing her confusion. "She said you two have a date. Don't worry; I'll make sure everyone gets the tea they like, and steep it like you both showed me."

He looked excited about handling the shop alone.

Reyna still hesitated. "We can't just leave—"

"Why not?" Kianthe stepped into the storage room, scooping up the picnic basket with a grin. "We always used to leave everything behind. You'd sneak out and we'd hide in the forest near the Eastern Ocean. Listen to the waves, talk about whatever, home by dark."

"Those were during my days *off*, love." Reyna couldn't hide her exasperation. "Now we manage a shop."

"And you haven't had a day off in ages. You think I can't see the bags under your eyes? Cya, you're working too hard."

Was she? It didn't feel like work, not when she had complete control over her schedule, their shop's success, and her own happiness.

"I'm not—"

"You helped me, and you helped Gossley, and now we want to return the favor." A gleam overtook Kianthe's expression. "Come on. You've *earned* it."

They'd left that argument behind, but occasionally, it would resurface—like a mold Reyna couldn't seem to eradicate. She wrinkled her nose, even as embarrassment flooded her skin with heat. Gossley was watching, oblivious and utterly hopeful.

It was just a day, she supposed. And a picnic did sound nice.

Reyna heaved a long-suffering sigh. "Fine. But next time, warn me, and I'll set it on our schedule."

"You know why I love you? Your spontaneity." Kianthe's tone was bone dry.

Reyna smiled. "You knew what you were getting into, darling." And she stepped past Kianthe to change into something more suited for a day out. Gossley waved cheerfully as they left the shop with Tarly and Matild, both of whom were holding new tomes. Kianthe wasted no time bidding their friends goodbye, towing Reyna toward the forest to the southwest.

About fifteen minutes from town, it was evident they were walking the entire way. There was a small path, and now that the snow had melted, Tawney was surrounded by massive fields of straw-like grass. Above them, a gorgeous blue sky stretched on forever.

"We're having a date without Visk?" It was supposed to be sarcastic, but Reyna's curiosity won out. They almost always flew (or in her case, rode) to their date destinations.

Kianthe stretched her arms above her head. She'd offered to hold the picnic basket, but once they were alone, she'd complimented Reyna's muscles—which made Reyna want to show them off. Few things delighted Reyna more than knowing she was appealing to Kianthe on every level.

Now the mage hesitated. "Truth be told, there's an ulterior motive to today's date."

"I feel so appreciated," Reyna drawled.

Kianthe nudged her playfully, grinning. "Listen, there are two important beings in my life. You, and Visk. You're always my top priority." She paused now, squinting at the coniferous trees in the distance. "But when I released Visk to the wilds outside of Tawney, I honestly didn't expect him to be gone *so* often. He comes when I whistle, but it takes a bit of time. Almost like he's busy with other things."

"Do you think he's . . . in trouble, somehow?" Reyna wasn't sure how a griffon, even a tame one, could find trouble—unless he was captured by poachers or the like. But he'd responded to a summons recently, so that probably wasn't the case.

"Trouble?" Kianthe laughed out loud. "Hells no. Stone help the poor soul who tries to contain him against his will."

Reyna had seen Visk's powerful movements during the dragon attack. Watching him work, she'd developed a newfound respect for the creature's bravery, but in the same way she respected the power of a bear on a solitary trail.

Cautious, with a healthy dose of fear.

Well, that wasn't true anymore. After seeing his dedication, Reyna couldn't argue he was an excellent mount and an even better companion. It was something she'd pointedly avoided acknowledging, because then she thought of Lilac.

Lilac, who, despite intensive training for battle, was only a horse—and when horses were scared, they threw their riders. Reyna didn't fault her for wariness around Visk, or a startle response to battle. But something sour and bitter seeped into her veins whenever she thought of riding Lilac again.

Fear.

Kianthe noticed none of her contemplation. She continued breezily: "But I do wonder if my little stud has found himself a mate. He's about that age, you know, and griffons naturally tend to roost in places like this." She gestured at the vicious snow-capped mountains west of them.

Reyna shoved down her thoughts. Lilac was happily stabled for now, and the horse had always preferred relaxation over action. Reyna would work on rebuilding that trust soon. Now she let amusement filter into her voice. "So, you want to spy on him."

"*Check up* on him, love. There's a difference."

"Something any concerned parent would note, I imagine."

Kianthe snapped her fingers. "Precisely."

And so they hiked, chatting away the morning. They passed the spot where Kianthe had expelled the dragon magic, and she shuddered, towing Reyna farther into the trees. "Let's not dally here. I can still taste that magic." She looked a little nauseated, so Reyna picked up the pace.

The forest was gorgeous. Towering pines blocked all but the bluest sky, and this time of year, even the ground was vibrant green. There was plenty of space between the trees; Reyna had visited forests farther south and felt claustrophobic with all the tangled undergrowth. Here, she could see far into the distance, and appreciated the deer, foxes, and squirrels that crossed their path.

The conversation lulled at one point, and Kianthe restarted it by grabbing Reyna's arm, towing her toward a tall pine with rough, scaly bark. "Smell it."

"What?" Reyna quirked an eyebrow. "The scent is all around us, darling. I hardly think it's necessary to physically smell a tree."

"She didn't mean that. You've done a wonderful job." Kianthe stroked the tree fondly, then shot Reyna an exasperated stare. "You're offending it. Smell the bark, Rain."

It looked like the pines Kianthe had grown behind their barn; nothing special. But Reyna supposed this was the price she paid for dating an elemental mage. She forced a smile and pressed her nose into the bark. It tickled her skin, and she inhaled deeply.

Vanilla. Or molasses, but hyper-sweetened. It smelled like something she would bake into cookies.

"It's nice," she admitted, surprised. Suddenly, she regretted never smelling the pines on their back patio. This tree seemed to swell at the praise, its needly branches lifting imperceptibly higher.

"A ponderous pine. You're smelling the resin, which is distilled for some of the salves Matild makes." Kianthe grinned deviously. "It's also highly explosive when ignited."

"Explosive." Reyna couldn't tell if she was joking. "You can't be serious."

Kianthe cackled, patting the tree once. "You may never know." They continued.

By midday, Reyna was starving. Kianthe pressed a hand to the ground and asked it for the prettiest spot nearby—and no, that wasn't a joke—and then confidently led her to a quiet meadow beside a gorgeous stream. The towering mountains were visible uphill, and the sun warmed the brisk air.

Kianthe spread out a blanket, and together they sat shoulder to shoulder. The mage smoked the cheese with a burst of flame, spread it over a thick slice of bread, and added a few apple slices to the top. She presented it to Reyna as if it were a royal's crown.

"For you, my dear."

Reyna's heart fluttered, and she accepted the meal. "I'm having a wonderful day, Key. Thank you for coordinating this. I mean it."

The heartfelt gratitude was too much for Kianthe. She squirmed, busied herself in preparing her own slice of bread. "You want to joke about earning it, Rain? This barely scratches the surface of what you deserve in life."

Reyna kissed her, the juice of the apple making it taste sweet.

"I'm beginning to realize that you're everything I deserve."

Kianthe looked like she might faint from happiness. "*Finally*. I thought I'd have to propose to get you there." She paused, even as Reyna took a careful bite of her bread. "What are your thoughts on that? Proposing?"

Reyna's hands trembled, and she swore she felt her blood pulsing. It took every conscious thought to keep her voice level, casual. "Are you inquiring for the future, or for the present?"

The mage cleared her throat, turning her gaze to the sky. "Um— the future? Mostly because coming to a proposal empty-handed isn't romantic. Proposals should have forethought. Meticulous planning."

"By that measure, perhaps I should be the one proposing to you."

They stared at each other for a long moment.

"Are we getting engaged?" Kianthe asked, and she seemed genuinely confused.

The thought made Reyna's heart soar, but she tamped it down. Now wasn't the time—not with Queen Tilaine blackening the edges of their happy life. She squeezed Kianthe's hand. "Not yet. How about this? Let's finish the year in Tawney and reassess."

"I mean, I'm marrying you anyway. It's just a question of when." Kianthe spoke so confidently, it was like their entire life had already been carved in stone. And maybe it had—maybe one of their deities had determined this path.

Reyna was keen to find out, but not today. She laughed. "I would agree. My final concern was how we'd fare living together, and clothes on the washroom floor aside, that's been everything I hoped. So . . . surprise me with your meticulous proposal." She offered a weighted pause. "But you'd better hope I'm not struck with spontaneity and ask you first."

"But—but *I* want to propose."

"You don't always get what you want, dear." Reyna took another bite, supplementing the savory cheese with a grape, mulling the flavors on her tongue. Truthfully, she had no plans to propose, but it was fun to let Kianthe think she might.

The mage smirked, and they returned to their meal with the warm content of mutual love.

※

Much later in the day, they scaled a cliffside to find a griffon's nest.

Reyna was far better at climbing than Kianthe, her fingers strong from years of swordsmanship, her muscles toned from extensive drills. Of course, comparing her climbing ability to the Arcandor's was like comparing a horse to a griffon. While Reyna gripped outcroppings and chose her path up, Kianthe just spread her arms and the rock *carried* her up the cliff.

It grabbed Reyna too, almost as an afterthought, and spit them out on a deep ledge. She yelped, pushing upright, spluttering at Kianthe. "I was managing—"

And then a furious griffon nearly barreled into her.

It was a flurry of wings; the attack so fast Reyna didn't have time to draw a blade. Sharp talons glinted near her face—but before the creature could make contact, a powerful burst of wind knocked it back, slamming it into a shallow cave. Rock surged to pin it in place. The griffon screeched, furious, writhing as Kianthe helped Reyna stand.

"Are you all right?"

Her body was buzzed, hyper-focused and prepared for a fight, but Reyna drew a steadying breath. "Well enough." She moved away from the ledge, squinting at the griffon Kianthe had trapped. "That's—not Visk."

"Of course it's not Visk. He would never attack us." Kianthe sounded offended at the very thought. She strolled toward the new griffon, examining it. "Ha! A female. I knew it. You're Visk's mate, aren't you?" She waved a hand, releasing the creature from its stone prison.

Reyna tensed, reaching for one of her daggers, but the griffon just fluffed her feathers and screeched disdainfully, like this mage entering her space was an absolute insult.

Stepping closer, Reyna saw why. Four eggs were perched in a grassy nest, gleaming white in the afternoon sun. She nearly laughed. "Key—"

"*Eggs?*" Kianthe exclaimed gleefully. "Stars and Stone, he didn't waste any time, did he? Look at these beauties." She dropped beside them, and the female griffon flexed vicious claws, but stopped when another griffon screeched overhead.

Visk appeared, his massive wings flashing, a fish dangling from his beak. He landed hard, dropped it at the female's talons, nibbled her feathers. She preened under his attention, then pointedly turned away from the humans intruding on their space.

Visk, meanwhile, shifted to nuzzling Kianthe. Almost like he was pleased to finally show her.

Kianthe was equally delighted. "I knew you were up to something, kid."

Visk shifted, and if a griffon could look abashed, he did.

The female huffed, scarfing down the fish. It was a bloody experience, and she did nothing to temper the gore. Reyna wrinkled her nose, but Kianthe was still stroking the eggs, awed.

"They're stunning. Two males, two females." How she knew that, Reyna had no idea, but she'd learned long ago not to question the Arcandor about magic. "What a brood you'll have. Do you know how rare griffon eggs are, Reyna? Even with our tame griffons in the Magicary, the waiting list is ten years long. This is incredible."

Reyna peered around her, lips tilting downward. "She had four of them." Her words were unspoken: it didn't seem like a rare resource.

"They're the only eggs she'll have in her lifetime. Griffons mate once, and only once." Kianthe bounced on her toes. "Stars and Stone, the babies are going to be so *cute*."

Visk tilted his head, looking between them, then chittered to his mate. She screeched something back. Kianthe was only half paying attention as she talked, still stroking the eggs. In the end, the female puffed, spread her wings, and took to the skies.

"Are all wild griffons that averse to humans?" Reyna asked.

"No, she's a special case. Most love bonding with us." Kianthe made a face. "Ugh. Now I'm the terrible in-law, aren't I?"

Visk chirped, like a griffon laugh, then stepped to tug on Reyna's shirt. It was a gentle pull, nothing like the firm yank he'd done during the dragon attack to get her to Kianthe. This was more of a pleased lead-in, with his head high and a bounce in his step.

"Ah—" Reyna let herself be towed closer to the nest. "Key?"

"Well. This is interesting." Kianthe assessed it with a wry smirk. Her gaze cut to the eggs, then back to Reyna, and a laugh bubbled in her chest. "Very interesting." Without offering anything else, she stepped back, giving them space.

Visk, meanwhile, seemed immensely pleased. He released Reyna's shirt and nudged the egg on the far left. Looked at Reyna. Stared at the egg.

Reyna hesitated, glancing at Kianthe for instruction, but the mage was watching them as she might a show in a theater. In fact, she swung her wrist and spelled a rock-chair into existence, draping over it with a satisfied smile.

"I'm a bit confused," Reyna said. "What's he doing?"

Visk chittered, almost like he was exasperated, and tugged Reyna down. She fell hard to her knees. His wings pressed against his body, and he slid his beak under her hand, guiding it to the egg.

"They're very nice," Reyna said hesitantly. Cautiously.

Visk swiveled to look at Kianthe, his stare deadpan.

From the chair, Kianthe snorted. "He wants you to take an egg, Rain. That egg, specifically."

Reyna reeled backward like she'd been burned. "I can't take one of his eggs."

"Mages and their mounts bond for life. The only way for that to happen is if the griffon imprints on you when it hatches." Kianthe crossed her legs, leaning back in her stone chair. Near the nest, Visk preened his wings, growing bored with her apprehension.

Reyna felt like they'd both lost their minds. "Kianthe. I can't *steal* a baby griffon from its parents."

"Well, Visk is around me all the time anyway, so it'd hardly grow up unsupervised." Kianthe chuckled. "This might be Visk's way to ensure he gets to spend time with one of them forever. Usually griffons leave their family nest in the first year and never return." Now a sly smile overtook the mage's features. "Or he's just welcoming you into the family. Either way, I'd accept the offer."

"The—" Reyna pushed to her feet, raking a hand through her hair. It was coming loose from its typical bun, and she felt equally frazzled. "What offer? I'm not a mage. Isn't this blasphemy?"

Visk lifted his head, his golden eagle eyes unblinking.

Kianthe pushed off the chair, draping herself over her mount. "Mages just bonded with them first; we hardly own the species." His tail swished in pleasure, and he began grooming Kianthe's hair instead. She giggled, pushing his beak away. "This is a really rare opportunity, Reyna. A griffon parent chooses their broods' riders. After that, it's a lifelong bond. That griffon will go to the ends of the world for you."

"But won't his mate be upset?"

"Pretty sure he just asked permission, and she gave it." Kianthe smirked, ruffling Visk's feathers. "He wouldn't do anything to jeopardize his relationship with his mate. He'll be with her a long time."

Reyna dubiously stared at the egg.

It would be convenient to cut travel times, too. Right now, even with Lilac at a full gallop, Visk drifted casually through the skies. He and Kianthe took detours, scouted ahead, and generally treated their journey as a slow vacation.

She could get her tea shipments much faster with a flying mount. Maybe even visit Leonol for some rarer blends. And there was something romantic about soaring the skies beside her partner, rather than galloping below her.

Kianthe's gaze had turned contemplative. "Plus, think of the money you'd save on stables."

That startled Reyna into a laugh. She glanced at Visk again, questioningly, and he nudged the egg a third time. Hmm. It wasn't like this griffon would replace Lilac right away. Even once it hatched, it'd be some time before it could bear her weight.

If this truly was a once-in-a-lifetime chance, Reyna didn't care to pass it up.

And the Gods knew Lilac would *love* to nibble away her days in a lovely pasture.

"You'll have to help me train it. I'm not sure how to tame a griffon."

The mage laughed out loud. "Well, they aren't *tamed*. It's a mutual agreement between us and them. Go ahead. He thinks that one is the best for you."

Hesitantly, watching Visk carefully in case he rescinded the offer, Reyna lifted the egg from the nest. The weight of it was surprising. The shell was leathery, almost soft, and very warm. Inside, the baby griffon shifted, and Reyna was shocked to admit that something protective sparked in her, there and gone like a flash of lightning.

A bond, indeed.

"Can this be our engagement present?"

Reyna didn't bother hiding her smile. "Darling, we're not getting engaged four hours after deciding to wait."

Kianthe sighed. "That would have been romantic as hells, though. I always wanted Visk to help me propose." She swung her legs over her mount's back, settling in. "I don't know about you, but I'm ready for a wash and a good book on our patio. Care to take a faster route home?"

Visk spread his wings, as if anticipating a nice flight. Overhead, his mate circled the nest, watching, but not interfering. Maybe he really had received permission somehow.

Reyna pressed the egg to her chest, holding it carefully. The weight and warmth made her ridiculously happy. One day soon, she wouldn't have to watch Kianthe's shadow from the ground.

Soon, she'd fly too. It was a freedom she hadn't even realized she wanted until it was within her grasp.

"I'll travel any way you like." And she let Kianthe hold the egg while she mounted Visk. Visk chirped a goodbye, then leapt off the mountainside and angled toward Tawney. Behind him, his mate landed near the nest again and resumed eating her fish.

With the wind ruffling Reyna's hair, the weightlessness in her stomach, the egg warm against her chest, she laughed.

What a wonderful life.

28

Kianthe

Kianthe felt smug, watching Reyna mothering her griffon's egg. Reyna refused to name it, not until she could meet the beast, but she created a literal shrine in their bedroom. She started with a wooden box—"In case it rolls," she'd said firmly, which was absolutely hilarious—padded it with a pillow and blankets, and insisted Kianthe spell an ever-flame to keep it warm.

Kianthe grumbled. "You know griffons thrive in cold climates, right? Their eggs don't need to stay warm."

"Maybe not, but it can't hurt," Reyna replied, readjusting the ever-flame. Normally, ever-flames were free-floating fireballs, but at her behest, Kianthe had placed this one inside a glass container. It pleasantly warmed the glass, and by extension, the egg, especially when Reyna tucked both into the blankets.

Pampered child.

Kianthe crossed her arms, squinting at the setup. "The light will keep us awake. Can't we move it into the storage room?"

Reyna offered a deadpan stare. "You want to put *my griffon* into the cold, half-abandoned storage room? Key, I will remind you that Visk entrusted me with this. If you keep pushing, you'll be the one testing the storage room's comfort level."

"Yes, dearest." Kianthe pinched the bridge of her nose.

Reyna smiled and patted the egg, then crawled into bed.

The ever-flame burned all night, as expected, and Kianthe slept with a blanket over her eyes.

❧

Three days later, Kianthe perfected her plant spell.

Gossley was sick with a cold, nursed by Matild and coddled by Tarly, so it was just the two of them manning the shop. They'd finished their morning rush and now settled into a smaller crowd for midday, but that was fine. A test group, Kianthe reasoned, to see how her spell would be received.

She revealed it with a flourish, setting a luscious philodendron on a table in the center of the barn. Their patrons craned their necks to see what the Arcandor was demonstrating.

"I call it the ever-plant," she declared proudly.

At the counter, drying a set of mugs, Reyna raised one eyebrow. "Ever-plant?" Her eyes drifted to the rafters, the perpetual glow of firelight that drifted aimlessly among the foliage. "So, you modified the ever-flame spell?"

"Modified the—" Kianthe spluttered, wholly offended. "The ever-flame was created eons ago. We're taught that spell as children. Fire craves life. Light. Warmth. Encouraging fire to burn in perpetuity is like encouraging a griffon to fly."

Reyna's eyes cut to the bedroom. She'd decided to keep her griffon a secret from the town for its own protection. Kianthe wasn't about to argue with her motherly instincts.

Not again, anyway.

That comparison was clearly distracting to Reyna—but then again, it had been a *whole hour* since she'd checked on the very immobile, very unhatched egg. Kianthe made a mental note to keep griffons out of her vocabulary, and redirected Reyna's attention back to the conversation at hand.

"The point," she emphasized, "is that flame wants to burn, but plants are temperamental. They need persuasion to thrive. That means my spell, my ever-plants, are one of a kind: only my magic is strong enough to coat their leaves with the nutrients they need to flourish."

Now she fluffed the leaves of the plant, as if it would prove her point.

A few of their more curious customers moseyed over while she spoke. They ooohed and aaahed, and Kianthe basked under the praise . . . right until Reyna slid her arm around the small of her back, leaned against her, and said, "Love, I mean this in the nicest way . . . but this looks like a normal plant."

A few of the customers snorted, which turned into coughs and exclamations of "Oh, look at the time." A few scattered, returning to their seats and burying their noses in books and mugs.

They didn't understand, and it offended Kianthe to her core. She hefted the plant into the air. "A normal plant? This is so much more. This plant doesn't need water, sunlight, humidity, proper soil . . . it literally can't die. My magic nourishes it from the moment I cast the spell until I recall the magic."

It was impressive. They had to see it was impressive.

But one of the more cynical patrons, an older teenager who apprenticed in the butcher's shop, crossed her arms. "Sounds implausible."

"Ever-flame is implausible," Kianthe sniped back, jerking a thumb at the firelight in the rafters.

The balls of fire were a crowd favorite, and one of the aesthetic indicators of New Leaf Tomes and Tea. The girl barely glanced at the ceiling. "Exactly. A flame that doesn't burn, or burn out, is already intense. You just finished telling us that this spell is harder. I don't believe it."

"I meant that ever-flame is rare, and yet, there it is." Kianthe glared at the kid. "Where's your sense of wonder?"

Reyna squinted at the plant. "You have to admit, one is flashier than the other."

They couldn't see the magic laced into her creations. The fire-lights in the rafters were mere sparks of yellow, shifting as they burned and reignited in perpetuity. But this philodendron was covered in magic as intricate as lacework, golden threads spreading like a doily over the leaves. It was *beautiful,* and no one could tell but her.

She twisted out of Reyna's hold, clutching the plant. "Well. That's the last time I try to solve a problem for you people." Wounded, she carried her ever-plant behind the counter. The crowd dispersed with various degrees of proffered sympathy.

Reyna alone followed her. She retrieved a dripping mug as Kianthe stared glumly at the philodendron. The moments passed, and then Reyna ventured, "So, it won't ever die?"

Kianthe tapped a leaf, watching the magic bounce like a spiderweb in the wind. "Not if I did the spell right. Maybe in a few weeks they'll believe me."

"You should leave them around town. Spell a few as sample products, then attach a card directing townsfolk here to purchase. Houseplants that never die . . . it's an intriguing business model."

Kianthe perked up. "You think so?"

Reyna kissed her, then retrieved the rag to keep drying the mugs. "I do. But I suspect you'll need word of mouth to truly market them."

Kianthe opened her mouth, but cut off when the barn door opened. Feo and Wylan strolled inside, shoulder to shoulder, a united front—except they were never united. Kianthe elbowed Reyna, and they shared a private smile as the leaders approached the counter.

"Pack a bag, Cya," Feo said, their voice nearly inaudible. "The council wants to see you." Their eyes shifted to the mage. "Not you, Kianthe. You'll stay here."

"What?" She bristled.

Feo heaved a sigh, like this was exhausting to explain. "The Arcandor is neutral in terms of the Realm's governing bodies. If you're seen begging the council for her immunity, you'll open a slew of political problems. The council requested you stay here."

Kianthe pouted. "Tell me you got something on the dragon eggs, at least."

Now Lord Wylan stepped into the conversation, rubbing the back of his neck. "I wanted to provide an update . . . which is that there *isn't* an update."

"Comforting," Kianthe drawled.

"We found logs from the sheriff at the time, submitted to my father for approval." Lord Wylan offered an old journal for their perusal. "Feo determined the age of the alchemical spellwork— apparently the linguistics have changed in the last generation."

"It isn't linguistics, and they haven't *changed*," Feo said curtly. They looked exasperated, like the pair had repeated this discussion sixteen times already. "The principles of alchemy are always the same. But spells are a vehicle to tap into that magic, and the physical representation of a spell circle has been refined in recent years."

"So, it adapts . . . just like our language." A ghost of a smile crossed Wylan's face. "How isn't that linguistics?"

Kianthe, meanwhile, wrinkled her nose. "Alchemy is the worst." Elemental magic never changed. There was no *refining* anything— just adding persuasion to her spells and hoping the elements responded favorably.

Reyna squeezed her arm, then reclaimed the journal. She flipped to the bookmarked page, scanning the logs. Kianthe peeked over her shoulder. The pages were brimming with handwritten logs: locations, times, names, shipment items. It looked boring, but Reyna was engrossed. She tapped one page. "So, all we need to do is identify the shipments leaving Tawney around the time of the dragon attack, and trace them across the Realm."

"In theory," Lord Wylan agreed. "But the records aren't complete. It's going to take a while."

Feo leaned against the counter. "We've decided to pivot to something more urgent. Wylan will keep working, but in the meantime, you and I need to get to Wellia."

Wylan seemed to notice they'd earned the townsfolk's curiosity. He straightened his shirt, turned to address them. "The tea here really is excellent, isn't it?"

A few murmurs of agreement. They weren't close enough to eavesdrop, not with how quietly Wylan and Feo were speaking, but the patrons still looked between the two leaders in utter confusion.

Reyna sighed, taking the hint, and handed Feo back the logs. She began heating water for two cups of tea. As she worked, she said quietly, "I still doubt this request of immunity will stop Her Excellency. I fear it's a fool's errand."

"It's worth a try." Wylan frowned. "Especially with the queen's men prowling town."

His words stopped Kianthe cold. Reyna's shoulders stiffened, even as she casually scooped tea leaves into a linen bag. After so much time enjoying their shop, their new lives, and a dragon-free environment, Wylan's words slammed things back into focus.

Kianthe leaned forward, her expression stormy. "Then her guards have been back?"

Lord Wylan pressed his lips into a thin line. "Not to see me. But Sigmund and Nurt report to me regularly, and they've seen some strangers enter town, poke around, and leave again. Nurt suspects there's a camp nearby."

"The queen's spies don't *poke around,* and especially not where anyone notices them." Reyna frowned.

"I don't believe it's her spy network. I think it's the man who confronted me before the dragon attack."

Venne. Kianthe had never wanted to stab a man more. Maybe she could borrow one of Reyna's knives.

Reyna was calmer. "To Wellia, then. At the very least, it'll get me out of town for a short while. Maybe the time away will convince Venne I've moved on."

"Our thoughts exactly." Feo seemed pleased to get the conversation back on track. "And the council is expecting you. We don't have time to waste."

"Now I feel like I should come too. I don't like that Tilaine's men are so close." Kianthe frowned.

Reyna offered a comforting smile. "Perhaps you can determine a way to throw him off my scent. In the meantime, Gossley is sick. Someone needs to tend the store." Now Reyna offered a pointed stare. "And monitor our bedroom."

The griffon egg. Kianthe almost groaned. "That thing will be fine. It's nowhere near close to—"

Reyna's gaze sharpened, cutting her off. "Dearest, please stop calling my pride and joy a 'thing.'"

Kianthe was beginning to regret taking one of those eggs.

The mage set her jaw. "Fine. But take Visk. Don't ride on horseback; it's too easy to be followed."

Feo, who'd been raised in the Magicary and was very familiar with griffons, shrugged.

"If that's your preference." Reyna kissed Kianthe's cheek, offered a weighted look. "Lord Wylan, the Arcandor will be happy to get your tea. Perhaps she can even show you her undying houseplant."

"It's not undying—" Kianthe cut herself off, because that wasn't *technically* untrue. "Ugh. Go get your sword. What kind of tea do you want, Wylan?"

"Ah, steeper's choice."

The young lord took a seat at a nearby table while Reyna disappeared into their bedroom. She resurfaced with a travel cloak, a leather satchel, and her sword. Kianthe trailed behind her and

Feo as they headed outside, then offered a sharp whistle to summon Visk.

While they waited, Kianthe pulled Reyna into a hug.

"Be careful."

"I'm always careful." Reyna searched Kianthe's eyes. "Are you worried about the dragon eggs? Or . . ." She trailed off, noting Kianthe's wince. "Love, we'll face her together. No matter what."

No one needed to clarify who she was referring to.

Heavy wingbeats echoed, and Visk soared overhead. He screeched hello, then landed with a plume of dust. Next door, Sasua's son poked his head through a window, laughing in delight. They waved at him, and Kianthe stole another kiss before Reyna swung her legs over Visk's broad back.

"Take care of her, okay?" Kianthe told her griffon.

He ruffled his feathers, tilting his head. In the dirt, vicious claws flexed.

"Good boy."

Feo carefully climbed on too, and Reyna patted Visk's neck. "All right. We're heading to Kyaron first, then south to Wellia." Then, to Kianthe: "We won't be long. A few days at most." She tugged a necklace out of the folds of her shirt, revealing the moonstone. She hadn't had much reason to wear it in Tawney, but the sight made Kianthe relax. "I'll be in touch."

"I know." Kianthe smiled.

But as they took to the skies, a wave of unease swept over her. Kianthe cast a glare across the open field south of Tawney and decided she'd light Venne on fire if he showed his face. Grumbling, she stomped back inside.

29

Reyna

Diarn Feo was a terrible travel companion.

They were well versed with griffons, so the flight didn't seem to bother them. But they also weren't inclined to conversation—Reyna tried a few times, and each time she was met with grunts of acknowledgment that dissolved into silence. Eventually, she stopped trying.

So, when Diarn Feo gasped in excitement and leaned over Visk's broad wingspan to squint at the landscape below, Reyna flinched. "What?" Her nerves sang, and she braced for a hit, gripping Visk's feathers harder than necessary. "Are we being attacked?"

It'd take a master archer to hit them at this height, but it'd happened before.

Diarn Feo scoffed. "No, nothing of the sort. That clock tower—"

Reyna followed their gaze. The geography had transitioned from harsh forests and icy plains to rolling hills of grass, half-way hidden by thick trees. The sun was setting, casting everything in a brilliant orange hue. It took a moment of searching, but eventually her eyes landed on a crumbling tower nestled in a valley.

They weren't far from the town of Kyaron, but it still seemed odd.

Diarn Feo was silent for a moment, then sounded almost vulnerable. "We're staying in Kyaron overnight, correct? Would it be a terrible inconvenience to stop here first?"

Visk was listening, and had shifted from an arrow's path to a lazy circle above the clock tower. His powerful wings beat every few moments, but occasionally he found a breeze to drift on.

"We can stop," Reyna replied. "I don't assume a short detour would affect the council's decision."

The grin on Diarn Feo's face made her glad she'd agreed. Visk gently drifted to the ground, landing lithely in the clearing with the clock tower. The trees here were pines mixed with deciduous flora; in Tawney, any trees that shed their leaves were just starting to grow again, boasting tiny leaves of vibrant green. Here, that had obviously happened much earlier in the season—the canopy was thick, casting the entire area in shadow.

Reyna rested a hand on her sword, because this was prime bandit territory. But the clearing was quiet, a calm hush interrupted only by the chirping of crickets and occasional owl's hoot.

"This seems like an odd place for a clock tower." Reyna followed Diarn Feo to the crumbling structure. It wasn't a hazard, not yet, but it had obviously fallen into disrepair. The clock's face was a vertical sundial, and a discolored bronze bell loomed in the tower's center. She squinted through the trees, but there were no signs of civilization. "Who's it meant for?"

"There are farming fields all around this area. Orchards and the like. This tower was used to help the farmers track time." Diarn Feo approached the heavyset wooden door with confidence, testing the handle.

Locked.

Their expression crumbled. "Shit. I can't believe he locked it." "Who?"

The diarn startled, like they'd forgotten she could hear them. "Ah—no one."

Reyna frowned. Visk was stretching his wings after the long flight, and seemed happy for the break, so Reyna strolled to the door. Mutely, she plucked a lockpicking set from a pocket in her trousers.

Diarn Feo stared like she'd just produced a mewling kitten. "Uh, what are those?"

"Lockpicks?" Reyna pressed her ear to the lock, listening, feeling the pins shift under her touch. After a breath or two, it clicked, and with a satisfied smile, she heaved open the wooden door.

Diarn Feo sounded suspicious. "You possess a myriad of odd skills."

Reyna was startled into a laugh. "The queen doesn't approve of locked doors." That was all she said on the matter. "So. Care to explain why we're here?"

They hesitated, stepping into the space. The base level of the clock tower was an old apartment, clearly long disused. A few tattered curtains divided a large bed from the rest of the room. A makeshift kitchen with scuffed counters and an old stove took up the room's corner, and another area was lined with heavy bookshelves and a few chairs.

Diarn Feo stepped to the bookshelves, retrieving an old tome and dusting off the leather cover. "This is where I grew up. My fathers were the bell-ringers." They ran a finger almost reverently along the book's spine, then set their jaw. "One died in a bandit attack when I was a kid. The other passed while I was at the Magicary, trying to become an elemental mage."

Elemental mage. Kianthe had briefly explained the path to mage-hood: interested children, or those who showed magical inclinations, had the opportunity to study at the Magicary. But some never formed a connection with the Stone of Seeing. They had the option to convert to alchemy at that time, accept a life of research in the Magicary's extensive libraries, or . . . leave.

"I've never seen you use elemental magic," Reyna replied neutrally.

Diarn Feo scoffed, bitterness in their tone. "Astute observation. When it became apparent I had no natural aptitude for the elements, I trained in alchemy and wasted years studying the Stone's scripture—only to realize it was written by a bunch of ancient, biased mages." They stuffed the book back on the bookshelf, almost aggressively. "My father died of sickness while I squandered that time."

Diarn Feo shoved past her, climbing the staircase with old familiarity. The steps were rotted now, but held their weight. She followed silently, being more careful about her own foot placement.

The second level of the clock tower was much smaller, with a tiny bed perching in the corner. It was draped in colorful fabric and had its own bookshelf, brimming with the picture books meant for children. Diarn Feo barely glanced at it, scaling the tower's staircase with purpose.

The top level was open to the elements once they moved through its trapdoor. The sun had shifted from orange to purple, and the stars were beginning to show in the inky night sky. A cool breeze rustled Reyna's hair.

Diarn Feo contemplated the rope hanging in the center, just beneath the bronze bell. It was fraying from the elements, but looked solid enough.

"I'm sorry," Reyna replied. "My mother also died when I was young."

"That's life. I shouldn't care. But I couldn't even get home for the funeral." Diarn Feo clenched their jaw. "They buried him and seized the chance to build a new clock tower closer to Kyaron."

Reyna leaned against the stone half wall that surrounded the square space. Far below, Visk had somehow captured a squirrel, and was tearing its flesh with gleeful abandon. The juxtaposition of that to this conversation made Reyna chuckle.

"Sometimes I feel like I wasted years of my time serving Queen Tilaine." She hadn't admitted this to anyone—hadn't been willing to voice it aloud before now. She wanted to be proud of her service, but . . . serving a murderous queen wasn't admirable or honorable. "There are days where I feel such crippling sadness, thinking of the years lost in that ridiculous palace. I wonder who I could have been otherwise."

Diarn Feo didn't look at her. They leaned against the opposite wall, their back to her, forearms resting against the stone. "You'd probably be unrecognizable. Everything that made you, you. Gone."

Reyna thought the same. She hummed. "I suppose we can't change our pasts. But it's okay to mourn the people we miss. My mother loved her job; I do believe she died feeling like she made a difference."

"Perhaps." Diarn Feo hesitated, then plowed ahead. "Reyna, has anyone in the Grand Palace ever contemplated overthrowing Queen Tilaine?"

The conversation shift made Reyna blink. "Officially? No. We know firsthand what happens to dissenters." Reyna turned her attention to the sky, watching the stars glimmer far overhead. For a brief moment, she wished her Gods were as visible.

"How about unofficially?" Diarn Feo turned to face her, tilting their head.

Sneaky, indeed.

"Her family has been ruling the Queendom since it separated from Shepara and declared independence." Reyna's voice was neutral, a perfectly amicable response. "Only a blood-related heir would be able to seamlessly take control of my country, and Her Excellency knows it. That's why she's postponing children until the very last moment."

That was a whispered fact. Typically, from the time of adulthood, a queen attempted children—continuing the bloodline. Queen Tilaine was boldly ignoring tradition, and every year, it strained her court.

She wasn't expecting Diarn Feo's sly smile. "A blood heir. Interesting."

"Why?" Suspicion laced Reyna's voice.

Diarn Feo shrugged. "Some believe Queen Eren took a year-long sabbatical four years after Tilaine was born. That she left a lookalike in control, vanished to the countryside, and returned the following year as if nothing was wrong."

There was a long stretch of time when Reyna's mother had left the Grand Palace; Reyna had barely been old enough to remember it. The only reason it lodged in her brain was because she'd spent them training with her uncle instead, and that was unique.

But Reyna had seen Queen Eren in the palace halls that year . . . hadn't she?

Her skin prickled, and she rubbed her arm. "What's your source?"

Diarn Feo stepped forward, running their fingers along the thick rope in the center of the clock tower. "The same as always. Journals of the time. Testimony from captured spies. Eyewitness reports. I'll collect them for your perusal." Now Diarn Feo paused, their gaze sharp. "You were in the palace at that time, weren't you? Surely you noticed. It was a whispered theory in Shepara for years."

Reyna would have been five years old—she was very close in age to Queen Tilaine. But her memory of that year was fuzzy at best, framed around learning to ride a horse, picking up her first longsword, and cooking with the palace chef—who was an old friend of her mother's, and had taken pity on her in the woman's absence.

What Reyna remembered of Queen Eren was a beautiful woman swathed in royal green robes, commanding her crowds from afar.

Which *was* odd, since Queen Eren had prided herself on an up-close and personal mindset after that.

Reyna didn't love how suspicion caressed the corners of her

mind, didn't love considering that she may have been misled all her life. "Queendom law is that the oldest daughter inherits. If there was another child, why wouldn't she be raised alongside Queen Tilaine?"

Diarn Feo rocked back on their heels. "Unknown. It's wholly possible we're mistaken. It's just a rumor, after all."

It didn't feel like just a rumor. Now it felt like someone had shattered a pane of glass over her head.

"Anyway. For my dads." Diarn Feo yanked the rope downward, ringing the bell.

Its clear sound echoed across the countryside, loud enough to shake Reyna's bones. Diarn Feo rang it loudly enough that no one in the surrounding areas could write it off as a mistake—long enough that everyone would remember the sound of his fathers' home, even after they left.

In the ringing silence that followed, Diarn Feo clapped their hands together. "Thanks for stopping, Reyna. I'll buy your room tonight at the inn. My treat." With a satisfied smile, they strolled through the trapdoor, down the staircase.

Reyna followed, more than pleased to leave the discussion of a supposed secondborn royal for another time. Hopefully far, far in the future—she didn't have the capacity to consider this now.

"You don't have to do that. We have plenty of coin." It was a lie; they were regaining profits, but it'd be a while before her savings were rebuilt after the construction of New Leaf.

Diarn Feo stopped by the bookshelf of their youth, plucking a few tomes and slipping them into their satchel. They left the rest as a memorial, untouched except by time, and strolled back to Visk. "Please, it's my pleasure. I found inconsistencies in the Stone of Seeing's scripture. The Magicary offered me a sizable fortune to keep my heresy to myself." They chuckled. "I know Kianthe thinks I want control of Tawney to secure title and fortune, but trust me, it's more of a passion project."

Reyna mounted Visk, helping Diarn Feo climb up behind her.

The griffon cleaned his beak against the grass, leaving the carnage of the squirrel behind. "Is that passion Lord Wylan?"

Diarn Feo flushed. "Don't push it."

Reyna laughed as Visk leapt into the air, angling confidently toward Kyaron.

30

Kianthe

The day after Reyna left, Venne arrived at the bookshop.

The morning dawned bright and cheery, as summer days in Tawney apparently did. Kianthe started by checking Reyna's griffon egg—which, surprise, had not moved at all, since it was an *egg*. Satisfied her girlfriend wouldn't be irritated at her "neglect," Kianthe slipped the moonstone around her neck, prepared a cup of tea, and retreated to their back patio to bask in the sun.

She absently tapped against her moonstone, a long-distance "good morning" to Reyna, and enjoyed the nice weather until Reyna tapped a response. The pendant thrummed warm against her chest, and Kianthe smiled into her mug.

If all went well, they'd be leaving Kyaron today and heading southwest to Wellia. Another long day of flying would get them there, and then they'd be at the whim of the council. To keep busy, Kianthe was planning to visit that secret room below the church, hunt for more information on the dragon eggs. If alchemy was involved, Kianthe wouldn't be able to help much—but there was a small chance her connection with dragon magic would offer new insight.

Plus, she really wanted to see the creepy underground room.

Hopefully that alchemy spell just stored the magic, and forced the dragon babies inside into a state of stasis. That would explain why three newly hatched dragons weren't terrorizing some innocent town yet.

With her tea finished, her moonstone silent, and little else to do, Kianthe went about opening the shop. Matild had offered to deliver fresh bread while Reyna was gone, since no teashop should lack food. Kianthe was wiping down the tables when the midwife strolled inside.

"Delivery," Matild called, then chuckled. "Place is busy, I see."

Unlike Reyna, *Kianthe* didn't open a bookstore at the crack of dawn. She wrinkled her nose. "A few people stopped by, but now they know better than to show up early when I'm watching the shop. How's Gossley?"

"Oh, sneezing up a storm." Matild tutted, setting a basket of scones on the counter. "Keeps trying to get out of bed and help, though. He's a good one, I'll admit. Got a crush on the carpenter's daughter—I think that's why he likes working here."

Kianthe grinned. "Oh, does he now?" There was something deeply pleasing about being in a committed relationship; it meant she could turn her attention outward to play matchmaker. Reyna had taken that new hobby and run with it, constantly pairing the townsfolk up in her mind.

She controlled herself most of the time . . . but it was a near thing.

Matild drummed her fingers on the counter. "Apparently, she left Gossley a book in the lending center. I wonder if they're communicating that way."

"They'd better not be writing in our books," Kianthe said hypocritically, since she wrote in her personal tomes all the time. It was the best way to remember her favorite lines, or emotional moments that really punched her in the gut.

But she *paid* for those.

. . . Mostly.

The midwife laughed, a bright sound. "I'll tell him. I should get back, anyway—Larson's triplets went swimming in the glacier lake, which is a bad idea even in summer. I need to create a tonic for them too, or half the kids in this town will be sick."

She'd barely stepped toward the barn doors when Nurt burst through, Sigmund hot on his heels. The two men gasped for breath, but Nurt recovered first. "Your friend is back!"

"What friend?" Kianthe said sharply.

"Goes by the name Venne," Sigmund offered, wheezing. The pair must have run all the way here. "He isn't visiting Lord Wylan's, either. This time, he's coming here, and I don't think he's leaving without a fight. Got four men with him, armed to the teeth."

Five of the queen's men total, heading straight for the barn.

Kianthe was immensely relieved that Reyna was gone.

She waved the three of them toward the back door. "Clear out, quickly. Matild, bring the sheriff and Wylan—I won't need backup, but this could get tricky. Politically speaking."

Sigmund and Nurt scrambled for the back exit; it was clear that they preferred watching these situations from a distance, not involving themselves. Honestly, it was impressive they took the time to alert Kianthe at all, with danger impending.

Matild, meanwhile, hesitated. "I shouldn't leave—"

"You knocked out a soldier and escaped the palace, once upon a time," Kianthe said hurriedly. "Venne is one of the queen's private guards. Get out of here before he recognizes you."

Matild paled, spun on her heels—but it was too late.

"Everyone, stop! In the name of Her Excellency Queen Tilaine, sovereign of the Queendom in which you reside, you will cease movement at *once*."

Matild, Sigmund, and Nurt froze, steps from the back patio door.

Disgust raced up Kianthe's spine, hot and furious. Shit, she hated this guy.

She faced the entrance of the bookshop in time to see Venne leading four heavily armed guards through the barn doors. They wore the crimson cloaks of the royal guard, adorned with golden armor that was more decorative than practical. The four behind Venne held glaives: long staffs with vicious blades attached at the tip.

Venne rested a hand on his sword, which matched Reyna's perfectly except in size. Since he was taller, bulkier, Venne had been given a slightly longer blade with a heavier handle.

Kianthe wished he'd stab himself with it.

"Hello, Venne," she said, sounding far calmer than she felt. Fury coursed through her: here was the source of all their stress, arriving years ahead of schedule. All because he was so Stone-damned obsessed with Kianthe's partner.

She wanted to ignite him where he stood, and that wasn't an exaggeration.

Behind her, Sigmund and Nurt were inching toward the door—but their steps made the guards shout warning and surge forward. Sigmund yelped and dropped to the ground, and Nurt froze like a deer under a predator's gaze.

Venne held out a hand to stop his backup. For a long moment, everyone was silent, still. Kianthe didn't attack; these were the queen's men, after all, and Tilaine would throw as many bodies as needed to solve a problem.

If Kianthe played this poorly, Tawney could become the site of a massacre. The council's precious immunity wouldn't come fast enough to save them now.

Venne assessed her. "The Arcandor, Mage of Ages. So, our spies' reports were true."

"Depends on who reported and how recently," Kianthe replied.

He chuckled, pacing toward their bookshelves. His fingers trailed a lengthy strand of ivy that fell from the rafters, and the plant's leaves began curling around his hand, feeding off Kianthe's hatred. It would choke him if he got too close.

Good.

Venne immediately shook the ivy loose, stepping back with scowl. "We knew the Arcandor was in Tawney. Everyone heard about the dragon attack, and how you fought them. Her Excellency was perplexed when you refused her invitation to the ball this spring. Since you couldn't deign to attend that, she thought your time must be valuable—yet here you are, squandering your days in this backwater town."

Kianthe wouldn't offer more details than necessary. "I came to Tawney to address the dragon attacks. If magical creatures attack the Queendom's capital city"—*What luck that would be,* she thought drily—"I'll take the same intervening action. But a ball holds no interest for me."

"Ah. You'd rather be here, tending these plants? Receiving books from Wellia, teas from Kyaron?"

He shouldn't even know about those shipping routes.

Kianthe *hated* him. She'd tolerated him before, but now she just flat-out loathed this intrusion. She didn't bother keeping the venom from her tone. "You'll have to forgive me if I find books and plants more enticing than your queen."

Behind her, Matild gasped.

It was bold. And stupid. But Kianthe didn't regret it.

Venne narrowed his eyes, his fingers tightening around the sword's hilt. The blade would be poisoned, Kianthe knew. If he drew that weapon, someone would die, and she'd demolish the building to ensure it wasn't one of her friends.

"Where's Reyna?" Venne's voice was hard as steel.

"Who?"

He didn't entertain that. "You know exactly who, Arcandor. You courted her in the palace, right under Her Excellency's nose. You'd visit her late at night, give her flowers off the back of your griffon."

Kianthe stiffened, but stayed silent. Denial until the very last moment.

She wanted to sneer, *Are you jealous?* She wanted to kiss Reyna, watch his face crumple with the realization that the woman was never his to love. She wanted him to suffer. She wanted to gloat. Her anxiety was far, far from this moment—now she was entirely focused on acting . . . violently, if necessary.

Kianthe's palms warmed with magic, fire preparing to burn.

And then he continued, low and dangerous: "You put her life at risk for selfish interludes, and then you somehow convinced her to flee." A cold laugh. "Queen Tilaine never dismisses those in her service. It's treason, Arcandor, but if she returns willingly, Her Excellency promised to stay the execution."

Stay the execution. Not dismiss the idea entirely—merely postpone it under the queen's ever-shifting whim.

Tilaine would get ahold of Reyna over Kianthe's dead body.

The Arcandor's palms ignited with fire, scenting the air, burning in a way that would scorch anyone else's hands. Gone was Kianthe, and in her place stood the Mage of Ages, the most powerful being in the Realm. At her feet, the wood warped upward, as if preparing to launch her forward. The plants came to life, reaching for the guards, vines and branches trapping them, smothering their cries. The air dropped several degrees, and the guards found themselves gasping for breath.

Venne had the decency to look alarmed.

Kianthe stepped forward, her dark eyes as tempestuous as a summer storm. "You seem to misunderstand. Reyna isn't here— but even if she was, she wouldn't be going anywhere with you. Sorry, but she's mine." A pause, a laugh. "You're welcome to a cup of tea. I'll try not to poison the leaves."

"You are going to get her killed." Venne bristled. He cast a glance at his backup, then lowered his voice. "The queen knows she's here. Her spies are circling town. My men volunteered to retrieve her first, because we worked with her for so many years. But if she doesn't return with me, someone far less kind will drag her back by force. Soon."

Kianthe bared her teeth. "Somehow, that's a risk we're willing to take. Make your choice, Venne. Reyna isn't here, but I'm itching for a fight."

Venne scowled. His eyes fell on Matild, and recognition flashed. In the next second, a smile split his face. "You might be able to protect Reyna, but can you protect your friend, too? I heard what you said: she fled the palace." Now he squinted, rubbing his jaw in contemplation. "You were a midwife, weren't you? You attacked my brother-in-law."

Kianthe yanked the pine floors up, creating a literal wall to hide Matild, Sigmund, and Nurt from view. "If you're this easily distracted from the true threat, it's no wonder Reyna was the competent one. Queen Tilaine must be aching to get her back."

"Queen Tilaine wants her dead. I've negotiated for her life. You have one day, Arcandor. Send her to my campsite in the forest south of here, or the queen's spies will swarm this place. She'll be killed on sight." Venne paused, tapping the scabbard at his hip. "Maybe you save her—or maybe someone gets a lucky hit. Are you willing to take that chance?"

Kianthe glowered. "Get *out*." And she shoved the very air at them, forcing them violently into the street. They fell in front of a few patrons who'd moseyed to Lindenback Road for a cup of tea, and the Queendom citizens recognized the uniform. They scattered in fear, leaving the queen's guards to pick themselves out of the dirt.

Venne cupped his mouth and hollered, "One day, Arcandor. I'll be waiting."

And he swept down the street, his men at his heels.

Once he was gone, Kianthe slammed the barn doors closed, then tugged the wooden floors back into place. They still buckled unnaturally where she'd ripped them, but she would address that later.

"Are you three all right?"

Sigmund coughed. "N-No offense, Arcandor, but I'm gonna make myself scarce. Tell Cya—uh . . . Reyna . . . good luck."

Nurt muttered agreement, and the informants fled.

Kianthe turned her attention to Matild. "You're safe in Tawney, Matild. I promise."

For the first time, the midwife looked scared. She'd faced Reyna with a fever, Kianthe with magic drain, the debt collector . . . never once did she flinch. But now, her eyes were wide, and her voice shook. "M-My only chance was that I'm too anonymous to be remembered." Fat tears trailed down her cheeks. "It's not your fault, Kianthe, but . . . Gods, I have to tell Tarly."

Kianthe's heart ached, and she caught Matild's arm, squeezing it comfortingly. "Hey. Look at me. Nothing will happen to you or Tarly, okay?"

Matild didn't seem to hear.

So Kianthe stepped into her space, forced her to focus. "Matild. *Nothing* will happen to you two."

"You can't know that. Her spies—"

This was spiraling out of control, and in that moment, Kianthe wanted nothing more than to storm the Capital, pin Tilaine to her pretty, bloodstained marble floor, and force her to grant immunity to everyone Kianthe loved. Fuck the council—Tilaine was always going to be the source of this.

But that display wouldn't work; otherwise, Kianthe would have done it a season ago. Matild needed to feel safe, so despite fear curling in her own chest, Kianthe interrupted: "They're after Reyna, not you. We'll handle this, Matild. I promise."

"Okay." Matild drew a deep breath, even though she sounded far from convinced.

Kianthe pulled her into a hug. "Trust me. I've dealt with bigger problems. You two will be safe."

"We have a good life here, Kianthe. You do, too. I just—I can't lose it." Matild wiped her eyes with her shirt, then edged around

Kianthe. "I need to see Tarly. We may take a vacation." She choked on a sob. "An extended one."

"Do what you need, but I *will* resolve this."

Matild didn't ask for more reassurances. She was out the back door in moments, cutting through the patio to get home faster. Once she was gone, Kianthe sank to her knees, fumbling for the moonstone pressed against her chest. Anxiety washed over her like a tsunami; her hands shook, and her breath was coming in short gasps.

But if there were ever a moment to get a hold on this visceral reaction, it was now. Fierce, angry determination settled in her veins, and she acknowledged the panic—and shoved it aside.

She needed to focus. If she didn't, everything could be lost.

Emergency. Come home, now.

The moonstone glowed white-hot in her hands, sending the message. Somehow, Reyna couldn't return fast enough.

31

Reyna

Reyna was not ashamed to say she abandoned Diarn Feo in Kyaron.

Her moonstone heated enough to burn her skin, and she yelped, wrenched it from her shirt. Something had gone horribly wrong at home. Within seconds, she was abandoning Diarn Feo as they checked out of the hotel, sprinting into the street, whistling for Visk.

The griffon landed a few stones away, and Reyna swung onto his back. A few concerned shouts and alarmed cries of bystanders faded as Diarn Feo caught her. "Whoa, hey! Where the hells are you going?"

"Something's happened." Reyna was itching to leave. Visk must have sensed it, because he spread his wings, seconds from taking off. "I'm going home. Are you coming, or staying here?"

"Am I—" Diarn Feo cut themself off. "You need to get to Wellia! The council is waiting."

And they would continue to wait. All this time, and Reyna had only felt this red-hot pulse of her moonstone once before. That time, Kianthe had been captured, and she'd had to rally the queen's entire army to rescue her. The mage had barely been conscious when Reyna stormed the complex.

If Kianthe was in danger, some politically granted immunity wouldn't matter. There were bigger issues now.

"I'm leaving. Make your choice." Her voice was sharp.

Diarn Feo floundered, then stepped back. "Forget it. I'll head to Wellia and speak on your behalf. I'm sure I can borrow a horse."

Reyna didn't even apologize. She nudged Visk with her boot's heel, and with a screech and a flurry of feathers, they were airborne. He angled toward Tawney, flying as fast as he was able, and Reyna clutched the moonstone.

On our way.

It was the longest ride she'd ever endured, but finally, the town was in sight. Dragon country stretched beyond it, and for a moment, Reyna imagined the town under siege yet again. But the bindment ensured Kianthe's deal, and the skies were clear.

So, if it wasn't dragons, it had to be Venne.

Visk landed hard outside their shop, and Reyna was sliding off his back before he'd folded his wings. To her immense relief, Kianthe burst through the barn doors, appearing in one piece. The mage grabbed her arm, towing her inside.

"Keep watch, Visk," Kianthe ordered, and he fluffed his feathers, his lion's tail swishing in agitation.

Reyna closed the barn doors behind her and locked them, pressing her back to the wood. The shop was empty, which was concerning this time of day. The curtains had been drawn. In the back, the flooring buckled, and if plants could bristle, theirs were doing it.

"What's happened, Key?" Reyna's heart was pounding.

"Venne, of fucking course." Kianthe paced, and her feet singed the floor where she stepped. She was acting fidgety, but didn't seem to be breaking down. That was optimistic. "He came into the shop with backup. Matild was here, and Sigmund and Nurt. He—I mean, he didn't care about them, but he saw Matild and—" The mage cut herself off, drew a shaking breath. Reyna was silent while she collected herself.

Kianthe's voice was stronger when she resumed. "Tilaine knows where you are, Rain. Venne said that if you rejoin him, return to the Capital voluntarily, she's agreed not to kill—kill you outright." She stumbled over the word.

Reyna crossed her arms, her own alarm solidifying into cold fury. "How very generous of Her Excellency." Her sarcasm was scathing.

Kianthe laughed, the sound anything but humorous. "I almost killed Venne for saying it. Truly, Rain, I almost burned him to a crisp." She stared at the buckled floor, then paced to the kitchen counter and back, like she didn't know where to stand.

"I believe you." Reyna intercepted her, pulling Kianthe into a hug. The mage was trembling slightly, but it wasn't a full-on break-down. Reyna smoothed her hair, keeping her voice level. "You're doing so great, Key. I'm sorry I wasn't here when it happened."

Kianthe clenched her eyes shut, burying her face in Reyna's hair. "Stars and Stone, I'm not. If you'd been here, things would be worse. He might have tried to take you by force."

"Well, I'd have gone with him, in that case."

It was an honest answer. If someone threatened her loved ones, Reyna would acquiesce with the order given. She'd probably stab them in the back while they slept, but she wouldn't cause a fuss in the meantime. Anything that avoided violence just bought more time to formulate a plan.

Kianthe clenched her hard enough to make her grunt. "Don't say that, Rain. He thinks you'll be safer with him than chancing the queen's spies."

He's probably correct, Reyna thought, but she kept quiet.

"I think you'll die either way. Do you think the council's im-munity will really help?"

"No. Maybe if we had more time, but now . . . no," Reyna an-swered honestly.

Kianthe grimaced, like she'd been thinking the same thing. "Shit. Then we should flee. We'll grab Matild and Tarly—and maybe Gossley too—and the five of us can—" A pause. "But then Wylan will be at her mercy. And any other Queendom citizens she dislikes. Fuck, I don't—"

Reyna had seen Kianthe descend into thought-spiraling like this, but it wasn't usually verbalized. Hearing it actually made it easier to understand, easier to interrupt. Reyna moved automatically, pulling Kianthe into a kiss.

Kianthe exhaled and melted against her. "Sorry," she mumbled against Reyna's lips.

Reyna pulled away, but tangled her hand in Kianthe's hair, pressing hard with the five points of her fingers. Almost like a massage, but something grounding—here and now, to keep her partner's focus. Their noses brushed.

"I have another solution," Reyna said simply.

And she did.

Because unlike Kianthe, who'd ignored this problem and hoped it'd go away, Reyna had spent the time strategizing. She'd always known her freedom wouldn't come easily, or without a fight—but the Arcandor was supposed to be neutral, and thus, a fight wasn't truly an option.

Two people couldn't topple a country.

And even if they could, all Reyna wanted was to sip tea and read books.

"A solution? To this? Why didn't you pitch it before?" Kianthe demanded.

"It's risky, and there wasn't a reason to attempt it before now." Reyna brushed her lips to Kianthe's nose. The mage had once admitted that physical reminders of the present moment helped temper the panic. Reyna played into that, trailing her fingers up Kianthe's bare arm, offering her scents and sights and sounds that had nothing to do with the cacophony inside her head.

It worked. Kianthe kissed her back, drew several shallow breaths, and responded in a measured voice, "Okay, I'm intrigued. What's your thought?"

Reyna tugged Kianthe to the armchair beside the fireplace. The hearth was dark and empty, and the room was slightly chilled. She sat in the chair across from her partner, took her hand.

And then Reyna laid out her plan.

By the end, Kianthe's jaw was unhinged. She gaped at her girlfriend, a mix of adoration and horror on her face. It was an amusing combination.

"You've—you've thought about this before."

"From the day I contemplated leaving, yes." Reyna smiled, perching on the armrest of the opposite chair. "I'd hoped it wouldn't be necessary for a few years, and then I'd hoped the council's immunity would stay the plan entirely . . . but we're clearly out of time."

The mage had gotten a handle on her anxiety, finally focused on the here and now. She massaged her temples with two hands, slumping into the armchair. "I don't like it."

"I know." That was always Reyna's hang-up—because the plan was dangerous. She would have to present herself to Queen Tilaine, and everything depended on the queen's mood that afternoon. It was a calculated risk, but it was still a risk.

And it all hinged on Kianthe's willingness to partake.

So, she was pleasantly surprised when Kianthe muttered, "I guess we have no other option. Venne recognized Matild. He knows she fled the Grand Palace, and he's going to tell Tilaine if you don't visit his camp."

"Well, that's easily fixed," Reyna said. "If we kill him, he can't tell anyone else."

Kianthe spluttered. "W-What?"

Reyna forgot, sometimes, that Kianthe was a pure soul who didn't resort to murder. And sometimes, the mage seemed to forget *Reyna's* background—that her sword was a deadly extension, that there was a reason she kept so many knives hidden in sheaths across her body.

She couldn't feel ashamed about it, not now. Reyna tapped her foot impatiently. "Never mind. Even if we eliminate Venne, her spies will discover the truth sooner than later. If this works, I can secure Matild's future too. But it all depends on you, love. If you don't agree to this, we'll have to brainstorm something else."

Kianthe groaned. "My issue isn't with *my* role in this plan. My issue is with you, presenting yourself on a fucking platter to a murderous royal."

"And that's why it will work. I've taken exactly one risk in life: fleeing the palace to live here, with you. Her Excellency would never expect more."

Kianthe was quiet for a moment. Then she ventured, almost nervously, "Can I follow with Visk? Just in case things don't work?"

"I'd feel much better if you would, to be honest."

They stared at each other.

Kianthe said, "In case you care, I think this is insane. Brilliant, but insane."

Reyna kissed her, then strolled for the bedroom. "Our life is brilliant, but insane. And I wouldn't have it any other way."

❉

And so, Reyna turned herself in.

It was a rather anticlimactic affair. She removed Lilac from the stables, swallowed her fear, and mounted her horse. Lilac nuzzled Reyna almost like an apology, and Reyna whispered, "I know it wasn't your fault, girl. You did your best."

Lilac puffed in agreement and trotted toward the forest—and the camp beyond. The horse's eyes turned to the sky for just a moment, and Reyna braced herself—but Lilac seemed to accept there were no griffons or dragons to be seen. From there, it was a nice, steady ride.

Kianthe stayed home. This only worked if Venne never suspected the Arcandor's involvement.

Lilac's hooves thundered against the dirt road, leaving Reyna plenty of time to collect her thoughts. At home, she'd stayed calm, confident, because Kianthe needed that. Here, alone on a moonlit road, Reyna's fear was all-encompassing. Her chest felt tight, and her palms sweated against the leather reins.

This might not work. If it didn't, if she couldn't persuade Tilaine—she'd be trapped in the Grand Palace, left to Her Excellency's nonexistent mercy. Kianthe was planning to follow behind as added protection, but if the Arcandor was forced to invade the palace, the battle would be devastating.

This required a delicate hand. And Reyna was the only one who could manage it.

She thought of the assassin's blood staining the ballroom floor, what felt like eons ago. Of his sword pressed against her neck, of Queen Tilaine's dismissive wave. Sentencing her to death even when she'd been unerringly loyal. The woman was unpredictable, but this . . .

It *had* to work. Not just for Matild's safety, but for everyone they'd grown to love.

If she fought for anything, Reyna would fight for Tawney.

And so, despite the cold fear gripping her soul, despite her heart longing to curl up beside Kianthe and read near the fireplace, Reyna directed Lilac into the trees. Visk had already scouted ahead, located Venne's camp, so Reyna knew exactly where to go.

A cheery fire burned, surrounded by five of her old colleagues. They tensed, reaching for weapons until they saw who it was.

"Hello, folks." She dismounted, spoke with exasperated confidence. "That was a bold move, Venne. You win. Take me back to the Capital." And she offered her hands.

Venne blinked at her. He looked just as she remembered, the same eager eyes, the same wry smile. Once upon a time, they'd been best friends, inseparable partners. For a few confused years growing up, Reyna thought maybe she could be happy with him—someone who always watched her back, protected her from evil.

But evil turned out to be a lot closer to home.

A relieved smile split his face. "Thank the Gods and the queen herself that you came to your senses. Put your hands down, Reyna; we're not going to bind you." He offered a glass bottle. "It's a long ride back to the Capital; we'll get started in the morning. Care for a drink?"

Her colleagues were watching her with various degrees of relief and irritation. They were, admittedly, the closest friends she'd had within the Grand Palace—which only meant they were the least likely to backstab her.

Did they begrudge her for escaping a life they probably hated, too? Or did they loathe her now for the blatant display of disloyalty? Her actions after the ball had put everyone at risk; Queen Tilaine almost certainly tightened security standards after Reyna fled without warning.

Well. They'd rethink their opinion of her soon.

Reyna dropped beside Venne, slipping into the most important role of her life.

"Hells, you know it." And she took a deep swig.

It was easy to fall back into her old ways. She remembered their families, their passions, and used that information to lighten the mood. Venne seemed pleased that she was the same person, that she apparently didn't hold a grudge for his earlier threats. He kept nudging her shoulder, putting his arm around her in a joking manner, and for once, she didn't stop him.

Time spent acting as Cya had loosened her for this moment. She drank just enough to be convincing, and played these people like instruments of her own musical inclination.

When one ventured to ask why she'd left in the first place, she merely smiled and replied, "That's for the queen's ears alone."

And eventually, they stopped asking.

32

Kianthe

Kianthe was meditating.

That might be dangerous, while soaring so high above the clouds that ice crystals kept collecting on her eyelashes. But Visk couldn't fly lower, or Venne might notice they were being followed. The only chance they had of staying secret was if Kianthe whipped the clouds into a dull gray smear, then danced in their shadows.

Occasionally, she'd pull a hole open, catch a glimpse of the procession far below. Six horses—six Queensguard. All but one wore crimson cloaks, but even so high up, she could hear muted laughter and casual chatter. It was comforting that Reyna had rejoined her colleagues so easily.

But their journey back to the Capital felt like a funeral procession.

The only good part of this had to do with the ley lines. The farther south they got, the more powerful the ley lines became . . . and their sunshine magic filled Kianthe's reservoirs to bursting, calming her mind in a way that seemed out of reach in Tawney.

Reyna wasn't safer here, but surrounded by the Stone's blessed magic, Kianthe felt a lot more confident in her ability to intervene.

With this magic, she could topple mountains, or barricade cities. With this magic, Reyna would be safe, no matter what.

But Stars and Stone, she really hoped she didn't need to use it.

"It's a dangerous idea," she told Visk.

The griffon chittered, the noise lost over the wind. Even he knew to stay quiet, operate in stealth.

They continued that way for days, camping near enough to track Venne and his crew, but never getting so close as to reveal their position. Visk kept Kianthe warm at night, curling into a tight ball and draping his wings over Kianthe's body. She had a harder time sleeping, but gave it her best attempt—and in the mornings, they were back in the skies, watching Reyna creep closer to enemy territory.

When Reyna rode through the gates of the Capital, Kianthe almost expected Queen Tilaine to greet her with the gallows. She canvassed the city twice just to make sure none were set up, coaxing Visk to fly so high the air thinned and she was shivering.

Finally, Reyna and the other guards thundered through the palace gates, and Reyna dismounted. Kianthe squinted, watching over Visk's back as Reyna strolled inside with immense confidence. The mage's heart clenched in fear, but now wasn't the time to break down.

Now, she needed to get in position—just in case. She directed Visk to the tallest tower's flat roof, manipulating the cloud cover with a wave of her hand. No one saw as she dismounted her griffon, released him to the skies, and felt the parapets for the secret passageway.

The stone shifted to reveal a thin trapdoor, just as Reyna said it would.

And so Kianthe delved into the Grand Palace's labyrinth of hidden corridors, descending tight staircases, eavesdropping on servants and guards and noblefolk as she followed Reyna's careful instructions toward the throne room.

"Don't dawdle," Reyna had warned back at New Leaf, "but the

queen likely won't see me right away. She'll want me to sit in fear, reconsider my actions. Stay alert for anyone else in the tunnels."

Kianthe stepped lightly now, pausing on occasion to feel the magic swelling around her. The stone, simultaneously aching at being ripped from the earth, and proud to be admired by so many, swelled in spirit to greet her. "Keep people from finding me," she told the walls, and far away, she felt the granite close off other entrances to the tunnels.

Finally, she reached her destination. It wasn't even the end of the tunnel; this one ran alongside the throne room, although there were no doors to enter it. Slivers of space between the granite bricks offered glimpses of what lay beyond: a space absurd in its opulence.

The throne room's gold and crimson accents bordered on blinding. A thick, plush carpet led to the throne, which was carved in the image of two dragons, their skulls baring fangs as long as fingers, golden wings flaring, fake tails curling around the chair's feet. Heavy chandeliers of waxen candles hung low, and along the west wall were thin windows carved into the stone, casting shards of light on the marble floors.

Kianthe wrinkled her nose. The only reason she appreciated this room was because she'd met Reyna here, all those years ago.

Now, her eyes traced the space where Reyna had stood— replaced by some no-name guard standing at perfect attention. Did that person yearn for a teashop at the edge of the world, too? Or was Reyna just that special?

Kianthe knew her answer, however biased it was.

Her girlfriend hadn't arrived in the throne room yet, but within seconds of Kianthe taking position, the double doors swung open and Venne stepped inside. He strode swiftly to the center of the room, dropped to his knee in a deferential bow, and said, "Your Excellency, we've secured Reyna."

Queen Tilaine was lounging on her throne, reviewing a thick set of parchment. Now she flicked her staff away, offering the guard her full attention. "Hmm. Last I heard, you'd confronted that silly lord in his estate, and returned to your camp empty-handed."

Venne stiffened, and Kianthe stifled a laugh. Amateur mistake, assuming he wasn't also being watched by her spies. It left Kianthe wondering who these spies were, and how they'd circled Tawney for so long without anyone noticing.

Of course, if Reyna's plan worked, those details wouldn't matter.

"I needed to gather more information, Your Excellency."

"You were buying her time." Tilaine pushed off her throne, taking measured steps toward her guard. The folds of her ridiculous dress trailed behind her, and her crown gleamed with rubies, like pinpricks of blood atop her dark hair. "I know you fancy her, and I do appreciate a love story—however uninspired it may seem. But that delay borders on disobedience."

Venne stiffened. He didn't seem to know how to respond, except to keep his gaze lowered in respect.

Tilaine circled him, a wolf waiting for her prey to bolt. Her other guards subtly moved behind Venne, surrounding him as if he were a prisoner. "Where is she?"

"Awaiting your summons, Your Excellency," he replied. A pause, a bold move: "She returned to us willingly, with full apologies for her behavior. You promised mercy."

Thunder overtook Tilaine's face. She flicked a hand, and her guards sprang into action. Within seconds, one had a knife to Venne's throat, the other muscling him into a submissive hold. The blade against his neck was obviously tipped in poison, because even without breaking the skin, it caused a dark red welt to rise.

Tilaine presided over it all, her smile never wavering. "Do you remember which of the Gods offered me favor upon my coronation day?"

Venne didn't dare respond.

"The God of Mercy. It bestowed a vision upon me of mercy

for this blessed land. When I reached for my mother's scepter, it burned my hand." She raised her right hand, gently peeling off her silk glove. The skin on her palm was bright red and grotesquely warped. Kianthe winced, but Tilaine merely stroked the injury fondly. "I was wounded, yet left to lead. That is mercy. Sometimes, a wound must be endured for the country to survive."

Kianthe would never understand Reyna's Gods.

Venne, meanwhile, looked nervous now. His breaths were coming in shaking pants. "Of course, Your Excellency."

"Reyna abandoned her post, which is treason in every sense. She is the wound to be endured—and now it is time to place salve on the wound and move forward with our lives. But since I am curious, I will allow her to plead her case before the execution. That is my mercy."

Kianthe stiffened, her mind scattering conscious thought. She almost—almost—tore the wall apart and attacked the queen right there.

But Reyna knew what she was doing. She expected to be killed on sight; that's why *Kianthe* was here—to prevent a tragedy. If there was a slight chance this would work, they had to take it. It could mean the difference of years uninterrupted, or all-out war.

Venne wheezed, paling, but didn't try to break the hold. Behind the queen, two guards stepped closer, as if Venne might attempt to break free and stab Tilaine where she stood.

Kianthe wished he would. It would redeem him. Not entirely, but a bit.

"Please, Your Excellency," Venne gasped. "P-Please."

Tilaine smiled wider and slid her silk glove over the wound. At an inclination of her head, her guards tossed him to the ground. Venne struggled back into a kneeling position, his fingers brushing the angry red mark on his neck.

"Another display of mercy, to please the Gods." Tilaine strolled back to her throne, settling into the deep seat. Her fingers traced one of the dragon's heads adorning her armrests. "Reyna's actions were inexcusable, but I know my patron deity. As I said, she may plead her case . . . after which, she will be killed."

Tilaine gestured at one of the guards on her left. "Retrieve her. Say nothing."

The Queensguard dipped low and left the room.

Kianthe drew a shallow breath, clenching her hands together to stop their shaking. This was a bad idea. But now it couldn't be stopped. Feeling like she'd just been buried alive in this cramped tunnel, Kianthe awaited Reyna's fixed trial.

33

Reyna

The palace was cold.

It was ironic, considering that the Capital was much farther south than Tawney. And yet, at home, they were surrounded by good company, warm hearths, hot tea, cozy books. At home, all Reyna had to do was lean against Kianthe, and the mage would give her a hug so tight she'd lose air.

Here, everything was stone. It was, after all, the Queendom's primary export, a testament to the strength and power of the royal family. The walls were granite, polished to a shine to reveal the natural movement of the stone. The floor was marble, gleaming under the firelight. The statues were gold, which was more common in Leonol, worth the handsome payments Queen Tilaine offered to import it.

But more than the physical stone were the *people*. Reyna was raised here, had played in these hallways, crashed into the kitchens, and tested weaponry in the training rooms. She recognized every single person she passed, but after the first five gave her the silent treatment, Reyna stopped trying to say hello.

They were afraid; she understood.

It still hurt.

And so, she kept her gaze locked on the guards she'd arrived with, who'd shifted from colleagues to captors the moment they entered the Capital. They wordlessly put her into a small waiting room near the throne room, removed every weapon she had—even the hidden ones—and finally left her in silence.

She expected her summons to take longer. Days, maybe. Queen Tilaine would find pleasure from the expectation of interaction, only for Reyna to be stalwartly ignored.

But Her Excellency's curiosity must have won out, because Reyna had barely settled onto the uncomfortable chair before a guard rapped on the heavy door, then escorted her to the throne room.

Venne was against the far wall, standing at attention. His neck was splotchy and red; whatever conversation they'd had, it must not have gone well. Reyna swallowed past a dry mouth and thought, *That's what you deserve for making a deal with the queen,* then realized she was about to do the same thing.

At her chest, the moonstone warmed, a bare nod to Kianthe's position behind the walls. Reyna didn't look toward the slivers in the stone, didn't acknowledge the mage's presence at all. It was insurance, nothing more; if this conversation went poorly, Kianthe would rip apart the walls, tear the air out of everyone's lungs, and they'd be on Visk's back before Her Excellency could respond.

But that was a temporary solution to a long-term problem.

Across the room, Queen Tilaine drummed her fingers on the carved dragon's head, one Reyna knew held a dagger sheathed against the dragon's tongue. How would Her Excellency fare against a real dragon? Reyna wondered. The ones on her throne were poor interpretations.

She knelt in the room's center, bowing her head—half expecting to be beheaded right there.

Nothing happened.

Long beats passed, and finally Queen Tilaine said, "Well, well.

Reyna. You were a rising star. Your mother served mine well, and it leaves me wondering where *I* went wrong."

Amusement tilted the sovereign's words.

Years of conditioning came back, and Reyna fought the subservient impulse that told her to apologize profusely, beg forgiveness. Her mother used to say, *"If you have to beg, Reyna, it's already too late,"* and that was the only thing that stayed the apology on her lips.

Focus. This was acting. Instead of Cya, the blacksmith's daughter from Mercon, she was Reyna: loyal Queensguard. And she'd had years of practice with that attitude.

Imagining that fake persona, it was easy for Reyna to keep her tone level. She didn't drench the words in respect or apology, because that wouldn't intrigue the queen. This was a knife's edge, and she would walk it perfectly.

She had to.

"Your Excellency, I wholly understand my misstep."

"Your misstep?" Queen Tilaine asked mildly.

Reyna kept her eyes on the floor. "Abandoning my station. Fleeing your palace in the middle of the night, with no word. I recognize my treason." She wouldn't apologize for it; after all, *this* Reyna hadn't committed treason. Queen Tilaine just didn't know it yet.

The queen laughed, a sound like a wind chime signaling a coming storm. "Then you know what your punishment is. It truly is a testament to your upbringing that you returned at all. I honestly expected my spies would have to poison you one night."

Reyna dared to meet her gaze now, her face coolly impassive. "Your Excellency, with all due respect, you will not execute me."

The gambit.

Queen Tilaine blinked, taken aback by her boldness. And just as Reyna expected, intrigue took hold. She leaned over her knees, steepling her fingers. "No? And why shouldn't that be your fate?"

Reyna offered the barest hint of a smile. "Your guards found me in Tawney. They've been inside my bookstore. They've met my partner. Surely, someone reported back that I'm dating the Arcandor."

"A threat? My dear, how uninspired." Queen Tilaine pushed off her throne, waving a hand. As she approached Reyna, two guards moved into position behind her, their poison-edged swords drawn. "You'll be dead before you hit the floor. We'll have the mess cleaned in moments."

The moonstone pulsed against her chest, but Reyna didn't break stride. She didn't flinch, didn't clench her fists, didn't argue.

Instead, she held Queen Tilaine's gaze.

"Your Excellency, my plot was a success. That is why I returned. My purpose in fleeing the palace was not to spite you. My *purpose* was to secure the Arcandor's loyalty, trust, and love . . . in the name of your crown."

Everything stopped.

Against the far wall, Venne looked stunned. Several of the Queensguard shifted, breaking their stoicism to exchange perplexed glances.

Queen Tilaine paused, waved her hand again. The guards flanking Reyna sheathed their swords, stepped backward, offering the sovereign space. Meanwhile, Queen Tilaine chuckled. "You expect me to believe that you abandoned my service to woo the Arcandor—all for my benefit?"

"No, Your Excellency. By the time I left, I had already wooed the Arcandor." Reyna smiled now, like they were sharing a private joke. "I caught her gaze in this very throne room, but her temperament is . . . difficult. It took years to persuade her to trust me. Midnight rendezvous. Vacations together. My queen, you've known me since childhood. I never take anything but calculated risks."

Queen Tilaine tapped the side of her cheek. "You are meticulous, it's true."

Reyna bowed her head in appreciation. "I kept our relationship hidden, never encouraging her more than needed . . . until she offered to run away with me. And even then, I spent half a year refusing the invitation, enticing her further." Reyna paused. "When she ignored your summons for the ball, I realized that her formal relationship with you is tenuous, and always will be. But if I could gain her favor, make myself indispensable in her life, you would be presented with a rare opportunity to alter her perception of the Queendom, and you as its ruler."

"Why *ever* would I care to alter her flawed perception of my magnificence?"

The queen was still feeling snubbed from Kianthe's silence after the ball. That might make this more difficult. Reyna infused an appropriate amount of disgust into her voice. "My queen, Shepara considers the Magicary part of its rule simply because it's within their borders. But the Arcandor is the living embodiment of the Magicary—wherever she goes, their mages follow."

"And with them, comes power," Queen Tilaine mused. Suspicion flashed across her features. "If this is true, why didn't you brief me on your plan?"

"I wasn't sure it would work. Rather than disgrace you with failure, I wanted to ensure success. Your spies poking at our new shop only offered authenticity, in the Arcandor's eyes."

It was a bit of a stretch, but Queen Tilaine did love success. If she could boast, she would—but if she boasted too early and was later faced with an unfortunate surprise, it was disgraceful. Humiliating.

Queen Tilaine contemplated her. "So, it was a success. The Arcandor is in love with you."

"Precisely." Reyna held her gaze. "When I fled, I signed my death warrant—but it was entirely to present you with this decision. If you stay my rightful execution out of the kindness of your heart, I've ensured that you will earn the Arcandor's favor. She will feel indebted to you, and *that* is how we will secure the Queendom's prosperity."

And there it was.

For a long moment, the throne room was drenched in heavy silence. Sweat trickled down Reyna's neck, but discomfort didn't show on her face.

And then Queen Tilaine laughed, and laughed, and didn't stop laughing. For a moment, Reyna thought her story was falling to pieces, that she'd seen through the lies—but this entire plan hinged on one thing: Queen Tilaine's conceit.

If there was a character trait Her Excellency possessed, it was that one.

The queen offered Reyna a hand, helping her stand, gripping her arms like they were best friends. "This is delicious. The *Arcandor*. You've swindled the Mage of Ages. Oh, the Sheparan council is going to be furious." And she laughed again, louder.

Reyna smiled, and this time, she didn't have to fake it. "Your Excellency, please accept my profuse apology for the secrecy. My intention was never disloyalty."

"You truly are my most loyal guard." Queen Tilaine patted her cheek. "I suppose it wouldn't cost me to allow your freedom, with the assumption that you're seeding my merits throughout the Arcandor's life. How much does she love you?"

The moonstone glowed warm against Reyna's chest, right above her heart. Reyna chuckled slyly. "She's mentioned proposing. I suspect we'll be engaged by year's end."

"Incredible. If this weren't such a long game, I'd reemploy you as my spymaster. Locke is getting far too old now." Queen Tilaine seemed giddy. She waved her guards off, then glanced at Venne. A cruel smile flitted across her lips. "Oh, but this must be truly terrible for you. Allow me to be clear: Reyna is now under my protection. If you pursue her, confuse her, or otherwise intervene, you will be killed. The Arcandor is a far more valuable resource than your male desires."

Venne just looked bitter, confused, and a little angry—but he had no way of disproving this ruse. With everyone watching and his life on the line, he dipped his head and murmured, "As you wish, Your Excellency."

Reyna seized the opening. "My queen, Venne placed us in an awkward position. Your spies may have reported that there's a woman in Tawney who worked as a midwife here. She fled the palace years ago."

Queen Tilaine's expression soured. "Oh, I know of her. You cannot expect me to stay *every* execution."

Reyna's heart thrummed in her chest, but she channeled the ice of Tawney in wintertime. Here, she would be an impartial informant. "I would never presume. However, this woman is one of the Arcandor's dearest friends. If anything happens to her, my sway won't be enough. The Mage of Ages will take it personally, and everything we've accomplished to this point will be a waste."

Reyna forced herself to breathe, to furrow her brows like this was a puzzle they were solving together. It was risky as hells, bringing up Matild—but it was better to label her off-limits than refrain from mentioning her at all.

Queen Tilaine mulled it over, pacing back to her throne. "My spies lost her trail, so I was impressed you'd led us right to her. If she's significant to the Arcandor, I suppose I can make two exceptions." She glanced at her right-hand guard, a man with more years' experience than Reyna had lived. "Inform Locke immediately."

He bowed deeply, and the moonstone tapped against Reyna's chest. Relief.

"I will offer a full pardon in writing so the Arcandor cannot dispute my generosity." Queen Tilaine faced her now, and she looked every bit the impending royal. "But allow me to be clear, to you and everyone else in this room. This is a unique circumstance. Reyna, you have presented me with something more valuable than your death—and for that reason alone, you will be spared. Consider this an act of mercy."

Now her expression shifted; the storm had arrived. A shiver ran up Reyna's spine.

"The moment that becomes untrue, I will not be so kind."

Reyna lowered her head in submission, even though her hands trembled—in fear, or fury, it was difficult to tell. Her mouth was dry, but her voice was strong: "I understand, my queen. My loyalty is true; everything I do is for the Queendom, the Gods, and your venerated name."

"We'll see." Queen Tilaine glanced at the windows, at the afternoon sun streaming through them. Light flashed on the rubies in her crown. "But Reyna? The next time I throw a ball for the Mage of Ages . . . I expect her to attend."

"It would be her pleasure, Your Excellency. If you have orders in the meantime, you know where to contact me. Although I'd appreciate if Venne weren't the one delivering the report; the Arcandor is not fond of him."

"She doesn't like the competition," Queen Tilaine replied, amused now. "This is suitable. You are dismissed."

Reyna bowed again, caught Venne's perplexed gaze one final time, and left the throne room on her own free will. Lilac was already saddled and waiting when she arrived in the Grand Palace's main courtyard, and with little delay, she thundered out the gates.

This time, with full permission to live her life as expected . . . at least until Queen Tilaine decided to call in a favor. But that was a problem for another time. Now, her freedom made her light as a feather, bright as sunshine.

Later that night, Kianthe and Visk caught up to her under the low-sitting pines, and they laughed until they cried.

34

Kianthe

It was getting cold, and that pissed Kianthe off.

Summer in Tawney was gorgeous and brief—and as fall neared, so did the snow. Dark clouds hung in the sky, people shed thin straps for longer sleeves and heavy cloaks, and New Leaf Tomes and Tea's fireplace burned all day.

Kianthe hunched under the folds of a blanket she'd tied, very stylishly, around her neck. It trailed behind her like a child's cape, and she grumbled as Gossley chatted with his girlfriend—he'd somehow wooed the carpenter's bookish daughter—near the open barn doors. He'd shaved his sad little beard, grown some muscle, and wasn't half bad with a sword anymore.

Maybe he was a catch, but to Kianthe, he was the reason their shop was dropping in temperature.

"Gosling!" she called grumpily. "Close the door!"

He flinched, the carpenter's daughter laughed, and they ducked outside. His arms wound around her waist as they resumed their conversation.

On duty, Kianthe noted.

Behind the counter, kneading dough, Reyna chuckled. "Darling, it hasn't even gotten cold yet. Matild said the winters here will freeze you the moment you step outside. Wind so cutting it ices over your lungs."

"You're not helping." The mage stomped back to her partner, slumping against the counter. She'd left a book there, and absently leafed through the pages. "Aren't we due for a vacation? We did a lot in summer. I say we go somewhere warm."

"And leave us without tea?" Matild called from the bookshelves. She was perusing the romance section, yet again, although this time Tarly was absent. After Reyna won the arm-wrestling contest, Tarly had poured himself into his work, determined to beat her in a rematch.

It hadn't happened yet, but who knew.

Matild, meanwhile, moved with a bounce in her step. The threat of the queen discovering her had clearly been a years-long weight, and now that it was resolved, she smiled bright and laughed loud. At Reyna's subtle suggestion, she also started visiting the bookshop more, making a point to be vocal friends with Kianthe.

It amused the mage to no end. "Look, there's still tea. We'll give you access, and Gossley can supervise the shop. I bet he and his new friend would love the privacy."

Reyna hummed, dipping her hands into a jar for more flour. "I don't particularly want two teenagers roaming the barn alone, Key."

"What do you care? We'll be basking on some Leonolan beach."

"How about scouring the Nacean riverside, instead?" a voice called, and they glanced up to see Diarn Feo and Lord Wylan strolling into the shop. Wylan had spoken, and now he waved at a few regulars. They cheerfully waved back. Seeing the two leaders together now was commonplace—and frankly, had made life in Tawney far more bearable.

They hadn't declared a relationship yet, but they spent an awful lot of time "discussing" the town's future. Kianthe shot Reyna a sly smile, which she returned. The mage stepped behind the counter, abandoning her book to heat some water in the copper kettle.

"What's this about a riverside?" Matild said, tucking two tomes under her arm and joining everyone at the counter. "Because when I hear rivers, all I think are mosquitoes."

"Not this time of year." Kianthe smirked. "Picture towering mountains and green meadows giving way to thick forests filled with changing leaves. And just when you start to feel claustrophobic, the trees part to reveal the prettiest rolling hillsides you've ever seen—all the way to the ocean itself."

Reyna tilted her head. "Well, that sounds magical." She shaped the dough into a sphere, offered it to Matild for approval, then set it on a metal tray for baking. Kianthe moved to poke it, and Reyna slapped her finger. "If you leave holes in my bread again, Key, I'll let Ponder nibble your hair while you sleep."

The baby griffon, a contemplative, quiet female, was currently sleeping the day away on their back patio. Visk checked his daughter from time to time, but the bond had formed with Reyna when the griffon hatched—and Reyna took it *very* seriously. Training and play sessions had been constructed into a rigid schedule, and Stone-forbid Kianthe try to say it was lost on a griffon this age.

Kianthe wrinkled her nose.

Before she could retort, Feo, who'd stayed quiet as long as they cared to, cleared their throat. "If we can return to the topic at hand. Kyaron's diarn finally found the documents we needed." They lowered their voice, adding, "Only took her the entire summer, but that's the price of poor management, I suppose."

"So, the dragon eggs were taken to Shepara?" Reyna asked.

"Shipped to the Nacean River," Feo confirmed, their jaw set. "Unfortunately, I won't be traveling further; Tawney can't be without its diarn that long."

Wylan snorted. "Tawney will survive with me."

"Or, Gods forbid, we survive without either of you," Matild drawled.

The leaders shot her identical glares.

Kianthe drummed her fingers on the countertop. "So, they found records that the dragon eggs were shipped to the Nacean River, in Shepara. Which means . . . we have a built-in excuse to flee the winter and take an extended vacation." Now she gave Reyna a pointed glance.

Reyna pressed her lips together, wiping her hands on a rag. "Ponder's awfully young to be uprooted. She's comfortable here. This is a nice environment for her to be nurtured."

"Griffons crave adventure, Rain." Kianthe rolled her eyes. "And it's not like she won't have Visk for stability. Not like she wouldn't have you."

Reyna sighed. After a moment, she said, "I suppose we must locate those dragon eggs, one way or another. But promise me that we won't be gone all winter. Gossley is still young to be handling the shop alone."

"Maybe Feo can help with that. Or Wylan."

"We can all help," Matild said, before the leaders could vehemently oppose the idea. "It takes a community to keep a place like this afloat, and we all understand the necessity of your investigation."

Feo grumbled, but handed off a letter to Kianthe. "There are the details. Let me know when you leave." And they about-faced, stomping from the shop.

After they were gone, Reyna caught Wylan's gaze. "Any news from the Capital?" She meant news from the queen, who'd been eerily absent from their lives after Reyna's little acting experiment.

But the lord just shook his head, wonder in his tone. "Nothing. It's like Tawney was erased from the map." He smiled wryly. "Can't thank you enough for that, Cya."

"Please. There's no risk to calling me Reyna now." She'd been slowly spreading the name around, gently correcting backstories, and eventually the town narrative shifted. More people called her

Reyna than Cya, and some assumed Cya was a nickname she'd tired of.

Lord Wylan nodded, took his mug of tea, and joined a table in the corner with two Sheparan folk and one Queendom citizen. They welcomed him boisterously into their conversation, and he was laughing soon after.

Reyna covered her dough with a light cloth, then said, "Matild, you're still welcome to borrow those books. We don't need payment."

The midwife already had five pents out, sliding them across the counter. "That follows the assumption that I'd care to give them back." She laughed loudly. "These romance novels are far too engaging. Tarly's been impressed with all the ideas they've spurred." They chatted for a few minutes more, and then the midwife had to return to the clinic. She waved and left.

Gossley came inside a few moments later, his cheeks colored with the glow of young love. It was sickening. Kianthe grimaced and said, "Isn't it time to check on Ponder?"

Reyna glanced at her, then at Gossley making loving faces at his girlfriend through the window. She laughed. "I suppose."

"Gosling, watch the shop," Kianthe called.

He huffed, tearing his eyes away as his girlfriend strolled down the street. "My name is Gossley."

Kianthe waved him off, trailing after Reyna. She stepped onto the back patio just in time to see Ponder leap at her girlfriend. Even young griffons could fly, and although Ponder was newly hatched, she managed to stay airborne until she slammed into Reyna's chest.

Reyna caught her, coddling the tiny creature. "Hello, Pondie. I told you I'd be back after I made bread."

The griffon was the size of a housecat right now, growing larger every day. Soon, she'd be bigger than Lilac, although Kianthe doubted she'd ever reach the size of Visk. Her feathers were deep black, closer to her mother's coloring than the brown of her

father's, although her lion's coloring was still a beautiful gold.
Her yellow eyes gleamed as her tiny beak nibbled at Reyna's ear,
hair, and chin.

Reyna squealed in delight. "Dearest, we talked about this. No
nibbling!" But she didn't exactly push the griffon away.

"I remember when *I* was called 'dearest.'" Kianthe kissed the
griffon's tiny head, then kissed Reyna for good measure. "How
fast things change."

"Why can't two things be dear to me?" Reyna kissed her back,
nearly squishing the griffon between them. Ponder chittered in
exasperation, clawing her way to Reyna's shoulder, then launch-
ing toward the patio table on shaky wings.

Kianthe wound her arms around Reyna's waist, happiness
bubbling in her chest. For a long moment, she just searched Reyna's gorgeous ash-brown eyes, struck again with how lucky she
was. Tilaine was out of the picture. They finally had a lead on the
dragon eggs, a mystery Reyna was thoroughly enjoying. Their little family was growing, albeit oddly, and Tawney had become a
true home.

Kianthe kissed Reyna again, just because she could.

Reyna laughed against her lips. "Tell me what you're thinking,
Key. I know that look."

"I'm thinking"—Kianthe pulled back, pinned her with a bright
smile—"that it's time to propose."

Her partner laughed—then stopped when Kianthe didn't join
in. They hadn't discussed marriage since that day in the forest. It
hadn't been mentioned at all since the throne room, but Kianthe
was aware of the timeline Queen Tilaine expected.

There was no reason not to oblige, now.

Kianthe pulled back, reached into her pocket, and produced
a seed.

Reyna squinted at it. "I was under the assumption you'd give
me jewelry."

"You don't like jewelry. I ask you to wear that moonstone

whenever you leave, so I wouldn't dare clutter your body with more." Kianthe grinned, offering the seed. "This is an ever-seed. I spelled it like my plants; it'll grow as long as there's magic on earth."

"What kind of plant is it?" Reyna took the seed reverently, examining it. She couldn't see the magic laced over its small form, but it was beautiful—almost as beautiful as Reyna herself.

A fitting engagement present from an elemental mage, Kianthe reasoned. A chill swept through the air, and the mage wished she'd thought to bring her blanket-cape outside.

Then again, that might make this less romantic.

"It's a pinyon pine. A seed from the tree where we met when we fled the Capital—the night you made my dreams come true." The mage paused. "Sorry. This is sappy."

"Is that a tree pun?" Reyna's tone was bone dry.

"Maybe. But don't worry, I'll leaf it at that."

Reyna choked on a laugh.

This was going about as well as expected. Kianthe's heart fluttered as she took Reyna's hands in hers, felt the power of the seed pulsing between them. "Reyna, the Stars to my Stone, the roots of my tree, the clouds of my sky—"

"Oh Gods," Reyna said, but she was smiling wide.

"That too. Will you marry me?"

Reyna bounced like a kid in a bakery. Her eyes were alight as she threw her arms around Kianthe's neck, kissed her passionately. "Of course I'll marry you, you ridiculous mage. It took you long enough to ask."

"You told me to wait!"

"Well, I got impatient."

On the table, Ponder screeched and shook her feathers, as if upset Reyna was getting all the attention. But the griffon could wait; Kianthe only had eyes for her girlfriend. No, no. Her *fiancée*. It made the mage warm from the inside out, and magic flecked the air around them, sparkling like the night sky.

This time, Reyna didn't wave the sparkles away. Instead, she gasped: "We have to tell everyone."

"They can wait. Let's make this official." Kianthe towed Reyna to the back of the patio, the space between the two towering pine trees. They knelt together, and she coaxed the ground covering back with a wave of her hand. It receded, leaving a bare space of dirt. The soil was icy, but that, too, melted with a thought.

"Would you do the honors, Rain?"

Holding her breath, Reyna scooped into the soft soil and gently placed the seed. Together, she and Kianthe covered the hole again, patting it resolutely. Their fingers brushed, and they shared a private smile.

"Now you're almost stuck with me," Kianthe said.

"That is the idea," Reyna teased, and pulled her into another kiss. Dirt covered her fingers, but neither of them cared. Together, they laughed and whispered and kissed in the shade of the pines.

On the metal table, Ponder curled up for a nap.

And all was well.

Epilogue

In the late fall, far from the quiet town of Tawney, a dinghy thrashed on a river of rapids. On that boat, a young woman named Serina stood alone, surrounded by sealed crates, desperately trying to regain control.

And all she could think was, bitterly: *The river is supposed to be safer than the open ocean.*

Clearly, this stretch of the Nacean River didn't give two shits about that. Serina yelped as her tiny boat pitched to the left. Rain poured in sheets, coating the deck in slippery water, but it was nothing compared to the rapids washing overboard. This stretch of river was riddled with murk: moss and grime towed up from the riverbed to make her life miserable.

"I just swabbed the deck," she shouted at the water.

The rapids raged, and she squeaked as the boat plummeted down a short drop. Apparently, the Stars didn't care that she took pride in a clean workspace. She also took pride in her continuing existence, and they didn't seem to care about that either.

"Serina!" a panicked voice called from far, far away.

She wrenched her head up to see Bobbie thundering along the river's edge, the sheriff's horse puffing smoke in the icy rain. That was dangerous, running a horse this fast in this weather, but Serina was more indignant about the fact that Bobbie had somehow caught up to her at all.

Again.

"Can't you leave me alone?" Serina grasped at the helm. The dinghy lurched on another rapid, and the force of Serina's hold shattered the ancient wood. It sliced deep into her hand, spilling warm blood. She hissed and raised her voice. "Pirates are people too! Just because I pillage doesn't mean I'm breaking the law."

Bobbie bent low over her horse, and even from this distance, her irritation was evident. "That's *exactly* what it—" Then she cut herself off, her frustrated groan blending with a rumble of thunder. "Never mind. Serina, you have to get to shore."

"Nice try."

"You're coming up on a waterfall!"

Serina squinted downriver, and realized with dread that the thundering wasn't thunder at all.

Well, shit.

She spun the wooden wheel, felt the boat lurch left. It tilted dangerously, and devastating splashes cut through the air. Her cargo. *No.* She'd just stolen that, a shipment of wheat that would help the people in Lathe survive the winter. Serina cursed, spun the wheel back to save the crates still left.

It meant she couldn't quite correct her angle, and the current dragged her to the river's raging center.

Everything after that happened in quick succession:

The boat listed to the side, and finally tipped.

Water flooded everything, and Serina heard Bobbie's devastated cry right before she was dragged into the depths.

Her chest ached but she couldn't gasp, or she might drown, and by the Stars' grace, *how* could she drown with the shore so close?

Somewhere in the dizzying tumult of a swollen, icy river, she tipped off the edge of a waterfall—

—and rough claws buried into her clothes, and she was flying.

Serina lost track of what happened then, but soon the wind stopped howling in her ears, and she coughed hard enough to black out, and then she gasped to life on hard, solid ground. The thunder of the waterfall was very distant, which was either good or bad. A figure loomed over her, and Serina's scattered mind suggested: *Bobbie*.

She didn't know whether to be relieved or irate.

"Y'can't arrest me," she mumbled, but the words slurred together.

The woman standing over her was blond, with pale skin. So, not Bobbie. It was raining all around, but the rain didn't seem to reach them, for some reason.

Serina blinked to clear her blurry vision. "Who—"

"Just once," a dry voice said from nearby, and a mage stepped into view. Serina knew she was a mage because her *hands were on fire*. "I'd like to have a vacation without mortal peril. I don't feel like that's too much to ask."

"Darling, this isn't a vacation." The blond woman sounded affectionate, but her gaze was no-nonsense as she turned Serina onto her side. "And you should probably learn to sail better."

Serina couldn't stay focused. Her brain had been left on the riverbed, wrenched to pieces in the current alongside her precious little dinghy. Without that boat, pirating would get a lot more difficult. And her wheat—

Well. The wheat was gone. Which meant she'd have to pillage more. Eventually.

Now, her vision was blurring. "T-Thanks," Serina mumbled. "If you see a mean-looking sheriff, tell her to fuck off."

And the world went black.

Meet and Greet

A Tomes & Tea One-shot

Queen Tilaine smiled, and Kianthe contemplated what it would be like to punch a royal.

Well, okay. That was a bit much. Kianthe wouldn't call herself a *violent* person, per se . . . but she could fight when needed. And considering her magic was intended to quell tsunamis, raise crops for an entire country, tackle magical beasts of all manners . . . it was hardly ethical to use on a single person.

Although, if anyone was an exception to that rule, it was the Queendom's sovereign.

"It's truly a pleasure to host you, Arcandor," Queen Tilaine crooned. She was perched on a ridiculously large throne, elevated above the rest of the room. She'd chosen crimson and gold accents, with a special theme of dragons—ironic, since dragons resided far to the north, and didn't bother with human affairs. "I've been anticipating your arrival."

Kianthe sniffed haughtily and almost replied: *I haven't.*

But the Magicary would throw a fit if she demolished global relations with a sentence like that. Instead, Kianthe matched Tilaine's pleasant smile, right down to the malicious undertone.

"I wholly agree. This visit is long overdue . . . especially with the recent riots."

Behind Tilaine, her royal Queensguard—eight in total, as if eight trained soldiers could stop the Mage of Ages—bristled at Kianthe's implied threat. Cute. The mage met their gazes steadily, one by one.

Good luck stopping me if I decide to act, her dark eyes promised.

Each of the guards glared back . . . until Kianthe locked eyes with the one perched against the huge bank of glass windows.

And time seemed to stop.

Fuck. Kianthe hadn't realized she was so gorgeous.

Oblivious to the mage's sudden panic, the female guard merely stared past her—watching without *watching.* Everything about her exuded cool professionalism. Her stance was loose, her hand resting on the sword strapped to her hip. Her ash-brown eyes were stunning, and their color contrasted nicely with her pale skin and ice-blond hair.

A lifetime flashed between them. Kianthe saw it all, with such vivid clarity that the Stone of Seeing itself must have placed her in this woman's path.

What could they become if Kianthe was brave enough to introduce herself? Not here, obviously, but perhaps she could linger around the palace after this meeting. Maybe fabricate a chance introduction, or—

"—with me. Arcandor?"

Ah, shit. The meeting. Right.

The queen was talking, because of course she was. Tilaine was enamored with her own voice.

Recognizing the brief distraction, Queen Tilaine cast a dark glance at whatever was stealing the Arcandor's attention. "Is something wrong?"

The female guard by the windows looked blankly ahead, so carefully detached that Kianthe almost snorted.

Better be present to this conversation—anything else could endanger the guard. Tilaine was known for being a brutal sovereign. If she thought one of her Queensguard was intervening on this meeting, she might have the gorgeous guard . . . beheaded, or some shit.

So, Kianthe addressed the question head-on. "Oh, things are definitely wrong. In fact, let's get riot down to business."

She held her breath.

Instead of laughing, the queen quirked one delicate eyebrow.

"Because of the riots happening in the Queendom?" Kianthe ventured, gesturing with a hand. "Come on. That was comedy gold."

By the windows, the female guard smirked. It was such a brief motion, gone in a flash, but it warmed the Arcandor like a blazing sun.

The guard thought Kianthe was funny.

She'd *laughed*.

Sort of.

Ugh. Bad mage. Focus.

Kianthe plowed ahead: "Okay, listen. Not even your network of spies can contain the fact that your citizens are rebelling. I'm sorry for the loss of your mother, but the months after your coronation haven't been smooth. People are taking notice."

On her throne, Queen Tilaine's painted lips tilted upward. Her skin had been powdered to hide the pink undertone, her eye makeup applied to imply elegance and dominance all at once. "You are mistaken, Arcandor. This so-called uprising is merely a few dissatisfied pockets of citizens, most of whom have already accepted the new regime." Now Tilaine pushed off her ornate throne, strolled like a peacock to the bank of windows.

The female Queensguard moved seamlessly out of her way, taking a deferential position in the shadows.

Stars and Stone, she was so professional.

Tilaine gestured beyond the glass, at her stone city far below. "You flew here on a griffon, did you not? Surely you toured the city from above, noticed the lack of . . . how would the Sheparan council frame it? 'Blood in the streets'?" Her voice was lilting, almost amused. "I understand the Mage of Ages has a duty to intervene when injustice occurs, but your sword is pointed in the wrong direction."

Kianthe didn't use a sword, and she didn't appreciate the manipulation. From her current position in the center of the huge room, Kianthe twirled her fingers, summoning a fireball that burned merrily in her palm. "Oh, I don't bother with weapons."

Tilaine stared at the flame, almost greedily. She swept the folds of her dress around herself, shoulders back, chin high. "Indeed. Once I've settled into my position, I would absolutely love to discuss how mages are born. It seems unfair that the only mages in my country are visiting citizens of Shepara and Leonol."

"All mages are citizens of the Magicary, regardless of where they're born." Kianthe didn't mention that the Queendom worshiped a pantheon of Gods, not the venerated Stone of Seeing or adjacent Stars. She didn't mention that even if mages were born here, they'd never amount to much without training—and Tilaine almost certainly wouldn't let them leave.

Tilaine's gaze was sharp. "And why aren't any of my people magic users? It's beginning to feel like a conspiracy."

Now Kianthe shrugged, almost amused. "The only way to source magic is through worship. But I'd be happy to get you a pamphlet on our venerated Stone of Seeing, if you're interested in converting."

In the corner, the female guard's shoulders shook. It was nearly imperceptible, utterly silent, but her golden pauldrons—sculpted into a ridiculous dragon skull that matched the queen's throne— were shaking just a bit.

Playing it up for this woman, Kianthe extinguished her fireball, swept her arms wide. "Listen, Tilaine. Your time is valuable. The sooner we conclude our business, the better for us both, right?"

Let's finish this so I can meet that guard.

"Our gathering is long overdue, as you said." Queen Tilaine stepped back to her throne, settling onto the red velvet cushion. The dragon statues that made up her throne were absurd—too large for human décor, too small to truly represent dragonkind.

She'd probably never even *seen* a dragon. The thought made Kianthe chuckle.

Until Tilaine said definitively: "I've cleared my schedule to give you the attention you deserve, Arcandor. I expect the same courtesy."

Her words had concealed venom, much like the poison that coated the palace guards' blades. Like it or not, the Arcandor was the most powerful mage in the Realm, and Kianthe cared far less for politics than her predecessor. Queen Tilaine wasn't the only ruler vying for her time.

It must kill her slowly, bowing to someone else.

Kianthe smirked, momentarily forgetting the cute guard. She strode forward, getting close enough to the throne that Tilaine's front guards stiffened, bracing their weaponry.

"Regrettably, I don't extend that courtesy to many. But as I said, our business is short. Stop massacring your citizens." Kianthe paused, as if she'd just had a revelation. "So simple, isn't it?"

Tilaine drummed her fingers on the skull of the left dragon statue. "Mmm. Simple to you, perhaps, swathed in magic and untouched by reality. But a true sovereign doesn't let pockets of disorder infect an otherwise healthy nation."

"Okay. This might seem wild, but hear me out. How about you listen to them . . . and respond to their complaints with actual change?" Kianthe's voice was low now, dangerous. The air around them dropped several degrees. Magic followed her whim, and Kianthe was all about dramatic flair.

"You are overstepping, Arcandor." Tilaine narrowed her eyes.

She rocked back on her heels. "Oh, I doubt that. I don't answer to your country, or Shepara, or Leonol . . . but I guarantee *you* will answer to *me* if we have a problem. Is that clear?"

Silence.

The queen sighed. "I'd hoped we could be civil, but I'm beginning to think you've already formed an opinion of me."

Kianthe laughed, icy and unfeeling. "I form an opinion of anyone who treats human life callously." Without giving the queen a chance to respond, Kianthe spun on her heel, turning her back to the sovereign. Over her shoulder, she called, "You have one week to stop the riots—*peacefully*—before I return with more firepower. Literally."

And with a wave, Kianthe strolled through the double doors of the throne room.

No one stopped her.

⚘

Reyna wasn't sure what she was expecting of the Arcandor, the Mage of Ages, the most powerful magic user in existence, but a stunning young woman with a fiery temper and a dry sense of humor wasn't it.

The guard moseyed back to her quarters after an early dismissal. Queen Tilaine was huffing and puffing about the Arcandor's threats, her attitude, her lack of respect. And when Her Excellency was in a mood, the whole palace paid attention.

Queen Tilaine had promptly summoned her advisors and spat, "Out. All of you, *out*," to everyone but her most trusted guards.

Reyna was not one of those, despite her family history, despite the fact that her mother served in Queen Eren's shadow before Reyna was even born. Alongside the others, Reyna bowed and wasted no time obeying.

As she strolled back to her quarters, Reyna contemplated what had just happened.

The Arcandor was powerful, but the extent of her power inside the heart of the Queendom was shocking. The woman had exuded brazen confidence as she spoke in tones of treason, fatal words. Anyone less would have wound up in chains, or bleeding from a poisoned wound.

Apparently not even Queen Tilaine was willing to test the Arcandor's temper.

A ghost of a smile tilted Reyna's lips. The Queendom was a bloody place by nature: Queen Tilaine's mother, grandmother, and royal ancestors weren't known for their compassion. Worse, the God of Mercy itself had blessed Tilaine on her coronation day—which she'd twisted to her own, vicious accord.

Her Excellency would have a difficult time obeying the Arcandor's order without losing the fear of her staff and citizens.

What a beautifully curious dilemma.

Either way, it resulted in a free day for Reyna, and she didn't get many of those. She unclipped her heavy crimson cloak as she walked, folding it over one arm. Her gold-plated armor was aesthetic more than functional, and Reyna anticipated stripping it too, maybe sinking into a bath. A cup of tea on her small balcony sounded like the perfect end to an interesting afternoon.

And then she turned a corner—right into a young woman.

Reyna leapt backward soundlessly, lithely, one hand on her sword. It dropped immediately when she registered just who she'd almost plowed into.

The Arcandor.

The *Mage of Ages*.

And Gods damn it, she was more beautiful up close. Her skin was the color of wet sand on a sunset beach, contrasting with dark, inquisitive eyes. Deep brown hair fell in a long, messy braid, and unbidden, Reyna ached to comb it out, rebraid it more carefully.

She didn't, to be clear.

Instead, Reyna bowed, neck burning, heart pounding. "My sincerest apologies, Arcandor." Wordlessly, she pressed against the wall, stiff as a tree while she waited for the Mage of Ages to pass.

Where was she going? Reyna set her jaw, staring straight ahead. It didn't matter where the Arcandor chose to walk—if she offended the legendary mage somehow, if Reyna interfered with this political firestorm, Her Excellency might consider it a grievous transgression.

Never mind the dungeon. Reyna could be killed on the spot, years of loyal service be damned.

Already, she was gauging ways this could go wrong, mapping out the areas of risk. This hallway had two entrances: the one she'd just cleared, and another at the far end. Six doors lined the stone corridor. One was Reyna's own bedroom. Two belonged to Her Excellency's personal guards, who'd stayed in the throne room when her advisors arrived. Another room belonged to Venne—but he had a personal day, out hunting with his cousin.

That left two doors with Queensguard potentially inside. Colleagues who could get curious if the Mage of Ages caused a commotion.

Cohorts who could become witnesses, *informants,* if they thought it'd earn an ounce of Queen Tilaine's favor.

Sweat dripped down Reyna's neck.

She needed to get out of here.

Unfortunately, the Arcandor didn't move. Instead, a wide smile split her lips. "Please, don't apologize. You're gorgeous, you know that?"

To say Reyna was taken aback was an understatement.

"Ah—thank you, Arcandor. That's very kind."

"Huh. You must not get compliments often. It seems like I caught you off *guard.*" She emphasized the last word, this goddess of a human, then spread her arms as if waiting for Reyna to laugh at the joke.

No, not a joke.

A pun.

And Reyna laughed. Not because it was funny, but because it was fucking absurd that the *Mage of Ages* was delivering puns when she was supposed to be brokering peace in the Realm and keeping all magic and magical creatures in harmony. Whatever

Reyna had expected from the woman, that joke wouldn't have even graced her list.

And Reyna's lists were meticulous.

But her surprised snort was apparently tinder to the Arcandor's fire, because the mage bounced on her toes and kept going. "I sword of guessed that you'd enjoy humor. You seemed a bit on edge—get it? Because of your sword? Anyway, I hoped I could lighten the mood." At that, the mage summoned another ball of flame, the fire dancing over her knuckles like a party trick.

Reyna forgot the dangers.

She laughed, bright and bubbly.

The Arcandor's eyes widened, her smile brightening like she'd been gifted a deity's favor. And down the hallway, a doorknob turned. Reyna noted both things in immediate succession, then did something that rarely happened: she made a snap decision.

She unlocked the door to her quarters with a heavy key, grabbed the Arcandor's wrist, and towed her inside.

The door slammed shut, and only in the privacy of her bedroom did she breathe easy.

And then realization settled in her bones.

Reyna's breath seized, and she spluttered an explanation: "I'm so sorry, great Arcandor. I didn't mean—here, you're free to leave—of course you are—"

"Wow, your place already. I must be fantastic at flirting." The Arcandor whistled, spinning around the space. Reyna's private quarters were three rooms: a living area, a bedroom, and a washroom. The living area was sparsely decorated, with a single window and a wooden door to the small balcony along the back wall, but it was hers, and it suddenly felt intimate to share with this woman.

The Arcandor failed to notice her panic. She simply grinned, which was also inappropriately adorable. "Or you're just really into puns. Tell me the truth."

"I'm not—" Reyna drew a short breath, struggling to compose herself.

"Did I already leave you breathless?" The Arcandor rocked back on her heels, clearly satisfied.

Any negative response might offend her. Reyna considered her words as she draped her crimson cloak over a chair, then removed the heavy pieces of armor and her poisoned sword. Half of her wanted to say something witty, engage in banter—and the other half remembered that this was the *Mage of Ages,* and one did not simply *banter* with her.

But her silence was just as telling. The Arcandor raised a hand. "Hang on. You are enjoying this, right?"

"It's a pleasure to be gifted with your presence, Arcandor." Reyna defaulted to her old state of bowing deeply, one breath short of kneeling before this mage like a true knight. "But I never should have dragged you in here. Please, excuse my grievous offense—"

"Grievous offense?"

For the first time, the Mage of Ages seemed alarmed.

Reyna hesitated, keeping her eyes downcast, her tone neutral. "Her Excellency expected your time. If she discovers I'm stealing it, especially after—well, after your meeting, she won't be pleased."

"And you'll be hurt." The Arcandor wheeled backward, fingers trailing along her braid like a bad habit. No wonder it was so messy. "Shit. *Shit.* I should have thought—but of course I didn't, because that's just me. I'm so sorry. I thought you were cute, and now I know your laugh is fantastic, but that's no reason to stalk you through the palace. I'll leave." And she spun on her heels, heading straight for the balcony.

It was a seven-story drop, but that didn't seem to faze her. She tossed open the door and stepped onto the small balcony, pressing her fingers to her lips like she was about to whistle.

The Arcandor traveled via griffon—most mages did. She was probably about to summon her mount and fly away. Panic seized Reyna's chest. She had a mere breath to intervene, or this woman would be lost to her life forever.

It shouldn't have bothered her. Reyna's life in the Grand Palace was stable, predetermined decades before she was born. She'd trained for this career her entire life, and it fitted her well enough.

And yet . . . here was a woman not only brave enough to stand up to Queen Tilaine, but powerful enough to back up her words. The Arcandor had traveled the world. She'd seen everything Reyna dreamed of, far beyond the palace walls, things outside carefully curated diplomatic visits . . . and for a brief moment, Reyna wondered what it would be like.

Testing boundaries.

Becoming someone new.

Maybe Reyna could be like that too. Someone who took risks. Who accepted dangerous liaisons just because they presented themselves with a smile and a few puns. Reyna had never wanted anything more, in that moment.

And so, she took a chance.

"No one knows you're here. You don't have to go." Her fingers reached for Kianthe's arm, but withdrew at the last moment. She couldn't expect the most powerful mage in the Realm to acquiesce to a lowly guard's request.

The Arcandor paused at the doorway, slowly lowering her fingers from her lips. She looked wildly conflicted. "I don't want to put you in danger. This was selfish."

"Maybe we all deserve to be selfish once in a while." Reyna felt bold saying the words, but she didn't regret them.

The Arcandor relaxed, smiling bright, and stepped back inside the living room. She closed the balcony door firmly, then drew the curtains over the window. Complete privacy. It should have made Reyna nervous, but all she felt was excitement—especially when the Arcandor offered a hand. "Call me Kianthe. That's my real name."

Reyna had never considered that the Arcandor would have a given name . . . but of course she would. The Mage of Ages wasn't gifted power until the old Arcandor died or was killed, which meant she had a life before gaining her immense magic.

It felt so special. Reyna didn't think anyone *knew* the Arcandor's name. At least in the Queendom, she'd never heard it.

Kianthe. Key-an-th. It rolled through her mind like a dewdrop on a leaf, crisp and lovely. Everything here felt tenuous, on the cusp of something grand. Reyna shook the young woman's hand, feeling dazed. They must be about the same age.

"I'm Reyna."

The Arcandor—no, Kianthe—repeated her name, tasting each syllable. "Reyna. Like rain. That's beautiful." She was an elemental mage, so she probably had to say that. Reyna still blushed. Kianthe noticed, smirked knowingly, and diverted the subject. "Have you always been a Queensguard?"

"I form an opinion of anyone who treats human life callously," Kianthe had said.

Guilt and doubt churned in Reyna's chest. "Callous" wasn't the word Reyna would use to describe herself or her talents—she only killed when absolutely necessary. But "necessary" was defined by her job parameters: protecting Queen Tilaine.

Which meant her body count was far higher than the Arcandor would expect.

Reyna hated that, for the first time in her life, she doubted her own actions. Hated that one conversation with this woman was enough to tilt her world on its axis. She responded with her default, because it seemed less complicated.

"My mother served Queen Eren, and I am proud to serve Queen Tilaine."

She waited for judgment.

Kianthe didn't offer any. She simply asked, eagerly, "Do you like to read?"

Dazed, Reyna replied, "Ah, a little. I prefer baking, I think." This was so awkward. They were just standing in her living room. She gestured at the chairs by the hearth, hesitantly. They weren't luxurious by any means, but hopefully the Arcandor didn't care about that. "Would you like to take a seat?"

Kianthe contemplated it, then cast a cautious glance at the door. "Ah—yes. So fucking badly. But now I'm paranoid that someone's going to interrupt, and you'll get in trouble." She rubbed her arms, suddenly nervous. The change in demeanor—especially since it was due to concerns about Reyna's safety—was endearing. A thrill of affection raced through Reyna's veins.

"I can leave the palace tonight, after most of the Queensguard are asleep? There's a nice spot in the forest west of here. I think you'd like it." Reyna tensed, waiting for Kianthe's reply.

To her shock, the Arcandor squeaked.

Actually *squeaked*.

"Yes! Ahh, I'll make a picnic. I bought some cheese in Wellia—I can share that. Do you have any allergies? Or—or food preferences? Shit, though, a midnight picnic in the forest is pretty romantic. Is this a date? Would you like that, or do you prefer to take things slower? Hang on, are you single? Because you seem fantastic, and I'd love to take you out—but if you're in a relationship, this will get really awkward—"

Reyna burst out laughing. It was so freeing, pulling fond amusement so deep from her chest that it startled her. She scrubbed her face. One of the Gods must be playing tricks on her, because this was so absurd.

"I'm single. But this doesn't have to become a grand gesture. Let's just . . . eat. Okay?"

Simple.

Kianthe squinted at her. "I'll have you know, Reyna like rain, that you're pretty special. And I've been alone long enough to seize *special* when I find it." A pause, a wry smile. "If you like me after tonight, you may never get rid of me."

That sent another thrill up Reyna's spine.

What the hells was happening?

Of course, before she could reply, someone rapped on her door. "Hey, Rey," Venne called through the wood. "I heard the Arcandor was here, and it didn't go well. I'm going to need all the details." He lowered his voice, petulant. "This is why I shouldn't have agreed to go hunting. Stupid."

"Ah, one moment," Reyna called, eyes widening.

"See you tonight," Kianthe whispered, and with a *swoosh* of her cloak, she stepped onto the balcony and closed the door behind her. When Reyna peeked a moment later, she was gone.

Heart pounding in anticipation—and the thrill of almost getting caught—Reyna smoothed her shirt and let Venne inside.

Tonight couldn't come fast enough.

❧

Kianthe dressed to impress.

Granted, to her, that was a nice vest, a high-collar shirt, and a bow tie. She pulled a sheet of ice from the creek where she was changing, admiring her reflection, then grimaced and tugged the bow tie loose. "It's too much," she told her griffon.

Visk chittered, far more interested with the rabbit hiding nearby than anything Kianthe was doing. He bent low near a fluffy bush, his haunches poised, lion's tail swishing. It was adorable—but Kianthe didn't have the time.

The moon was already starting to rise, and the stars had come out. Reyna could leave the Capital's gates any second—and if Kianthe wasn't waiting, she might get bored and go home.

What a travesty that would be.

So, Kianthe let the bow tie hang, pinched some color into her cheeks, and smoothed her scraggly braid until it looked somewhat decent. Then she released the ice so it wouldn't freeze the stream and patted Visk's flank. "Come on, bud. We have to go."

The griffon screeched indignantly, but a stern look from her had him puffing. She mounted him, and he cast one glare at the bush before spreading his wings and leaping into the air.

Reyna appeared exactly on time—Kianthe added *punctual* to her growing list of Reyna's traits. There were guards manning the gate, archers perched in the parapets. Everyone in the Queendom seemed poised for an attack, which felt ridiculous. Kianthe circled high overhead as Reyna walked with confidence toward the forest's edge, a lone figure on a long path.

When she stepped into the tree line, Kianthe landed nearby and dismounted Visk.

"Reyna! Over here."

The Queensguard didn't seem startled. She did, however, seem very concerned about the griffon. "Ah—is he friendly?"

"Friendly to my friends," Kianthe replied lightly, petting the tiny feathers along Visk's head. He preened under her touch. "But he'll keep himself busy tonight, if you're uneasy." With a quick dismissal, Visk took off again—undoubtedly to catch his own dinner.

It left Kianthe standing awkwardly in the clearing, hoping the evening light was doing her favors.

Reyna was dressed in a silk shirt and deep black trousers. Casual enough to appear normal for a Queensguard, but the materials were definitely a step up from her uniform.

A flush crept over Kianthe's face as she admired how they hugged Reyna's toned muscles. "You are beautiful."

Reyna flinched. "Stop—please stop saying things like that."

Shit. Kianthe backtracked hastily. "Ah, I mean. You're . . . okay-looking."

Now Reyna stared at her, deadpan. "Thank you."

"Y-You're welcome." Kianthe tugged at her collar. Why did she go with something so high? And her bow tie hung uselessly. Should she tie it? Her frazzled thoughts made her laugh, self-deprecating. "I don't think I'm very good at this."

That seemed to give Reyna some courage. She smiled warmly. "If you were good at this, Kianthe, I'd be concerned you do this with every cute person who crosses your path."

"No," Kianthe yelped. "Stars and Stone, it's just you. I don't—I honestly don't even know what possessed me today. You just looked so regal standing by the windows. Like you were the queen, not Tilaine."

That made Reyna wince, even as she started leading Kianthe deeper into the forest. She was carrying a picnic basket, its handle set over her arm. "I would never presume to outshine Her Excellency, our blessed sovereign."

It felt like a perfectly regurgitated response. Something honed over years to caress Tilaine's ego.

Doubt flickered in Kianthe's mind. Maybe this was a bad idea. The Queendom wasn't known for allowing individuality—what if Reyna was just like the other Queensguard after all? A mindless creation of professionalism and flattery.

Kianthe had sought *Reyna* out, but . . . for a moment, her walls slammed back into place. Because if Reyna was this dedicated to Queen Tilaine, maybe she was using Kianthe's favor to earn the queen more power. Maybe this whole thing was orchestrated, and Kianthe played right into it.

Sweat trickled down her neck.

But Reyna added another trait to Kianthe's ever-growing list: keen observation. She stopped short, frowning. "Are you worried about this?"

"No," Kianthe lied. "Not at all."

Reyna's hand tightened around her other arm, hugging the picnic basket to her chest. "I mean this in the nicest way, Arcandor, but your entire body tensed when I said that." She lowered her gaze, like she was embarrassed. "This is a bad idea. If Her Excellency knew we were here—"

"She won't hurt you," Kianthe swore fiercely.

She couldn't stomach the thought of putting this woman in danger.

But Reyna just sighed. "I don't think you can control that. Today was an impulse—but it's okay if you've changed your mind. You're allowed to walk away."

Kianthe didn't want that. The very suggestion of leaving Reyna now, sitting with Visk all night, venturing on yet another lonely journey tomorrow, made Kianthe cringe. All those seasons spent alone, wishing someone would take an interest in her.

She'd finally broken today, and seized the courage to start a conversation. It had paid off in the greatest way, and now she had the opportunity for a maybe-date with an intriguing woman.

Or she could live in fear of her magic being misused.

It seemed like a simple choice.

"I want to stay." Kianthe paused. "Do you?"

"This is the most exciting thing that's happened to me in years." Reyna was breathless. "But . . . can we try something? Can we pretend you . . . aren't . . . the most powerful mage in the Realm? Just for tonight?"

Thank the Stone of Seeing itself. Kianthe breathed a sigh, her shoulders relaxing. "Absolutely."

Reyna seemed equally pleased. She resumed walking down the forest path, her tone teasing. "What would you like to do, Kianthe, now that you're unemployed?"

The moon was bright enough overhead, but Kianthe wanted to see her smile. She created an ever-flame, holding it casually in the palm of her hand. "Honestly? I've always wanted to open a bookshop. Something with a cozy hearth and lots of armchairs and good company."

In her mind, it would never be empty. People would know her real name, not her title, and she'd have real, honest friends again.

"A bookshop?" Reyna sounded intrigued. "Can it have a kitchenette in the corner for tea? All the best bookstores have food and drink, I believe."

Kianthe grinned. "Either tea, or liquor."

"I thought mages didn't drink."

"I wouldn't know. I'm not a mage tonight." Kianthe winked.

Reyna's lips tilted upward. "Well. That's very concerning, considering your hand is on fire."

Against her better judgment, Kianthe snorted, and a glob of

saliva slid down her throat, and she dissolved into a coughing fit that doubled as wheezing laughter. Reyna started laughing too, patting her back almost sympathetically, and once Kianthe regained her composure, they moved on.

❆

When they arrived at their destination, Reyna bit her lip, truly hoping it was impressive to an elemental mage. The space was surrounded by rock on three sides, with a short waterfall cascading into a burbling stream. A few pine trees blocked out some stars, but for the most part, the sky opened above them.

"My mother used to take me here," Reyna admitted. "It's my favorite spot in the Queendom."

"Used to?" Kianthe tilted her head.

Reyna's lips curved into a fond, sad smile. "She was killed when I was young. Assassination attempt."

Kianthe winced. "Shit. I'm sorry, Reyna."

"It's an honorable death." Reyna untucked the thin blanket she'd draped over her picnic basket, unfurling it. It settled over the dirt—which smoothed itself out magically fast. At the same time, a glimmer of firelight spread around them, flickering like dozens of tiny candles.

Reyna stared at them, eyes wide.

Kianthe had her arms spread, conducting whatever spell she deemed necessary—but stopped short when she saw Reyna's expression. "Ah. Too much? I thought it felt a bit romantic, but the moon is probably enough—"

"No, it's . . . it's really beautiful." Reyna didn't hide the wonder in her voice. When Kianthe smiled, she continued, amused, "Shockingly so for someone who isn't a mage."

Kianthe rolled her eyes, grinning. "Okay, okay."

They settled down to eat. Kianthe offered cheese and fruits, and Reyna had smuggled smoked elk from the kitchens. Kianthe *wasn't* a vegetarian, which surprised Reyna—although the mage drily pointed out, "I have more of an affiliation with plants. Some mages try the opposite; no vegetables or fruits at all." She tilted her head back, sarcastic: "It doesn't end well."

"I can only imagine." Reyna waited until Kianthe had helped herself to another slice of apple before reaching back into her picnic basket for the final item inside. "This is probably silly, and I'm sure you don't need it. But you mentioned reading back in my room. I thought you might like a copy of my favorite tome."

She pulled it out of her basket, face hot with embarrassment. It wasn't a popular tome, or even one aimed at adults. No, this book was a short story, barely thicker than her pinkie, with a stiff leather cover. The handwriting inside was smudged, nearly illegible in places.

Kianthe's jaw dropped. "You brought me a *book*?"

"It's my favorite nighttime tale." Reyna ducked her head. "I have two copies, so I won't miss it. But I rewrote this one myself when my best friend wanted to borrow it." She rolled her eyes. "He called it 'boring,' so I challenged him to a duel over the main character's reputation."

Kianthe gasped, gleeful now. "Tell me you beat him."

Reyna drew a demure sip from her flask of water. "He's always been second-best with a sword." Now she tapped the cover, pointing to the gold title. "He paid me accordingly, and I used the coin to bind the book. I thought you might like it."

"I *love* it." Kianthe looked like she was a second away from hugging her.

Or kissing her.

For a charged second, their eyes met, and Reyna held her breath—waiting. She wouldn't make the first move, not on their first "let's just eat" date, but her body felt warm with anticipation anyway.

Kianthe broke the spell, clearing her throat as she flipped open the novel. "What's it about?"

It took Reyna precious breaths to regain her composure. For an intriguing moment, she realized that the heaviness in her chest was *disappointment*. Very interesting. "Ah, a princess—who decides she'd rather be a commoner. She leaves the palace for a day beyond the gates."

"Let me guess. It doesn't go well?"

Reyna tilted her head. "No, it's everything she wanted." She left it at that, not wanting to descend into spoilers. "It was such a comfort to me as a kid. The thought that someone could leave a preordained life to find happiness elsewhere."

"That is the dream." Kianthe stroked the cover, staring at the tome. "Thank you, Reyna. For this, and—well, everything."

"I've hardly done anything, Kianthe."

"You're sitting here with me. That's pretty nice."

Reyna hated her defeated tone. "Nice to spend a rare evening off with excellent company and fine food? I completely agree." She left no room for argument.

So, Kianthe didn't argue. Now, her smile was genuine, and she tucked the book into her bag. "Yeah. That. Okay—you mentioned a mother. What about a father? Siblings?"

"Never knew my father, but that's not uncommon in the Grand Palace." Reyna shrugged. "Siblings, none. My best friend, Venne, is closest to it—but I figured he'd be my eventual match." She'd discounted it a long time ago, and today had only confirmed that choice. "I'm far happier to be sitting here, with you."

Kianthe grinned. "Oh damn. Now *I* feel special."

Reyna shoved her arm, taking another bite of elk. "How about you?"

"Parents, back in Jallin. An old friend, but I haven't spoken to him in years. Other than that, no one, really. Lots of diplomats and diarns and other leaders vying for my attention. Not much time for this kind of thing." Kianthe gestured at the picnic.

The stream beside them burbled, and Reyna lapsed into silence for a moment. "Sounds lonely."

"It is."

They sat with that for a minute.

Finally, Kianthe clapped her hands. "Have you ever wanted to fly? Visk is a sweetheart, I promise."

"I'll believe it when I see it," Reyna replied, only half joking. But something about the thrill of flying was exquisite, brightening her gaze, lightening her tone.

Kianthe seemed elated. "I'll call him. Just a quick one, don't worry!"

The date progressed, and Reyna found herself enjoying every minute of it. By the end of the evening, she'd befriended the Arcandor, the Mage of Ages. Within days, they were confidantes. Within a season, they were dating . . . in secret, always in secret.

Reyna didn't regret taking a chance.

❦

Much later, Reyna stepped into their new bedroom at New Leaf Tomes and Tea to see Kianthe hunched over the deep windowsill. Through the glass beyond, their patio glimmered in the early-morning light. Dew glistened on the metal table and chairs, and a soft fog hung over the space.

It was cold this morning, so Reyna stepped to their wardrobe to retrieve a knitted sweater. "Ah, dear? What are you doing?"

"Well, *we* need a bookshelf," Kianthe said resolutely, stepping back to show what she was organizing. She'd stacked several books vertically, pressed between the windowsill's wall and—what looked like a heavy glass orb.

Reyna squinted at that second piece.

"It was a gift from a councilmember in Wellia," Kianthe shrugged. "Some artifact his family has held for generations. Kinda stuffy. But it has these cool gold flecks, so I figured we could display it."

"Ah." Reyna browsed through her sweater options, choosing one that had stretched over the years. It was dyed deep blue and hung to her hips—it always felt like wearing a warm hug. "And what tomes have made the cut for our private collection?"

Kianthe grinned. "Some raunchy ones, for sure. Might need some evening inspiration."

"Dear." Reyna rolled her eyes.

"And some nice ones!" Kianthe tugged out two, showing them off. "Look, these are nonfiction. Matild gave me this one on human behavior."

Reyna pulled the sweater over her head, shifted it so it was comfortable, and fixed the strands that had pulled loose from her bun. "Put that one aside for me; I'll read it next." She turned for the door, paused in thought, and pivoted to Kianthe instead.

The mage had just set that tome on Reyna's bedside table, and jumped a bit when Reyna snaked her arms around Kianthe's waist from behind. She hugged Kianthe, rested her chin on the mage's shoulder. "I'm really happy to be here with you, Key. I'm glad you got your bookshop."

Kianthe turned so they were facing each other. Her arms draped over Reyna's shoulders in a close embrace. "Check the tall book on the windowsill."

Reyna glanced at it.

A familiar tome—one handwritten by Reyna herself and bound by a leatherworker with Venne's hard-lost coin. A fond smile tilted her lips. "You kept it. After all these years, I wasn't sure."

"I locked it in the Magicary, in a vault."

"You did not."

Kianthe raised one eyebrow. "Rain. You handwrote that. I most assuredly did."

A flush crept over Reyna's cheeks. "Well. That's . . . impressive."

"After the unicorn incident, I figured it was time to retrieve it—

put it on display. Maybe a reread." She leaned in close, pressing a kiss to Reyna's lips. "I thought all stories needed heart-pounding action, but that one proved me wrong. You're right; the princess lives her best life by abandoning it all."

"Mmm. They say the stories we love share a bit about our-selves," Reyna murmured, feeling warm in all the best ways.

"They do." Kianthe pulled away with a hug. "You ready to open the shop?"

Reyna followed her out of the bedroom, casting one last glance at the book she'd gifted Kianthe on their first date. Fondness swept over her in a wave, and she gently closed their bedroom door.

"Always."

$\mathcal{A}$CKNOWLEDGMENTS

Update: Spring 2024

When I self-published this book in 2022, I was just hoping for a bit of side income and a fun experience as an indie author. Instead, this journey allowed me to become a full-time author. (What the hell is happening. Seriously.)

This book isn't perfect, but this story, these characters, mean everything to me. In helping Kianthe and Reyna pursue their dream life, I somehow stumbled on mine, and I'm so, so grateful for it.

All of the acknowledgments below still apply, but I have a few new ones to add.

Thank you *so* much to my literary agent, Taryn Fagerness, for randomly agreeing to represent me. I'm still not quite sure how this happened, but I know a sign from the universe when I see one. Your unrelenting determination to sell this book, your enthusiasm for my upcoming projects, your advice as we navigate this business . . . I'm so lucky to have you in my corner. (Special shout-out to Rebecca in the UK, and all the other coagents around the world who helped make this a reality!)

The biggest, most heartfelt thank-you to the folks at Tor, my dream publisher, for taking a chance on me. Bella, you fought for my book in the very beginning, and I'm so lucky to have met such a powerhouse in this business. And then to have Monique (and Mal!) offering incredible support on the US side . . . incredible. To everyone else on the Tor team who worked hard to make this book a reality—Holly, Lydia, Grace, Sarah, Christina, and so many others—*thank* you.

To Jessica Threet, for offering her voice to these characters—I can't express enough how grateful I am for your passion (and patience)!!

Now back to our regularly scheduled programming.

Original Acknowledgments (2022)

I'd be lying if I said this book wasn't directly inspired by Travis Baldree's incredible cozy fantasy, *Legends & Lattes*. Travis, thank you for all your incredible kindness and encouragement. And thank you for giving the cozy fantasy genre a name, so authors like me can rally behind it.

Next, shout-out to Irene Huang (artist name: Illulinchi) for bringing this incredible cover to life. Added thanks to Amphi for helping with the lettering, and drawing that adorable image of Visk on the front page. Almost certainly, this cover is why people read this book at all.

Huge personal thanks to Audrey, who read every chapter of this book as it was being written, helped me brainstorm plot progression and character development, and then—as if she didn't do enough—came up with the incredible title and, like, half of Kianthe's puns. I appreciate you putting up with me!

I'd also be nowhere without my family: my parents (who always had a book in hand), my sister (the best friend a girl could want), my grandparents (who still have my first self-published book sitting on their coffee table), and the extended family (who support me always).

Next, my friends: the Breckenridge girls (and Kayleigh, who's always there in spirit), the NaNoWriMo pals past and present, the writers from my Discord servers, my college and high school friends, and anyone else who's supported me. Special shout-out to Krissy (the OG beta), Alex (the sunshine friend), and of course, Paige, who deserves two shout-outs after the dedication in *The Secrets of Star Whales*.

Finally, I'd like to acknowledge the TikTok crowd. You inspired me to create this. Without your enthusiasm and support, I would never have been brave enough to try something new. Thank you to my beta readers, my ARC readers, and anyone else kind enough to hype this book on social media. (Please use the hashtag #tomesandtea, if you post about this series!)

Until next time!

About the Author

Rebecca Thorne is an author of all things fantasy, sci-fi, and sapphic romance. She thrives on deadlines, averages 2,700 words a day, and tries to write at least two books a year. (She also might be a little hyper-focused ADHD.) When she's not writing (or avoiding writing), Thorne can be found traveling the country as a flight attendant, or doing her best impression of a granola-girl hermit with her two dogs.